A HERO'S CHOICE

Book 4 ✦ A Hero's Choice

Tommy Kerper
AKA SourpatchHero

For Sarah:
You motivate me when I'm lazy and call me out when I'm wrong. Whatever I did to deserve you wasn't enough. You'll always be the best choice I made.

For Oliver and Milo:
I hope you never grow too old to play video games with Dad or snuggle watching cartoons.

Cover design by Art of Neight

ISBN: 978-1-0394-9425-1

Published in 2025 by Podium Publishing
www.podiumentertainment.com

Recap

When a truck jumped the curb to hit his best friend, Orrin valiantly tried to save the day.

Instead, they both woke up in a forest, naked, afraid, and with magic powers. Orrin and Daniel stuck together and did their best to learn how to survive. Orrin gained the ability to buff and heal—he could make a person slightly stronger or quicker and later added amplified magical potency. His spells cost less and hit harder. He even found ways to infinitely loop his health and mana, making his utility near limitless.

Daniel was the [Hero]. Stronger, faster, better-looking. It would have made a lesser man jealous, but Orrin was ready to help his friend defeat the Demon Lord. Together, they agreed on three simple rules for surviving their own isekai: First, survive. Second, stick together. Third, find a way home.

In Orrin's opinion, they'd done a shitty job.

Both Orrin and Daniel had almost died multiple times. Within minutes of arriving, Daniel was attacked by a vine monster that tried to carry him away into the trees. Orrin's abilities to increase a person's strength and heal had kept them alive . . . barely. As they made their way to the closest civilized town, a chance encounter resulted in the rescue of a not-quite princess, Madi, and her [Knight], Brandt.

Everything was coming up positive until Madi threatened them with imprisonment and execution. Daniel's Quests were negotiated to save their lives, but further attempts to test their prowess almost ended in their deaths anyway. Orrin and Daniel had just settled into their new lives of leveling up and working for the Guild when Orrin broke the second rule.

After a fight with his friend, Orrin teleported away, separating their group. His new powers came with a price, and luckily, he met Tony, a [Mind Mage], who taught him how to not kill himself with his unique set of spells and skills. Finding his way back to Daniel, the friends reunited and made a deal with Madi's father, one of the lords of Dey. The trio battled their first dungeon, drank some coffee, and started to trust each other a bit more.

But then Daniel was kidnapped right in front of them. Orrin and Madi gathered their allies and went on the hunt, discovering a hidden plot and a traitor in their midst. Saving Daniel wasn't the end, as more pieces of the puzzle were revealed. A daring rescue attempt for a friend's family members ended up drawing the most powerful leaders of the city out into open warfare. Orrin and Daniel survived the fallout, gaining powerful friends in the process.

One of those allies offered the opportunity to destroy a new dungeon. The rewards for doing this would be astronomical, but Orrin feared it was just an attempt to learn more about their hidden spells and skills. They accepted the challenge, but with a secondary goal: A neighboring country, Odrana, had declared war on the elven nation. Daniel and Orrin had a Quest to end the war and the dungeon was close to the elven forest. After they raided the Guild's storeroom for all the supplies they could take, the two boys and Madi entered the dungeon known as the Crumbling Waste. Two friends-slash-spies accompanied them. The monster battles were fierce but ultimately victorious. The dungeon core was ready to be destroyed. Everything was coming together.

Orrin discovered a new ability, something that had popped up from time to time in the past with varied results. His Administrator power was unlike anything else. Absorbing the dungeon core gave him access to administrator points, a secondary set of abilities that even the [Hero] didn't have. Leaving their new friends, Orrin set out with Madi and Daniel to help the elves rebuff the invading Odranan forces.

The elven council cared little for the new [Hero], but one elf found Orrin intriguing. Stories of Administrators of old brought up new questions, but a sudden attack from the leader of Odrana, Lord Sanerris, wreaked havoc with Orrin's plans to unite the elves and Dey. The elven council sold them out, and only quick action from Daniel and Orrin kept Lord Sanerris from capturing the [Hero] for his nefarious plot. The fight was not as one-sided as Orrin had thought it would be, leaving him questions about how and why his spells worked better against certain people.

The newly appointed council members helped rebuild relations with Dey, promising to help fight off the Demon Lord on his way. Orrin began using his Administrator powers and found himself used as a shuttle for messages between the two countries. When Daniel and Madi brought him news of an imprisoned Brandt, they raced to save their friend. The mission went sideways from the beginning.

Followed, discovered, and attacked, the trio made their way into the heart of Odrana to rescue Brandt. Their escape seemed within reach when Lord Sanerris returned. Orrin watched Daniel die and come back to life thanks to the use of one of his skills. Quick thinking and a little luck got his friends out of the Odranan dungeon sewers, but Orrin was left behind and enslaved.

When he awoke from his beatings, Orrin was shipped off to a remote villa, where he met Lady Sanerris, the recently deposed leader of Odrana and mother of Lord Sanerris. Between playing board games and learning the intricacies of magic, Orrin discovered her plan. She meant to use him as a spy and pawn within an elite magical academy. To live, he had to make friends with her political rivals and help maneuver her back into power.

Orrin attended class, plotted his own escape, and made friends before stumbling into an assassination attempt. Using every bit of cunning he possessed, Orrin united his new friends and old for a takedown of the entire rotten Odrana leadership. Finding his way back to Daniel, the celebration is cut short. The Demon Lord is on the move and Dey is not ready. With all his new magical knowledge and little time to rest, Orrin and Daniel must stand with their new friends against the impending Horde.

A HERO'S CHOICE

Chapter 1

Orrin watched the innumerable forces of the demon Horde approach from the south. Thousands of figures marched near the mountains, alongside wagons and horses. As the sun rose slowly into the sky, Orrin squinted against the first rays of light and reassessed his initial deduction. *Those aren't horses . . . those are monsters.*

Some of the larger beasts pulled wagons or large contraptions on wheels. Demons sat astride the more normal-size monsters, but two colossal beings in the back carried full-size houses on their backs. The Horde was still miles away, but the smooth plains on this side of the Pass gave the people of Asmea ample time to watch and quiver in fear.

"The final count is just under seven thousand, not including the monsters they've tamed," Daniel said from Orrin's side. "I call dibs on taking down one of the big spider houses."

Orrin's best friend wore gleaming new armor supplied by the lords of Dey. His massive sword, Gertrude, rested on his back. His clean-shaven face and easy smile had been put to use over the last few days, as he'd been dragged in front of every group of power in the world as a showpiece. They both stood on the Outer Wall, a new fortification built at the end of the Pass. If the Horde broke through these defenses, the army could retreat to the next. Even as they watched, additional fallback positions were being erected closer to the city of Dey itself. The humans, orcs, dwarves, and elves of Asmea had worked tirelessly through the night and wouldn't stop until the Horde was repelled or the demons killed everyone.

"Spider houses? You can see that far?" Orrin asked, his voice wooden. He was numb, letting [Mind Bastion] run to keep his voice from shaking.

Daniel shot a glance at Orrin and popped him on the back of the head with his open palm. "Stop doing that, it freaks me out."

Orrin slowly turned [Mind Bastion] off as he rubbed his head. "Sorry. I'm stressed we didn't do enough. We needed more time."

Daniel stared at Orrin and slowly raised his hand to point at the masses beside and behind them. "We've got five thousand troops from Odrana and Dey, a thousand elves, and hundreds of orcs and dwarfs. There are more walls and barracks built into the path behind us than I even know about. You figured out a way to make everyone stronger. What more could we need?"

Orrin smiled ruefully. "I notice you didn't mention yourself, [Hero]."

Daniel shrugged. "I don't think I'm needed here. You made this possible. They don't stand a chance at making it to Dey."

Orrin turned red but kept his head up. He had spent the prior week making spell orbs and preparing in a hundred small ways. The little glass balls could store a spell for release by anyone. His specialty was stat buffs—he could cast spells that made a person stronger or quicker. He could also increase a mage's mana pool or even the intensity of their magic. In a world where a person had a limited amount of magic they could cast in a day, Orrin's help increased the output of thousands of people by an unfathomable amount. His spell orbs were directly responsible for the Outer Wall and all the traps they'd built in the Pass.

His knowledge of the Pass was also second to none now. Lord Catanzano, one of the leaders of Dey, paid special mages called [Locationists] to teleport Orrin all over the Pass. Once he'd seen a location, he could return himself using [Teleport]. The Pass was an eighty-mile-long path through the mountains that separated civilization from the demon lands. It tapered from ten to fifteen miles wide at the ends, with a massive forty-mile-wide section near the middle. The best [Locationist] in Dey could travel to ten spots in one day by himself. Orrin used [Teleport] ten times before lunch, moving groups of people out to the Outer Wall and back.

Orrin reached up to touch his hair, missing the length. He'd not had it cut for months, but Madi had insisted he sit still for twenty minutes last night and let her hairstylist clean him up. He'd gone back to clip some additional ingredients from his penidrop mothershroom for potions. Just one potion, really. Early on in their adventure in Asmea, Orrin had found a recipe for a potion that increased the regeneration rate of a person's mana. He'd made as many as he could and started handing out single doses to the most powerful spellcasters he could find.

"Madi should be here," Daniel muttered darkly as they watched the human generals conferring with Leanthun. The beautiful elven man carried his Citrandish bow in one hand, while his khopesh and magical mace rested against either hip. "The humans are trying to boss the elves around again. I better go deal with this."

Orrin watched Daniel move down the steps of the fortress. The mouth of the Pass was closed by the Outer Wall, but a tower, rooms, and stone stairways along the southernmost part of the structure gave Orrin pause. This was nothing more than a fantasy castle. The battlements were wide enough for the elves to stand five deep and shoot their arrows in volleys. Orrin was surprised at Daniel's knowledge of siege warfare and the recommendations his friend had made. Roofless towers within sight of each other would give the illusion of entrances, but each gate had no stairs leading up. Instead, a single [Earth Mage] could drop tons of stone down a trapped chute while archers and mages sent arrows and spells flying from the top.

He leaned back and slid down the wall, checking his stats. He was ready and buffed with his daily [Utility Ward] but would need to top off his stats before any real battle began. Orrin kept one eye on Daniel as he yelled at the humans the lords of Dey had put in command. The last time demons were this close, Daniel had lost his senses and run into danger. Half the reason Orrin was allowed to be on the front lines next to Daniel was to keep him from doing the same again.

If it was up to the other leaders of Dey, Orrin would be locked in a room, churning out spell orbs for everyone to use . . . or, in a few already-discovered cases, stolen for later resale. With the massive number of [Increase Will] spell orbs that he'd created, Orrin knew someone would figure out his spell sooner rather than later. After his stint at the Sanerris School for Spells in Odrana, he knew how smart the people of this world could be when they wanted to be.

Twenty minutes later, a runner approached Daniel's group and spoke with some of the attendants near the edge. Orrin raised an eyebrow when Leanthun turned and said something before pointing toward Orrin's dark corner. As the dark-haired man made his way to Orrin, he recognized him. Dale, one of the [Locationists] that Silas had hired to ferry messages between the two ends of the Pass.

"Orrin, you're needed in Dey. Lord Catanzano requests your immediate presence," Dale informed him when he was close enough. "I can bring you back so you can conserve your mana."

Orrin waved at Daniel and pointed two fingers at his wrist when his friend granted him a moment of his attention. *Spare two minutes?*

Daniel held up his hand to forestall whatever the younger general was saying. Orrin didn't care enough to keep the different men's names straight, but this one was particularly annoying. Raymond Hayder wanted to rush the demons on the field and use Orrin's spell orbs to rain hell from above before swooping in for the kill. A decidedly insane way to get everyone killed.

"It's over, Raymond. We have the high ground," Orrin murmured to himself as Daniel jogged back to him.

"Excuse me? Did you say something?" Dale asked as Daniel closed the distance.

"Sorry, it was nonsense. Forget it."

"What do you need?" Daniel demanded a minute later.

"Silas wants a word, I guess." Orrin shrugged. "Want to come with?"

Daniel leaned over the edge of the crenellation and shook his head. "If they keep moving at this rate, we'll have our first encounter within an hour. Is this necessary?"

"Dale? Did Silas say what this was about?" Orrin parroted Daniel's annoyed tone but wagged his eyebrows in an exaggerated form so Dale knew he was playing.

"Lord Catanzano did not give me a reason but did say that it was an urgent matter. He doesn't need the [Hero], though. I was told to bring Orrin back quickly."

Orrin held Dale's gaze as the man answered. When Silas had hired the man a few days ago, Orrin traveled the Pass with him. He'd been calm and without fear. Right now, he was sweating.

"I'll go with you in a minute then, Dale," Orrin said. "I just need to go tell the generals that I'll be right back."

"Orrin, we don't have time—" Daniel started to argue.

"D, if Silas says it's urgent, I should go," Orrin interrupted his friend. "I'll come with you to tell Leanthun he needs to keep Raymond from attacking."

Daniel cocked his head but didn't argue.

"Dale, wait here," Orrin ordered and walked away, not looking back. Daniel followed.

"What's going on?" Daniel whispered.

"Silas wouldn't ask us to meet him without giving a reason. Dale wants to separate me from the group. The Hospital might be making a play, or shit, it could even be Anabella."

"She wasn't executed?" Daniel nearly tripped in surprise. "Fuck."

"I could be wrong," Orrin conceded. "Silas could need me, but he'd send Madi. She's supposed to be here by now anyway."

"What's the plan?" Daniel's fist clenched.

Orrin smiled at the instant trust of his best friend. "Leanthun has the teleport wards set up, right?"

Daniel nodded. "Yeah, but they haven't activated them yet."

Orrin turned and waved at Dale, who was still standing behind them undecided on if he should stay or hurry after them. "Tell him to get close to Dale and use one. If we can pin him down, we might have a chance to get some information from him. If he runs, we won't know who sent him."

"You're sure?"

Orrin frowned. "No, but I'd rather tell him sorry than walk into another trap. He's nervous, and the man travels alone for a living. Something has him rattled."

Orrin smiled and shook Leanthun's hand while pointing at the young general. His words did not match his actions. "As soon as I return to that man, get someone sneaky over there as soon as possible and set up a teleport ward. Something is about to go down."

"Why are you pointing at me? You might be in the [Hero]'s party, but I'm—" Raymond started belligerently. Daniel cut him off. Orrin ignored the conversation and waited for Leanthun to nod slowly.

"It'll be done. Don't move too quickly. He appears to be ready to run." The elf's gaze flickered over Orrin's shoulder for the barest of seconds. "I need ten seconds to get someone in place."

Orrin nodded and raised his hand to Daniel for a high five. "If I'm not back in twenty minutes, kill some demons for me," he nearly shouted, trying to be overheard. "Silas better have a good reason for calling me away right before the fun starts."

He made his way back to Dale, moving as slowly as he could without giving himself away. He counted to twenty in his head before he got close. "I can [Teleport] back if you want. You can save some mana."

Orrin prayed that Dale would accept the offer. If they were truly going to Lord Catanzano's house, his base of operations, the saved spell would let Dale continue to work today.

"It's fine, he's at a different location with the other lords. You wouldn't know where it is," Dale said with a sigh of relief. He believed Orrin was coming with him. "Here. Accept my party invite."

Orrin felt nothing different in the air but trusted Leanthun. "No, Dale. I'm not going anywhere with you. Tell me who really sent you."

Dale didn't wait. He blinked once, realizing his [Teleport] had failed. The man's green eyes widened in fear but to his credit, he reacted quickly. Raising his hand toward Orrin, he cast a spell.

Orrin expected to be attacked. Dale was an adventurer at heart, someone who traveled to new places to see different sights. He had to have a way to defend himself. The wards that Orrin cast would protect him from nearly every type of damage, but what he hadn't expected was a simple [Wind] spell.

The air gathered and pushed into his chest. Orrin stumbled back, his knees buckling as he hit the edge of the wall, and he fell backward off a fifty-foot drop.

Chapter 2

Of course, it was Daniel who came to the rescue and saved Orrin from becoming the first to die outside the Outer Wall. As Orrin's thoughts jumbled into a half dozen plans that would inevitably end with him flattened against the hard-packed dirt below, Daniel leaped toward his falling friend, reaching out his hand. Orrin just made out multiple bodies tackling Dale, which stopped the wind magic's intensity. It was too late, though. Daniel's hand was out of his reach.

Orrin didn't notice that his descent had slowed. His eyes were wide as he stared at Daniel's face, covered with sweat, as he slowly bounced up and down in midair.

"Push air behind you, idiot," Daniel growled through clenched teeth. Vessels in his right eye burst. "Hurry."

Orrin jerked and pointed his left hand down, pushing mana into a cast of [Gust] as he bobbed again. The spell rocketed his body forward into Daniel's arms. Orrin wrapped his arms around his friend as he pulled him back on the wall.

"Thanks," Orrin said, breathing heavily. He quickly dropped his arms from around Daniel and watched his friend dry heave, his hands on his knees. "How did you do that?"

"[Gravity Well]," Daniel got out before he spat bile on the ground. "I figured if it can pull monsters toward me, it might stop your dumb ass from falling to your death."

Daniel grinned up at Orrin and the worry melted away. Daniel had used his skill to pull the attention of nearby enemies his way. The added effect of physically dragging monsters toward him was a gentle tug for a second, but Daniel had held him there over fifty feet of unimpeded air for much longer. *The stress of the skill started hurting him.*

Orrin cast a [Heal Small Wounds] on his friend, ignoring the scuffling of the man who'd tried to kill him nearby. He trusted Leanthun and the other elves had it under control.

"Don't waste your mana," Daniel grunted as he stretched and rolled his neck. "I'm not hurt; I bottomed out my stamina. Don't try flying again, please."

"It's not like I did it on purpose," Orrin complained. "He attacked me."

"Why?" Daniel asked. He was winded like he'd run for an hour.

That spell is dangerous, Orrin thought.

"I have the same question." Leanthun appeared behind Orrin, making him jump. "Easy, Orrin. No more heroics from you this morning."

"Sir, he's resisting still," one of the elves shouted. "Permission to knock him out?"

"No," Daniel answered before Leanthun could give the order. "I want to talk with him."

Orrin took a step, but Daniel put an arm out and stayed in front of him. "I'll do the talking this time."

Dale's fear was palpable as they approached. The dirt tracked on the walkway of the Outer Wall stuck to his face where he'd been shoved to the ground. Blood leaked from a wound under his hair, matting it all into a dark tangle. Orrin checked him over with [Identify], but overall, the elves had been gentle.

I could have died. The shock wore off and the fear hit him. Orrin cast [Calm Mind] on himself, staving off the trauma for later.

"Who sent you?" Daniel crouched and grabbed Dale's head, pulling it back so he had to look Daniel in the eyes. "Why did you try to kill Orrin?"

Dale's eyes moved frantically in any direction but toward the [Hero]. "I—I told him. Lord Cat . . . Catanzano wanted to see him, but he attacked me."

Daniel raised an eyebrow at Orrin. "How's his health?"

"He's mostly fine, why?" Orrin asked before stepping back in surprise.

Daniel smashed Dale's face into the stone twice. He calmly brushed some leaves from the man's mouth and shook the blood from his fingers. "I'm not going to ask again. The next lie earns you a jump off the edge."

Orrin clenched his fists until his knuckles popped. He hated this. A few months ago, Daniel never would have done anything like this. A few months ago, Orrin would have tried to stop him.

Now, he kept an eye on the man's health and waited to see if healing would be needed or not.

"Please, please just come back with me. I'm dead if you don't," Dale cried around his broken nose.

Daniel shook his head and stood up. Dale let out a sigh of relief that turned into a strangled yell as Daniel grabbed his collar and walked toward the edge of the wall. "I warned you."

"No. No, wait." Dale tried to pry Daniel's hand off his shirt but Daniel's strength was buffed beyond what anyone could gain naturally in Asmea. "I'll talk. Promise you'll protect me. I don't want to die."

Daniel casually threw Dale against the battlement and drew Gertrude. "A name or you go over the edge in pieces."

"I didn't get a name, but they work for the Hospital. Two [Teachers], I think. They wanted Orrin. I had to get him to them or else they'll blacklist me from any healing. One of them said I'd be better off dead than running. I swear that's all I know," Dale whined as he shrank against the stone, beaten and broken.

Orrin knelt beside him and started healing his wounds. "Where did they want me?"

Orrin felt the stillness of his [Calm Mind] spell fade as anger built inside.

"Are you sure we have time for this?" Leanthun whispered from under Orrin's [Camouflage Ward]. "The Horde could arrive any minute."

"If members of the Hospital are operating in open sedition of the rulers of Dey, we must immediately root out the snakes at our back," Madi answered in a near-perfect copy of her father's voice. They'd found her returning to the Wall just in time to join their adventure. "Dale, you will point these two [Teachers] out, and if you try to give us away, you better hope the demons kill us all or I will find you and make you regret it."

Dale shivered next to the twenty members of the guard and Daniel, who kept a close eye on the man. "I gave my promise to your father. I had no power to reject their request. How was I supposed to know it wasn't an official order?"

Orrin ignored the man. He'd listened to his story again when they'd brought Dale to Lord Catanzano's manor. Orrin had used [Teleport] to bring Daniel and Leanthun with them. He'd hoped to drop Dale into Silas's lap and make him deal with it, but the politics of the ruling class of Dey and the Hospital left much to be desired.

Madi's intervention was all that had kept Daniel from throwing her father and his wheelchair out a window. An accusation by a single [Locationist] was hardly viable proof of an attempted kidnapping. A full retinue of guards, the [Hero], and the daughter of a lord of Dey witnessing the attempt would give Silas the political capital he needed to force the Hospital to help more with the demon Horde.

Or so they hoped.

"I don't like this," Daniel said for the tenth time. "You don't have to walk out there with him. He can say he failed and we can move in."

"That's not going to work," Orrin whispered, putting his finger to his lips in silent rebuke at Daniel's loud voice. "We don't know what they want me for. Silas needs evidence of wrongdoing. Dale attacked me in panic, not in an attempt to kill me. We need more."

Orrin wasn't happy about playing bait yet again, but he had more tricks up his sleeve this time. Literally. He carried two of his new spell orbs that reduced a target's dexterity when hit. Nobody would run away. His practice in Battle Class at the Sanerris School improved his reflexes and use of [Gust] to move around. [Way of the Water] kept him agile and hard to hit. His own buffs to his dexterity and strength made him quicker and stronger than almost anyone in the city.

In short, Orrin was ready to kick ass.

"I still don't like it." Daniel's hand reached over to touch his sword's bone handle, checking it was ready to draw. "I trust you, though. Be careful and remember the signal."

"The signal that is literally me running away?" Orrin deadpanned. "How ever will I remember that?"

The plan was simple enough: Guards and his friends surrounded the coordinates where Dale had been ordered to bring Orrin. Orrin and Dale would [Teleport] a few feet in and set off whatever trap had been laid. The cavalry, namely Daniel, would then rush in.

Orrin pulled up his [Map] and let out a sigh of relief.

"What?" Daniel turned at the sound.

"No traps. I just had the thought, what if they set something up to explode and kill me."

"Damn it, Orrin. Stop coming up with terrible ideas."

Madi chuckled. "That's kind of his thing."

"Be quiet, all of you," Leanthun whispered. "We are in place."

Besides the guards, Leanthun had his best scouts hidden on the roofs around them. Orrin trusted the elves more than the guards. His eyes hurt as he glanced at Daniel and Madi's blurry shapes through his spell. *I trust them more.*

"Let's go, Dale. Just hand me over and get back to the Catanzano manor. You'll be protected," Orrin said, trying to calm the man. He'd already tried his spells, but Dale was too used to having his ability to teleport away from danger. Walking headfirst into it went against every fiber in his body. Orrin was surprised the man was still there. "Do you need me to [Teleport] us in?"

"I can do it," Dale said, reaching up to touch the healed wound on his head. "I'll do what I can to apologize for almost killing you."

Daniel growled. Madi shushed him. Dale and Orrin disappeared and popped into existence fifty yards away.

"Hello? Anyone here?" Orrin spoke loudly. "Dale, I thought you said Lord Catanzano wanted to talk with me?"

"Thi-this is where I wa-was told to bring yo-you," Dale stuttered.

His acting is worse than Daniel's. I'm not seeing anyone new on my [Map] yet. I think every one of these dots is someone from our group. Oh, there we are.

Orrin turned toward the new dot on his screen and waved. "Hi, who are you?"

The man stepping out of a nearby building stopped in the doorway for a moment before continuing his quick gait toward Dale and Orrin. He was wearing a dark cloak, but Orrin saw the white robes of the Hospital underneath.

"I've brought the kid as requested, so I'll be leaving," Dale said when the man was about twenty feet away. He was supposed to [Teleport] away and get out of the danger zone.

Dale scrambled backward and cursed. "Not again."

He turned and ran.

"Not a very bright man," the approaching figure commented. "He should know better than to run."

Orrin sighed dramatically. "Is this the part where you threaten me? I'm getting very good at being threatened, you know. You're not Silas. Who are you?"

The man pulled back his hood, revealing brown hair tied in a bun. He smiled. "You know who I am?"

"Should I?" Orrin asked honestly. "I haven't dealt with the Hospital much. So sorry if that offends you."

The man laughed, a quick, sharp sound like the last breath of a dying man. "I am Principal Viccio. You may call me Logan."

Orrin said nothing.

"You truly do not know me?" A hint of annoyance tinged his voice.

"No, dude. I truly don't," Orrin answered in his most obnoxious voice. "If you wanted to speak to me, you didn't need to trick me. I'm pretty easy to find."

Principal Viccio sneered. "You are protected by Silas Catanzano and impossible to approach. A [Healer] who is not a [Healer]. A member of the [Hero]'s party. A friend to the heretic who upends our work in the city. If this was not so urgent, I would tell you of the hundred ways we've tried to contact you and been ignored. But time is short. What do you know of the negotiations between the lords of Dey and our great organization?"

Orrin didn't let his guard down but was happy that Viccio didn't attack outright. "The Hospital wants a healing monopoly and is using the demon Horde to negotiate in bad faith. I'm not part of those talks. Bring it up with Silas."

Viccio kept his distance, both hands in his sleeves. "Naive boy. We need [Healers] who are schooled in the way the body works. If we allow anyone to—"

"I'm going to stop you before you get all worked up," Orrin cut him off. "I don't give a single shit what the Hospital wants. Why did you trick me into coming here? You know the Horde is almost at the Pass, right?"

The man waved a hand in obvious dismissal. "I don't care about the Horde. We have a [Hero] on our side. They always turn back the

Demon Lord. I'm worried about these new magics you've introduced. Do you have any idea what is going on within our ranks? The chaos you are spreading throughout our young recruits?"

The turn in conversation confused him. "What? What do my buffs have to do with the Hospital?"

Viccio laughed. "This is the problem. You don't even know. The schism already runs deep, and you've set a charge between the members that will soon explode."

"What. Are. You. Talking. About?" Orrin said slowly, enunciating each word.

"You bring doubt into our believers' hearts. If Silas lets [Healers] run wild from our control and you create the means for them to do so, it will end with a crusade. Please. You must—"

Viccio gagged when the first arrow hit his throat. He clawed at his neck, mana flashing to close the wound, but more sprouted from his back.

Orrin stepped back, looking around. Those were not elven arrows. He'd paid too much attention to the man and not enough to his [Map]. Ten red dots filled his view.

White robes swirled around corners as more arrows and magic rained down on the square, but Orrin was not the target. They were attacking each other.

Chapter 3

Orrin thought Logan was an asshole, but if he was pragmatic, the city needed every [Healer] it had left. The man's health was plummeting as spells started flying their way. Orrin saw Daniel, Madi, Brandt, and the guards moving in and pinning down some of the white-robed members of the Hospital, but enough slipped through to be a threat.

"If I heal you, are you going to be an asshole about it?" Orrin closed the distance and started casting before Logan could answer. *If he can talk at all. Gross.*

Orrin flinched at the mass of scar tissue forming around the man's throat. The shaft of the arrow was still clutched in his bloody hand. He'd yanked it out before healing.

Orrin trusted his friends to subdue the attackers, but more white cloaks swirled into their location. The small plaza between two intersecting streets seemed defensible with their original numbers, but Orrin counted close to forty dots that blinked red and gray.

"Why are your people fighting each other, Logan?" Orrin asked as he yanked arrows out of the man's back and healed the bleeding wounds until they closed. He slapped on a few wards for good measure.

"You . . ." Logan rasped and coughed hard. Orrin felt along the man's throat and pushed mana into the puckered divot left along his Adam's apple. Logan's eyes widened a bit as he stopped choking. "You are the reason. Half want you dead and the others think you are some sort of hero for the [Healers] to rally behind."

"I'm definitely not the hero," Orrin responded between Logan's screams. A few of the spells had left burns, frostbite, and a tacky green substance that Orrin used [Identify] on. "One of them got you with acid. I'm going to—"

"Cut the skin quickly before it gets deeper," Logan interrupted, pulling a dagger from his waist and holding it up.

The battle around them was a mass of confusion. The guards were trying their best to subdue the two sets of attackers, but each side was bent on killing the other. Daniel was using the flat of his blade to bash people apart.

"I can use [Remetabolize] and decrease the efficiency. Would that work?" Orrin asked as he took the knife. "If I make it—"

"Acid is not a toxin or poison. This is why training is essential to ah—" Logan screamed as Orrin dug the blade into his shoulder and carved.

[Mind Bastion] kicked on.

Orrin quickly cast [Numb] on the affected area, but carving out the skin was taking up time when he could be helping in the fight.

This is taking too long. He looked around and noticed Brandt bodily throw a woman screaming and casting fire from her hands at another man holding a bow. "Brandt, get over here."

The knight watched to make sure the tumble of limbs wasn't getting up and jogged over. "You don't do things halfway, do you?"

Orrin handed him the dagger. "His health is fine. Get the acid cut out. I'm going to end this."

"Orrin, as strong as you are, this is a lot of people. I've sent one of the men for reinforcements, but this is madness." Brandt grabbed the knife and paled at the sight of Logan's shoulder. "I'm not a [Healer]. This looks bad."

"Trust me, he's fine. Just cut the skin there. Everything else I've healed," Orrin said distractedly as he pulled his [Map] up. "I only need a minute."

Orrin glanced at the two people Brandt had taken down. They were starting to stand up after getting themselves untangled. He cast [Decrease Dexterity] on both, and they fell like marionettes with cut strings. "Maybe less."

Orrin's dexterity was at one hundred, and he'd practiced with the increased stat relentlessly. He used [Gust] as he ran. A push here and a pull there knocked most of the attackers around him to the ground. A few casts of [Decrease Dexterity] on the prone bodies kept them down. He flitted around the streets, leaving anyone wearing a white robe laid out.

A few of the quicker ones began to target Orrin, but his wards kept the attacks from harming him. An arrow from a roof activated [Side Steps], which made him stumble as he regained his balance. Orrin looked up and saw five elves jumping from other buildings to subdue the lone high sniper.

Two of the smart mages on the periphery retreated, but Orrin wasn't about to let anyone get away. He charged down the street, barely hearing Daniel shout after him.

Slapping feet behind him turned his attention from his [Map].

"Orrin, stop. Let them go," Daniel shouted. He was sprinting behind him, but Orrin could tell he was falling back.

"There's only two. One is right around this corner," Orrin yelled, turning his gaze back to his [Map]. His brain stuttered, and he almost fell as he tried to stop. "Daniel, turn back."

Orrin skidded along the cobblestones as he failed to arrest his momentum. He'd been ignoring the flood of white dots around town, focusing only on the fleeing red enemy spots. A crowd down the next street turned red as he cleared the building's corner and came face-to-face with a dozen people wearing white robes and holding staffs and wands, open hands pointing toward him.

"Fire!"

Orrin felt the heat of mana racing toward him. He knew his wards were lower, having taken a beating from the few enemies able to take a shot before he brought them down. He'd underestimated them. They'd planned a trap in their retreat.

I can survive this, Orrin thought. He cast as many spells as he could. [Gust] combined with [Fire Sword] to explode out and stop any ice magic attacks. He summoned [Ice Swords] and threw them at the fire before ducking down and making himself into the smallest target he could.

Orrin closed his eyes as he waited for the pain to hit.

And waited.

He opened one eye and was surprised to see he was still alive. Scorch marks, pitted stones, and two arrows were scattered around him, but nothing had struck him. A shield of multicolored light hung over his body. It was translucent but shimmered with an opal sheen.

"Orrin, get back here."

Orrin snapped his head around and saw Madi breathing heavily next to Daniel. They stood by the corner, and Madi's outstretched hand gave him a hint at what had happened.

She stomped her foot in agitation. "Now! I can't hold this for another volley."

Even as she spoke, a few of the quicker mages were sending more magic at him. Orrin scrambled from his squat into a full sprint and only took a single glancing shot of a stone fired at incredible speed to his leg.

"Thanks, Madi. Whatever that was . . . thanks." Orrin peeked around the edge of the building but was yanked back before another missile took a chunk of the wall off.

"Orrin, I swear I'm going to put a leash on you," Daniel threatened. "Why do you always run into the danger zone? Stay away from the danger zone."

"We should get back to the others," Madi said, breathing heavily. "Brandt is going to be pissed we left him behind."

Orrin reset his buffs and wards on the three of them, checking his mana. A large portion was burned from all his casting, but he could always chug a regen potion if he needed it. He'd drunk his last one yesterday morning.

"Don't." Daniel glared at him. "Drop it."

"Will you stop talking to me like I'm a dog?" Orrin asked before rolling his eyes. "Fine. I don't use [Mind Bastion] all the time, and it triggered itself when I almost threw up on Logan's acid burns."

"That was Logan Viccio that you were talking with before everything went sideways, right?" Madi asked as she brushed some building dust off Orrin's shoulder. "Never mind, you can tell me later. Cast [Camouflage] on us and let's get out of here."

"There's still a bunch of enemies, literally right there," Orrin said. Then he realized what he'd said. "Fuck, I'm stupid. Maybe I should get a leash."

"Whatever you're into." Madi smirked. "They don't matter. We need to get back to my house. This isn't an isolated incident. We got reports of fighting all over the city."

Daniel frowned before he pushed Orrin to the side. With a big step, he lifted his other foot and kicked. The chest of a man with a sword held overhead connected with the [Hero]'s boot. He was thrown back with the distinct sound of breaking bones. "We should go."

Orrin cast [Camouflage Ward] and they backed away from the intersection. "How did the demons get into the city? They weren't even close to the Outer Wall yet?"

Madi's voice drifted from his right. "It's not the demons. The Hospital is fighting. [Healers] and their support. All the members that guard the buildings and accompany the [Healers] for experience raids are up in arms. We got reports right as Principal Viccio approached you."

Orrin thought back to what the man had been saying. He'd mentioned a schism and a crusade, but Orrin had thought it was hyperbole. *I didn't do anything that would start a civil war between healers. That makes no sense.*

Brandt orchestrated the guards as the now-prisoners were arrested and brought to jail. Fighting in the streets during a Horde attack was a major crime, no matter what side these Hospital members were on. Madi stopped to talk with some of the guards, giving orders and taking her place as the daughter of Lord Catanzano.

"I don't get why they're fighting," Daniel muttered, echoing Orrin's thoughts. He dropped the spell as they approached, and Brandt sighed in relief.

"Where did everyone go?" Orrin joked.

"We've cleared most of them here, so I sent most of the other guards to reinforce elsewhere," the knight explained. "This is terrible timing. Principal Viccio demanded to go with them. Leanthun and his elves went to find a jump back to the front. I'm not sure what I'm supposed to do here."

Madi approached and put her hand on the tall man's shoulder. "It'll be fine. My father is sending more of his guards into town to help."

"That's good, but what should we do, Madi?"

Madi looked at Daniel.

"I trust your dad can get this under control. I don't think Orrin started this fight for once"—he threw an exasperated glance at his friend—"so we can all head back to deal with the Horde. That Viccio guy didn't want to talk with us more?"

Brandt shrugged. "He said it was too late now and climbed on one of the wagons with the accused. By the way, Orrin, that was incredible how you knocked them all out. You've been going easy on me."

Orrin scratched at his neck. "If you guys are ready, I'll [Teleport] us back. Brandt, are you done here?"

Madi half-heartedly raised her hand. "Actually, if Orrin can spare an hour . . . I just received word that the Wellans finished collecting the ingredients needed for the [Purify] potions. I know you've never been to Ceraun, but there is a [Locationist] who . . . no, it's not the same man. Will you at least hear me out?"

Orrin and Daniel stared at each other.

We said no more getting separated, Daniel said with a small head shake.

You can't leave the front line right now. Nobody else will have the storage ability to carry the amount we need. Plus, who would we trust to get the ingredients back without the Hospital fucking it up? Orrin answered with a wry smile and shoulder raise.

It's not up for discussion. No. Daniel straightened his spine so he stood taller than Orrin.

"When you two are done posturing at each other," Madi ridiculed, "I want to go with Orrin. Brandt and Daniel can return to the Outer Wall. We can be there and back in an hour or less. We need those potions for the soldiers. More now than ever with the [Healers] fighting."

Viccio said the "schism already runs deep." Orrin remembered the words clearly now. *What does that mean?*

"Orrin?" Madi tilted her head. "Are you in there?"

Orrin gave an apologetic grimace to Daniel. "Don't let the demons kill everyone before we get back."

Chapter 4

Orrin worried that the demons would arrive before they made it back, but Madi assured him the entire trip wouldn't take more than twenty minutes. Brandt guaranteed him that the town guards could take care of the remaining Hospital members, as well.

"I'll watch Daniel's back," the knight promised.

"It's not his back that I'm worried about," Orrin muttered. He leaned in close to Brandt. "Make sure he doesn't charge the demons or something. His class makes him reckless around them."

Brandt's eyes flicked toward the [Hero]. "I'll tap another guard to join me."

"I'm literally standing right here," Daniel complained.

Madi shook her head. "Orrin, you can [Teleport] us back and we can join Daniel as soon as we drop off the supplies. If we leave now, we might beat them to the Outer Wall. There are only so many people who can [Teleport], and nobody has the mana stores that you do."

Orrin agreed and sneaked in a few last-minute pieces of advice to Daniel as they walked toward Madi's house. Brandt reappeared with a guard wearing robes and wielding a staff. Daniel waved as they walked inside to wait for their own [Locationist] to arrive.

Orrin and Madi's [Teleport] to Ceraun required two jumps. The [Locationist]'s spell wasn't as strong as Orrin's, but she'd been to the breadbasket of Odrana before and he hadn't. They stopped in a field near a river and waterwheel. Orrin saw a farmhand straighten and shade his eyes with his hand before they disappeared as quickly as they arrived.

A moment later, they stood outside sand-colored stone walls that rose fifteen feet into the air. A gate with a handful of merchants waiting to be let in was a few minutes' walk away. It seemed quaint.

"Thank you. You can return," Madi said as she handed over a bag of clinking coins. She glanced around nervously before pulling her hood up over her head.

Orrin briefly wondered how much he could charge to zip people around the world. *I need to travel to more places first and learn the rules. Like, why are we outside and not in the city?*

"Is this Ceraun?" Orrin stared up at the walls. "I thought it would be bigger."

"Ceraun is the province. This is the closest thing to a capital city. Terraco. It's where Maeve said to meet."

"Why couldn't we jump into the city?" Orrin asked Madi as the [Locationist] disappeared. She must have been eager to get back to Dey. She didn't say goodbye. In fact, she hadn't said a word the entire trip.

Madi rolled her eyes. "Orrin, think about it. Odrana is undergoing a political upheaval. A Demon Lord is invading Dey as we speak. The elves are jumpy after being harassed, and I'm not even going to get into the situation in Veskar. Major cities that can afford it are on lockdown. I doubt the Wellan family can afford teleport wards to cover all of Ceraun, but they'll have trackers set up. Any unauthorized [Teleport] into a city is targeted as a hostile act. Why do you think my father always has you report your jumps to the elves?"

Orrin scratched his neck. He'd assumed Silas was anal.

"You thought he was being a dick," Madi said exasperatedly. She adjusted her shortened spear to hang within easy reach and walked by him. "Keep up. We need to make this quick."

The line into Terraco moved quickly. Orrin paused as he took in the view.

With the height of the wall, Orrin had assumed he was entering a medium-size city, something smaller than Dey. He was wrong.

Vast fields stretched far into the distance. He saw enclosures with different livestock, including sheep, cows, and a hybrid pig-donkey beast he hadn't seen before. The lack of buildings nearby confused him until he noticed that multiple hills had windows.

"Do they live underground?" Orrin asked as they moved down a packed dirt path. Something big in the distance rumbled and one of the hills moved. "What is that?"

Madi laughed and pointed. "Ceraun has to protect the crops and livestock from monsters, but the land is too vast to fully enclose with walls. See those buildings?"

"That's a building?" Orrin squinted into the morning light. The hill stopped.

"Ceraun has created the best earth and plant mages in the world. All construction is made using the magic of hundreds of people working together. They are made to look as natural with the land around them as possible. Some of the buildings are sloped so livestock can climb and eat from the grass covering the outer layers. From what I understand, the buildings move and create links with each other. The walls around Terraco are in the least defensible areas, and the buildings create a barrier around those portions not protected. Any two buildings can connect with magic. I've seen it once or twice. They can call up a wall of earth between two of them or even an electrified fence. It's all moving and rearrangeable so the lands can be rotated for maximized use."

"And everyone lives under a hill?" Orrin moved to the side of the road as two smaller wagons pulled by a single horse each passed in the opposite direction. "That doesn't seem healthy."

Madi shook her head. "These are mostly processing and work quarters. The people of Ceraun are agricultural and live outside the main enclosed spaces. There are some small towns and villages, but the vast majority of work is done here. I'm sure a few people live here full-time like the Wellans, but even they have a castle a few miles to the north."

Orrin watched a woman in a field spraying water from her hand like a hose. She waved at them as they passed.

"Maeve will have the supplies for the [Purify] potions for us in that plant," Madi said as they walked toward the nearest hill/building. "We'll grab what we need and go."

The disguise failed to hold up as they got closer to the hillside. It still resembled a hill, but Orrin could see the ziggurat structure underneath as they approached. Windows dotted the outside and figures moved within. A massive barn door slid open from the side and people dispersed, going about their duties.

A single guard in full plate and a giant sword that would have put Gertrude to shame waited outside the opening. Once Orrin and

Madi were close, the hand on the sword let go of the handle and moved toward the helmet's facemask. A small hook flipped and the helmet's mask came up. The woman inside smiled and waved.

Orrin forgot to breathe. She was gorgeous.

Sweat dripped from her brow, likely from standing out in the morning sun, but that didn't detract from her beauty in his mind. From inside the helmet, her short brown hair fell in light curls that framed her face. The light reflected off the metal helmet, and he noticed a run of burgundy streaked throughout as well. Her sky-blue eyes sparkled as she reached out to clasp Madi's hand. Orrin's heart pounded, and he was forced to cast [Calm Mind] on himself.

"Little Catanzano, I haven't seen you in years. When Maeve told me you were coming, I made sure to change my shift. How have you been? Where is Brandt?"

"It's good to see you, Rae. I'm well," Madi answered, pulling the tall woman in for a hug. "Brandt is keeping things in check back home. I can't believe you are still working for the Wellans. You know my father would pay anything you wanted if you came to work for Dey. Brandt would be happy to see you, too."

Rae laughed, waving a gloved hand. "You know that's not true. He'd send me away quicker than a Veskarian mercenary retreats."

She noticed Orrin standing beside Madi and took her helmet fully off, putting it under her arm. "Who is this handsome man that you've brought me? This isn't the [Hero]. I heard he has a sword almost as big as mine." Her eyes widened. "Is this Casimir? Or do you go by Orrin? Maeve told me a little about you."

Orrin nodded and shoved his hands in his pockets.

Madi nudged him with her shoulder. "Yes. This is Orrin. Maeve is expecting us. We need to get back to Dey with the shipment she's got for us. Is she inside?"

"She's about," Rae answered, leaning over to look at Orrin. "Maeve told me you were cute, but I thought you were older from her description."

"I'm old enough," Orrin stammered.

Madi coughed as she tried to stifle a laugh.

Rae put her hand on Orrin's shoulder. She had to be over six feet tall. In her full plate armor, the guard made him feel tiny. "I owe you for saving my cousin."

"Your cousin?" Orrin felt the hand on his shoulder squeeze.

"Iona. She sent me a letter," Rae said as she ruffled his hair. "After you push the demons back, you should come back and visit. I'll buy dinner."

Orrin blushed. Madi let her laughter escape and slapped Orrin on the back.

"Let's get inside before you catch fire," she teased.

Rae smiled and waved toward the entrance. "Go ahead inside."

Madi didn't say a thing as they moved into the building. Orrin caught her glancing at him, but he ignored her.

Inside the sliding barn doors, a dozen pathways split off, with signs posted at each entrance. The floors were grass, but the walls were solid metal. Orrin read, "Laboratory," "Irrigation," "Border Control," "Planning," and "Quarters" on a few of the signposts before Madi walked down a hallway marked "Management."

"Have you been here before?" Orrin asked as he jogged to keep up.

"Not this particular location, but I've visited Ceraun before. They like uniformity in their houses," Madi replied. "Their guards, on the other hand, get bored easily and like to try new and exciting things whenever they get the chance."

"What?"

Madi elbowed him gently in the ribs. "Daniel is right. You're oblivious. Maeve will be in the management area. She'll have the shipment location."

Another three turns and they walked into the last thing Orrin ever would have expected: a cubicle farm. A flurry of paper moved around, and Orrin saw firsthand a new type of magic: competent administration. Small desks were lined up with dividers giving only the barest modicum of privacy between them. Men and women sat briefly in chairs, scribbling furiously, before running down the middle aisles to ask questions to someone else. Messengers came in with more paperwork that was promptly sorted and moved to the correct desk. The entire thing was surreal. If it wasn't for the grass under his feet, Orrin could have been back on Earth in a corporate office.

Maeve sat at a desk near the back, flipping through a folder. Three workers stood around waiting for her to look up.

Madi grabbed Orrin's hand and pulled him along the outer path. Maeve glanced up and said something to one of the waiting workers, who replied and left the room in a hurry. His awkward friend from school caught them getting closer and waved.

"Madeleine! Orrin! Welcome," Maeve said, standing up and leaving the other two waiting workers behind. "I'm glad you made it safely . . . and so quickly, too. Let's get you those potion supplies you need. How is the Horde repulsion going? Did the elves join the fight? I would love to talk with one of them someday."

"Hi, Maeve," Orrin answered but she kept talking and asking questions until Madi stopped her.

"Maeve, I'm sorry, but the demons are moving toward the Pass right now," Madi interrupted. "We need to get back. This isn't a social visit. I'm sure we can figure out a way to get an elf to talk with you about trees after we stop the end of the world."

Maeve nodded seriously. "That would be best, I suppose. I'll show you to storage room twenty-two B-four. That's where we've collected as much of the ingredients as we could. I'm not sure we'll be able to get much more within the next week or two."

Maeve brought them down more pathways and up three flights of stairs. She talked as they moved. "We had a few of the things you needed on hand already but had to pull a few of our senior plant mages in to speed up the creation of some parts of your request. We've dedicated about ten acres to growing more of each item, but that could take anywhere from one to two months to go into full production."

"Maeve, we told you that we only needed what you had on hand," Madi chastised as they climbed the last steps. "It's an emergency order, not an ongoing production line."

Maeve waved a bracelet over a door labeled "22 B-4" and pushed the heavy door to the side. "I find overpreparing is best."

Orrin watched the lights flicker on and groaned. Hundreds of pallets were stacked in a room that could hold a small airplane. Each box was marked with the ingredient name and when it was packaged.

"Madi, I'm not sure I can carry all of this," Orrin complained. "This will take days."

"Grab what you can for one trip and we'll come back when we can," Madi answered after a long moment. She played with the strap holding her spear to her side. "Make sure you get a few boxes of everything."

Orrin sighed and began walking through the room. From what he could gather, there were a half dozen different ingredients the potion makers needed to create the [Purify] potion. The wooden boxes looked heavy. He picked one up and pushed it into his pocket using [Dimension Hole]. It moved into his storage space with ease, but he still had to do the initial lifting.

Orrin grabbed two more at once and paused when he heard Madi talking behind him.

"Thank you, Maeve. This will help. While he's busy . . . is Rae seeing anyone right now?"

The top box slipped off and fell with a clatter.

"Are you okay in there?" Madi yelled into the room.

"Fine," Orrin replied loudly as he healed his broken toe. "I'm fine."

Chapter 5

Orrin exited the now-empty room. His arms were sore from lifting all the containers and he cast a [Heal Small Wounds] on himself to relieve the dull throbbing. Madi smiled mischievously at him as he walked by her and Maeve. Orrin pointedly ignored them both.

"I'm sorry this is all we could do," Maeve said, glancing back and forth between Orrin and Madi. "These aren't products that we make on a regular basis."

"It's enough to get us going. We owe you one." Orrin smiled at Maeve. "This will be a huge help. Are you doing all right here? Are you keeping safe?"

Maeve blinked in confusion. "I'm home. Why wouldn't I be safe?"

Orrin forgot who he was talking to. "I meant, have there been any further attempts on your life since Anabella was put in prison."

"Oh, no. That sort of thing has stopped," Maeve answered while pushing the door to the storage room closed. "Though Lady Sanerris isn't in prison anymore. She made a deal."

Orrin stopped moving. "She what? Why would you do something so—"

Madi grabbed his hand and squeezed. "Maeve, what kind of deal?"

Maeve waved her bracelet back over the door. She shook her arms to let her sleeves fall back over her wrists. "I don't know the details."

"She tried to kill you all," Orrin growled through clenched teeth. "Why would you let her go free?"

"She's not free," Maeve said, looking up in shock. "Oh, I'm sorry. I've upset you. She's confined to the school. I think she has to wear a necklace like yours, Orrin. Did you know that with the death of her son, she is the last member of her family? My father said that some of the others wanted her executed, but then we'd have to rename the Sanerris School. I suppose it could have been renamed . . ."

Maeve tapped her finger on her chin in thought. "I don't think that had any bearing on her predicament, but I'd imagine it didn't hurt her case."

Orrin stared as his mind raced. "Madi, we need to leave Odrana."

Madi still held his hand, which Orrin realized when she stopped him from storming off. "Orrin, wait. We need to know more." She turned to Maeve. "Dey was told she was sequestered and awaiting trial. She plotted to kill you all."

"All I know is she pleaded innocent and blamed everything on Arvin. She is not the lord of Mistlight and has a teaching position of some sort. This happened yesterday. I'll go find my father and have him explain."

Orrin shook his head. "No. We're leaving."

Madi's fingers were a vise on his wrist. "Maeve, she kidnapped Orrin. She tried to kill Orrin and Daniel. She tried to kill Finley. She probably sent assassins to kill you."

Maeve nodded along with Madi's argument. "I'm not a chancellor, Madi. I don't know what happened. I'll tell my father you're upset and make him send a letter. If Orrin wants to have charges brought against her for what she did to him, I can see what I can do to help, but he's not from Odrana. He's not a noble. You know how that complicates things."

Orrin cast [Calm Mind] and began to peel Madi's fingers off his wrist one at a time. "We're wasting time, Madi. There's nothing we can do now. We have bigger problems."

Now that his fear and anxiety were riding back seat in his mind, Orrin saw the tense posture of Madi's shoulders. He healed the bruises on his wrist where she'd grabbed him. He also used [Calm Mind] on his friend.

"Madi, we have to help Daniel."

That snapped her out of it. She sighed. "I'm sorry, Maeve. Please tell the chancellors that Dey is very interested in whatever deal Anabella made. We'll talk."

Maeve smiled and waved for them to follow her. Her normal obliviousness was on display. Orrin kept casting [Calm Mind] on himself and Madi. He cared for Maeve. They'd become friends, but her tendency to ignore topics that didn't interest her was something that he needed to keep in mind. She started telling them about an experiment she was running with growing different fruit types in seasonally inappropriate climates.

"We need to get word to Finley," Orrin whispered to Madi as they moved back toward the entrance of the building.

Finley Madvarr was the son of the chancellor of Ronden, the Odranan province that bordered Veskar. He'd helped rescue Orrin after discovering a possible assassination attempt, and he'd been in the room when they'd fought the Sanerris mother and son. If Anabella was free, Finley might be in danger.

"I spoke with him last night," Madi said softly, slowing her stride and letting some distance grow between them and Maeve. "He traveled to Dey with some of his best fighters and mages to help with the Horde. Odrana supplied reinforcements already, but he said he felt honor-bound to help you and Daniel."

Orrin smiled. He'd made more friends than just Maeve at the Sanerris School. "At least he'll be safe in Dey. We can protect him."

Madi kept quiet.

"What is it?"

Madi slashed her hand down. "Later."

Orrin followed her eyes. Two guards that they'd not seen before waited by the exit. Maeve was still explaining her newest project, oblivious that they'd not heard a word of what she'd said.

Orrin kept a [Decrease Strength] spell primed, but the guards simply watched them walk through the doors. The heat of the sun beat down relentlessly as they exited the building. *I'm getting paranoid.*

"Rae, Madi wanted to know if you're seeing anyone?" Maeve's question broke the tense atmosphere.

Orrin choked and coughed.

Rae raised her helmet up and winked. "Sorry, Lady Catanzano. You aren't my type."

Madi laughed. "I asked for a friend."

Orrin stood between the three women, sweating.

"In that case, I'm single." Rae kept her eyes on Madi, not acknowledging Orrin standing right next to her. "If your friend wants to get a drink sometime, I spend most nights at Rocza's pub. It's not hard to find."

"Good to know." Madi beamed. "I'll make sure to let them know."

Orrin was red as he walked away.

"Sorry if I embarrassed you too much," Madi said with a grin as she caught up to him outside of town.

Orrin paced and tried to bring his emotions under control. He wouldn't really [Teleport] back to Dey without Madi. That didn't mean he couldn't enjoy the fantasy. He didn't mind her teasing. Daniel had done worse for years. It was part of the reason that he'd never confessed his crush on Daniel's sister to his best friend.

Orrin also didn't care that Anabella Sanerris was alive. This wasn't Earth. Even there, criminals went free and people got away with bad shit. He was old enough to know that things didn't work out all the time but still . . . he'd hoped the leaders of Odrana were smart.

What bothered him most was the million little things that went along with the demon Horde. Orrin was stretching himself thin. He woke up each morning and made spell orbs. He trained with Madi and Daniel. He watched his back for the Hospital, which it seemed was now in the middle of a civil war. He worried about Tony and Amir staying safe. The faces of a dozen acquaintances that he hadn't checked up on since he got back from Odrana ran through his head.

"Orrin?" Madi nudged him in the ribs. "You ready?"

I don't have time to break down. We need to get these ingredients back for the [Purify] potions and I should go check the third wall in the Pass. I think it should be done by now. I wonder if Daniel is—

"Orrin, snap out of it and talk to me," Madi demanded, interrupting his spiraling thoughts.

"What? Sorry." Orrin tried casting [Calm Mind] again. It wasn't working as long for some reason. "I'm going to [Teleport] us back to Dey. We can make another jump to the Outer Wall unless you nee—"

Madi grabbed his shoulders and made him face her directly. "You're shaking. This isn't because I joked with Rae, is it? I was trying to lighten the mood like you and Daniel do. I'm going to find out everything I can about this deal with Anabella as soon as I can. Don't worry about this. I'll handle it."

Orrin held out a hand. Madi was right. A slight tremor passed along his fingers. He considered turning on [Mind Bastion], but the last thing he needed right now was cold logic. He might convince himself that storming off to kill Lady Sanerris was the best course of action. Plus, he'd promised too many people to cut back on his use of the skill. It made him distant and kind of an asshole.

"It's not just Anabella," Orrin finally got out. He forced his hands into his pockets. "I think I just need to rest for a few minutes when we get back and sort out my thoughts. I'm a bit frazzled, is all."

Madi cocked her head to the side. Her hair was tied into small bundles on top and they waved in the air when she moved. "Talk to me. Let me help you for once."

Orrin felt the weight crashing back down on his shoulders and sat down against the wall outside the city. He plucked a few blades of grass and twisted them together. Madi sat on her heels next to him.

"I think I'm overwhelmed," he admitted. "I'm spreading myself thin. I'm worried about everything and I can't control it all. We have plans on plans on plans and then the sudden addition of a free Anabella sent me over the edge. How should we change the Horde retreat plans now that she's around? How many of the Odranan troops that were sent are her spies and should we try to find out who is who before giving out information to them? How should I spend my administrator points? Should I buy something that could help us or wait for an emergency?"

Orrin watched his fingers braid the three strands of grass together into a rope the length of his middle finger. *How do I knot the ends together? I used to know this.*

"I have ability points to spend, but I'm paralyzed with indecision. It's just like when I played video games. I'd collect every special spell scroll or invincibility potion and not use them because I might need them in the next fight. Did I tell you that I completed all four of my buff spells? I capped out the experience in each. Now I've got a mystery skill that costs fifty points sitting there like a weight on my chest. It could be a strong spell. I'm scared it's going to be [Utility Ward]—I never bought level three because the mana price would be absurd compared to the payoff. What if I waste the points? I could use them to get [Alchemy] and make my own [Purify] potions, but that would be one more thing that I have to worry about doing. I know everyone is pulling their weight and doing what they can, but damn it . . ."

Orrin threw the broken grass strands down and rubbed his fist across his eyes. "Never mind, you don't need to listen to me bitch."

"Shut up," Madi said calmly. "You are allowed to complain. You are allowed to feel overwhelmed. You should know that you aren't the only one feeling that way, Orrin. I'm terrified of messing up, and there is no doubt in my mind that we all will make mistakes before this is over. It's good to admit it, though. I can't help you make the perfect choices for your points, but I am here to talk things through. Daniel and Brandt are, too. If you want, my father would carve time out of his day to discuss spells and skills with you. I used to get so caught up in what spells I'd purchase at my next level-up that I'd get indecisive. My father gave me advice that he said he uses every day: Fight one battle at a time. Give each task your full attention until it is defeated."

Orrin grinned involuntarily. It was nearly the same advice his mom gave him when he had too much homework piled up at the end of the weekend. "*Start small and knock it out one at a time.*" Orrin could hear her voice.

I miss you, Mom.

"What do you say? Pick one thing and we'll figure it out together," Madi said as she stood up and reached out her hand.

Orrin slapped his palm against hers. She pulled him up and he felt lighter than he had in days. "Thank you, Madi."

She smirked evilly. "First task, ask Rae out for dinner."

Orrin narrowed his eyes. "Maybe I should leave you here. You can run back to Dey."

Chapter 6

Madi laughed at Orrin's threat and pointed at his chest. "If you leave me here, I'll have to pay to get back. Daniel will send you back right away. I'm half kidding about asking out Rae, but I really am here for you if you want to talk through anything. Daniel is the [Hero] and is an important figure for the fighting forces we've assembled to push back the Horde, but Orrin . . . you're just as important."

Orrin scratched at his neck and turned west. He couldn't see Dey from where they were, but his [Teleport] spell would let them step through the miles in a second. "That's nice of you to say, Madi, but—"

"But nothing," she said, stepping around to get in his face again. "Your help will save hundreds if not thousands of people. My father and the other lords know who you are and how hard you've been working for us. Everyone has seen how much of the Pass you helped map by yourself, and that's not mentioning your spell orbs. Leanthun respects you more than half of the people in charge. Maeve and Finley consider you a friend. Putting aside the Anabella issue, Odranan leadership is terrified of being on your bad side. Not the [Hero]. You."

Madi rested her hand on his shoulder and waited for him to look her in the eyes. "If you have a problem, we all do. Let me help."

Orrin's mind ran through a dozen things he'd been putting off, ignoring, or hadn't been able to get to lately and he sighed. For all the shit she was giving him about his little crush, Madi was being a friend right now. "I don't know where to start," he admitted.

Madi crossed her arms and tilted her head. Orrin recognized the stance and tried to head off the lecture.

"I'm serious. I have a lot of points to spend, both administrator and ability points, but there isn't a guide to help for my class. There isn't much you could do to help me with that."

"You idiot." She put her fingers on her eyes and rubbed hard. "I just spent days researching possible spells and skills for myself. Did you forget that you gave me a class straight out of myth? Is there anyone better than me that can understand what you are going through? I spent years plotting my course for [Prism Conjurer] and even longer slowly leveling up. My spell list is a mess. I have to level up spells before I can unlock things I've lost. I've gained spells that I thought weren't real."

"I hadn't thought of it like that," Orrin admitted. "I'm sorry. I shouldn't— Ow!"

Madi knocked on his head hard. "Don't be stupid. I knew it wasn't going to be easy starting over from level one. I didn't expect this huge jump a few days later, either, but at least I can help during the Horde attack. We aren't talking about me, though. How many ability points do you have?"

Orrin checked his status screen.

Orrin	**Utility Warder Level 31 (18,245/23,000)**	**Ability Points: 71 Administrator Points: 23**

"I have over seventy," Orrin confessed. "I know that seems like a lot, but I'm trying to make sure I get a ward for every type of magic."

Madi shrugged. "I'm not judging you, O. You don't have to spend the points until you are ready. When we get back, we can go over the spells you have and any weak points I can find. I doubt I'll find anything, though. I'm glad you're on our side."

Orrin smiled. "Thanks, Madi. I am sorry that you lost some of your spells, though. Maybe I can figure a way out to help you get them back."

"I appreciate the thought, but for everything I lost, I gained more." Madi held her hand up in the air. Her arm's shadow cast a long black spot along the grass, but around the edges, a pool of different colors shimmered. "I've been experimenting, and my new class is everything I ever hoped it would be. Give me a year or two and I might even give you a hard time in a fight."

Orrin tried to see the mana around Madi. He was getting better at isolating the waves around cast spells, but other than the addition of his [Time Ward], he'd yet to unlock more spells.

"Why are you looking at me like that?" Madi asked as she dropped her hand.

"Trying to see the mana around your shadow. I can't place the magic type," Orrin explained. "It doesn't matter. We should get back. We've been away for long enough."

"What do you see?" She raised her hand and the shadows crawled again.

Orrin was about to cast [Teleport] but paused at the quiver in her voice. He studied her for a minute and looked back down at her shadow. "There is light mana there for sure, but it moves and seems to be changing into . . . something I can't figure out. There's something else there, too, but I can't see it fully."

Madi bit her lip and then stepped closer. "Don't tell anyone. I trust you, but nobody else can know. I think I can use shadow magic now. I've always been able to curve light into different frequencies, but it only affected the strength of the spell a little either way. But now . . . if I hit the right spot . . . I can't explain it yet, but I think I can cast different magics. I tried pushing it all the way and the light twisted in a weird way. I splashed a training dummy with light and it was covered in black darkness."

"That sounds powerful. Good for you," Orrin said, missing the fear in her voice. "I wonder if you could cast that on someone and make them blind."

"No, Orrin. Shadow magic is the opposite of light magic. I shouldn't be able to cast it. If I force a bit of shadow through my spells, I can twist it around and do weird things. My father doesn't own any shadow magic books. What if he thinks less of me for this?"

Orrin cast [Calm Mind] on Madi. She stopped hyperventilating and smiled weakly.

"Thank you."

Orrin hesitantly reached out and grabbed Madi's hand. Their Guild rings clinked together, and he noticed a dainty silver ring on her hand as well. "I won't tell anyone, but this is not a bad thing. I'll find some books when I have a minute and we can work on it."

She squeezed his hand back. "I appreciate that."

"We should get back," Orrin said, noticing how close they were. He dropped her hand and shuffled away.

Madi chuckled and they disappeared from Odrana.

Orrin unloaded the supplies in the Catanzanos' receiving foyer and Madi ordered people around storing some and moving more to the appropriate parties. Orrin sat in the corner of the room, drinking his second cup of coffee of the day. The entire trip to Odrana had wasted an hour, and they needed to get back to the Wall soon.

Orrin toyed with his status screen and read the same box again. After he leveled all four of his increase-stat spells to ten thousand experience, he received a cryptic upgrade option.

4/4 Completed
Would you like to upgrade for 50 AP?

Some of Orrin's spells earned experience for every point of mana he spent casting the same spell. When Orrin spent the first thousand points of mana on [Increase Will], it moved from level one to level two. However, when his stat-increasing spells reached level three, they plateaued with no additional level increase. Instead, he'd received a one-of-four notification that grew with the completion of the four stats: intelligence, will, dexterity, and strength.

He'd never received the option to upgrade something without a complete description of what he was buying. Now he had a dilemma.

Even if I spend fifty points, I'll have twenty-one points left. That is more than enough to buy anything I might need on the fly. Madi's right. I should knock these things out one at a time. My increase-stat buffs are my most powerful spells. What if this gives me a way to cast something like [Utility Ward] but without the need to be in my party?

Orrin hovered over the purchase button.

"Screw it."

New Spell Purchased:
[Increase Constitution] increases target Constitution by +1 per 10 MP variable without return.

"Huh?" Orrin poked the screen, hoping it would give more information. "That's not the same as the other ones."

[Increase Will] increased a target's will by one for five minutes with a base cost of five mana points. It said nothing about "without return." While it was awesome to find a way to increase his health and potentially the health of everyone around him, Orrin was concerned with the changed wording of this spell.

"Variable, I understand," he muttered to himself. "I can spend fifty MP and get a plus-five constitution, but I've never seen 'without return.'"

He watched Madi giving the last orders about the boxes of plants needed to brew more [Purify] potions.

Might as well. Orrin cast the spell on himself using the minimum mana cost of ten.

Orrin	Utility Warder Level 31 (18,245/23,000)	Ability Points: 21 Administrator Points: 23
HP: 340/340	MP: 490/500	
Strength: 9	Constitution: 34	Dexterity: 11
Will: 40	Intelligence: 11	

His constitution went up four, which grew his health points an additional forty as well. This would give him even more shield options for himself and his friends. He hadn't cast [Utility Ward] this morning and his buffs had worn off while waiting around. *If I increase my will and intelligence to a hundred, I can increase my constitution by ten for a single mana point. That is crazy!*

Orrin stood to tell Madi that he'd gone for it and it had worked out. He took two steps and frowned. He waited and watched.

"Fuck."

"Orrin?" Madi swept across the room. "What's wrong?"

"I bought a new spell. Have you ever heard of a spell that costs mana variable without return?" Orrin asked, hoping he was wrong.

"I . . . I don't think so. What spell?" Madi waved a courier away.

"[Increase Constitution]," he answered, ignoring her gasp. "The problem, though . . . once I cast it, I don't get my mana back."

The notification in his status that showed his mana pool was blinking with an exclamation point. It was stuck at four hundred and ninety.

"Turn it off," Madi suggested. "That should fix it."

Orrin poked around and sighed. "I can't turn it off."

Madi pursed her lips in thought. "Maybe it'll wear off? If not in a few minutes, then after you sleep. That's how your other spell works, right?"

A swell of hope filled his chest. "Damn, that's probably it. I was terrified for a minute."

The courier hopped from foot to foot behind Madi. She turned and rolled her wrist at him.

"Lady Catanzano, we've received word. The Horde has set up camp half a mile from the Outer Wall. Your father and the [Hero] request your presence," he said. "Do you have a response message?"

Madi slowly shook her head and the young man didn't wait around. As he left, Madi turned back to Orrin. "You mentioned once that a higher constitution would affect all the other stats, right?"

Orrin stood straight in pride. "You listened."

"Right?"

"In theory, yes. I know that it makes it harder to heal for sure. I think a high con stat would make a person harder to do damage to with spells."

"What about handling the stress of higher-powered spells?"

Orrin narrowed his eyes. "It should . . . why?"

Madi barely looked at him as she grabbed his arm and dragged him from the house. "Get us to the front. You can buff my constitution so I can cast [Sunbeam] for longer than a few seconds. If the Horde pushes in, I want to cast it with everything I've got."

Chapter 7

Daniel and Brandt stood at the forefront of the Outer Wall when Orrin and Madi arrived. The elven leader, Leanthun, was close by, talking with Madi's father, Silas Catanzano. Men and women lined the Outer Wall every fifteen feet or so for as far as Orrin could see. He knew the choke points would have more clustered troops, but this was the first defense, and they'd spread thin in an attempt to keep watch over the entire entrance to the Pass.

Over the edge of the stone wall, far in the distance, Orrin could see the Demon Lord and his troops had set up camp. Tents were erected and defenses of their own were built. They were far away still, but Orrin could just make out a palisade of angled wooden sticks around the front of the encampment. Bonfires roared high at spaced intervals, and a larger cluster of tents sat toward the back.

"What did we miss?" Orrin asked. They'd [Teleported] in nearby, been pointed in the right direction, and climbed the circular stairwell to the commanders' location.

Daniel's drawn face brightened for a moment at hearing Orrin's voice. He stepped in Orrin's direction, but Brandt grabbed Daniel's arm and shook his head.

"I'm not having this discussion again, Brandt," Daniel snapped and pulled his arm away roughly. "He'll see it himself soon enough."

Orrin felt a pit form in his stomach. "See what?"

Silas wheeled himself over to the group, with Leanthun trailing behind him. "Daniel, we've been over this. It does not matter what—"

"Orrin, what do you think a demon looks like?" Daniel interrupted the man. Silas frowned but stayed silent.

Orrin blinked at the unexpected question. "I don't know for sure. I remember Tony told me about them once." Orrin tried to pull up the memory but only remembered pieces. "Some have horns but not all of them, I think. Maybe different color skin?"

Daniel shook his head. "There are thousands of troops out there, and with [Telescope], I can see them all. Orrin, they're almost all humans. There are a few elves in there and a group of orcs, too. For every person with red skin or small goat horns on their head, there are a hundred that look like someone we'd pass on the street. I was told these were monsters coming to invade and kill. The Quest lied."

Orrin pulled the Quest box up and read. He shook his head. "No, Daniel. The Quest said a dark army was assembled. This is a Dark Horde, not a demon Horde."

Daniel turned and punched the stone wall behind him. "I can't kill regular people again."

Orrin glanced around and saw that everyone else had backed away from the raging [Hero]. A few people down below had stopped in place, holding supplies or weapons. The fear in the air was palpable and Orrin didn't know what to do. Daniel knew when Orrin cast [Calm Mind] on him. He was on edge about something, and the last thing anyone needed was an unhinged [Hero].

"D. Does it matter? They're here to attack us. We know nothing about these people other than that. They came here." Orrin moved closer and sighed. "It sucks what you went through and it sucks that this world keeps kicking us when we're down, but those are the bad guys out there."

Daniel's fists clenched and went slack. His voice was a faint whisper when he spoke. "Orrin, you weren't there outside the elven forest. It was tough getting used to killing monsters, but those are people out there. I . . . I'm not sure I can keep killing people."

Orrin moved in front of his best friend and peered out across the razed ground separating the Outer Wall and the Demon Lord's camp. "If you can't, we might die."

Daniel stiffened behind him.

"I wish I could tell you that I'll figure something out, but I've already thrown everything I've got at this problem, D." Orrin pushed his sleeves up to his elbows to cool his arm. The sun continued its slow crawl into the sky above, beating down with relentless fury. "If I thought all the people behind us would follow me or Madi or even Silas, I would tell you to get back to Dey and wait . . . They won't do that, though. You are the [Hero]. You are the one that the elves, Dey, and even Odrana rally around. At some point, you are going to have to fight."

"Maybe we could convince them to leave?" Daniel said in a hopeful tone. "We could go out under a white flag and try to negotiate with them. Nobody knows why they always attack Dey. We could make a treaty or something."

Orrin paused. "Daniel, do you remember the first time Mark Lenoti pushed me on the playground? Your parents talked with his parents and he stayed away from me for a few weeks?"

Daniel didn't answer, so Orrin continued.

"When Mark started tripping me in the lunchroom, you told him to stop. He said sorry, but a few days later, he did it again. We tried every way we could think of to get him off my back, but he kept coming at me," Orrin said, remembering the weeks of torment. "He kept doing it until you tackled him, sat on his chest, and told him that if you ever saw him near me again, you wouldn't hesitate to beat him up. Mark was still a dick and never stopped being mean to me, but he never touched me again after that."

"This isn't a bully, Orrin. We can't threaten them or hit them a few times to make them run away. There are thousands of people down there and behind us who will die," Daniel said softly, shrinking into himself. "I'm not stupid. I know they're coming to kill everyone, but . . . I'm scared, man. It's too easy to kill people, and I don't want to lose myself. There has to be another way."

Orrin glanced back at the group around them. A space had formed where they'd backed away, giving room for him to talk with the [Hero]. Orrin could see the frustration on Brandt's face. Brandt was a knight who had dedicated his life to protecting others. Silas sat watching intently, probably thinking of ways to use the panicking [Hero] and make things go the way he wanted. Leanthun whispered to another elf but took the time to check in every few seconds on what was going on.

Madi appeared torn, constantly shifting her feet. She wanted to join this conversation but was giving them space. Orrin had to give her credit. She was working hard on boundaries with them and trying not to be demanding.

"Madi, come here, please." Orrin waved his hand and she practically jumped the few feet distancing them.

"What's up?" she asked. She'd even started using some of their phrases. "Are we attacking?"

"Daniel didn't know the demon Horde was made up of regular people," Orrin explained. "He doesn't want to kill more innocents. How many people died when those two demons attacked Dey?"

Daniel's head snapped up. When Madi answered, he looked away again.

"Is that all you need me for?" Madi asked. "Did you tell him about my idea?"

"Not yet," Orrin answered. "He's got his head up his butt and is scared to fight."

Daniel was in his face so fast that Orrin almost used [Gust] to launch him off the wall. "I'm scared to fight? Of course I am. I've never wanted to fight, but I've been fighting every day since we got here, Orrin. I've killed people. I'm good at it, even when I don't want to be. I know that there are some actual demons down there. I can feel it. There's a pull in my chest to go out there and slaughter everyone. I'm not scared for my safety; I'm scared of how badly I want to do it. I'm scared that I won't be able to stop myself until everyone is bleeding under my sword."

Madi pushed her way between the two men, holding a hand on Daniel's chest but also keeping one on Orrin. He was surprised to find he was pushing into her palm, ready to push Daniel back.

"You two are friends. Stop right now," she ordered, looking back and forth. "Orrin, apologize. That was uncalled-for."

"What?" Orrin sputtered. "There is an army right there and he's saying he doesn't wan—"

"Apologize to Daniel. Of course he's scared. We all are." She turned to glare at him and Orrin stepped back. "You aren't listening to him."

"I am listening," Orrin countered. "He wants to go parley with the demons and—"

Madi didn't say a word, but the lightning that flickered in her eyes gave him pause. He cleared his throat and mumbled, "I'm sorry, Daniel."

"Now, you. Apologize," Madi said and gave Daniel a push in his center mass. He barely moved an inch.

"I'm sorry I got in your face," Daniel muttered. "You don't have to be an as—"

"Finish that sentence and so help me, I will send you both back to Dey. You two are our best hope of getting through this alive. Not one of you. Both of you. Daniel, I know you are worried you'll go off on your own. We've talked about this. Brandt is not leaving your side." Madi dropped her hands to her hips. "Talk to us. What are you worried about?"

Daniel deflated again. He turned back to look over the expansive, barren field separating the enemy camp from the Outer Wall. He took so long to respond that Orrin wasn't sure he was going to answer at all.

"I've been ignoring the fact that I'm a murderer for a long time. I hoped that this enemy would look different enough that I could ignore it. I'd built it up and justified it all in my head," Daniel explained, still not looking at them. "When I saw all the humans down there, I saw the group outside the forest again. I heard the screams and the blood. Then I felt the call of a demon."

Daniel's hand reached up to touch Gertrude on his back. A comforting habit that he'd picked up along the way. His security sword. "I wanted to jump down there and rush the Horde . . . It's more than that. I needed to attack that demon. I thought about how powerful I would feel taking them out and how weak the obstacles in the way would be."

He sank to the ground and turned to put his back to the battlements. Daniel's head hung between his knees. "Obstacles. That's all those people are to me now. Weak speedbumps on my way to kill a demon. Something is wrong with me."

Madi moved before Orrin, sitting down on his right side. She put her arm over him and hugged him awkwardly, as his giant sword got in the way. He waved a hand and it disappeared, gone into his own dimensional space.

Orrin watched them silently. He knew that Daniel was dealing with the trauma of killing people. He'd struggled with it more than Orrin had. It wasn't something that he thought about much, because he was scared of the answers he'd find. A vague hand wave at [Mind Bastion] worked in the past, but Orrin was better at controlling the skill now. He rationalized his own kills while not under its mind-cooling effects.

Orrin remembered the way Daniel had abandoned them after

their first dungeon run to attack a rumored demon. He'd had to rescue his friend that time. Tony had confirmed that a [Hero] would have a natural urge to hunt down demons, but Orrin had thought it was controlled. Now that Daniel knew about it, it would be easy for him to ignore the instinct. Right?

He brought up the Quest.

> **Defeat the Demon Lord—In the southern lands, the Demon Lord has risen. The dark armies have been assembled. Seek out and defeat the Demon Lord before the Dark Horde attacks.**
> **Reward: 1,000,000 XP and Dark Essence Unlocked**

"Defeat the Demon Lord . . ." Orrin muttered. "That's it! Daniel, can you see the demons?"

Daniel's dark eyes blinked back tears. "I can feel them, Orrin. They stand out like fires on a snowy field."

"Can you tell which is the Demon Lord?" Orrin stood and narrowed his eyes, trying to see the large tents at the back of the camp. "Maybe toward the back, there?"

"They're all too far away to [Identify], O." Daniel wiped his arm across his face, expertly dislodging himself from Madi's hug in the same motion. He recognized Orrin was on to something. "What is it?"

"We don't have to defeat the entire Horde. The Quest says we have to defeat the Demon Lord. Madi, I'm sorry, but I don't think you'll need to burn everyone to the ground. We might be able to take out the Demon Lord with a precision strike." Orrin spoke faster as the idea formed in his mind. "Leanthun. Silas. How many scouts are out there, and do we have eyes on the Demon Lord?"

The two leaders moved closer as Orrin asked his questions. Both sent runners to track down anyone who might have answers. Madi's hand briefly rested on Orrin's shoulder and squeezed. He smiled and went back to giving orders.

"If this works, the Horde might retreat," Daniel said slowly. The life in his eyes returned as hope sparked. "They might leave and not attack."

Orrin doubted the plan would work. Something always went wrong. He kept his mouth shut anyway.

Chapter 8

Orrin's plan was simple: Kill the Demon Lord.

Simple if they ignored the thousands of enemies between them and their target. Simple if the Demon Lord wasn't at level one hundred. Simple if a dozen things didn't go wrong.

The Quest only required the Demon Lord to be defeated, not the entire army. Orrin assumed that meant all the people mustered up in front of the Demon Lord would scatter at his death. Using [Camouflage], he could sneak into the middle of the army and incapacitate their leader.

"Walk me through it again," Silas said as he rubbed his eyes. "But tell me why you need to go alone?"

"He doesn't," Daniel grumbled, his arms crossed. While he had originally agreed to Orrin's plan, once the topic of his demon-lodestone issue was raised, everyone unanimously voted the [Hero] was to remain back on the Outer Wall. "He just likes being the center of attention."

"You know me so well, Golden Daniel," Orrin shot back but cringed when Madi narrowed her eyes at him. "Sorry, D. You know that if you go, it puts the entire attempt in jeopardy. You said yourself that you were having a hard time staying away from the demons from this far away. What happens if you get close and lose control? You need to stay here."

Silas raised his hand to interrupt. "Why you? We have people at higher levels and with better subterfuge spells than you. If it is as you say and the Horde will disperse at the Demon Lord's death, we can send multiple attacks in at the same time."

Orrin agreed with Silas in theory. Multiple attacks would allow for contingencies that he alone couldn't pull off. The problem was with the information brought back by the various trackers and hunters watching the traveling Horde.

"You heard Leanthun's man. Nobody could get close enough to the army. Every single time, they were spotted. I'm not saying we shouldn't have them ready to attack, but there's a better chance that I can make it through."

"Why you? We have others that have [Camouflage] or can move quicker than you. At least take Madeleine. Her powers are growing daily," Silas said, trying again.

Orrin held down his smile. That was Silas's angle. He wanted Madi to be part of the attack group. He wasn't stupid and knew the reason it had to be Orrin. Leanthun had seen it at the first explanation and accepted it with cold stoicism. Sure, he'd asked Orrin if he was okay with taking the risk, but he'd moved on to getting all the information gathered on troop movements and layout that he could.

"Orrin explained it already," Madi said finally, exasperation in her voice. "We have individuals who are better at one area, but nobody can move quickly, heal, dodge, [Teleport], and take someone down. He's a team in and of himself. Stop arguing and help figure out things he might have overlooked."

Silas might as well have been slapped. His daughter talking back to him in front of hundreds of onlookers was not a good look for one of the men in charge of the defense of Dey. Lord Catanzano recovered quickly and nodded his head toward Madi. "As ever, I'm amazed at how well you grasp the problem at hand, Madeleine. Blunt and to the point as well, when it is needed. Your mother would be proud." Silas raised his voice. "Orrin, I give you this task and ask that you protect Dey and all the life beyond that we defend. Strike into the heart of the enemy and destroy the Demon Lord. End this threat to our families and return victorious."

Daniel's mouth dropped open and Madi rolled her eyes.

Of course, Silas tries to take credit for the idea, Orrin thought as he ignored the clapping behind him. *If I come back with a win, he looks like the genius behind it all. If I die, I'm an expendable part of the army. I'm not the [Hero].*

Orrin forestalled Daniel's disconcerted response before he could begin. "Daniel, it doesn't matter. I'll be back in an hour or less if I'm lucky. Madi, I'm counting on you two."

Madi's role was simple but could mean the difference between Orrin surviving and not. Daniel had [Map], the same skill that Orrin used more than anyone else they'd heard of. With a single ability point, Daniel could now find anyone in his party with [Party View]. His range gave him enough to watch that Orrin's dot on his [Map] should stay visible.

Orrin would cast [Camouflage] to avoid some of the troops, but it was his combination of [Gust] and [Boost] that would let him move quickly enough to find the Demon Lord. The multitude of different wards that he created around himself would hopefully stop any attacks from landing. Plus, he had [Side Steps]. The skill only had a small chance of activating and making an attack miss, but every little bit added up when facing an entire demon army by himself.

Leanthun and Silas's spies were trying to pinpoint the exact spot where the command tents were set up. If somebody could confirm the Demon Lord's whereabouts, the mission would be much easier.

"I still think you should increase my stats and let me blast them all," Madi said as she moved closer to him. Daniel was going over a map with Brandt and arguing about the location of the next choke point on the Wall. The crews would continue to build as many stopgaps in the Pass as they could.

"It's not about killing them," Orrin said, sitting back and taking a bite out of a sandwich. There was a table of food set up nearby for the leadership, but Orrin didn't see anyone else eating the food and helped himself. "They'll have a dozen ways to stop spells and another dozen ways to catch you."

"What if they can stop you?" Madi whispered hesitantly. "You convinced my father and Leanthun because you can move so fast and you can [Teleport], but the demons have had all morning to set up their defenses. They'll have [Teleport] wards and guards watching every direction."

Madi was worried for him. Orrin pulled an extra sandwich that he'd stolen out of his [Dimension Hole] and offered it to her. "They're pretty good. Eat."

When she took the bread and cheese layered together, he told her the part of the plan that he'd kept hidden. "If we can't find a way for me to [Teleport] into their camp near the Demon Lord, I'll try to run in while invisible. If they try and stop me, I've got [Way of the Water] to avoid them. If I can't find the Demon Lord and need to escape, I'll blood cycle and drop half the army. I don't even need to spend a lot of mana to do it."

Orrin bounced as he got into the math. "With my stats all maxed out, I can cast a level-three [Decrease Strength] that normally costs fifteen mana points for only one point five . . . well, rounded up to two points, because of my intelligence. Instead of dropping the target by four strength points, it should reduce each person's strength by forty because of my will. I can use [Split Spell] for a single extra point and bounce that off a few people each time. I tried it with the Hospital people we fought and took them down quick."

Madi crossed her arms and stared at Orrin, unimpressed. "So, you can take down a hundred enemies. That's not enough. You'll be overwhelmed before you make a dent in their forces."

"It's a lot more than a hundred people. I have almost five hundred MP in my mana pool. I can do close to a hundred and sixty casts, each hitting a few extra people. Even if it only bounces to two each time, that's four hundred and eight enemies that are down. That's before I blood cycle. But I don't need to make a dent in their army, just a line to escape. That's where you come in. If you see people falling, you need to cast your spell and put down a wall of fire. I can push the prone bodies out of the way and we'll avoid killing anyone if we can. That's for the worst-case scenario. If I fail and have to run, we don't want to murder half the army and have them rush the new wall here. We want to keep our strategy the same: keep them away and pick them off a few dozen at a time. Wear their spirits down. They are the invaders here and don't have the infrastructure that we do. They don't have enough food for a siege, but now that we have the Outer Wall and all the other traps set up, they can't rush straight through to Dey." Orrin tossed the last bit of bread in the air and caught it in his mouth. "If I can drop the Demon Lord, we win. If I can't, we demoralize them. Either way, Daniel doesn't have to fight as many people."

Madi took a single bite from her sandwich before answering. "You have a habit of rushing into danger. I'm not sure we should let you do this. Daniel is going to try something, I know it. When you suggested an assassination attempt on the Demon Lord, he thought you meant as a group."

"That's why Brandt is going to have to keep him back," Orrin said, checking on the other two members of their party. "Daniel needs to stay on the wall. How far can you cast your new spell? Did I give you enough constitution?"

Orrin's new spell, [Increase Constitution], was a give-and-take spell unlike anything else he had. For every ten points of mana he sacrificed from his total mana pool, he could increase a target's constitution by one. When he'd tried the spell on himself, the plus one turned into a plus four. He'd forgotten to fully buff his stats. A mistake that he'd rectified before casting another twenty points' worth of the spell on Madi.

"Twenty extra points of constitution? Yes, Orrin. I think that's enough. I can cast [Sunbeam] for almost two minutes like this," Madi said, preening. "I'll use up most of my mana even with the increased will and intelligence."

Daniel and Brandt walked up. Orrin noticed that Brandt was taking his guard-the-[Hero] job seriously. He never looked away from Daniel.

"Have the scouts reported in yet?" Daniel asked, handing the rolled-up map to Brandt. "It shouldn't take this long, right?"

"Not everybody has your stamina, Daniel," Madi chastised. "As long as the demon Horde stays put, we have time. They weren't expecting to find a new wall built up. I don't think we've ever had this much advance notice of a Horde in the history of Dey."

Brandt made a series of knocks on his leg and another knight ran to him. Brandt spoke out of the corner of his mouth, and the woman took the map before darting off again.

Daniel turned at the sound of armor moving. "Who was that?"

"One of our squires," Brandt told him. "She'll bring your markups and changes to the builders."

"I was hoping you could do that," Daniel sighed. "I explained it to you so that we could get it right."

Brandt shook his head. "I'm not leaving your side, no matter how hard you try to get rid of me."

A moment of awkward silence fell over the four of them as the whistling wind pushed its way down the ramparts.

Daniel grumbled something, but everyone ignored him.

Orrin patted his back. "If I can't kill the Demon Lord, I'm sure you'll get the chance. It's not like this plan is a sure thing, either. If the scouts can't find him, then the entire thing is off and—"

"We've found him," Leanthun gasped as he ran up the stairs. "We've found the Demon Lord and have his location. Let's go."

Chapter 9

"It's strange," Leanthun explained as he led Orrin and Madi down the stairs, leaving Daniel and Brandt behind. "I would have expected the demons to attack by now. All they've done is dig in and fortify, which is not something I've ever read about."

Orrin noted with some surprise that he was easily keeping up with the swift elf. All his training was paying off. "How many Dark Hordes have you helped fight?"

Leanthun threw a desperate grin over his shoulder. "This is my first. It's been a long time since we've helped the humans."

Orrin exchanged a glance with Madi, who shrugged before she answered. "Demons rarely attack en masse and there hasn't been a Demon Lord in a millennium. There have been a few demons that attack from time to time, but nothing like this. I've never seen my father so nervous."

Orrin scoffed but kept his mouth shut. He saw no difference in the man's face.

"We pressed in on the camp from different directions and found one safe approach from the north. One of the human scouts has [Camouflage] like you. She was able to make it to the edge of the camp and return without being seen. A large group of demons were kneeling in front of a seven-foot-tall demon with red skin and massive horns. She doesn't have [Identify] but hurried back before she was caught."

Orrin followed Leanthun as they ran along the inside of the Outer Wall. "Then you're not sure it is the Demon Lord?"

"It's a calculated guess, but demons don't kneel to others without a huge power differential," Leanthun said. His curved sword bounced on his hip as he jogged. "Even if it's not the Demon Lord, you should take him out. Someone that can direct demons will be a high-ranking officer in their army."

"It's a Horde, not an army. We can't be sure they have a structured hierarchy." Madi spoke up from behind them. "Orrin should not attack anyone except the Demon Lord. This is not a suicide mission. If you can't confirm it's the Demon Lord, get out of there."

Orrin didn't have to answer. He wasn't stupid. His entire plan was an attempt to short-game the Quest and hopefully end the threat of the Horde before it attacked.

"I have to disagree," Leanthun replied, bringing them to a stop in front of a blank section of the Wall. "If you can weaken them in any way before they attack, it will save lives."

"This will save lives," Orrin said, patting the stone Wall beside him. "Now that we're away from Daniel, I can say this freely. If someone in that camp looks at me funny, I'm getting the fuck out of there. I expect this entire thing will fail and we'll have to fight from the walkways up above."

"What do you mean?" Leanthun asked with a frown. "That's not what you said—"

"Daniel is impatient." Madi started first, surprising Orrin. "Orrin came up with a plan that keeps him waiting but for a reason. Sitting up there with his thoughts and fears about fighting humans was going to end badly for everybody."

Orrin laughed. "How long did it take you to figure out?"

Madi smiled and ran her hand over her braided hair, checking that it was still tied down to her head. "How long did it take me to figure out you were distracting Daniel? About three sentences into your plan."

Leanthun's frown deepened. "We sent people out into danger and you two never planned on following through on this?"

Orrin waved his hands. "No, no. I'm going to try, but I hoped they would attack before you found anything. It would be easier to fight them from afar. If we found out where the Demon Lord was, Madi and I already have a plan on how to go scorched earth on that part of the battlefield."

"Scorched earth," Madi said slowly, tasting the words on her lips. "That's an apt description of my spell."

"Should we return, then?" Leanthun asked, uncomfortable with the subterfuge.

"Yeah, sorry. How much farther?" Orrin scratched his neck.

Leanthun reached up to one of the blocks of stone that made up the wall and pressed it. Multiple blocks turned and shifted, cascading away to reveal an archway through the wall. "This is one of multiple inner rooms we built. It's dark inside."

Madi held up her hand and a ball of light appeared. "Will this work?"

Orrin entered behind them. The wall was hollow here, allowing the three of them to move around. As soon as he entered, the bricks moved themselves back, closing the room into darkness. Madi's spell kept the shadows away.

"What is this?" Orrin whispered. Somehow it felt more appropriate.

"At various points throughout each wall, we've made these rooms," Leanthun explained, walking up to a small lever on the far wall. "This will open a window where a defender can cast spells from below or, in your case, crawl out to get where we need to go."

Orrin groaned.

Leanthun explained their location and where Orrin was to go. Now that he was here, Orrin's stomach tightened at the prospect of soloing the big bad evil guy.

"You don't have to go," Madi said quietly. "We can wait for them to make the first move."

Orrin considered it. It would be easier to return and say the plan wouldn't work. They could make up any number of excuses. It wasn't the Demon Lord. His [Camouflage] didn't work as well as they'd hoped. Someone attacked Orrin as soon as he got close and he needed to run. Daniel wouldn't need to know, either. He would believe Orrin. They could devise a way to distract Daniel until the demons attacked. His friend's fear of harming more people wouldn't matter as much if he was reacting in defense.

That's a lie. You know Daniel won't forgive himself. Orrin closed his eyes and tried to think of another way.

"Be ready for my signal, Madi. I'll be back before you know it." Orrin forced a smile and nodded at Leanthun. "Throw the lever."

"You have to go through fast. We don't know if they have spotters out watching us."

Orrin cast his spell. Madi blinked and rubbed her eyes, staring at the ground. Leanthun activated the switch and a small opening appeared. Before he could doubt himself again, Orrin jumped through.

Running north along the Outer Wall, Orrin considered his life choices.

"I'm running. Into danger. Again," he muttered to himself. "I'm an idiot."

The idiot who kept running toward the edge of the mountain line for his friend's mental health. As much of a long shot as this plan was, if he could take out the Demon Lord, there was a chance that Daniel wouldn't have to kill all the people to his left.

With his increased dexterity, Orrin made the mile run in only a few minutes. Running that fast would have set records at his high school but now, he barely noticed. He was looking for the clump of bushes that would hide his contact. It took him a full minute before he felt his eyes slip past a certain part of the mountain for the tenth time.

He approached slowly and whispered the code phrase that Leanthun had given him. "No rest until sunrise."

"Breakfast will be late." The countersign came from the brush that Orrin would not have called bushes in his most forgiving mood. "Are you Orrin? The [Hero]'s party member?"

A slight woman with darker skin and a shaved head climbed out of the ground, breaking rock and dirt as she straightened up. At least, that's what Orrin saw. When he blinked, the ground was level again.

"That's a cool trick. I'm Orrin. How'd you do that?" He crouched and touched the ground. The grass was uniform.

"[Earth Mage] trick of the trade," she answered with a slight smile tugging at one side of her mouth before her eyes darted around. "I'm Valerie. I was told to point you in the direction I went and then get back over to safety. You have a plan, right? The [Hero] is going to stop the demons?"

She stooped low and kept looking around, her hands pushing into the pockets of the overalls she wore. Orrin saw no weapons but wondered more at the jitteriness of the scout. This was who they were sending out to check the Horde's defenses. She looked like someone's mom.

"We're all going to do our best." Orrin spoke in his most soothing voice. He decided not to cast [Calm Mind] on a person he just met. "Tell me where to go and get yourself back over the wall."

Valerie nodded and showed Orrin the path she'd taken. Every few steps, she cast a spell that left a divot in the ground. It was small enough that unless you were looking for it, the small clumps of dirt would look like large anthills. "I left a hole right by the fence line they put up. You can't miss the demons. They have a tent set up almost near the front. The Demon Lord is huge. He has a two-handed sword that is as long as he is tall. It scratches the ground when he walks sometimes. I counted six more demons with him. Three were kneeling when I got to the fence, but I got out of there. This is crazy. I shouldn't be out here. I search for good farmland in the wilderness. I'm not a soldier."

"Valerie, you did great." Orrin rested his hand on her shoulder to calm her and stop her talking. "I'll take it from here. Go."

She squeaked and nodded. Orrin tried to watch her mana, but the quickness of her spell in combination with her reactivating [Camouflage] kept him from figuring out what she did. He watched the trail on the ground as she left.

It looks like a gopher is digging under the ground, but she's actually walking . . . isn't she? Orrin put the issue out of his mind. He could ask her later if he survived.

Shut up. Of course I'm going to survive.

Making sure to keep his wards up, his stats buffed, and his [Camouflage] running, Orrin began to make his way toward the Horde.

As soon as I get close and someone sees me, I'll use [Gust] to rush in. I'll use [Identify] to find the Demon Lord and take him down. Quick little adventure. In and out in ten minutes. What could go wrong?

Finding Valerie's trail was harder than he thought until he started trying to find the mana signature left behind. The ground lit up like a Christmas tree and Orrin made a mental note to have a talk with whoever trained the mages of Dey. They were criminally undertrained compared to the students of the Sanerris School. Anybody with the least amount of training would be able to see someone had come this way. He did his best to step on each mound of dirt, crushing the magic underfoot.

The camp looked even more slipshod the closer he got. The posts were uneven and the fence was made of a dozen different materials. Some portions were wide enough for a carriage to go through, but twenty feet away, the wooden posts had been driven into the ground at knee height and touching for several yards. There were a few people standing around, arguing. A raised area closer to the Wall served as a watchtower, even though it was only three feet off the ground. Nobody noticed Orrin as he crept in.

He found Valerie's hole marker and kicked some dirt into it, smothering the last bit of mana she'd left behind. Orrin couldn't see any demons. Humans outnumbered everyone else, but he saw two elves pulling a tent up together. A group of orcs walked. One held a small calf over his shoulders. Figures moved everywhere, but no demons were about.

I'm going to need to get deeper into the camp. Orrin grimaced and slipped between two posts. He ducked behind one tent, then another. Slinking through the camp reminded him of playing assassin games. If he messed up here, he couldn't hide in a clump of hay and wait for people to stop looking for him, though. He would have one chance.

Orrin waited as two men wrestled a cauldron down the dirt path between the patches of tents. Once they'd moved away a bit, he stepped out, moving quickly across to the next area. Maybe there would be demons over here.

"Hey, give us a hand, would you?" One of the men turned and looked directly at Orrin. "Wait, who are you?"

Chapter 10

Orrin paused for a heartbeat as he let the chilling power of [Mind Bastion] speed up his thoughts. He was in danger now, but how much was up to what he did next. The man's question wasn't one of challenge but genuine curiosity. All of the elven scouts and the scouts of Dey had failed to get close to the camp in their probing attacks, with some complaining the demons had an unnatural ability to detect them before they could gather useful information. Silas's theory was the Horde had unique markers of some sort that identified friendlies from enemies. How Valerie had made it so close was anyone's guess.

The slightly bored look that was directed in his direction right now squashed that idea. They were looking right at him but not screaming out in alarm.

Orrin's heart dropped at the sudden realization. *I'm still running [Camouflage]. How can he see me? Oh. Shit.*

The spell, along with most of his protection wards, were no longer active. His stats were still boosted and [Mind Bastion] seemed to be working as well, but his protection and stealth spells were deactivated. *When I passed through the barrier they made? I didn't know that was a possibility.*

"Buddy?" The man cocked his head as he rested an arm against the big metal bowl the two of them were moving. "If you're busy doing something else, it's not a big deal. Which camp do you belong to? That last push to get here quicker created a lot of chaos. You're in Support Squad C right now."

"I'm Casimir," Orrin lied, using the name he'd gone by for a few weeks recently. "I'm . . . delivering messages. Where's command?"

Orrin was proud of himself. The off-the-cuff story would allow him to roam the camp as long as nobody looked too closely. The lie of being Casimir rolled off his tongue after all his practice.

The second man sighed and slapped the talkative one. "Stop trying to get other people to do your job, Joss. If he's Messenger Corps and you delay something important, the brass will double your taxes."

The man, Joss, rolled his eyes and continued to lean lazily against the cauldron. "Shut up, Deacon. Nice to meet you, Casimir. If you need Supp C's command, that would be Janelle over that way. Dark-green tent. You can't miss her. Why anyone would waste a messenger on us, though . . ."

Orrin nodded his thanks and left Joss and Deacon to continue their task alone before he was asked to help again. He walked in the direction offered but ducked behind a row of full wagons as soon as he lost line of sight.

"Come on," Orrin muttered, trying to reactivate [Camouflage]. The spell triggered. It ate his mana. Then it disappeared. It was similar to the feeling of using [Teleport] when a teleport ward was on—he could cast the spell but nothing worked.

Don't panic. You can't stay invisible, but you knew that was a possibility going in. The Demon Lord is around here. This isn't a problem. Keep going.

A smaller part of his brain considered what would happen if all his spells didn't work in the camp. Without [Teleport], his plan would be to run, knocking people out as he got away. If [Gust] or his decrease-stat spells were taken away as options as well . . .

Orrin used a single mana point to push the wind at some tent support lines in the distance. The long leather straps spiked to the ground rippled in the air for a moment before going still.

At least I have that. My stats are still up, so I'll hope I can still debuff others. It's not like there's a good option to test that out.

Orrin knew he could debuff himself and then bring his stats back up, but he wasn't going to mess with his own points right now. He could take someone out but without knowing who his random target was, and that chanced letting the entire camp know that something was wrong.

He rocked on his ankles and waited another minute, sorting out his choices. They'd hoped he would find the Demon Lord here, but enough time must have passed that he'd moved. With a sigh, Orrin crawled out from between the wagons and continued walking toward Janelle's green tent. Leadership would mean information. He smiled and walked with purpose, trying to act like he belonged. If he put up the persona that he was part of the camp, maybe he could get in deeper.

The support camp appeared to be mostly grunts. They ran around carrying heavy boxes and supplies or unloaded the same from different wagons. Most worked in groups of two or three. The deeper he walked toward command, the more it felt like a parking lot than a camp. Without warning, he was forced to turn left at a barricade and was in a clearing with twenty wagons in a circle. Three tents sat in the middle, the tallest the dark green he was looking for. A long line of people, including a few demons, stood in front of him.

A short and stout woman with short, bright-red hair, pale white skin, and a long, forked tail waving behind her sat behind a desk. She barked orders to each person as they approached. The members of Support Squad C would snap to attention and run off to fulfill whatever task they'd received.

Orrin couldn't help but be impressed with the order and precision. He stood in line behind a tall human man with blond hair down to his ankles and studied everything around him.

Using [Identify] would be the quickest way to find the Demon Lord, but if he used it on the wrong person, they might have a skill that let them know they were being investigated. He was hesitant to use the skill this early, but curiosity got the better of him. He used [Identify] on the man in front of him.

He froze and shook his head. *That can't be right.*

He tried again. It didn't change.

Orrin moved slack-jawed as the line continued to crawl forward. He could hear the orders better now. The orc didn't complain as she was told to bring extra shovels to Waste Administration. He blinked and used [Identify] on her as well. Maybe it was an anomaly or something.

Nope. What is going on? Orrin used [Identify] three more times. The lowest level he found was in the sixties. The man in front of him was at level eighty-five.

If this is their third-string support squad, what level is the Demon Lord at? Orrin worried that the entire camp was at a higher level than most of the Dragoon squad.

With that worrying thought, he risked using [Identify] on the demon Janelle.

Janelle Drakestone	Supervisory Assistant Level 122

Even with [Mind Bastion] running, Orrin's brain short-circuited. The cap for leveling was one hundred. That was what he'd been told. That was common knowledge.

Knowledge that was now proven wrong.

Orrin had hoped to walk up and ask Janelle for directions, but at seeing her level, fear slipped in, bypassing [Mind Bastion]. She was so much higher than him that his version of [Identify] couldn't grasp her stats, but the pit in his stomach told him her stats would be higher than he'd expected as well.

He was getting closer to the front and needed to get away. Orrin slapped his forehead like he'd forgotten something and ran off, back to his secluded spot between the wagons. Nobody paid him any attention.

Think. Calm down. This changes nothing. I can still reduce their stats . . . I hope.

He needed to know for sure that he could use [Decrease Strength] or [Decrease Dexterity]. With the level disparity of that demon, he had to assume the Demon Lord would be at a higher level as well. That also meant that his constitution was going to be stronger than normal.

Orrin didn't use strength in his fighting and decided to take the chance. He selected level-one [Decrease Strength] and cast it on himself. A sigh of relief escaped before he could help it. It worked.

Now for the real test. Orrin selected the opposite spell and buffed himself. The missing points reappeared on his status screen. *So my buffs and debuffs still work. I can do this.*

Orrin hoped he was right as he squeezed out the back of the clump of wagons and made his way back to Janelle. He wasn't going to talk to her but instead just listen. If she gave a directive to one of her underlings that sounded important, Orrin could follow. It was always a long shot that the Demon Lord would stand around in one place. If he went where the action was, he might get lucky.

Not that lucky! Orrin thought as he pushed his way back between the two open-bed wagons. Several red-skinned demons were walking down the path he'd almost escaped to. Several had bowls of food and were eating as they strolled. Orrin counted twenty demons. The majority had red skin and horns, but three or four could pass as human if not for a tail or horns randomly dispersed.

"—telling you it's true. I heard from Grappor that these walls weren't here a few weeks ago. The damn scum pushed out beyond the border and cut down trees to build it, too. It might be the biggest excursion of them recorded in thousands of years," a demon with horns that curled down like a ram said to another demon. The second demon was taller than the others, with a robe that had runes and script along the sleeves, hem, and neckline. His horns were small and pointed back along his bald head.

"If they have united together enough to build in the Pass, perhaps we should push for a full extermination. The topic has been broached in the past, but this is not one or two of them exploring out into the world. This may give them ideas of expansion," the tall demon answered. They were moving quickly down the road, and Orrin stood still as they passed.

"The Accords say that if—" the ram-horned demon started.

"Damn the Accords," one of the smaller demons cut in. He'd finished slurping up noodles from his bowl and tossed it into the back of the wagon nearby. It clattered against the wood side next to Orrin's head. "If the Accursed don't follow the rules, then we have no reason to keep to it. You know, it's like my da always said. If someone hits you, don't hesitate to put them down. They broke the peace. If they'd stayed on their side, we could keep ignoring them. Look how close they are. The bastards could make it to Tasmus in a few hours. I'll vote for extermination."

Orrin didn't breathe.

"We have a meeting at noon to discuss the new challenges. Find any of the Pure that you can. He wants everyone there," the ram demon ordered. "Do not bring up extermination at first. We must see if the votes are on our side before we make any moves."

"Votes won't matter if Mr. High and Mighty decides against it," the bowl thrower complained. "Don't call them Pure around him, either. He hates that term."

A few chuckles escaped from the red-skinned demons while the ones with white and darker skin tones dragged their feet. One of them almost spoke, but another grabbed her arm and shook his head.

Internal strife between the different ones, Orrin noted. *That could come in handy.*

"It will not matter what he decides if the new [Hero] comes out to fight," the ram demon laughed. "He will only be in charge as long as that child is alive. If we can get him to attempt a parley with this [Hero], we could end both threats at once."

"We can't attack the Dem—"

"Shut your mouth before I do it for you." The demon's robes swirled as he descended on the smaller demon. "None of us would or could hurt the Demon Lord. That is the law. However, we can target enemies with any spells or weapons we have. Accidents happen."

The group silently moved on as they digested the demon's words, leaving Orrin shaking in fear, rage, and confusion.

What was that all about?

Chapter 11

Orrin crawled under one of the wagons and thought through his situation. It might be time to give up and get out of here. He'd learned too many new things and failed to find the Demon Lord, which was the entire point of this anyway. For whatever reason, the Dark Horde had failed to notice him creeping around the camp. The group of demons that Orrin had just finished eavesdropping on was likely the same one that Valerie spotted. The Demon Lord was not here. The information he was working with was flawed, and continuing on at this point was dangerous and reckless.

Like that's stopped us before, Orrin ridiculed himself as he dragged his body through the mud and away from the main thoroughfare. *If Daniel was here, he'd at least do some damage before he left.*

The things the demons had talked about ran through his mind. They hadn't known about the new Outer Wall until they'd arrived. That meant a lack of scouts and spies. *Something made them come all this way, though. What could that be?* Orrin stopped crawling to swipe a beetle off his hand. *As far as I know, Dey doesn't send invading parties out into the demon lands.*

While he was curious why the demons thought they were going to be invaded, Orrin could barely contain himself in his desire to ask Silas about demon cities. He'd always found it a bit odd that nobody knew much about this side of the world, but there were always bigger problems to solve. From the few descriptions he'd heard of these lands before, Orrin thought it was a wasteland filled with wanton murder and mayhem.

That one guy talked about taxes. They don't seem much different than the people of Asmea, except for the higher average level.

Orrin shook his head as something dripped on his head. He glanced up. Some of the sauce from the demon's bowl was getting through the slates of wood. Orrin hesitated before running his finger against his hair and bringing a red-tinged finger to his tongue.

I can heal myself if it's poison, Orrin reminded himself before he took a lick. *Spaghetti? Really?*

The fact that these invaders could level beyond one hundred was cause for concern in the short run. The majority of the defenders would be lucky to reach level forty before they died. What worried Orrin most was whether those in charge knew and had lied to the general population.

If people believed they could reach level one hundred and never progress farther, it set a limit for humanity. True or not, people would set the timeline of their lives to reaching that target. As far as Orrin knew, nobody in Dey had reached level one hundred. In fact, he didn't even know who held the highest level. What would it do to society when they found out that level one hundred was not only attainable but surpassable?

But why would my stats only increase to one hundred if it wasn't the max level? Orrin second-guessed himself. *Maybe one hundred is the* stat *maximum and people got it confused over the years?*

He was of half a mind to use [Identify] on a few more people. The level disparity made it difficult to gather more information. When Orrin read the level of someone around his own level or lower, he could gather information about their stats, skills, and spells to a frightening degree. However, he'd learned early on that when someone had more levels than him, the blue box showed less. That was why the demon lady's stats hadn't shown up. He'd gotten stat blocks on only a few of the random people in the supply line, but nothing jumped out at him as strange or abnormally high. It was just the actual levels.

Of course, none of his theorizing mattered in the long run. The group of demons wanted to exterminate them. Anytime someone talked about "Pure" in regard to other people, that was a bad sign. Luckily for the people of Dey, it seemed the demons were as united under the Demon Lord as everyone thought they would be.

Silas will know about the Accords and have some reason for not telling us, Orrin thought as he waited for a dozen orcs carrying huge wooden boxes on their shoulders to walk by. *How many more secrets is that man going to keep from us?*

There was no reason to continue searching the camp. The Demon Lord wasn't nearby. Orrin's [Camouflage] wouldn't help him if he decided to continue his search, and without a clue as to why he hadn't immediately been spotted as an enemy while the other scouts had been, staying longer was an unnecessary risk.

"At least Daniel will be happy he didn't miss any action," Orrin muttered, just before someone grabbed his foot and pulled. He scrambled for a hold on the ground, but the wagon wheels had turned up the grass into a muddy sludge. Orrin was unceremoniously dragged from his hiding space and held upside down by his ankle.

"Look what I found." A grating voice accompanied the smell of rotting fish as Orrin was turned in the air. A massive orc, maybe ten feet tall, held him out with one hand. A two-handed battle-ax was gripped in his other hand, looking more like a toy in the meaty-fingered grip. "Another shirker? Where are you supposed to be, little one?"

Orrin barely kept himself from blasting spells at the orc. If he could talk his way out of this, getting back into the camp was still a possibility. Once he went nuclear, there was no going back.

"I . . . I was trying to clean up someone's mess," Orrin lied quickly and pointed at his head, still slick with red sauce. "There's a bowl somewhere around here and I need to get it back for cleaning."

He was proud of his quick thinking. He was less pleased with the result.

"Kitchen scullery workers don't leave the cleaning area. Jehap is big, but that doesn't mean stupid. Who are you?" The orc narrowed his eyes as he leaned in.

"I'm not on duty right now," Orrin answered, readying his spells. *This isn't going to work.* "I was passing by and saw a demon throw the bowl. It was—"

"Oh. Why didn't you say it was one of them bastards?" Jehap the orc used his other hand to turn Orrin in the air and place him right side up. His massive blade came within inches of Orrin's scalp. "They're always lording over us all. It makes sense they'd treat the entire camp like their personal trash heap. Oh. You were looking in the wrong place. The bowl is in the cart, not under it."

Jehap reached over the side and picked up the still partially full bowl. He thrust it into Orrin's arms. "Get going then. Maybe put in a good word for Jehap. A double ration here or there would be nice."

Orrin nodded and bolted. He wasn't sure if he was heading in the right direction to sell the lie to Jehap, but the more distance he made from the tall murder machine, the better. He tried going hazy with [Camouflage] again, but it continued to fail until he crossed the border fence. Orrin used [Gust] and practically flew back to where he'd left Valerie what felt like hours ago.

Checking the position of the sun, it couldn't have been more than half an hour. He renewed all his wards and kept an eye on [Map] as he made his way back toward the Outer Wall. It was only when he got closer that he realized they'd never talked about how he should get back over.

Brandt kept his eyes on Daniel as he argued with another [Builder]. They'd descended from the Outer Wall to discuss the fallback walls that were being built even as they spoke. A simple wooden table groaned under the massive amount of paper plans. The dwarf shouted as he pulled out a different blueprint.

"Here it is. This contradicts what you want. Why have a wall that falls down on the enemy? That is a waste of time. We could slow them down even more with a sturdy wall to—"

Daniel leaned forward and flicked the dwarf between the eyes. The smaller man blinked twice and tried to tackle Daniel over the table. Brandt was a tad quicker and held the snarling dwarf back.

"I don't care who you are, I'll kill you and bury you," the man shouted as he struggled against Brandt.

"Daniel, please apologize to Urtrat," Brandt said in short bursts as he tried to hold on. The dwarf was more agile than he appeared. "You didn't need to do that and you know it."

Daniel ignored Brandt and moved closer to Urtrat. He raised a hand, fingers folded to deliver another flick. The dwarf flinched.

"There," Daniel said softly and stepped back again, dropping his hand. "That is why. You've been arguing over and over against my suggestions, Urtrat. I know you want to build a big strong wall and repeat it over and over. I want the Horde to flinch and pause at each wall, not knowing if this one will fall on them, burst into flames, be filled with our troops, or just be a big boring wall. Every moment they waste considering is another life saved because we have more time to prepare. Do you understand?"

Brandt was impressed at how well Daniel was learning to deal with the dwarves. Urtrat grumbled but stopped tugging forward. When released, he grabbed another rolled-up wall plan and spread it on the table to ask more questions. Neither one spoke of the flick.

Daniel glanced back up toward the wall behind him multiple times. Brandt knew what he was worried about. He was scared for Orrin as well. The unassuming kid had grown on him even before he rescued him from more torture and certain death. This plan they had come up with was stupid. Almost as bad as his own attempt to kill Lord Sanerris. At least Brandt had training for that sort of thing. Being a [Knight] wasn't all about protecting in the light. He'd carried out his share of cloak-and-dagger missions for Lord Catanzano. Brandt had simply underestimated his target.

Madeleine . . . Madi, as she was increasingly making everyone call her, was up above, he knew. She stayed close in case Daniel tried anything. The relationship between Orrin and Daniel was a tricky one. Brandt had seen something similar in brothers who joined the guard together, but these two were nothing alike. Madi was keeping watch for any signal from Orrin. She had a [Locationist] ready to [Teleport] her closer. Daniel didn't like that part of the plan, either—something that Brandt very much agreed with. Sending Orrin in was a calculated risk. Letting Madeleine Catanzano, the daughter of a lord of Dey, go close to the demon camp was suicidal.

Yet, somehow, Brandt felt at ease watching Daniel explain how traps should be set at random intervals in the Pass with markers that could be removed quickly by retreating troops. He knew fighting was coming, but this [Hero] and his friend kept saving them all.

"Attack from above!" A clear voice rang out from the ramparts. Echoes of the same repeated a moment later.

Urtrat scooped the papers up into his arms and ran. Daniel's large sword appeared in his hand, his feet already hitting the stairwell up to the top of the Outer Wall. Brandt charged behind him, taking the steps two at a time. Not for the first time, he wished his armor was lighter, but he would have to cut quality or pay triple the price for better materials. Sweat ran down his back as he burst through the door at the top a second after Daniel.

"Where?" Daniel's question turned a few heads, and swords and staffs pointed north where several men were grappling on the ground.

Daniel and Brandt ran forward to find Madi bodily throwing their own men to the side. Broken glass on the ground told Brandt they'd used the spell orbs meant for use in emergencies. What confused him was that the same men and women he knew had the orbs were lying prone where Madi rolled their breathing bodies to the side.

"Brandt. Daniel. Good. Help me get them off him. They tackled him as soon as he jumped up here," Madi said as she pulled on a foot. "Idiot."

Brandt was still trying to figure out what was going on when he saw a familiar face in the middle of the bundle of limbs.

"Sorry, guys, I used [Gust] to send myself up the wall, but I overshot it a bit. I didn't mean to fall on that guy, I swear." Orrin smiled guiltily from under six fully armored warriors. "At least we know their response time is good."

Chapter 12

The more eager of the defenders needed some healing and buffing after Orrin had had to drop them. He didn't hurt anyone, but having their feet stop working because their strength dropped to one made a few heads bounce off stone.

He wasted no time telling Daniel everything that happened. Brandt listened in but stayed quiet. Orrin did notice the knight making hand signals at two other guards who ran off at a sprint, but he kept talking.

"Hold on, O," Daniel said, stopping Orrin's multitude of theories about level caps. "That's a lot of information that you threw at me in one long sentence. You didn't find the Demon Lord, but demons are all over level one hundred?"

"Not all the demons, I don't think," Orrin answered. He pulled a bottle of water out of his [Dimension Hole] and poured it over his hair. It still stank of tomato sauce. "It's weird, right?"

Daniel said nothing as he gazed into the distance. Brandt shrugged when Orrin raised an eyebrow.

"Has he been brooding a lot?"

Brandt held back a laugh, but his eyes shone with merriment. "Isn't that what a [Hero] does best?"

"If we can't find the Demon Lord, we might be able to sow a little discord between the demons," Daniel said, ignoring them. "Brandt, our scouts can't approach the camp like Orrin. Why?"

The knight scratched his cheek. "I have no idea. Nobody does."

"Do you think our scouts could find one of these demon cities? If we can cause some chaos at one nearby, the Dark Horde might break up a bit. Nothing huge, just some quick destruction and then running back here."

Orrin looked at his friend. "You want us to attack their settlements? Did you not hear the part of my story where I said they didn't know the Outer Wall was built and think we're invading them?"

"They are here now," Daniel said, his voice unwavering. "I don't care about anything but defeating them."

Orrin couldn't think of a polite way to tell his friend he was being a dick but was saved when Madi arrived.

"Why didn't you meet back at the rendezvous point?" she asked Orrin, punching him in the shoulder. "Do you have any idea how worried we've been? You were gone for way longer than we planned and there was no sign of a struggle in the camp. We thought you'd been caught."

Daniel told her what Orrin had seen and heard, leaving out a lot of key information.

"He didn't tell you that the demons think people from Dey are invading their lands," Orrin added when Daniel stopped talking. "Have you heard of demon cities before?"

Madi shook her head. "The little information we get back from adventurers who go into the Pass is usually about the Pass itself. As far as I know, no one has come back from out there in a few hundred years."

Silas rolled up and Orrin tuned out as Daniel began delivering the same stilted information again.

Is he being weird because he wants to attack the demons? Orrin watched Daniel's body language but didn't see the same slightly shifty behavior he'd shown before he ran away from Dey to fight the demons in the Pass all that time ago. *He might be better at hiding his desire to fight demons now.*

"I'll get this information to the others," Silas spoke slowly. "However, nobody should mention anything about demons with a higher-than-cap level until we've confirmed it. We don't want to cause a panic."

"I confirmed it," Orrin said. "Don't you think lying to pe—"

"Orrin, I'm not saying you are wrong. It goes against everything I know about magic, but I believe you when you say you saw what you saw." Silas held up his hand to forestall Orrin's raised voice. "There are multiple possibilities that we need to eliminate before we go to the worst possible option . . . that the demons have the ability to exceed the maximum level."

"What kind of possibilities?" Daniel demanded. "Because to me, it does sound like you are calling Orrin a liar again."

The man rested his hands on the wheels of his chair and rolled himself back and forth a few inches. Nervous pacing. "What if the camp perimeter, which has worked as a powerful deterrent for everyone we've sent through so far, creates a field that gives false information within? What if demons have an ability to skew [Identify] results? What if Orrin was hit with a spell that made him hallucinate the entire ordeal? While I, as someone who knows Orrin well and trusts him, believe him, I am still in charge of thousands of lives in Dey. I have to verify and exclude every conceivable variable. Until I can confirm that the worst-case scenario is true, giving that information to the people defending their homes would be foolhardy. I mean no offense by it."

Orrin put his hand on Daniel's arm. "D, he has a point. I didn't even think about half those things." He turned to Silas. "Sorry for raising my voice. I did check a few people out, and everyone was an abnormally high level. I can leave a list of what I remember."

"That will be appreciated." Silas gave a small nod to Orrin.

"Now tell me what you know about demon cities."

Orrin saw Madi roll her eyes.

"What?" Orrin challenged. "He has a history of secrets."

Silas let a smirk cross his normally passive face. "We all have secrets, Orrin. To answer your question, I do know that demon cities exist, though only by reputation. In the past, expeditions were sent to destroy any deemed too close to our territory. I've never sent anyone to antagonize the demons, though, nor do I know of any sent in the last thirty years. Sometimes groups of adventurers go out for a clear-the-Pass quest from the Guild and don't come back. They're marked as killed in action, but we know that some simply left the Pass in search of their fortunes in the demon lands. None return."

Orrin was stunned. A straight answer from Silas was rare.

"I wish someone had told me about this," Madi said, crossing her arms. "If we didn't attack them but they think we're a threat, maybe a truce could be on the table?"

Silas and Daniel shook their heads at the same time, but Silas spoke first. "There's no way they'd back down. We built these new walls to protect against their attack, but from their perspective, we now have a forward operating base to strike from. I fear that the time for negotiations has passed."

A guard was speaking into Brandt's ear when he turned and nearly shouted, "When did this happen?"

The young man holding a pike stepped back and paled a bit as he stammered, "A-about ten minutes ago, sir. We just got the report from the—"

"Sir, we have a problem." Brandt knelt and spoke quickly but quietly to Silas. Orrin caught a few words but not enough to know what was going on.

"Send in reinforcements, immediately," Silas ordered in a calm voice, but Orrin heard the despair underneath. "Will they make it in time?"

"We've already sent a runner for a [Locationist], sir," the young guard stepped up to answer. "ETA is three minutes."

"What's going on?" Daniel asked. "Are the demons attacking?"

Brandt glanced at Silas for permission but started speaking before the man nodded.

Small victories. Orrin pondered. *He's more willing to bend the rules for us.*

"When we started building the walls in the Pass, we called on the Guild to supply extermination quests. The more people we can send into the Pass, the more monsters we can clear to keep it safe for the builders and such," Brandt explained. "We have scouts checking every nook and cranny for monsters, and we send out teams specially picked for each type and level. We have [Locationists] ready for emergency jumps to bring in reinforcements or help with escapes."

"What happened, Brandt?" Madi prompted.

"A team that was sent in to clear some two-star Denclovers sent out a distress call. A [Locationist] went in with another five members. We got another distress call a few minutes later. The problem is nobody else was close enough to that area to get there quickly. It's been ten minutes since the second call. It's no longer a rescue mission but a recovery."

Everybody was quiet but Orrin. "Where is the call from?"

"Orrin, no." Daniel stepped in front of him. "We need to focus on the demons."

"I need to do something useful after that failed mission," Orrin said, turning back to Brandt. "Where?"

Brandt did wait for Silas to nod this time. Orrin noted the location. "I know the area. I'll be right—"

"I'll come as well." Madi stepped up and nudged Orrin. "You'll need someone to watch your back. Brandt, keep a close eye on Daniel. He's getting antsy for a fight, and we are not going to be the ones to throw the first punch. I'm not giving up on talking with the Demon Lord."

Orrin reacted before Silas could object and waved to the others. "Be right back."

He cast [Teleport] and brought Madi along with him.

They landed near one of the walls built already, near the middle of the Pass. It didn't run the length of the Pass, from sheer cliff to sheer cliff, but broke into several smaller section walls with odd gaps between that anyone could run through.

Except every third opening was trapped with hundreds of spells. Every defender was trained to watch for the markers that listed which were the safe passages. Luckily, Orrin landed on the correct side of the wall and they wouldn't need to pass through a potentially deadly section.

"You jumped quickly," Madi said, shaking her head. "I wasn't prepared for that. I thought you'd argue with me."

"I was worried your dad was going to say no."

Madi gazed down at Orrin with one of her piercing looks. "Do you think that would have stopped me?"

"Nope, but I didn't want to give him another reason to hate me," Orrin answered with a smile. "Brandt's map said they should be a minute or two this way. Are you still buffed?"

Orrin made sure to keep his friends buffed to their maximum sustainable capacity each morning using [Utility Ward].

"I'm good. I'll be right behind you."

Orrin pulled up [Map] and ran, wondering at the vast difference in red dots from his foray into the Pass to save Daniel. When he was searching for his friend then, the walls had been awash with hiding monsters, but now the few he saw moved away fast. They knew a predator was on the hunt.

He found the first body outside a cave. Orrin paused to check the wounds, only for some hint at what he might be facing, as the woman was dead. The crushed arms would have slowed down most people, but the several close stab wounds to the chest would have been enough to kill even a higher-level adventurer.

"Denclovers don't attack like that," Madi huffed as she arrived a few seconds later, her dexterity not as high as Orrin's. "They cast small poison clouds that you can step over. Is anyone alive?"

Orrin nodded. "I count about eight gray dots inside, but there are twice as many red. I can't [Teleport] that many out in one go, so I'll debuff the monsters first."

Madi gave a thumbs-up and they entered the cave.

They found fifteen monsters swinging their club-like arms at a wall of stone that chipped more with every strike. The hunched-over horrors weren't scary from the back, but when one caught their scent and turned to scream, Orrin's hackles went up.

The things had no head, and where their chest should be was an open orifice of teeth. To make matters worse, a dark-red prehensile tongue tipped with dozens of sharp quills swayed in front of the body, waiting to stab its victims.

Orrin made short work of the monsters. *Definitely not Denclovers.* He dropped them all with some debuffs and stabbed each one before letting Madi finish them off.

Experience Gained: 4,500 (300 XP x 15)

"You could make so much money bringing people out to farm experience," Madi complained. "This doesn't feel fair."

Orrin knocked on the stone wall. "It's all clear out here. Come on out."

Muffled words drifted back.

Orrin turned to Madi. "Did you understand that?"

"I think they said, 'We're stuck.'"

Chapter 13

Madi made a fist with her left hand and pointed it at the cavern wall. She spread her fingers and light appeared at each fingertip. Orrin watched the pretty light show as Madi's fingers glowed in an increasingly quick rainbow of colors. The sparkling lights settled into a lot of yellows with a few shades of green thrown in. With a push, Madi directed the spell into the wall where they'd heard the muffled sounds of the lost adventurers.

Where the lights touched, the rock melted until it became wet dirt. More dots of light drifted in the air, creating a halo of loose gravel and mud in the otherwise impervious stone. Madi kicked the center mass of the circle, and an impromptu window made of solid mountain fell into the empty space within. Lights from three different abilities and one torch shone inside the small, cramped room.

"We're saved," a female voice cried. A large arm swept out and blocked her way, as two men in blue robes stepped through first. The large arm belonged to an orc with a cleaver in each hand. A dwarf holding a shield and mace followed close behind. Both had blue strips of cloth tied to their own armor.

The other four adventurers were a group of women, mostly armed with swords and spears. Two had buckler shields strapped to their arms while one gripped a tall staff with both hands, looking around wildly.

"Be careful of the monster bodies," Orrin said, noting a few bruises and cuts. He sent a couple of [Heal Small Wounds] into the more injured of the rescued, mostly the orc and two of the women. "We should collect any of your dead friends. There's one body outside. How many of you were there?"

The man who stepped through first huffed and began to step daintily over the horrors Orrin and Madi had downed. His dark hair was tied back into a long ponytail, clasped with gold beetle pins. The second man, wearing the same blue robe as the first, stepped forward and shook Madi's hand.

"Lady Catanzano, your reputation precedes you. You saved our lives and destroyed these Denclovers without breaking a sweat. It is good to know that Dey is in such capable hands. My name is Jeremiah Francis Drambul, coleader of the Golden Beetles." Jeremiah spoke with the smooth and practiced cadence of a noble. "My team was misinformed of the strength of these monsters and the original group sent to take care of them. If not for our dwarven member's [Stone Barrier] spell, we would all be dead."

The four women in the group picked their way toward the back of the cave until one let out a cry of anguish. Orrin leaned back to see them pulling the half-devoured body of a man from behind a stalagmite.

Stalagmite, not stalactite, right? The g *means it comes up from the ground.* Orrin pushed the random geology lesson from his mind. *Was that guy in a party with all four of those gorgeous women?*

Orrin partially took in Jeremiah's tale of their daring rescue attempt of the other party. They'd lost the [Locationist] almost immediately upon arriving. He ignored the story and watched his other robed compatriot loot the body of a blue-robed human without a head.

Madi finally held up her hand to stop the man. "One party member lost from each group and the [Locationist] is dead. You failed to identify the monsters, which were not Denclovers. Why run into the cave and not leave for reinforcements?"

"We heard the fighting and moved into the rescue," the man with the ponytail said with a disgusted sigh. "If they had any strong men in their party, it would have been easy to fight these monsters, whatever you call them. You were able to take them down with just the two of you?"

The man's self-righteous voice and haughty attitude made Orrin want to punch his handsome face.

"Guild rules dictate you assess the situation before moving in. If you don't know what you're fighting, you're as good as dead," Madi said, turning to a crying woman and rubbing her back as she dry-heaved. The other three party members stood in shock. "We'll help you get back to the nearest Wall and you'll need to give a report."

"The women can give the report," Ponytail sneered. "We will push on to the front line."

Orrin frowned. "You four are not strong enough to fight the Horde. I'm glad you are all alive, but how did you get clearance for a rescue mission? You're both below level twenty." Orrin pointed toward the two humans. He turned to Madi. "I know your father is letting the Guild set monster clearance quests in the Pass, but this is borderline murder."

"We do not need anyone to tell us where to go," Ponytail spat, stepping toward Orrin. "We have come to rescue the weaklings of Dey from your own failures."

Madi dug her knuckles into her eyes. "If you are in the Pass, you are under our laws. Where are you from so I know where to send you back to?"

Jeremiah bristled but held a fake smile on his face that stopped before his eyes. "Veskar. The Gendy province. We answered the call to defend Asmea from demons but didn't realize we would be used to clear monsters away."

"Everybody is contributing," Madi answered, letting her own annoyance seep through. "If killing monsters is too much of a challenge for your group, I'm sure we can find—"

Orrin had pulled up his [Map] to make sure nothing else was in the back of the cave. The gray dot near the cave entrance flickered red.

He jumped, casting [Decrease Dexterity] at max power on Ponytail just as he turned and pointed a glowing wand at Madi. Mr. Ponytail crumpled to the ground.

The orc roared and charged Orrin, but he was already rolling away, casting more debuffs. The orc was already falling forward when the blunt end of Madi's spear hit his head, guiding him into the peaceful slumber of unconsciousness.

The dwarf dropped his mace and stepped back, hands in the air. "I'm not dumb enough to attack a Catanzano. That's how you end up dead."

Jeremiah closed his eyes and took a deep breath in through his nose before turning his gaze to Orrin. "You attacked the crown prince of Gendy, Ezra Egnatius Eochaid. You realize what this means?"

"His dad is terrible at picking names?" Orrin said as he set his feet to flip the orc over on his side. His face was in some of the dirt Madi had made with her spell and he didn't want the guy to suffocate.

"Orrin defended me," Madi said, her spear out and pointing toward Ezra's still body. "Crown prince or not, he attacked me, unprovoked. If this weren't the Pass, I'd place him under arrest and try him in Dey."

"Dey is not the Pass. There are witnesses here who saw you attack Prince Ezra first." Jeremiah's words were full of vitriol now. "You will regret this insult."

Orrin sighed at the cliché threat. He used [Identify] on Jeremiah, taking in his full stats and class before turning to the unconscious prince. Doing the same to Ezra, Orrin got some feedback damage from one of the man's skills. He gingerly touched his head and healed himself before turning toward Jeremiah.

"You're level fifteen. [Protection Emissary] sounds powerful, but your stats are shit. Ponytail here isn't that much better. You should go level up a few times before taking on Guild quests beyond your level."

"I told them the same thing, but they paid me a lot of gold to stop asking questions," the dwarf said. He had moved to the wall and kept his hands up and away from his weapons. "Now I'm thinking this job was a mistake."

"Shut up, dwarf. You are part of the Golden Beetles and will act with the decorum that is due," Jeremiah ranted, and Orrin turned away.

He whispered to Madi, "We don't have time to deal with this. Now that they're alive, can we leave?"

Madi nodded toward the still catatonic party in various states of grief around the chewed body of their teammate. "We can't leave them like that, and I don't trust the others to help out. I can send a message to have their access to the Pass revoked, but you can't [Teleport] this many people at once, right?"

"I'm also not going to leave you here alone with these dumbbells for even a minute." Orrin sighed and looked around. "Can you get the other party ready to go? I'll convince these guys to listen."

"Orrin . . . what are you going to do?" Madi shrank her spear down to its smaller size and crossed her arms. "Gendy is a smaller province, but they hold no small sway in Veskar."

Orrin held his hands up. "I'm not going to torture them. That would be bad. Do I look like a bad guy?"

Madi's eye twitched at the false grin on Orrin's face. She peered over Orrin's shoulder at Jeremiah. The man had stopped hounding the dwarf and was pale as he listened in on their conversation.

"I'm going to take the girls out into the Pass to get some fresh air," she announced loudly. One of the larger women in the group helped her pull the party away from their dead friend.

In the quiet cavern, the slow drip of water deeper inside echoed in time with the breaths of the orc. Orrin pointed at the dwarf.

"What's your name?"

"Drag Copperskull. [Earthshaper], tracker, and adventurer extraordinaire . . . when I'm not taking jobs that might get me killed or imprisoned," the stout man said with a bow. "If you don't mind, I would love a bit of fresh air myself."

"Traitor," Jeremiah hissed. "You would leave your party members alone and undefended?"

"You might be an idiot, son, but I'm not. This is the [Hero]'s party member Orrin. From the stories I've heard, when people get on his bad side, they end up dead. I won't lie and say the princeling didn't attack. Vet reacted poorly, but at least he went down before he got any attacks off. You paid me to lead you through the Pass and complete some quests for glory, not to die for his stupidity."

Orrin let the men argue. His plan was to buff the orc and Ponytail back into a vertical position and then convince them that leaving was their best option. He could drop them again if he needed to and even carry the orc if pushed.

"You are fired." Jeremiah clenched his fists but kept himself from striking at the higher-leveled dwarf. "Effective immediately."

"Hey, Drag, how much would you charge to carry someone back to the nearest Wall?" Orrin interrupted the fuming silence between the two.

"Huh? What?" Drag kept one hand on his hammer and turned toward Orrin. "Carry who?"

Jeremiah dropped like a sack of potatoes.

Orrin slapped his hands together like he was dusting them off, having debuffed Jeremiah's strength until he fell. "Any of these three. I don't have time to deal with their nonsense."

Drag carried both of the humans out of the cave, one over each shoulder. Orrin came out behind him with the orc draped over his back.

Madi took in the view and shrugged, but Orrin saw a tiny smile on her face. "Better you than me, I guess. This way."

Instead of going to the empty Wall they'd teleported to, Madi directed them toward Dey. She spoke with Drag at length as they moved. They approached one of the newly manned Walls and were spotted almost immediately. A scouting party met them and took the still-unmoving forms of Vet the orc, Ezra, and Jeremiah from Drag and Orrin.

"Make sure those two are deported from Dey gently but sternly," Madi commanded. "The orc should be questioned but left to the Guild to deal with. He tried to attack Orrin after he stopped an attack from the prince here."

The commander of this particular Wall saluted and had some of his troops tie up the low-ranking Veskarians. "Do you need any rest . . . or do you have any reports from the front line?" The man wore plate armor and towered over both Madi and Orrin but shrank before their combined power and reputation.

"We're heading back there now," Madi said as she tapped Orrin's shoulder. "Take care of that party, Captain. They lost a member and are mourning him."

"Yes, ma'am."

Orrin waited for Madi to turn away before he teleported them back.

Chapter 14

Orrin sat under the wide awning set up against the inside of the outermost Wall and watched Brandt and Daniel practice their swordplay. After he and Madi debriefed her father on their side-quest rescue, Orrin had asked the stern man the question weighing on his mind.

"Why hasn't the Horde attacked yet?"

Silas's answer was no comfort. "I don't know."

The glass of lemonade in his hand chilled his fingers, and Orrin swirled the cup to make the ice spin again. His thoughts raced each other as the sound of grunts and metal clinking echoed in the background.

"I feel it, too," Madi confided from next to him. When he frowned in her direction, she hurried to continue. "The pressure of this all." She waved a hand in the air vaguely.

"We're sitting here drinking your dad's lemonade while watching our two beefhead friends practice fighting," Orrin pointed out. "This is not pressure."

Madi sighed and put down her drink. "Maybe *pressure* isn't the right word. Everybody is tense from waiting for the demons to attack, Orrin. There are a lot of people in charge of this. You, me, Brandt, and even Daniel don't need to worry about the next move. We'll get our orders and move to help where we can. This is not like last time. We're a small piece of an army."

Orrin knew she was right, but something still bothered him. The Horde had rushed to the Pass, only to stop and wait. It didn't make sense. There was some kind of internal politics going on in the enemy camp, but that shouldn't stop them from putting forth a few probing attacks at the least.

"You should at least practice a bit. It might help you get out of your mind," Madi said as she stood and stretched. She reached down and pulled him up by the arm. "Teach Daniel a bit of humility. He's been beating Brandt nine times out of ten lately."

Orrin allowed her to drag him toward their friends, resting after Daniel had disarmed Brandt again. "I'm not fighting them. It makes no sense to do it. I shouldn't be fighting anyone. I can run through enemies and leave them either struggling to move or prone on the floor. If I'm fighting someone who can resist my debuffs, I'll just keep running and avoiding them until one of you can land a real attack. If all else fails, I'll [Teleport] away."

"What if you can't escape or we're not around?" Madi let her spear grow out. "Orrin, you're clever and powerful. That doesn't mean you should stop trying to improve. Fight me. I've got something I want to try."

Brandt and Daniel hurried to move out of the way. Orrin distinctly heard Daniel make a bet against him. He glared at his friend, who shrugged.

Orrin waited with his arms at his sides. If Madi wanted to spend the next few minutes on her back staring at the sky, she could have her wish. He didn't summon his [Fire Sword]. His wards were already set for the day, and their recent excursion hadn't shaved any points off his shields. His stats were maxed out from [Utility Ward].

Madi kept her spear pointed toward Orrin and began casting spells that flashed different colors. Her new class was a direct upgrade from her old one. Orrin had used his Administrator powers to give her the [Superior Prism Conjurer] class that everyone thought was a fairy-tale story. From what he'd seen so far, she had a bit more versatility in her spells with a few high-mana big-burst spells. It didn't matter against him. [Decrease Strength] would sap her ability to hold her spear or even stand upright.

Brandt glanced back and forth, waiting for their nods. The knight didn't seem worried, but Orrin counted that as trust that he wouldn't go too far. When Brandt gave the signal, Orrin cast [Decrease Strength] at the lowest level on Madi, expecting the duel to be over before his ice melted. With his increased will, the level-one spell would knock ten points off her strength. It wouldn't be enough to put her on the ground, but it would slow her enough to make her surrender the match.

Madi smiled as she charged at Orrin. He frowned and pointed again. A flash of light around her chest was the only hint he got before she was upon him.

The confusion at the spell not working was enough to put Orrin on the back foot, but he'd been training for months. [Way of the Water] still gave him the dodging skills he needed to keep from being skewered.

"I warned you," Madi huffed as she stabbed at him in rapid-fire motions. "You never know when someone will have a trick up their sleeve and surprise you."

She ran at him, holding the spear low. Orrin was forced to summon a [Fire Sword] and swerve to the side. As he moved, the spear and Madi's arms seemed to blur. Instead of the connection he expected as he parried her spear to the side, the attack came from above.

Madi rang Orrin's bell with the haft of her spear.

With his [Ward] active, the damage didn't harm him, but he still felt the pressure against his crown. "What the hell was that?"

Madi skipped out of range and smiled. "See if you can figure it out before I beat you."

Orrin pulled an [Ice Sword] out of midair and fell into Formless, the catch-all stance from his fighting style. He tried another debuff, which triggered Madi's attacks again.

While Madi was quick from her own boosted stats, she couldn't handle the backlash of a fully raised buff. As such, Orrin was faster without even using [Gust]. He sent his spell combinations through the swords, trying to freeze Madi or hit her with a burning gust of wind. Madi stepped out of each attack with a bigger smile and no wounds.

One of the reasons their party could train so hard was Orrin's healing. If one of them took damage, he watched close enough to hit a few [Heal Small Wounds]. With the amount of mana he was throwing out, Orrin was trying to minimize how much healing he would have to do after he won the fight. His movements became more frantic as he realized he might not win.

Madi scored a hit along his leg. It wasn't much, but coupled with the blow to his head from earlier, she was chipping away at his [Ward]. She kept from hitting him with magic, as his own mana pool dwarfed hers. If it came down to a slug match of who ran out of mana first, Orrin was confident he would win. Madi took a different approach, putting her years of weapon training into full effect as she dazzled him with bursts of light and conjured illusions that made her strikes come from different directions.

He couldn't use [Lightstrikes], as each time he tried, the spell fizzled against her skin. Orrin even tried to use [Camouflage], but Madi's eyes glowed like miniature suns as she kept her eyes on him.

"It's like you picked all the spells that would counter me," Orrin cursed. "You have to be running low on mana, though."

Madi's ferocious smile made Orrin's stomach flip. She charged again.

The fight was over when Orrin started running. Madi beat him with her spear a few times and then chuckled. She covered her mouth as her eyes danced, watching him stumble to a stop.

"What was that?" Orrin asked as he dropped the swords. "I quit, by the way, if that isn't obvious. You completely kicked my ass."

"If you paid attention, you could have won," Daniel said with a huge smile. Brandt was counting out silver coins and handing them over.

"Brandt! You bet against me?" Madi said incredulously, shrinking her spear down and hanging it from her hip.

"Daniel gave good odds, and I thought Orrin would be quicker on the uptake."

"Will somebody tell me what just happened? My confidence is taking a hit." Orrin scowled as his friends laughed. "I will [Teleport] back to Dey and let the Horde take you all, so help me—"

"I can deflect some magic spells," Madi explained, holding up her hands in surrender. "It's not perfect and I have to time it right, but I can even absorb some of the mana of an attack back into my own mana pool. You used mostly elemental magic against me, which I'm better at dealing with. If you kept hammering me with your debuffs, I'd have gone down with another few attacks. Those spells eat up my mana."

Orrin felt a little better about losing. "How did you move so fast? It's like you teleported your arms into new directions. I defended against you a few times, but sometimes when I thought I had you, the attack came from a different direction."

Madi was preening, and Brandt proudly looked on before explaining. "She can create illusory attacks."

"That's a simplification," Madi gloated. "My spell makes you see where I would attack while blocking your attention from where my spear is actually attacking. It's an illusion spell built into an attack. I can't use it every attack yet, but if I combine it with some feints I've been taught"—Madi nudged Brandt in the side—"then I can confuse the enemy . . . or friend, in this case."

"Can I see the spell you used to stop my magic?" Orrin asked. "Cast it and let me hit you with something? I want to watch the mana."

"He wants to watch the mana," Daniel mocked playfully. "Orrin, you got your ass kicked. You don't have to turn it into a lesson. Take the hit and try again."

Orrin shook his head. "Madi won fair and square. I still want to see it, if you don't mind."

Madi glared at him. "Are you just trying to find a way to win against me?"

"You already told me how to do that: I keep hitting you with [Decrease Strength] until you run out of mana. I also told you that my strategy is to run. I could have used [Teleport]."

"But you didn't."

"Because you told me you wanted to try something." Orrin squinted at Madi in the midday sun. "How long have you been planning this?"

Madi kept a perfectly straight face. "I don't know what you're talking about."

"Since she leveled up and unlocked the spell," Brandt ratted her out, which earned him a slap on the arm.

Brandt gave a few pointers on the technical side of their fight. He and Daniel were rested enough to have another session. Madi guided Orrin to the Wall and held her arms out to her sides.

"Go ahead and cast away. I can block another two or three attacks if you don't go all out."

Orrin used the smallest [Lightstrike] spell and focused on the magic as it hit Madi's body. The flash of light right before contact was the same as before, but Orrin watched the way Madi's spell worked. What appeared to be a translucent covering turned white when his spell hit, moving in ripples down her body. The majority of the mana from his attack was dispersed, but some of that magic moved to her eyes, where it disappeared into her body.

"That is amazing," Orrin said, explaining what he was seeing. "The shield turns the magic away and absorbs some mana into your eyes. I wonder if you would absorb more if I cast it closer to your head."

"You are not shooting spells at my head, Orrin."

"For science?"

"No."

Orrin summoned an [Ice Sword] and raised it toward Madi. She backed a step away.

"I'm not going to stab you. Try and activate it when I get close," he said, moving the tip to Madi's arm.

"Nothing?"

She pushed the sword away with the back of her hand. "I think it has to be a cast spell, not a summoned object."

Orrin used [Gust] through his sword and tapped Madi's arm again. The sword burst apart, and Madi's arm should have been covered in icy frost. Instead, her spell activated and a sparkle of blue light fizzled down her body.

"Was that necessary?" Madi asked, rubbing her arm. "It still hurts a bit to get attacked, you know?"

"Sorry," Orrin said distractedly. "Did the color change?"

Madi nodded and counted on her fingers. "Red for fire, blue for ice, and white for light magic. Daniel tried some space spell on me and Brandt said it looked like a shadow filled with stars swallowed my body for a second. I could only redirect some of that damage and couldn't absorb any of it. Light magic works best for me, obviously. Elemental magic, like fire, ice, water, and earth, is easier to deal with, too. That's not even the best part. I think the more I use the spell, the closer to—"

A cry from above them rang out. "Movement toward the Wall."

Daniel and Brandt moved to their side quickly enough that anyone outside their party would think they had teleported. Orrin checked over his party, rebuffing wards where necessary. Madi and Daniel drank a mana potion to cover the lost points from their fights.

"We shouldn't have trained so hard. We might need the extra mana," Daniel muttered.

"Maybe it's just a messenger saying they made a mistake and everyone is going home," Orrin said with no hope in his voice.

"And maybe a cute elf will fall out of the sky and ask me to marry her," Daniel said, rolling his eyes and unhitching Gertrude, his gigantic sword, from his back. "Let's go see who we're fighting today."

Chapter 15

Standing atop the Wall, Orrin watched a group of twenty or so demons jogging in their direction. The foremost demon held a spear in the air with a dark-green flag with black markings he couldn't make out rippling in the air above them. A smaller white ribbon was tied below it.

"A treaty delegation," Madi commented as they stopped about three-quarters of the way to the Wall. "The white fabric underneath their standard means they feel they are in the superior position to negotiate our surrender."

Daniel clenched his fists. "Maybe if I went down there and killed a few—"

Orrin slapped Daniel on the back of his head. "Control your emotions, padawan. Anger leads to suffering."

Daniel blinked and rubbed the spot Orrin hit. "That isn't the saying at all."

"This is why they made you stay back, D. You have to learn to control that rage against the demons." Orrin tried to use [Identify] on the demon in the middle of the group, but they were too far away. "The longer we can stall them, the more Walls we can get functional. You'll get your chance to knock some demons around."

Silas had point-blank ignored Daniel's request to go past the Wall and meet with the coming envoy. Orrin watched as hidden doors below them opened in the Wall and Madi's dad rolled his wheelchair forward. A smaller banner of white stuck up from a staff strapped to his chair. Lady Timpe, one of the other rulers of Dey, walked beside him. She wore her half-plate armor and kept one hand on the magical longsword at her hip. Leanthun, the commander of the elves sent to help the humans, followed behind them. He kept his arms crossed, but his curved sword, called a khopesh, and magical mace were visible as well.

"I think the three of them going out there alone is stupid," Daniel grumbled. "The demons sent that many as a show of force. We should respond in kind."

Madi put her hand on the brooding [Hero]'s shoulder. "Don't worry about my father and Lady Timpe. They can handle this."

Orrin watched the two groups cautiously approach each other and begin to talk.

"I can't make out what they're saying, even with [Telescope]," Daniel complained again.

"Can you read lips?" Madi asked in surprise.

". . . no, but I can't even see them talking."

Brandt shook his head. "Lady Timpe has a bracelet that creates a stasis bubble around her for when she needs privacy. I imagine she's using it now to keep all the people on the Wall without patience from learning piecemeal what will be shared in time. It wouldn't do for misinformation to be spread. Trust in the lords of Dey. They've kept the city alive for centuries."

Orrin chuckled. "Was that 'without patience' comment directed at anyone in particular or just in general?"

Brandt smiled and brushed his hair back. Standing on top of the Wall in his armor, he looked every bit the [Knight] that his class described him as. "Who is it that keeps running off with half-cooked plans, Orrin?"

Three minutes passed. Daniel growled and then huffed. "When they attack, I'll cast a spell on us called [Weightless]. We can jump right off the top of the Wall, but be quick. It only lasts ten seconds until I level it up a bit more."

"When did you buy Feather Fall?" Orrin asked. He didn't look away from the group below them.

"That . . . isn't what it is," Daniel answered shiftily. "[Weightless] makes things weigh ten percent of their normal weight at level one. I talked with Leanthun about it, and he assured me that I would be able to survive a fall at that weight."

Orrin turned his full attention to his friend. "Survive or land safely?"

"You can heal us if we break a leg."

Orrin covered his face with his hand and rubbed his fingers against his eyes in frustration. "Daniel. Please don't take this the wrong way.

Are you an idiot or are the demons affecting you more now that they're closer?"

"That's not fair, Orrin." Madi spoke up before Daniel could answer. The upturned corner of her mouth gave her away before she finished talking. "Why can't it be both?"

Brandt sighed. "Daniel, let's regroup downstairs near an action point. If someone does attack, we can safely move into the fray."

Daniel didn't object, and Brandt frowned at both Madi and Orrin as he guided Daniel away. "If you come with us, I want your word that you will both be better."

"He wanted us to jump and break our legs, Brandt. Maybe he should be better," Orrin said but followed behind the man.

Brandt held out his hand and stopped Orrin, letting Madi take the stairs down with Daniel. He waited until the two were out of earshot and turned on Orrin.

"When we arrived back in Dey after you were kidnapped, Daniel ignored his own pain and rushed back to save you. He felt guilty that he hadn't moved quickly enough to get everyone out. When we raided Lady Sanerris's home, we missed you again by a few minutes. Every time that young man has tried to do something lately, he has been late. Too late to save his friend. Too late to stop the deaths of innocents." Brandt was getting worked up but took a deep breath and stopped himself. "You know just as well as I do that he has a drive to attack demons. If I had known that when we first met, I would have kept him away from the city while the Fogbinder was attacking. I can't keep him away from this attack. We'll need him before this is over, but we need him with a steady mind. You are his friend. Instead of mocking him, you should help him keep his priorities straight. He respects you and listens to you more than you know. It's your greatest strength. Use it."

Ever since returning from his own capture and torture, Brandt was quieter. He spoke less and watched more, satisfied to wait in the background and go where the party led. The experience had given him a depth of patience and perspective that Orrin was only starting to see, but his speech now was the most he'd said since Orrin's return from Odrana. That it was a chastisement made it more remarkable. Brandt was a member of their party by default; he was a [Knight] assigned to keep Madi safe. He didn't add anything unique to their fighting abilities and had been absent for weeks after his friend Jude betrayed them. Brandt rarely tried to steer the team anymore, and for him to call Orrin out meant that Orrin had fucked up.

"I'm sorry, Brandt." Orrin focused on the tips of his boots. It had been a while since someone made him feel like an asshole.

"It's not me you should apologize to. Go talk with Daniel. I need to have a word with Lady Catanzano as well."

While Brandt reprimanded Madi outside, Orrin and Daniel waited in a dark room beneath the Wall. There were no windows, but a small button would open a hidden door to the western plains where the demons were. It would also lock behind them the entrance that let in the little light they had. Multiple staging rooms like this were built into most of the Walls in the Pass, and every single one on the outermost Wall was currently filled in the fear an attack was about to take place.

"Daniel, I shouldn't have—"

"It's fine, Orrin."

"It's really not. I'm sorr—"

"Seriously, forget it, man."

"I'm going to apologize and you're going to listen, damn it," Orrin yelled.

Daniel and Orrin looked at each other. Daniel chuckled.

"It isn't funny."

Daniel laughed harder. Orrin tried to keep a straight face, but a smile crept out.

"Never mind. You're an ass."

Daniel's laughter slowed, and he threw an arm around Orrin's shoulder. "It's just good to have you back."

Orrin looked at Daniel in the dark shadows of the room. "I am back, and I'm not going anywhere. We haven't really talked about . . . everything since Odrana. Between fighting with Sanerris and getting the Pass ready for the Horde, I forgot to ask how you are doing."

Daniel's arm clenched momentarily around Orrin.

"Right now probably isn't the best time to talk, but there will never be a perfect time. When have we had a moment to relax since we got here?" Orrin continued talking into the silent room.

"You're right." Daniel scowled, taking his arm off his friend and moving away. "This isn't the best time."

"Daniel, if you tell me you have the demon hate thing under control, I'll drop it. If you tell me you want to talk later, I'll wait. I know how much it sucked for you while I was in Odrana, because it sucked just as bad for me. I didn't know if you were safe. I knew you'd show up to save me at some point, because you always do. When—"

"But I didn't save you," Daniel snarled, his anger flaring as he talked. "I failed over and over. I was just a few minutes late every time until you strolled into camp with Finley, safe and sound. This"—Daniel gestured to the blank wall blocking them from the demon army—"isn't going to be like fighting a few monsters in a dungeon. This is a war. People are going to die."

He stopped and put his head against the stone. "We might die, Orrin. When we left you behind, I had to think about what I would tell your mom if I ever got home without you. I can't . . ."

Madi and Brandt entered the dark room before Orrin could respond.

"Daniel, Brandt says that I'm too harsh and need to be nicer," Madi playfully bantered as she came in, not able to see their faces clearly enough to read the room. "You're fine and will tell me if I go too far, right?"

"Yeah, Madi. I'm fine." Daniel's voice was flat.

"Daniel, I promise you—" Orrin started to talk but was interrupted by two horn blasts from above. "What does that mean?"

"Two is the signal for all clear. The negotiations are over and our people are returning to the wall," Brandt said, letting out a sigh of relief. "We can head back up."

"Daniel, did I really hurt your feelings?" Madi asked, finally catching on to his mood.

"Madi, can you give us a minute?" Orrin asked, nodding toward Brandt. "We'll come up right behind you."

Madi's hair swung as she glanced between Orrin and Daniel, her face filled with anxiety. "I didn't mean . . . I'm . . . I'm sorry."

Brandt took her by the hand and pulled her gently from the room.

"She's going to think I'm mad at her," Daniel muttered. "Another problem for me to fix."

"I'll tell her you're mad at me," Orrin offered. "It's basically the truth anyway."

Daniel pushed off the wall and was in Orrin's face before he finished his sentence. "I'm mad at myself, Orrin. The Demon Lord is here. I'm not level fifty and don't have the ability points to get [Demon Seal]. I spent too much time trying to save you. Not that I regret that. I would make the same choice over and over again. But I'm a failure of a [Hero]. I can't control myself when I see the demons. I want to run out there and kill them, and I don't even have a good reason for it. It feels like somebody is pushing my ribs out from the inside and I can't catch my breath."

Orrin hugged Daniel. "Shut up for a minute and take a few deep breaths."

He'd seen that frantic look in the mirror before. His panic attacks began in middle school. His mom tried talking with him for weeks before she brought him to a doctor. His half answers and shrugs throughout the appointment didn't deter the doctor. He gave Orrin a few breathing exercises to try and told him he'd see him in a few weeks.

A few days later, Orrin woke up sweating and shaking, gasping for air at whatever nightmare triggered his latest panic attack. Taking deep breaths and counting out with each exhale, he didn't get rid of his fear but brought it down enough to calm his body. He worked with Dr. Howick for a year to control his anxiety. He used what he could remember now for Daniel.

"Breathe in and out, counting to five. Don't think about anything else right now. We are safe and can figure out everything later." Orrin spoke softly and demonstrated with deep inhalations of his own.

"Orrin, you're squeezing me a little too tight, dude."

Orrin let go and stepped back. "Sorry."

Daniel kept his eyes closed and sucked in the air, blowing it out again. They stood in the room alone. Orrin could feel the tension leaving his friend's body. Daniel opened his eyes and grinned sheepishly.

"Thanks."

Orrin stuck out his fist. Daniel rapped his knuckles quickly.

"Let's go. Madi is going to be pouting until I tell her she didn't really hurt my feelings."

Orrin stopped Daniel with a hand on his chest. "No. It's time we talked."

Chapter 16

Orrin kept Daniel from walking out of the room. "There are a few things we need to chat about."

Daniel rolled his eyes dramatically. "Orrin, this is terrible timing. We should get up there and see what Silas learned from the demons."

Daniel tried to brush by Orrin, but he used [Way of the Water] to turn the [Hero]'s arm and gently shove him back.

"You are not leaving until we figure this out. You're stewing on things. Talk with me. I know you're worried about the Horde, that's a given. We all are. I know you're worried about losing it and letting your need to go kill the demons control you. We've got you, man. Brandt is watching over you literally all the time. You're pissed at me for doing dangerous shit. That's nothing new. I wish I could stay back and not do anything, but like you said, this is a war. There's something else bothering you. Talk to me, D."

Daniel rubbed his wrist where Orrin had twisted his arm and scowled again. "Orrin, you don't do dangerous shit, you do stupid shit. You constantly rush in without thinking and expect everyone to pull you to safety. I'm used to that. I don't like having a babysitter follow me around, but I accept it because I feel the pressure building inside to confront the demons. It's like a tic. If I let my guard down for a second, I start thinking of ways to get over the Wall. It's exhausting. But I'm handling it."

"Then why are you in such a rush to get into a fight with the demons?"

Daniel cursed and made gestures with his hand before a blue box appeared in front of Orrin.

> **Defeat the Demon Lord—In the southern lands, the Demon Lord has risen. The dark armies have been**

assembled. Seek out and defeat the Demon Lord before the Dark Horde attacks.

Reward: 1,000,000 XP and Dark Essence Unlocked

"Every time I look at this Quest, I worry. Do I have to defeat the Demon Lord or the Dark Horde? If the Horde attacks with the boss, do I fail the Quest? Am I already too late because the Horde is right there or do I just need to hold them back from Dey? I know you think of everything like a video game, O. You know what I do when I get stuck at some hard boss fight? I look it up on the internet. I don't like spending hours and multiple saves trying to figure it out myself. This is real and we don't have extra lives. What if I fuck it up again?"

Orrin focused in on one part of his friend's little speech. "Again? When did you fuck up?"

"Let me count the ways," Daniel said savagely, holding up his fingers one at a time as he counted off. "I left you all behind to kill some demons and got my ass handed to me by our own side. I got myself kidnapped and had to get rescued. I failed to protect you and almost lost you . . . twice. I killed people I could have saved . . . I know Madi told you about it. All of that together and the way everyone looks at me to help with this. I'll do what I can, but I'm not a leader, Orrin. Part of me wants to kill demons but a bigger part of me, the part of me I think is the real me, is scared I'm going to get someone killed. I'm terrified that I won't make the right decision and me or you will die before we get home."

"Shit. Now I don't know what to say," Orrin admitted freely as Daniel finally opened up a little. "I'm scared of that, too, Daniel. Every person on this Wall is worried they won't make it through this. There's nothing we can do but try our best. But you have not failed once. We got sucked into this world and didn't have a choice. We've been up against monsters and people stronger than us since the moment we woke up. We've killed people and made the best decision we could in the moment. It's easy to look back and think of all the ways we could do better, but that won't help us moving forward."

Orrin looked over his shoulder at the exit. Brandt and Madi were standing awkwardly far enough away to give some privacy. "Look at those two. They'd be dead without you. Remember when you made us save them on the road right after we got here? You acted and did what you thought was right. There's a reason you're the [Hero], Daniel. You are the kind of person who finds a way to save people, but this is bigger than a few thieves or monsters. Some of the people on this Wall are not going to live through the week. Don't isolate yourself from us because of that. Use it to push harder. Let it help you control that rage inside, because if you rush off to kill demons and we have to come save you, people will die. We got lucky with the Dragoon team. Having said all that, I am not worried about you."

The light hit Daniel's hopeful face as he turned toward Orrin. "Why not?"

Orrin punched him in the shoulder. "You're Daniel Kayson. You don't lose. It's super fucking annoying."

Daniel huffed in feigned annoyance as he rubbed his arm. "It doesn't feel like I'm winning, Orrin. Their levels are too high and I don't have the [Demon Seal]. I'm not sure I have to have it to beat him, but having a [Hero]-specific skill sure makes it seem that way."

"One step at a time," Orrin said. "I have an idea about that, but I'm hoping we can avoid it. I'm worried it would have consequences."

Daniel's eyes flared. "Tell me."

Orrin and Daniel joined Madi and Brandt as they moved to an open-sided tent where the various leaders defending Dey gathered. Silas and Lady Timpe were talking with the third leader of Dey, Lord Tarris, near a large wooden table covered in maps and small figurines. The generals of Dey talked with the leaders of Odrana's supplied forces. The actual leadership of Odrana was dealing with their own problems and hadn't bothered coming to defend the Pass themselves. Except Finley Madvarr.

Finley was the son of one of those missing rulers. His family's land bordered Veskar to the south, a country made up of multiple city-states, kingdoms, and despots working in a loose formation. The Madvarr family kept the borders of Odrana safe, and Finley had been raised to be a fighter among fighters. Orrin had met him at the Sanerris School for Spells, a place in Odrana for learning more advanced fighting and magic uses. Despite Orrin's predicament at the time, he'd made friends with Finley. Ultimately, Finley helped in his escape from imprisonment under the former Lady Sanerris.

Although she's probably playing all this chaos up to get herself reinstated somehow, Orrin thought bitterly. After Orrin and Daniel exposed the Sanerris family for their treachery, they'd been assured Lady Sanerris would be imprisoned, if not executed. Instead, she'd been freed to return to her eponymous school. *One problem at a time.*

Finley stood behind the Odranan generals but stretched over one of the shorter men to speak up from time to time. He noticed Orrin nearing the tent and waved, leaving the group to intercept them. "Casimir . . . Sorry, Orrin. How did your trip into the enemy camp go? There is some room for improvement with communication around here."

Leanthun was speaking quietly in turn with a row of elves that Orrin didn't know, sending each off one by one. He looked over his shoulder and shook his head at Finley's comment. "There's a reason we were called together here, Lord Madvarr. Patience would suit you well."

"Hey, Leanthun," Orrin said, waving at the elf. He reached out and clasped hands with Finley. "The demon camp was weird, but at least they haven't attacked yet. What did the treaty delegation say? Have they told us yet?"

Lord Catanzano rolled his wheelchair away from the other leaders of Dey and closed in on Orrin. "We were waiting for the [Hero] to arrive."

"I'm here now." Daniel spoke up, turning heads. Most everyone in the tent knew him at this point, but the myth of a [Hero] was still strong with even generals and elves.

"Then we shouldn't delay." Silas nodded at one of his men. Sheets rolled down the covered top, enclosing the tent. Magical lanterns lit up the inside. "To the table, please."

Everyone jostled for a spot, and Orrin ended up with Finley to one side and Madi at the other. Brandt stood behind Madi, peeking from over her head. Daniel was positioned near Silas.

The new parchment showed a rough drawing of the Pass. A few of the new Walls throughout the length of the winding crevice between the mountains were depicted on the map, but Orrin immediately realized a quite a few were missing. Some of the markings were outright wrong. His brow furrowed.

"Segmented knowledge sharing in case of infiltration," Madi whispered.

Orrin raised an eyebrow.

Madi sighed. "Spies have to work twice as hard to find actionable intelligence."

"Not just spies," Finley muttered. "Keeping information from your own allies can have dire consequences."

"Yes, Lord Madvarr. We recognize your concerns," Silas started from the other side of the table. "Lord Tarris, if you will?"

Lord Tarris wore a dark-green robe and a bad comb-over. The stress of his job was clearly getting to him. He pushed his glasses up his nose before putting his hands out over the map palms down. He clapped and put his fingers on the corners of the map. Electricity ran from his fingertips along the parchment, staining it in deep reds and blues. He nodded to himself and stepped back, gesturing for Silas to continue.

"Thank you, Lord Tarris. Those in this tent are the first and only members of our unified forces to see this map. The red lines highlight the multiple ruses and false markings we have put on every copy of our maps. The blue lines are the hidden camps, fallback points, Walls, traps, and force deployments that are never to be written down. Memorize quickly, for once we open the tent up again, I will burn this map."

Orrin smiled to himself. He'd known his own [Map] wasn't wrong. He pulled it up and noticed that some of the Walls were filled in on his [Map] as he studied the one on the table. Some of those hadn't been completed when he'd last run through the Pass.

"As you all know, I met with a delegation under truce a few minutes ago. Lady Timpe joined me, as well as Leanthun of the elven kingdom. The Demon Lord did not join but sent a message. The other demons had nothing of substance to say beyond their delivery of these words."

"One of the demons said we brought this on ourselves," Leanthun cut in. "I think that is worth noting."

Silas waved his hand in the air. "That statement does not help explain the Demon Lord's message."

"What did the message say?" Daniel said, his voice calm but carrying a menace that nobody in the tent missed.

Silas pulled a scroll of paper from his inner pocket and rolled it out on the table before he read it aloud. "'To the sequestered peoples of Asmea. We have forgiven your persistent navigation of the Pass, including forays into lands forbidden from you, for too long. Your attempt at summoning a [Hero] in your domain has not gone unnoticed and forced our hand. Surrender the [Hero] to our camp and raze every structure within the Pass within two days or we will crush your rebellion.'"

Silas looked up. "It's signed Demon Lord Niko."

Chapter 17

Silas met everyone's eyes one by one when he finished reading the Demon Lord's message. "It goes without saying that we will not be handing over Daniel. We are drafting a response to send back stating as much and laying the blame on the demons who attacked the Wall months ago. Dey is protecting its borders and its own. If I hear any talk of handing the [Hero] to the demons, I will personally throw you from the highest point of the Wall."

Orrin felt a rush of emotion for the man who had once tried to have him killed. Silas was a political animal, with snakelike cunning and the ability to shed his personal feelings for the greater good as he saw it. There were likely a half dozen reasons that Silas was protecting Daniel in this moment, but Orrin appreciated the immediate result. Daniel had tensed during the message but smiled with relaxed shoulders at Silas's addendum.

"Perhaps an acceptable compromise could persuade a peaceful resolution," Leanthun said, quickly holding up his hands in supplication at the angry looks thrown his way. "Nothing to do with Daniel. I merely think putting the offer of abandoning the Pass completely might placate the demons. His talk about forays into forbidden lands must mean the many expeditions into the demon lands that you humans have sent over the years."

"You've traded with the demons, too," Daniel said, placing his hands on the table and leaning forward. "Using the dwarves as middlemen doesn't make your hands any cleaner. It doesn't sound like that matters to them. What I'm stuck on is that the demons think you summoned me. Did you?"

Silence covered the room like a fog, heavy and thick.

"To summon a [Hero] is no easy feat." Lord Tarris spoke softly.

"The ritual requirements are costly and the knowledge closely guarded. In all of Dey, I can say that no single family or person in the last fifty years could accrue all they needed to perform the summoning. This I swear by the name of my family."

Silas nodded. "I searched and spent no small amount of time and coin in an attempt to find a source and can confirm that no one in Dey performed the summoning, Daniel."

Leanthun raised an eyebrow as everyone looked at him. "I can't speak for the council in this, but I doubt it was the elves. Summoning a [Hero] goes against much of what we believe is our role in life."

"We can't rule out Veskar," Finley said, drawing the attention his way. "I'll admit that I don't know much about the magical side of things, but if Odrana summoned Daniel, we would have made sure to get to him before anyone else did. From what I've heard, Daniel appeared in the Untamed Forest. The forest borders parts of Odrana, but mostly Veskar to the south of us. I wouldn't put it past one of the smaller powers to attempt a [Hero] summoning. There are attempts at unifying all of Veskar with risky plans every decade or so. You'll notice the more established states of Veskar have failed to send much help, if any at all. I've not seen any forces from Khubet or Karn. The few orcs I've met around camp are not from the Rinid empire, which isn't surprising, since they rarely leave or let others into their lands. Vas is too busy attacking Odrana to send fighters to save the world. My bet would be one of the kingdoms or city-states of Veskar is behind the summoning. Perhaps Karn . . . the mages there are skilled enough."

Silas sighed. "We've received supplies from Karn, as well as Khubet, Fanlo, and Spalril within Veskar. Vas and Rinid did not respond. Gendy said they would send backup, but until today, I didn't know for sure that they were sending anyone. I don't know the leader of Darmon, but we sent a message to him anyway. The messenger didn't return."

Finley winced. "Yeah, I could have told you not to send anyone to Darmon. Even the prisoners we get to talk from Vas don't know a thing about what is happening in those borders. Where are the Gendy forces? They're not the worst you could get from Veskar."

Madi cleared her throat. "Gendy sent the crown prince."

Finley groaned. "That psycho? That's a worst-case scenario. Every time his mother brings him to Odrana for diplomatic meetings, he gets into fights or seriously injures people weaker than him."

Madi grimaced. "We saved him from a Guild quest for clearing monsters in the Pass gone wrong. He attacked us and we turned him over to be deported."

Finley laughed and Silas rubbed his eyes. Orrin was lost. All the names of places within Veskar were new to him. He'd not had a reason to study the different city-states and kingdoms that made up Veskar. It looked like it still didn't matter if nobody was coming to help. Finding out who summoned them might be interesting to know, but it wasn't going to help them in their current situation. Something that Daniel picked up on as well.

"While I'd love nothing more than to know who to beat up for bringing me into this mess, I think we should focus more on what to say to the demons," Daniel said. "If we offer to pull back to Dey, what assurances do we have that the demons won't just attack anyway?"

One of the generals to the side of the table finally spoke. "Should we even make an offer? We could launch a preemptive attack. The camp is clustered together now that they've unloaded those monstrosities they brought with them. They have the spiders resting behind them. I would hazard a guess they are transports only and won't attack. A few high-powered attacks from our elites could take out thousands of the demons. Their defenses aren't strong enough to keep out a bombardment of various magic spells. They can't block a cloud of arrows falling upon them."

"That's a lot of assumptions," Orrin muttered.

He thought he said it under his breath, but every person at the table turned to him.

"What's that, young man?" the general asked. He wore dark-gray armor with golden embellishments down the sides. His long black hair and bushy beard helped mute the hawkish nose, but his piercing blue eyes glared at Orrin like he was a small mouse running across a field. "Speak up so everyone can hear you."

"General Andrew, that is Orrin. He is the one who scouted the enemy camp," Silas said quickly. "Orrin, do you have something to counter the general's plan?"

Orrin wiped his sweaty hands on his pants. "They have some sort of magical boundary set up around the camp that stopped most of my spells from working inside. You are looking at that camp like it's an invitation to attack, which is exactly what they want you to think. I would bet the moment a spell hits the perimeter, it fizzles out. I have no idea if there are protections from regular attacks, but if we send a cloud of arrows like you said, there are still way more of them than us. We'd need to bring our people out into the fields between this Wall and the camp to make any attack like that, and then we lose the only advantage we have—the protection of the Wall and the Pass. Some of those demons are a higher level than anyone I've seen in Dey, well above what I thought possible. We need to assume they will be able to take down dozens of people at a time, which means targeting any high-level attackers with designated groups. If we fight them on the field, it'll be a slaughter."

"I advocated for a first strike, not a full turnout of our forces," General Andrew said, tapping his fingers on the table. "How sure are you that their defenses would stop a concentrated magical attack? How many high-level targets did you see?"

Orrin answered as best he could, but after a few more questions, General Andrew shook his head in dismay.

"We don't have enough information, and the little we do have doesn't cover more than a small fraction of their forces. I withdraw my suggestion. We should spread our people out in smaller clusters to reduce casualties when they attack. This will be a fighting retreat with skirmishes if what this young man says holds true for the entire Horde." General Andrew tilted his head until his neck cracked audibly. "I'll compile a list of our stronger groups. Dragoon, Lily, Hornet, and Wendigo are set up already, but I think we could muster another three or four elite groups to hit these high-level demon targets outside of their protective circle."

He accepted what I said and didn't argue with me, Orrin thought in disbelief. He looked around for the other shoe that had to be dropping soon.

"Thank you, General. You as well, Orrin. Now, I'll explain the plan for the majority of our forces. Bring up any issues you see at the end."

Orrin listened as Silas explained the guerrilla warfare tactics that Daniel had pushed for, along with the experienced solutions to problems outside of Daniel's limited experience in warfare. Everyone was assigned specific duties to attend to, but the main idea was to harass the demons in a slow retreat to the original Wall. If they could not turn the Horde back before that point, the remaining combined forces of Asmea would make a last stand while the people of Dey were evacuated.

"It makes more sense to evacuate sooner, right?" Daniel argued after the final details were hammered out. "They can always move back into the city once we make it safe. Is there any reason to risk it?"

Lady Timpe indicated points around the city map. "These are manufacturing and processing plants for food, weapons, building materials, and more. If we abandon those points before the last minute, the infrastructure behind the entire war machine we've assembled is lost within days. Do you have any idea how much food it takes to keep this number of people satisfied? How many bandages for small injuries we've already gone through or the amount of money spent to keep tents over our people's heads and blankets over their backs? No matter the outcome in the coming weeks of this war, we've spent thousands of gold coins to fund this defense. Everything begins in the city. If we empty anyone out of the city, the chances of a mass flight from Dey could be triggered. Our families are still in the city to assuage the masses. Despite the fact that I want my children far away from Dey, we must risk everything to have a chance at victory."

Orrin watched the faces around him. The grim acknowledgment that they could die was written on every frown and furrowed brow.

"I will draft the response to the Demon Lord. If you feel you are needed elsewhere, attend to your tasks. Keep to your roles and show bravery for the common soldiers. The first battle for their hearts and minds has already begun. Remind them why we are in charge and be steady in the days to come." Silas spoke softly at first, his voice building up with a passion that Orrin rarely heard in the man. "This will not be our last strategy meeting, but the people in this room represent our greatest minds in leadership, tactics, and magical prowess. I respect each of you and know you will help steer our future to a safe harbor once more. Thank you for your time. Dismissed."

Most of the generals left at a brisk pace to set up their troops. Leanthun ducked out from the tent as well, moving toward his waiting messengers. The lords and lady of Dey whispered together over a blank scroll of paper as they discussed the best response to the Demon Lord's letter.

Daniel moved from the other side of the table and toward Madi, Orrin, and Brandt. "This is happening. We're about to be in some deep shit."

"You heard Lord Catanzano," Brandt said, his pride in the man obvious in his worshipful tone. "We have the best people on the job to defend Dey."

Daniel raised an eyebrow. "You realize he included you in that statement."

Brandt turned red as he stammered. "He meant the generals and other lords. If he meant anyone else, it would be you three."

Orrin threw his arm around Brandt's neck. "Either way, the guy is putting too much faith in our ragtag team of misfits."

Madi laughed and Orrin saw Silas glance their way. He smiled at his daughter, surrounded by friends, and noticed Orrin watching. Silas nodded his head at Orrin. Orrin smiled, tight-lipped, and raised his head in turn.

"It's funny. I thought Silas was smart," Daniel stage-whispered to Madi, "but then he has to go and ruin my image of him by saying Orrin is smart."

"I'm going to kill you and throw you to the Horde."

Silas closed his eyes and took a deep breath.

Chapter 18

"Orrin, wait up." Finley jogged out of the tent to where Daniel, Orrin, Madi, and Brandt were about to climb the stairs back to the top of the Wall. "Can you chat for a minute?"

Orrin waved his friends on and watched as Finley nervously let down his hair before weaving it back into a bun on the back of his head. "Sure, Fin. Aren't you supposed to be holding the next Wall?"

The few forces that Finley had brought with him from Odrana were elites from the Madvarr province of Ronden. However, Odrana and Dey's relationship was in a precarious position after the back-and-forth kidnappings, assassinations, and mayhem that started with Lord Sanerris working with one of the former lords of Dey in an attempt to capture Daniel and ended with that same man's death in the heart of Odrana's capital city at the hands of the [Hero] and another scion of Odrana.

Orrin might have helped a little, too.

The fraught and developing rapport between the two countries steered Silas to be cautious with any Odranan forces. They were integrated into existing frameworks of the Dey army, while kept away from any positions where indifference would be costly and far away from places where sabotage would be detrimental. Finley and his team were stationed one Wall back from the front line.

"That's not important. I can run there in a few minutes. I wanted to ask you something," Finley said, stopping close to Orrin and lowering his voice. "About what you said about the demon's camp being protected. Did you see any markings or try to find any mana flow around the perimeter?"

Orrin kicked himself mentally. "I didn't think to look. The fence that I passed through looked like shit. It was a bunch of wood fragments that wouldn't slow anyone and it was spaced out so far, I didn't think it could have been a magical boundary."

Finley sighed and gave Orrin a slap on the back. "Don't worry about it. Just try to keep a better eye on the details next time. You didn't have much time to study with Professor Galina, but she would have beaten that into you by the end of the semester. Did you feel anything when you went through the fence? Was there a moment you knew your magic was sealed?"

Orrin studied Finley. His eyes were constantly surveying the area around him, only meeting Orrin's eyes long enough to be polite. His hands rested comfortably on the knives strapped to his armor. He wore the same leathers he'd worn to Battle Class, but now the daggers strapped over his body made him look menacing. "You heard what I said in there, Fin. I didn't know until I realized my [Camouflage] failed. There was no single moment that I could pinpoint for you."

Finley kept staring at one spot on the Wall behind Orrin. "We're being watched, so don't react. If anyone asks, that's what we talked about. I slipped up and missed a detail in the tent. You filled the gap for me. Nod and smile."

Orrin's neck itched and he wanted to turn to whatever Finley was watching, but he controlled his urges and nodded with a smile. "What's going on, Fin?"

"This is terrible timing. I wouldn't even mention it before we go into battle, but I can't have you teleporting around Odrana without knowing. Lady Sanerris is teaching at the Sanerris School. I'm sure you've heard?"

"Yes," Orrin said through clenched teeth. "I thought you all would take care of her."

"The problem with being the chancellor of Ronden is the constant warfare with Veskar. My father has little time for actual politicking and sends me in his place more often than not. With this Horde threat, I gave my recommendation for Anabella's execution to the others and left to bring fighters here as quickly as possible."

"I don't get why she's alive or at least not in a dark hole," Orrin whispered, trying to keep the anger out of his voice. He nearly activated [Mind Bastion]. Anabella Sanerris had kept him in a slave collar and forced him to attend her magical school in an attempt to befriend the children of the other rulers of her country. It had taken them some time to figure out it was an elaborate setup to instigate a war with Veskar, blaming the Odranan neighbor for their deaths. Orrin had barely survived by killing her son, one of the rulers of Odrana. Anabella was captured as well. "She tried to kill half of the chancellors."

Finley flinched. "Don't blame the messenger. I'm on your side. My vote for death was a mistake. Lady Tonsa and Lord Wellan moved for execution as well. The three of us should have known what would happen. Lord Palmer voted for imprisonment. A supermajority is needed for the death sentence in these cases. The newly appointed lady of Mistlight voted to have her contained at the school, in a strictly advisory position. I'm sure you know how much Lady Sanerris is valued for her magical insights. She's using the position to quietly foment unrest in her supporters."

Orrin touched the back of his neck where he could feel the shadow of the slave collar still. "How does she have supporters? Her son started a fake war with the elves and she wanted to do the same with Veskar."

Finley toyed with one of the daggers on his chest. It clicked faintly as he clipped it off and on again to the leather indents that held the knives in place. "The specifics of what happened were not made clear to the general populace, against my recommendation. Everyone felt it would create distrust in the other rulers."

Orrin stared. "It should. They fucked up and let the Sanerris family manipulate them. You're all doing it again."

"Careful, Orrin. That includes my dad."

"Your dad is an idiot, then. She's going to come back twice as strong and finish what she started."

Finley clucked his tongue, tsking at Orrin. "I'll ignore what you said about my dad because we're friends and you're upset. There is another family in charge of Mistlight now. I received word that Anabella is working the populace of Mistlight into a frenzy over invading foreigners. She's pushing the narrative that her son was assassinated in a coup attempt by the other chancellors. We can't directly tie it back to her yet, but we will."

Orrin opened his mouth to again demean the man he'd never met but stopped. Finley was warning him for a reason. From what he said, Lord Madvarr was a respectable man who protected his country from raiding parties and spent little time playing politics. "Sorry, Fin. I shouldn't have said that. I've never met him. Please let him know to watch out for her. She's not happy with a win. She needs to crush her opponent. We played Kala and I never won, but if I got close or did something to set her back, she came at me with a cold anger that was scary. Anabella is going to be a problem."

Orrin trailed off as he had a thought. He'd been content to leave Anabella to the rulers of Odrana, but they were clearly not handling her well. He could get to Odrana easily with a few [Teleports]. It wouldn't be hard to kill her. He could drop Anabella's strength and toss her into the ocean. He knew the Sanerris School campus and could find out where she was within a few minutes. The only problem was she had access to the same spells he used to buff and debuff based on their last fight. If she was able to increase her strength back to normal . . .

"Orrin, you've got that look in your eye," Finley said with a warning tone. "What are you thinking?"

"Nothing, Finley. Thanks for the heads-up. I'm sure Rhys knows, but maybe send him a quick letter or something?" Orrin pointed up the stairs behind him. "I need to get up there and tell my friends."

"Orrin, don't try to go after her," Finley pleaded. "She's collared as of now, but if she survives an assassination attempt, they might let her free so she can defend herself."

"It doesn't seem like anyone else is going to take care of the problem. I'm not dumb enough to go in alone, Fin. If I do anything, I'll make sure she's put down."

"I didn't tell you this so you'd turn assassin."

Orrin whirled on Finley and got in his face. The older boy rocked on his heels. With Orrin's dexterity maxed out, he could move fast even without [Gust]. "I'm done letting people push me around and threaten my life, Finley. I'm not going to let anything happen to my friends. That includes you. If you don't want me to do something I don't want to do, then get your dad to put his foot down. She should not be in a position of power, no matter how much control you think you have over her. Anabella Sanerris will kill you, Maeve, Rhys, your families, me, and Daniel. It's not a question of if she can but when she can. Take away that power, or as soon as I get a chance, I will."

Finley reattached his knives into their holsters. He shook his head. "I'll do what I can, but I'm serious, Orrin. Don't go rogue. I have to protect my people, even those I don't like. We have laws for a reason."

"I'm not from Odrana. I don't have to follow your rules."

Finley's sad smile was enough to make Orrin back off a bit. "You're right, but like you said, we're friends. I'm asking as your friend. Don't attack a citizen of Odrana. Especially right now. My dad is close to getting a temporary treaty put through with a few states in Veskar that would let him move a lot more troops here to Dey. Let Anabella be tomorrow's fight."

Orrin stepped out of Finley's personal space and cast [Calm Mind] on himself. His prior abuse of [Mind Bastion] kept making his emotions flare when he wasn't using it. It was almost as if all the emotions he'd suppressed bubbled back up at the most inopportune times. His use of the [Calm Mind] spell was a temporary balm, but Orrin needed to figure out how to better control himself in the moment.

"You are a friend, Fin. I won't go after Anabella unless it's together."

Finley smiled and slapped Orrin's arm. "There he is. Thank you, Orrin. I'm sorry that I had to tell you."

Orrin waved him off. "Maeve told me she was alive, but I thought I could let it go. If she is going to keep playing games, that is when it becomes a problem. I'd still like it if you'd make sure Rhys knows. He struck the last blow on Arvin. Anabella likely is harboring a grudge against the guy who stabbed her son to death."

"Lady Tonsa knows. She's the one having Anabella watched. It's weird to me . . . calling her Anabella. She's always been Lady Sanerris my entire life. Even after fighting her and getting stabbed, a part of me feels like it's wrong to call her by her first name. I'll still reach out to Rhys. Although his mother probably has him locked away deep underground now."

Orrin chuckled and watched Finley retreat to his cadre of fighters. He felt bad misleading his friend. He'd told Fin that he wouldn't go after Anabella unless it was together. He'd let the blond knife-wielding mage assume that meant with him. He turned to look up at his party.

Chapter 19

Orrin finished telling his friends about Anabella as they ate a quick dinner sitting on the edge of the Wall.

"Orrin, we are not going to leave this battle to go kill Lady Sanerris," Madi said as she tossed an apple core over her shoulder. She leaned back and watched it bounce on the ground below. "Odrana can make their own mistakes. If she comes after us, we'll be ready and respond with force."

"I'm not saying we should go right now," Orrin said around a mouthful of the bean-and-beef mixture Brandt had scrounged up for them. The naan-like bread pieces soaked up the concoction. The food given to the militia farthest from Dey was usually soup or anything that kept well. A few patrolling guards sniffed the air longingly as they passed the group of four. Orrin savored the flavors before swallowing and finishing his argument. "I think we should make a list and move down it in a matter of importance. First, we take out the Demon Lord and his little Horde out there. Then, a quick [Teleport] to Mistlight for some light political murdering. After that, if we have time, we go kick the Hospital doors down and make sure they know who's in charge."

Daniel rolled his eyes. "I'm all for getting rid of a future problem, but let's not forget what's happened the last few times the four of us ran off to Odrana. I think we should trust Finley and let them deal with their own internal problems."

Madi and Orrin turned in surprise to look at Daniel. He was vocal about his dislike of Odrana. The country had been behind his kidnapping, the torture of Brandt, the false-flag elven war, and Orrin's enslavement. He'd even once chewed out a temporary party member simply for being from Odrana.

"What?" Daniel asked as they all stared at him. He rubbed his wrist against his mouth. "Do I have something on my face?"

"You're the one I thought I could count on to get some revenge," Orrin pointed out. "This new attitude of yours is not okay with me."

Daniel grinned in the fading light. "Finley can fight and I like him. If he can't put the screws to Lady Sanerris, then I'll gladly step in and wipe her line off this planet. Until then, we have a different problem."

Daniel waved his hand at the torchlights in the distance. "Silas said the letter will be delivered tomorrow at first light. That means the Horde will probably attack right after. Orrin . . . how sure are you about the seal plan?"

"The seal plan?" Madi asked, pushing the bowl of meat dip away. "What nonsense are you two plotting this time?"

Orrin was actually proud of his idea. At level five, Daniel had unlocked the ability to purchase a [Hero]-specific ability called [Demon Seal].

> **[Demon Seal] (Hero Specific)—Seal the Demon Lord. Only usable one time. The Demon Lord must be at low health when used. 300 AP**

There was no way Daniel could save up thirty levels of ability points before the fight tomorrow, but Orrin might have come up with a solution.

"Daniel can buy an ability called [Demon Seal]. It's like it was tailor-made for this fight, but it costs three hundred ability points," Orrin explained. Brandt whistled low. "Even if he had saved every point since he found out about it, it wouldn't be enough. Luckily, he's also got me."

"I'll admit, your class comes with some unique abilities," Brandt chimed in as he collected the earthenware plates they'd been using. "But if you start handing out extra ability points, I'm going to need to get in on that, too."

"Not yet I can't." Orrin smiled as he put a small kettle he'd pilfered over his heater cube. The small magical device gave off the same heat as a fire, and Orrin found the temperature was perfect for brewing up a small coffee. "I'm thinking of using my nonclass powers."

Outside of his self-made class, [Utility Warder], Orrin also had a secondary set of powers that named him Administrator. He'd been able to learn some about Administrators of the past from an elf—Arandir was Leanthun's uncle and one of the elves' council members. He'd told Orrin of the men and women of great power called Administrators who helped rule the world. Arandir had also admitted that he was an Administrator of sorts himself, cursed in a way through the generations to have diminishing powers.

Brandt perked up and tossed the plates into the mostly empty dip bowl. "You said you wanted to be careful using those powers."

Orrin had said that recently. His first conscious use of his Administrator powers was using Assign Class on his friend Amir. Amir's life goal was to become a [Healer]. Orrin used his Administrator powers to make Amir a [Healer] . . . the only one not controlled by the Hospital.

The fallout from that was currently playing out in Dey, with the Hospital strong-arming the governing lords for concessions in return for healing during the Horde attack.

"I know what I said but it worked out well for Madi," Orrin said, hoping to throw Brandt's judgment off. "Plus, I'm discussing options with you guys beforehand. This is me being careful."

Madi raised her hand to quiet Orrin as a patrol passed. She waited until they were alone and pointed at the ground. Madi's finger drew a circle of sapphire light around the four of them on the ground. "This will keep anyone from seeing or hearing us for a few minutes. You need to be more careful about talking about this stuff, Orrin."

"We are going to talk about your cool new powers," Daniel said, moving over and poking at the pretty blue light. "Isn't the color going to make it obvious you cast a spell?"

"Only those inside the perimeter can see it," Madi explained in an annoyed tone. "Orrin, you told me you didn't want to spend any more administrator points. What did you buy?"

"Nothing yet, I swear!"

Madi stared at Orrin and slowly nodded her head. "I believe you."

"It really doesn't sound like it," Daniel whispered to Brandt.

"I didn't buy one because there are a few ways of trying this . . . I think." Orrin pulled a bag of ground coffee beans out of his [Dimension Hole] and started measuring enough for a small cup. Brandt raised a finger and Orrin scooped a bit more into his press.

"I disagree, by the way," Daniel added. "I think he's got a surefire way to get us a lot of great things and also cheaper options he's going to try and convince you is the better way so he can keep more cash in the bank."

"What's cash?" Madi asked. "Never mind, don't answer that. Orrin, what are you suggesting?"

Orrin checked his kettle and poured the hot water over the ground coffee. "Daniel is being greedy because of the long-term benefits of the more expensive option, which I won't be able to afford because it uses almost all my administrator points."

Daniel flipped his middle finger at Orrin.

"Wait, I'll explain," Orrin cried and grabbed at his coffee press, but Madi was too quick. She held the precious liquid over the edge of the Wall. "Let's not do something we regret, Madi."

Madi growled.

"Fine. It's either Reset Class, Unlock Spell, or Assign Quests. Please don't throw that out. It's the good shit from Amir." Madi handed back Orrin's baby and he cradled the warm container in his arms. "It's okay. I won't let the bad lady hurt you anymore."

Brandt's laugh turned into a coughing fit when Madi glared at him.

"Would one of you take this seriously?" she asked, rubbing her eyes. One of her braids was coming undone and she flicked it off her face. "Orrin, clarify now or no more coffee."

Orrin doled out Brandt's cup and some fresh java. He raised his own cup to his lips for a single sip before he started explaining. It was all he felt was safe under Madi's gaze.

"Daniel wants me to buy Assign Quest and"—he paused for dramatic effect—"Edit Reward. He thinks that I can give him an easy Quest like the run to the Wall of Dey Quest we had before and tweak the reward to just give him the [Demon Seal] spell."

"Is it a spell or a skill?" Brandt interrupted. Orrin frowned in envy at the [Knight]'s half-empty cup. "You called it an ability earlier. Which is it?"

"I'll get to that," Orrin said, stealing another bit of coffee to wet his tongue. He sighed in pleasure and made a mental note to thank Amir again. "The problem with option A is it costs ten points per ability. I'll have three points left. If Assign Quests works like Assign Class, then I'll have to spend a point to just give the Quest. I'll likely have to spend another to use Edit Reward. Of course, there is also the chance that I can't give a Quest reward of a [Hero]-specific spell."

"You said 'spell' again," Brandt muttered before he slurped loudly.

"I think that route is too risky. I'd be out of points, and unless one of you has a fresh dungeon we can conquer in the next, I don't know, twenty hours, I'm not sure that's worth it." Orrin reached into his pocket and used his magic to pull out a small bag of cookies. Crumbs spilled down his shirt as he took a bite from one. More crumbs scattered on the stone between them as he pointed the half-eaten cookie at Brandt. "To answer your question, Daniel is pretty sure it's a spell. That's why I keep calling it a spell. If he's wrong, buying Unlock Spell is a waste of ten points. I'd have to buy Unlock Skill, likely spend another point to actually unlock the seal thing, and then I'm back in the same boat. Left with one or two points and hoping an Administrator can tweak [Hero] spells from that ability."

Madi reached forward and snagged a treat from Orrin. "What's the third option?" she asked as she bit into her own cookie. Her eyes widened as she chewed. "Where did you get these? They're amazing."

"Tony made them for me as a welcome-back present," Orrin said innocently. Madi's hand stopped its travel toward the bag for a second cookie. Orrin grinned devilishly. Madi was still slightly afraid of the mind mage. It was a testament to his baking that she took another anyway.

Orrin enjoyed the moment by drinking more of his own treat. *If I could store some of these beans and get them back to Earth, I'd put the other coffee chains out of business.*

"Orrin's third option is betting that Arandir is wrong about his own Administrator power and hoping he doesn't reset me to level one," Daniel informed them, tired of waiting. He was the only one not having dessert. "He wants to spend the least number of points possible and bet that I'm not turned into a weakling."

"Hard to turn into something you already are," Orrin said over the edge of his cup. He winked. "I'm messing with you, D. I explained it to you and you agreed it made no sense."

"Maybe explain it for the rest of us?" Brandt asked, holding out his hand. Orrin placed a single morsel in the man's palm.

"Arandir said he could reset an elf's class, but if he did, they were left without a class. At the time, I didn't know anything about my powers. I thought he was talking about Reset Class. Now, I think he has a broken version of Assign Class. Instead of picking a new class, he just wipes their previous choices away. Like how Madi went back to level one."

"That's a leap," Madi said.

"No, think about it," Orrin said, finishing his cup and setting it down. "I have two similar abilities, Reset Class and Assign Class. When I used Assign Class, it reset you to level one and I got to pick your new class. If all Reset Class does is make you not have a class, doesn't that seem duplicative? Why couldn't an Administrator just help the person get the class they wanted right away? Why reset them to essentially puberty and the need to undergo training? It got me thinking, and I tried to use Assign Class on Brandt—"

"You what?" Brandt scrambled to his feet and patted his body like something was missing.

"I didn't actually accept it, I was testing a theory." Orrin grabbed the man's hand and yanked, pulling him back down on his butt. It surprised him a bit, as he still thought of Brandt as much stronger than him at times. "Anyway, Assign Class lets me pick 'none' as an option."

Orrin waited expectantly.

"Get it?" he asked slowly.

"You think that since Assign Class lets you do what Arandir thinks Reset Class does, the second skill does something different?" Madi caught up. "Orrin, that is still a lot of guesswork. What if you're wrong?"

"Then I'm wrong and we go with the Unlock Spell option. But I think I'm right. I think Reset Class wipes out your ability point purchases. Daniel could beat the Demon Lord into the ground. I use Reset Class on him and he buys [Demon Seal]. The good guys win and the Horde runs away. But this is why we're talking. What do you think I should do?"

As Madi and Brandt thought it over, Daniel finally reached out and grabbed the penultimate cookie. He examined it before nibbling the edge. Time froze around them as Daniel shoveled the rest into his mouth.

A moment later, the [Hero] and his party scrapped like schoolchildren over the remaining contents of the small pastry bag.

Chapter 20

Orrin stared sadly at his gift from Tony, the remnants of an epic battle splayed out before him.

"Brandt, remind me to go ask Tony for the recipe. We'll need more provisions like that to get us through the upcoming fight," Madi grumbled.

Brandt's eyes were heavy-lidded as he savored the last cookie. "You still shudder every time we walk down his street."

Madi ignored Brandt and looked away.

"I think we should vote on which power Orrin gets." Daniel pouted, having lost the race. "All in favor of more Quests, raise your hands."

Madi gave Orrin a sheepish look before raising her hand with Daniel. "It makes the most sense, and even if you can't give Daniel this [Demon Seal] spell, there are other things we could get from having a Quest generator."

"That's all I would become," Orrin muttered darkly. "Your dad wouldn't let me out of his sight if he learned I could give Quests."

Brandt shook his head. "Lord Catanzano isn't that controlling. Madi still won't tell him how she upgraded her class. She only told me about your Administrator abilities once she ran it by you."

After Orrin changed Madi's class from [Prism Conjurer] to [Superior Prism Conjurer] using his Administrator powers, she'd left the party to return to Dey for a time. Her level had reset to one, and she'd needed the help of Brandt and her father's guards to raise her level safely. When Daniel and Orrin completed the Stop the War in Odrana Quest, Madi received credit as well and saw her way back to almost level thirty. The massive changes were not lost on Brandt or her father. Lord Catanzano asked but didn't push his daughter for answers. Brandt pestered her as well, but Madi had kept Orrin's secret until she could ask for his permission. Something that Orrin was happy to grant to their party member and friendly [Knight].

When Brandt learned of Orrin's Administrator status, he asked Orrin how he'd unlocked the same. Orrin explained how he'd come to Asmea with Daniel, which Brandt was strangely unfazed by. He muttered something about it being obvious in hindsight but was more interested in Orrin's ability to upgrade classes.

"While I appreciate Madi's respect for my privacy, there is a big difference between someone getting an upgraded class and the appearance of new Quests," Orrin reasoned. He scratched the back of his neck. "It wouldn't be only Silas I'd be worried about."

Brandt stuck his thumbs into the front of his metal chest piece. His fingers drummed on the smooth metal. "I don't think we should vote on something like this. It's Orrin's decision. It's the same thing as asking him to buy a specific ability for his class. We don't have the right to do that."

Orrin felt a flush of warmth for Brandt. The [Knight] was still recovering from his trauma in Odrana, but the calming presence that he'd always had was growing into a deeper foundational point of his personality. Brandt's higher level when they first arrived lent to his natural leadership in the dungeon they explored and against the monsters they fought. As Orrin and Daniel gained levels and became stronger, he gracefully sidestepped into a support role. His fighting prowess and knowledge were major boons to their party, but the new, quieter attitude he had begun to show lately was adding a level of wisdom to the party they sorely needed.

Daniel started to argue, but Brandt held up a hand. "My vote is to let Orrin decide. That means unless he chooses your way, it's a split vote. I'd argue that means it's solely Orrin's decision in either case."

Madi sighed. "I agree with Brandt. We can't force Orrin to make the choice we want. I'll make the argument that the Quest-giving option would help more in the long term. Resetting a person's class, even if it works the way Orrin thinks it will, is situational at best. There isn't a lot of demand for that kind of power, which might help Orrin's powers stay unknown if that is the way you want to keep it."

Orrin nodded at her when she glanced his way for confirmation.

"Daniel, what level are you now?" Brandt asked. "Would it even be worth resetting your class? You said the spell costs three hundred points? That's more than I've had my entire life. You'd lose most of your spells and abilities, too."

"I get ten ability points a level and I'm at level thirty-three," Daniel answered. "But when I first woke up, I had three hundred points."

Brandt blinked and shook his head. "I'm sorry, did you just say you started with three hundred points?"

Daniel grinned sheepishly.

"Blasted heroes and their stupid magic," Brandt muttered. "How have you spent so many points?"

"My space spells cost a lot," Daniel protested. "The spell I used to get us back to Dey from Odrana cost a hundred points by itself."

"Daniel, you went up almost a dozen levels from the Odrana war Quest," Orrin said slowly. "That's over a hundred and twenty ability points at least. Did you spend those?"

"Not all of them."

"Are you serious, D?"

"How many points do you have?" Daniel asked accusatorily.

"Twenty-one," Orrin said quickly. "I used up most of my new points buying spells to keep us alive. [Spell Orb] costs twenty-five and my new spell [Increase Constitution] costs fifty."

Brandt whistled low. "That's a hefty price. Is it worth it?"

"I don't know yet," Orrin admitted. "I cast it on Madi this morning. It gives the target more constitution but at the cost of a lot of mana . . . well, a lot of mana if I don't fully buff myself before."

"Broken cheater," Daniel said with a smile.

"Anyway," Orrin said pointedly, "I think making us harder to take down is worth a few less points of mana to use. If it resets after I sleep like I hope it will."

"We're getting away from the point." Madi directed them back to the task at hand. "Orrin, you seem pretty sure that the Reset Class option will let you reset Daniel to have . . . what . . . six hundred points? What about all his Quest rewards? Would those be lost?"

Orrin paused at the argument. Madi had kept her Quest rewards after changing her class, but Daniel had a lot more riding on it than she did. Half of his weapon proficiency skills were from the leveling Quests he received every ten levels.

". . . I don't know."

"What about his moniker?" Madi pointed out. "He's the Space Hero, right? What if resetting his class makes him lose that? Some of his powers are based on space, according to what you two say. I don't know what a black hole is, but one of Daniel's powers is called that. What if he can't get it again? He'd have to retrain under an entire new power set."

Orrin began to doubt his preferred option more as she talked.

"You said Unlock Spell was an option," Brandt said. "Does that make the spell available to a class or purchase it for the person?"

"Um, the second . . . I hope?"

Brandt shook his head. "From what you've told me about Administrators, they were there to help people correct mistakes. I don't think they could set a person's entire path by giving certain powers from the beginning. Think about it. If an Administrator could give [Fireball] to a level-one [Fire Mage] for no cost to them, why wouldn't they do that for everyone? It would upset the balance of classes and builds. It would make it pointless to practice the underlying principles of sword fighting before taking [Perfect Thrust]. It's more likely Unlock Spell will let you give me the ability to purchase [Fireball] with my class. Whether that would mean I have to split my focus and level up [Firebolt] or just make it possible to use the spell at a certain level, I don't know."

Orrin rubbed his hair in confusion. "You guys are making this too hard. You're basically arguing for the Quest option. Now I'm doubting whether Unlock Spell would even work."

"That's why you waited to talk with us, though," Madi said, comforting Orrin with her hand on his arm. She patted him gently. "You don't have to make the decision right now. Brandt is right, though. You get to make the final decision, and even if you pick something that doesn't work, it's okay. We don't need Daniel's ability to push the Horde back. Dey has survived for thousands of years without him."

"Somehow," Daniel joked.

They continued to discuss the three options as the sun set in the distance. Orrin noticed other clumps of people sitting together, chatting and laughing before the long day came to an end. Friends among the defenders of Dey, taking a moment of respite in the chaos of war.

"Look at them all," Orrin said softly, interrupting Daniel as he argued for more Quests. "Maybe a quarter of these people have classes suited for fighting. Most of them haven't held a sword or spear in their lives, and now they're at the front line, ready to stand between their families and the demons. None of them will ever receive a Quest or meet the [Hero]. Most of them won't know anyone in charge outside of their captain or group leader."

Daniel and Madi paused in their talk to see what Orrin pointed out. Brandt had a strange look of pride on his face as Orrin continued to talk.

"The only thing that matters is protecting as many people as possible. If the fighting starts tomorrow, we are going to see a lot of death. Not every demon was high level, but there were enough that I'm positive we will see areas of the defense wiped out to the man. Our orders are to protect a small stretch of the Wall, but I think we can do more if we [Teleport] up and down to find the weakest areas. We help save lives and give these people hope that the [Hero] might show up in their moment of need. Daniel, I'm sure you're wiped, but do you think you have it in you to do some rounds? Shake a few babies and kiss a few hands?"

"Why would you shake a—"

"Madi, that's just Orrin being weird," Daniel said with a grin. "That is a good idea, O. I'm sure talking with the mythical [Hero] for a few minutes will give them something to talk about besides fighting tomorrow."

Daniel stood up and stretched his arms high above his head. "Don't you think for a minute that this means I'm not going to keep pushing for the Quest option. We need to decide tonight. If the Demon Lord shows up on the field, I don't know if I can defeat him without the seal. I like the idea of running around to the areas being hit hardest. Other than the elite squads, I think we might be one of the strongest groups around. Madi, can you check with your dad and make sure it's okay for us to do that?"

Madi brushed her foot over the magical circle isolating sound from others and broke the spell. She, too, stood and arched her back side to side with her hands on her hips. "I can ask, but I don't know if they'll want us somewhere dangerous. If we lose the [Hero], it'll be over before the demons breach the first Wall. But don't worry about the Demon Lord, Daniel. We'll fight him together. No rushing in alone this time, though. We fight as a unit."

Madi and Daniel moved toward the nearest group of fighters. Daniel waved his hand and introduced himself as he sat down among them. Orrin watched as his friend turned on the charm. He was joking with the small group of three within two minutes.

Brandt sighed and smiled as they watched from a distance. "You did good there."

"What?" Orrin asked, jolted from his own thoughts. "Did good where?"

The [Knight] kept his fingers hooked in his breastplate as they watched Daniel and Madi bolster the spirits of the troops. They were only spending a few minutes with each cluster of men and women standing guard on the Wall, but the atmosphere change was immediate. The cooks, clerks, and workers of Dey were hardworking folk who were scared and in a dangerous situation. Most of them held spears or bows but had had only a few weeks of training with the weapons. Their nerves were shot after waiting around for days as the Dark Horde approached. Being granted a few minutes to talk with an actual [Hero] would be a talking point for them at parties and social gatherings for months to come . . . if they survived. For now, their thoughts turned from the unimaginable horrors of the next day to their bright, if uncertain, future. A future where they could brag about meeting Daniel and Lady Catanzano before they defended their city.

"You distanced Daniel from the problem he's fixating on and gave him a task that not only makes him feel in control but also helps make everyone else more at peace. Multiple goals accomplished with minimal effort."

Orrin frowned. "That's not why I did this. I thought these people could use a bit of good fortune and everyone loves Daniel. He's good with people."

Brandt looked down at Orrin and smiled. "I know you didn't mean to do it. That's why I said you did good. You do things like this without thinking about what you get in return. You came to rescue me in Odrana because you felt it was right. You had us pull resources to help that woman selling spell orbs because you felt she needed help. Daniel might be good with people, but you are good for people. I'm proud to fight beside the [Hero] and Madi. They save lives and move others with their words. But Orrin, I'm proud to walk by your side because you make everyone around you a little better."

Orrin's face turned red. Brandt complimenting him out of the blue was flustering. "I . . . I'm not trying—"

"Learn to take a compliment," Brandt chuckled, slapping his back. "Come on, keep up. They're moving to the next group."

Chapter 21

The following day, the Dark Horde advanced on the Wall as the sun reached its zenith.

Thousands of warriors and mages stood in loose formations among siege weapons built in mere minutes using magic. Dozens of flags depicting countries or battalions, nobody knew for sure, hung above the mixed troops of demons and humans. They marched slowly, sending no attacks toward the Wall.

"Target the scaling ladders," Lord Silas Catanzano yelled as he moved about on a floating wheelchair. Usually the wheels touched the ground, but today he was using what he called his battle chair. It floated a few inches above the ground with a steady flow of magic keeping it up. "Distance spells and arrows only. Save your earth magic until they've closed in."

Daniel's giant sword, Gertrude, was strapped to his back. His abilities were mostly geared for close-up use. Instead, he had a wall of spears standing up nearby to throw. Someone had given him a bow and arrows as well, but with his strength, a hurtling spear would do more damage.

"This is bullshit," he growled, raising his objections again as he raised a spear over his head like a javelin. "We should be down there fighting before they get too close."

Orrin cast [Calm Mind] on his friend for the tenth time in three hours. "Keep it together. You'll be fighting demons soon enough."

Orrin confirmed that his [Utility Ward] and other buffs were fully applied. His mana had been back to his normal amount when he woke up. Madi's constitution was back to her baseline as well. He was hesitant to fully buff her constitution to a hundred, despite her request. Orrin's plan was to experiment with a few extra points each day until they could figure out any potential side effects. Brandt requested a full constitution buff and [Utility Ward] increase of all stats, but only Daniel and Orrin knew they wouldn't suffer the backlash.

Instead, Orrin brought Madi and Brandt's constitution up fifteen points. He played with the math until he felt comfortable and left both of the other members of his party with nearly sixty points of strength, dexterity, will, and intelligence. Madi was practically giggling in glee as she prepped her [Sunbeam] spell.

Orrin also topped off his friends with every ward he'd purchased. He'd begun buffing them when the Horde first began to move. It took only a minute to get all three covered, but the demons chewed up the earth as they approached.

"Spell orbs ready," Silas shouted down the line. Mages using sound magic relayed his orders the full length of the Wall. Orrin heard someone mention the opening of the Pass into the rest of the demon country was one of the narrowest points. It would be the easiest Wall to defend with more consolidated troops gathered than any other planned defense. "Ranged attackers use the orbs and attack at will."

Orrin couldn't buff the entire army, but he'd done his best at creating a mountain of spell orbs with various increase-stat spells for Silas to hand out at his discretion. The vast majority would be used in the first attack, with the plan for Orrin to continue making more if they were forced to retreat.

A single arrow jumped out between the two armies. Streams of magic, more arrows, and what Orrin swore was a bag that exploded into several very angry badgers followed. The soldiers advancing on the Wall held up shields where they had them and cast spells in other places. Some enemy mages cast magic into the air that snuffed out the attacks. However, a number of enemies fell and the Wall erupted in cheers at the first casualties.

The majority of the Horde surged forward into a light jog, leaving the war machines to slowly make their way under the continuing barrage of arrows and spells. They were finally close enough that Orrin could use [Identify] on them. He let out a sigh of relief.

"I've used [Identify] on about ten different random demons. None of them are above level sixty."

Assigned to their same section was a squat, balding man wearing a white robe with silver trim. Black markings were embroidered on the silver background. His horseshoe of thin, graying hair did not match his youthful face or jovial attitude in their limited interactions so far. His spear was double-sided, but the man used it more as a walking stick. His name was Crius and he was Lady Timpe's Agent.

A ruler in Dey had the ability to give part of their power to a chosen representative. The last Agent the party had encountered was Samara, the woman who'd captured Daniel at Lord Wendeln's behest. Orrin and Daniel had killed her.

When Silas introduced them, Crius smiled and shook their hands, but Orrin noticed a slight unease behind his eyes. Agents were supposed to be nearly untouchable, the same as the lords of Dey. He'd been assigned to fight beside the party that had been the downfall of one lord and his Agent.

"That is what the few [Scouts] we have on the Wall are reporting as well. Most enemies are above level thirty, but the highest level we've found so far is seventy-five. Just two above level seventy so far," Crius said. He cast a spell and nodded as if listening to someone talking. "Yes. Three above level seventy but spread out. They are sending the infantry against us first."

Madi's eyes started to glow softly as she stepped forward. "Any of them close?"

Crius shook his head. "They're a few minutes away if we run, but not close enough to attack from here. We should stay until we're called to reinforce."

Crius didn't have the traditional [Message] ability, but he could send a ghostlike copy of himself to listen in and report to a select number of people giving orders. He'd been chosen to stay close to Daniel to lend tactical help.

Madi was now giving off a slight heat. "Orrin, point out any groups of higher-level demons."

Orrin nodded, understanding what she wanted. He got behind her and pointed to a group of mostly level-fifty to -sixty enemies. "There, the group of ten demons. The guy with the green armor and behind him to the red guy with two swords strapped to his back. That entire group is the highest level around here."

Madi nodded and held her hands up to the sky. Orrin watched the mana rip away from her body and explode at a point far above them. A solid beam of fiery light five feet in diameter appeared from the heavens. It struck wide from where Orrin had pointed, but Madi gritted her teeth and pulled her hands to the side. The impressive magic scoured the earth, looking like nothing more than a giant magnifying glass burning ants. It moved slowly and the men ran from the ray. Madi's spell followed them as it drew patterns in the earth, kicking up smoke in every direction.

She kept the spell going for almost two minutes. When the smoke cleared, only one of the ten demons in the group was still standing. His arm was gone, burned to the elbow. He still held his second sword but was on his knees screaming in pain. Three bodies were burned husks. The other six were ashen clumps on the ground.

Madi let out a cry as she fell to her knees, the spell faltering and fading. The afterimage of the bright line in the sky was burned into everyone's retinas, and many of those nearby stepped away from the awesome display of magic.

"Madi, are you all right?" Brandt asked as he partially caught her on her way to the ground.

"I overdid it a bit," she said, slurring her words slightly. "I couldn't get all of them. That swordsman is fast."

Orrin crouched and pulled a vial from his bandolier of potions. "Here. Drink this."

Madi tipped the potion back and squinted one eye as she swallowed. "Ugh. That's terrible."

"It's one of my regen potions. You'll be fine in a minute. You weren't supposed to push yourself that hard." Orrin rubbed her back as she began to shake. She'd used too much mana and was paying the price, but his mana-regeneration potion would give her a reprieve. Although it wouldn't work as well for anyone without [Meditate], the regen potion would still give Madi a point of MP every minute for the next hour. It was like getting [Meditate] for sixty minutes for the price of a few mushroom clippings and Orrin's time. "We really should get you [Meditate]. You could cast that again in a few minutes."

Madi gagged and almost threw up. "I can't even think about doing that again. [Sunbeam] is harder to control than I thought it would be. Every extra second toward the end felt like I was being turned inside out."

"Lady Catanzano, your father is coming," Crius said, taking his eyes from the battle.

Silas was rushing about the Wall, giving orders and using his own powers to bolster his troops. It wasn't the same as Orrin's buffs, but the man was able to project confidence through his voice in a literally magical way. Orrin watched him as he approached. Silas spoke to several groups of archers and mages, the mana flowing from his mouth to circle their heads. Orrin watched the spell coalesce around their eyes. Every fighter stood straighter as he left.

"Madeleine? How is she, Brandt?" Silas floated to a stop and touched her head hesitantly. "That was too much mana. How could you let her—"

"Father, I am fine. Don't berate Brandt, he did nothing wrong." Madi shook her head, letting her braids swing free from where she'd tucked them into her shirt. "How is the defense holding up?"

Silas sat back in his chair and moved his lips to argue but stopped. He reached out again and touched Madi's cheek. "You're right. I'm sorry. You did well. Your mother would be proud, as am I."

Silas dropped his hand, pointedly ignoring the tears that slipped past Madi's eyes, and looked at Daniel and Orrin. "The Horde has reached the Wall. A few were able to scale it without equipment, but we've held off any permanent incursion so far. We're seeing a few deaths but mostly injuries. We're evacuating the hurt for healing. We estimate they will begin escalating as soon as the ladders are set. Their mages are protecting those at all costs. I thought they would take longer to move, but they've attached the ladders to carriages or wheels. They eat up the distance without the need for horses. A few men pushing from behind is all they need, and they'll be here in a few minutes."

"We can go down there and take out those things," Daniel said, smashing his fist into his palm. "Orrin can [Teleport] us in and out."

Silas looked out over the fields below. Bodies stained the dirt, and the rolling ramps were within sight. "We aren't doing as much damage as we'd hoped. It might be necessary."

Crius muttered something under his breath and nodded. He glanced up, seeing everyone looking at him as he came back fully into his own body and smiled. "Sir, I've just received some news. Dragoon team took the initiative and jumped the Wall. They're attacking the ladder transports and moving their way south to us. They've taken down seven of them."

Daniel turned and hurled a spear. It struck a demon two hundred yards away and passed clean through. "We can work from here and move up to meet them," he said as he turned back to Silas. He reached over his head and touched Gertrude's handle. "Please, sir. I can't keep taking potshots from here."

Silas studied Daniel, turning to Brandt, who nodded. Madi pushed herself back to her feet and drank one of her mana potions.

"We can do it," she assured her father. "This is what we train for."

Silas ignored them all. He caught Orrin's eyes with his own. Orrin could see the man bolster his resolve before he asked, "Will you keep them safe? Can you handle the demons?"

Orrin summoned a sword in each hand. One was made from fire and the other was blue ice. "Yes, sir. We'll stop them."

Chapter 22

"What's the plan, Orrin?" Brandt asked as Silas and Crius discussed other logistical problems concerning the Horde attack.

Orrin noticed all three members of his party were staring at him expectantly. "Why am I automatically the one who makes a plan?"

Daniel laughed and pulled Gertrude from his back. He stuck his head over the side of the Wall and examined the hard dirt ground below. "We could make that jump with my—"

"Never mind, I get it now," Orrin cut his friend off with a heavy sigh. "Let's keep it simple. Stay close to each other. Brandt and Daniel, defend the group from any demons that get too close and keep them away. I'll debuff them as much as I can. Madi, you'll be in charge of figuring out the best way to destroy the ladders. They used magic to make those convoy things, but they had to use wood initially. See if you can burn them or bury them, I don't know. If we get overrun, we group up and I'll [Teleport] us back here. Daniel, pay attention, this is for you. No heroics. We have a job, and it is not to kill demons. Do not go out of your way to attack."

Daniel clicked his tongue. "You don't have to worry. Now that I know I get to bash some heads, I'm feeling strangely calm again."

"That worries everyone even more, right?" Madi asked, unclipping her spear and extending it to its full length with a flick of her wrist. "Brandt, be ready to knock him down if you need to."

"That's hurtful." Daniel pouted. "Don't you trust me?"

Brandt and Madi both said, "No," at the same time.

"After we take one down, I'll [Teleport] us down the line to the next ladder we can find," Orrin continued, ignoring their nervous bantering. "As long as the next wave of demons doesn't advance and those giant spider things stay away, we will be in between the two groups of demons. I don't know why they split the party into two, but we'll take advantage of the middle ground. Those transports are only a little slower, though, so pay attention. Yell out before things get out of hand. *Hit-and-run* is our watchword. Try not to engage longer than we have to."

Brandt nodded and drew his sword. "Do you want to go through one of the hidden gates or [Teleport]?"

Orrin watched the flow of demons rushing the wall. The groups were still more or less intact, but the invaders had the sense to spread out more to avoid single-fire cataclysmic magic attacks. Some demons were already at the Wall, although not within fifty yards of their own position. A few mages were casting spells on the stone, while others tried to climb the Wall itself. Orrin watched one demon mage sink into the ground. Luckily, the men defending the Wall pointed to the other side and some rushed off to intercept the attacker.

"[Teleport]," Orrin decided. "We don't want to spend time fighting."

"We could spend a little time fighting," Daniel complained, but only half-heartedly.

"We could also try to take down more ladder transports than Dragoon team," Madi offered. "It would be good to brag the [Hero] did more than ten of our elites."

Daniel's eyes flared with excitement. "Orrin, what are you waiting for? There's one over there. Let's go."

Orrin gave Madi a dead stare. "We talked about using your powers of persuasion for the forces of good, not inciting Daniel's competitive streak."

Madi kept her lips tight, trying not to smile at the [Hero] bouncing like a kid going to the toy store. "Sometimes you have to work with the tools you've got."

Orrin groaned. He picked a destination, locking the spot in his mind, and ran toward the stairs. They could [Teleport] once they were off the Wall. "Here we go."

The ladder transport appeared to be the bottom half of a wagon with long wooden steering prongs on the back end. A contraption of folded ladder rungs thick as Orrin's waist sat in a pile where the main cart would normally be and a wooden shield wall reinforced with metal bands stood tall across the front of the wagon to protect everything behind. It looked like a heavy door that had been secured to the front to block any attacks before the transport reached the Wall. The steering prongs had handles at various points down the length, at which demons and humans—Orrin still could barely tell the difference between the two in some cases—pushed the entire device forward.

It wouldn't make sense to use horses to pull it, Orrin realized as they landed twenty feet away. *They have to push from behind to keep it moving forward.*

Eight men pushed the ladder transport while another six moved slowly with the convoy. Orrin's [Teleport] landed directly behind them. Only one turned at the whisper of grass being trampled, but his eyes skipped off Orrin's party. He'd cast [Camouflage Ward] the moment they arrived. The spell only worked at level one for his friends, granting them a few minutes against detection that would end once they attacked. Orrin hoped to use it each time they moved along. It wasn't perfect, but it would have to do.

Orrin used [Split Spell] and [Decrease Strength]. He targeted the first five demons bundled together behind the transport. The spell modifier let him hit multiple targets with a single spell—instead of casting [Decrease Strength] five times, he spent the onetime fee of five MP to hit five people at once. He tried for the sixth but felt [Split Spell] reach its limit. With his intelligence at a hundred, the spell modifier cost a single mana point. He cast [Decrease Strength] at level two, which cost him one MP due to his high intelligence. The spell would normally take out two points from strength, but with his increased will, each demon went down twenty points.

Four demons turned around while one slipped and fell to his knees. Orrin cast the spell again. Only one stayed standing. She looked more human than demon, with black hair and a warhammer in each hand. Orrin cast a third time and the first five demons were incapacitated.

The sixth demon held a staff and pointed it at Orrin. Before he could react, something jumped from the ground in front of the man's outstretched staff and rocketed at Orrin's chest. Orrin looked dumbly at the pointed stone projectile at his feet. It had dented his leather armor. His [Ward] and [Mana Shield] saved him from taking much damage, but it still felt like a punch to the chest. Without his spells, the man's attack would have pierced his heart.

Gertrude came down on the staff, snapping it in two. Brandt's sword erupted from the man's chest a moment later.

Orrin shook himself from his stupor and cast [Split Spell] and [Decrease Strength] again on the eight demons pushing the convoy. Only some had reacted to the quick fight. Three stumbled immediately on his first casting, hands slipping on their posts. Two grunted and continued to push but went down with the second. Daniel and Brandt moved in, finishing the other three before Orrin could cast again.

The ladder slowed its forward momentum and Madi stuck her head out from underneath the wagon. "Orrin, can I borrow your [Fire Sword]? I think I can cut the axles down here."

Orrin tossed her the sword he had already summoned and made another appear in his hand. He began chopping at the rope supports on the folded ladder, making the entire apparatus tilt.

"Wait until I get out from under here, please," Madi cried from underneath. A moment later she popped out, dragging her body with an army crawl. "I'm in charge of destroying these, right? Don't do that again. I thought I was going to be crushed."

Orrin winced at the sound of swords rising and falling behind him. This was a war for survival, but the fight felt more like a slaughter when he used his debuffs. "Sorry, Madi, I'll wait next time. Want to set it on fire?"

Madi moved her hand in the air and a shimmer of light changed colors as she found the right frequency. Red light flooded through her fingers, pouring liquid fire all over the ladder.

Brandt walked up, wiping his sword clean on a piece of torn cloth. "Reinforcements are coming."

Orrin followed his gaze and saw a small platoon of about fifty heading their way. "Daniel, on me. We're leaving."

They were gone well before the demons arrived at the smoldering ruin of their ladder and comrades.

The second attack went smoother, with Daniel and Brandt timing their attacks to maximize confusion while Orrin dropped the demons. He waited for Madi to set it on fire before moving to the third. Each wagon took them two to three minutes to secure and destroy. Within an hour, they reached their goal. Hundreds of yards away, Orrin could see fighting. When they teleported close, Dragoon team was in battle with the last ladder transport.

Orrin noticed Sof, the leader of Dragoon, first. Sof's hand rested gently on the wooden frame of the ladder, the rungs growing and breaking from its design. The entire wagon lifted into the air and then collapsed on two demons fighting Bin, the giant man who fought with his fists. Bin pivoted from the abrupt end of his fight and turned to help Farah, the black-clad Goth girl swirling around with her scythe. Five demons were attacking Gracie, the giant of a woman who fought with a wooden club as big as Daniel. Their archer was sending arrows at the approaching reinforcements. Orrin couldn't remember his name and cheated with an [Identify]. *Clifford.*

Sof turned and held up a hand to attack but noticed Orrin waving. Brandt and Daniel ran in to confront the last of the demons. Orrin made the remaining demons fall before they made it close enough to help.

"Lady Catanzano and Daniel the [Hero]," Sof said with a nod as the groups converged.

Farah was breathing heavily and covered in sweat. *Wearing all that black in the direct sun is probably not helping,* Orrin thought. He considered trying to use [Gust] with [Ice Sword] to create a cooling breeze but decided against it. *Probably isn't the best idea to try new combos in the middle of a battle.*

"Orrin, well met." Sof reached out his hand to shake. His palms were surprisingly soft. "We were pleased to hear you've grown so much. Your spell orbs are being used to save many lives today."

Bin and Gracie stood quiet sentinels to either side of Sof. Clifford was shooting arrows into the distance still. "Three minutes, tops. We need to go, boss." Clifford's voice was hyperactive, like he couldn't get the words out fast enough. "There are too many of them for us to fight. We should move to the next climbing device. Oh, hey there. I remember you two. Is that Madeleine Catanzano? What is she doing off the Wall?"

"We appreciate the help," Sof said, holding his hand up to halt Clifford's tirade. "We have a mission and must continue. Do you need help getting back to the Wall?"

"We could ask you the same," Daniel replied with a smile. "We took out every ladder wagon south of here. Twenty-four of them. I'd guess about two hundred demons, right, guys?"

"Bullshit." Farah stepped forward. She grimaced and Orrin realized her heavy breathing was from an injury. "We've spent the last hour and a half taking out sixteen of these things. Even the ones that were lightly guarded took more time than you would have had to—"

She faltered and stumbled. Gracie caught her.

Orrin used [Identify] and found the problem. He cast [Heal Small Wounds], focusing on her right ribs. She had several fractures and a punctured lung. That she was still standing was a testament to her high level and incredible resolve.

Sof raised a wand at Orrin. "What are you casting?"

"I'm healing little miss dressed in black over here before she stops breathing altogether. Her ribs are broken and one is in her lung. I need to cast one or two more times," Orrin explained, trying to move around Sof.

"I vouch for his healing qualifications." Madi stepped forward. "We did take out everything south of here. There might be more beyond where we began, but my father sent us from there. He'll have contingencies for the rest of the Wall. We should return."

Sof's hard eyes softened for a moment and he shook his head. "I apologize. I remember now that you healed Ira as well. Farah, stay still, or so help me, I will build a cage around you and drag you home."

Orrin wisely kept his smile off his face as he worked. Farah's breathing smoothed out, and when she wiped her forehead clear of sweat, it didn't return this time.

"That should do it. Where's the rest of your team? Do you want a [Teleport] back to the Wall?"

Sof fussed over Farah for a moment before he responded. "Thank you, but no. We have secondary mission parameters we can focus on now that the ladders are taken down. Maya has our other half working on something. We can join them now. Good luck in your fight. We owe you a drink when this is over."

Brandt saluted and Bin returned the gesture before they ran back north, cutting toward the demons that were now fighting and trying to scale the Wall. Daniel kicked the burned wood at their feet.

"Is that it? Back to the Wall to wait?"

Madi studied the demons waiting in the distance. The group that Clifford had been holding back was advancing now, but thousands more demons were sitting just outside their camp watching the battle.

"Yes, Daniel. Back to the Wall."

Chapter 23

The Wall was cratered from attacks and magic, but the defenders gave back to the Dark Horde with a vengeance. Bodies littered the ground along with thrown weapons from above. The flattened earth around the Wall was scuffed from various magic spells, with fires burning in divots, icy patches the demons had to avoid, and quick-drop traps in the earth that swallowed the attackers without warning. Orrin landed behind the Wall and they swiftly climbed back to the top. Reaching the last step, Orrin saw other bits of magic that targeted individual demons as well.

The demons were suffering the majority of casualties everywhere Orrin could see. None of the men or women around them were injured, but more were peeling off from the attacks to sit down and rest. Those who weren't trained in fighting were helping others, tipping potions into the mouths of those who had passed out from mana exhaustion.

"They aren't trying to get through the Wall," Daniel realized, shading his eyes with his hand to peer into the distance. "These are the weaker fodder they're sending to wear us out."

Brandt rested his hands on the edge of the battlements, searching for areas that might need help. "What makes you think that?"

Daniel waved a hand at the fifty or so mages from Dey splayed out and breathing heavily. "It's been barely two hours and most of our magic users have spent all their mana. The demons keep attacking the Wall and retreating, but they've spread themselves thin against the entire length instead of targeting one area. If they wanted to punch through, it wouldn't be hard, even with the demons we fought, based on their numbers alone. Our fights out there were easier because Orrin was reducing their strength and buffed us up so we had higher stats than anyone else. This entire attack is a feint."

Madi nodded in the grim silence that followed Daniel's speech. She was nearly out of mana herself and unable to take another mana potion until she'd slept. "There's nothing we can do about it, though. We can't let them get through at any point or they can circle around and pincer us. We need to be more conservative with our defenses."

Orrin wished he could create enough regen potions for their allies, but the main ingredient was rare enough that he'd only been able to make enough to supply Madi and himself for a few days. It took time for the penidrop mushrooms to spore and regrow. The [Alchemist] that Orrin visited tried to take his mothershroom away from him when he realized that Orrin had never fed it. It needed straw and grain added around the base once a month to keep it healthy. Orrin also needed to feed the mothershroom by burying some raw strips of meat under the straw once the penidrops were fully harvested. The mothershroom would then refruit with the small bell-shaped mushrooms. Orrin was sure that he'd watched a video on growing mushrooms on Earth that conflicted with everything the [Alchemist] told him, but it was a magical plant in a magical world, so he'd shrugged and paid the man.

His plant was slowly adding more of the caps and Orrin bought all that he'd been able to find, but he had about thirty regen potions total. Not enough to supply an army. *Maybe Maeve could grow more or help me source them,* Orrin thought, kicking himself for not thinking of her earlier.

Before he could bring up his idea, Brandt waved down a young squire running down the stone path. "Where is Lord Catanzano?"

"North of here by ten minutes. Wendigo and Hornet are pushing for a direct attack on the camp," the young man yelled as he continued running. "I've got orders to deliver. Good luck."

"Wendigo and Hornet?" Daniel raised an eyebrow.

"Two of the strongest teams in Dey," Madi explained. "Wendigo is full of powerful melee and shield specialists. Hornet is a hit-and-run team with a few members who can fly. They don't usually work together."

"They can fly?" Daniel asked excitedly. "I haven't found a flight spell yet."

Orrin prayed Daniel never would find [Fly] or anything that let him be more mobile. They had a hard enough time keeping him under control without the power to soar off into the sky.

Brandt rested his hand on Orrin's shoulder. "How are you for mana? Can you [Teleport] us a mile north? We should report to him as soon as possible."

Orrin's mana was half-empty, but that left him with hundreds of points more than anyone on the Wall. He looked around in confusion. "I'm good to do it, but where is Crius? Isn't he supposed to stick around so we can avoid this kind of problem?"

Brandt shrugged. "It's a war, Orrin. He could have been called away for another mission, or maybe he is dead. You do what you can and adjust. Everybody ready?"

Daniel and Madi nodded. Orrin decided to forget about Crius for the time being and sighed as they made their way back down the stairs. A quick [Teleport] brought them north. Silas was easy to find with a few questions, and soon Madi and Brandt were giving their report.

"That is good news. Having their ability to breach the Wall is a stroke of luck right now." Silas turned and spoke to a lanky woman standing nearby. "Gloria, see to it that Wendigo and Hornet are given the all clear. They can proceed when they see an opportunity."

"Father, what's the plan?" Madi asked, fingers touching her shortened spear in anticipation. "Do you think the demons will continue the attack once the sun sets?"

Silas watched his messenger leave before he eyed his daughter. He turned away to Brandt. "Your orders are to rest for now. Have Orrin create more spell orbs, especially for mage use. Daniel and my daughter should try to sleep and reset their mana pools if possible. You four will be on the night shift watching for attacks. I'll send someone to get you if the situation changes."

Orrin felt Daniel bristle at being sidelined. "Sir, Daniel doesn't use enough mana to be worn out. Our stats are currently maxed out and we can go for a while longer. We should help now."

Silas grimaced. "I can't order Daniel to rest, but Madeleine needs to sleep. A spellcaster is weakest at the end of a long day when they have no mana left. We are beginning shifts for all mages and that should include you as well, Orrin."

"With all due respect, I'm not like other mages," Orrin answered before Silas could say anything else. "I can waste time making more spell orbs when we get back, but I'd like to know what those two teams are planning. At least let us help push the demons away from the Wall."

Silas rubbed his fingers over his eyes and sighed. "You two have never been easy to work with. Brandt and Madeleine, please go rest. Your night watch begins in eight hours. That should be enough time to reset your stamina and mana."

Madi shook her head. "No. I want to know what this plan is. I can take another mana potion if I need to. I've only taken one today."

Silas glared at his daughter as he addressed the [Knight] standing beside her. "Brandt, please escort my daughter to her tent."

Brandt glanced at Madi before he saluted his boss. "While I work for you, sir, I'm part of this team. I'll stand by Madi's decision."

Silas barked a laugh and tilted his head to the sky. "Just like her mother, turning people's loyalty to her alone. Have it your way, then. Hornet has agreed to drop Wendigo behind enemy lines. They are going to attack their transports and any demons they can."

"Their transports? You mean those spider monsters?" Daniel asked, risking a glance over his shoulder at the Horde's main army. "How do you even kill those? Wait . . . How are they getting back?"

"They won't come back," Brandt said softly. "They volunteered for a suicide run, didn't they, sir?"

Orrin felt [Mind Bastion] tickling his senses. It would be easy to see the logic in sacrificing some of their own major players to hinder the enemy. It made sense: Dey had multiple high-ranking parties. One team of fighters in exchange for the towering monsters behind the Horde should be an acceptable trade.

"No," Orrin growled in a deep voice that rattled even himself. "Bring them here. I can buff them up. They'll still suffer some backlash tomorrow, but at least they'll survive. I can even go with them and drop some demons. If the mission is to bring down their transport monsters, I can help with that."

Silas was already shaking his head. "They've been on standby. Gloria has already left to give them the go signal. I can't recall them now."

Orrin turned and looked at the demon Horde. "Daniel, are you with me?"

Daniel stepped up and slapped his back. He reached back and grabbed his sword. "Of course. Let's go— Ow!"

Madi reached up and pulled both their ears gently. "I thought we were done being dumb and rushing in?"

Daniel looked at Madi sheepishly, but Orrin glared at her. "We aren't rushing in. I have a plan. Just like I told your dad. I'm going to [Teleport] us over there and—"

"And get Daniel killed," Madi interrupted. "He'll be in the middle of a bunch of fighting demons and it'll be only you pulling him back. I can fight some demons on the Wall, but I can't do another extended fight, Orrin. Even if you bring Brandt and leave me behind, it's too dangerous for the three of you. Wendigo is a team that has worked together for years. They have teamwork ingrained. They don't know you or Daniel. Maybe one of them recognizes Brandt, but that will just confuse them in the middle of their mission."

"So, I go alone and bring something to prove I'm sent by Silas," Orrin countered, looking at Silas for help. "I can [Teleport] them out at least."

"Wendigo sent all ten members," Silas said sadly. "The main party and all five reserve members. They know what they signed up for. Hornet team is ready to suffer losses as well."

"I can make multiple trips," Orrin pleaded. "At least help me try."

Daniel's hand dropped from Gertrude's handle. "Orrin, we can't save everybody. We can do some good along the Wall at least."

Orrin clenched his fists and looked at the distant camp. He didn't have Daniel's vision power, so he couldn't see the flying forms of the Hornet team carrying in Wendigo. He knew they were there but couldn't even see them. "Silas, is there no way for me to help them?"

The lord of Dey spoke softly. "I appreciate your concern, Orrin. We did give them some of your higher-powered spell orbs to use. It's not hopeless and they volunteered the plan. As bad as those ladder transports are, those monsters could step entire regiments of demons directly over the Wall. It's critical they are taken down. You are of better use to me if you are rested and waiting for tonight, but if you insist, I'd ask you to reinforce the Wall in this area. It's why I'm here. The reports are the best climbers are in this area. We've had a few demons get over the top."

Orrin ignored the tears filling his eyes at the thought of people he'd never met rushing to their end. Brandt's words echoed in his mind. *You do what you can and adjust.*

I could [Teleport] that distance by myself, but Daniel would try to follow. Even if I got there, they wouldn't trust me. I can't take on the entire Horde by myself.

His palms stung in pain. Orrin blinked in surprise and opened his hands. He had squeezed his fists so hard that his nails made crescent cuts into his skin. He watched a single bead of blood pool and follow the creases that crisscrossed his palm.

I could use [Blood Mana]. Orrin realized he'd been forgetting about his greatest weapon. *I could drop every demon down the Wall. I could push into the camp, maybe retreat if it got too bad. Or I could be brave like the Wendigo team and push until every demon was on the ground.*

"Orrin, what are you thinking?" Madi stepped in front of him. "You can't go and leave Daniel. He needs you here. We all do."

Orrin ignored her as his thoughts started running away with the idea. *I can make it back to Tony and he can help me detox. I healed all those people in Dey after the Fogbinder attack. I've been training my resistance and know my rough limits. Even if I overdo it a bit . . . it'll be worth it, right?*

Chapter 24

One of the first powers that Orrin had received when he landed in this world was [Mind Bastion].

> **[Mind Bastion]—Individual is able to control his own mind and therefore part of his body.**

The ability allowed Orrin to use logic in stressful situations, ignore pain to an extent in order to continue fighting, and other things that he was still discovering. One side effect of using [Mind Bastion] was the normal limits on a person's mana use took a back seat as long as he kept the skill running. It allowed Orrin to draw his entire mana pool over and over without immediate repercussions.

Once he bought [Blood Mana] from the store on his interface, [Mind Bastion] became more powerful. The ominous-sounding ability [Blood Mana] was usually tied to outlawed classes. In fact, Madi had threatened him with death after their first encounter and learning of his skill. Usually, a [Blood Mage] would use the power to drain another person's health, sapping and swapping the health into mana to fuel their dark spells. Orrin used it to exchange his own health for mana on a one-to-one ratio. He also used [Heal Small Wounds] with his reduced costs due to [Increase Will] to cheat the system.

Whenever Orrin ran low on mana, he could use [Blood Mana] to give himself more fuel for spells. If he gave himself a hundred-point exchange, he could use [Heal Small Wounds] at level one to recover the hundred spent points of health. With his will increased to a hundred, the spell cost only a single mana point and would heal Orrin back to normal. It was a loophole he'd discovered that only grew larger the higher his level became.

Right now, I have three hundred points of health due to my thirty points of constitution. Orrin started running numbers. *If I use [Increase Constitution] right now with my will and intelligence already buffed to a hundred, my con would go up by ten for every point I invested for the day. I have eleven hundred mana points to work with, so dropping myself by seven MP in order to max my constitution out won't matter. Having that much con, my health will be at a thousand points. I can exchange my health and mana enough to cast spells forever.*

Orrin felt a chill as he finally realized how broken his class was becoming. "Madi, I can drop every demon out there if my math is right."

Daniel pinched his nose and shook his head. "You're giving me a headache. Are you going to stay here and help? Or are you going to ignore everyone and do your own thing again?"

Orrin ignored Daniel and turned to Silas. "How long until the two teams make their move?"

Silas remained silent for a moment, weighing the pros and cons of answering Orrin. He'd dealt with the man enough to understand that simply refusing to answer might be the best option to keep him in line.

"Lord Catanzano, I have a plan. I won't act without everyone's acceptance of it, but I need to know how much time I have."

Instead of answering Orrin, Silas turned to Madi. "Whatever he does, you will stay behind. You've done more than enough today. Agreed?"

Silas was talking to Madi, but Orrin knew the man was asking for Orrin's promise to leave her behind. Madi understood it as well.

"You would ask me to leave my party? I can fight without my magic. I'm not some helpless child."

Brandt placed his hands on Madi's arms and gently turned her until she faced him. "He's asking you to stay safe. I think Orrin is about to do that thing he does."

"What thing do I do?" Orrin demanded, crossing his arms.

"You make a plan, everything goes to shit, and you pull a win out of your butt using luck and a new power you discover along the way," Daniel stage-whispered. "Just tell us what you want to do, O."

Orrin felt attacked but told them his idea. "I'm going to use [Gust] to rush the length of the Wall and drop every demon on their back."

"You want to take down over four thousand demons, not even counting the beasts and monsters they control?" Silas asked incredulously. "I know you can do a lot, but that sounds like a death wish."

Daniel was shaking his head, too. "Orrin, you struggled to take down some of the demons we encountered with our ladder mission. Some people resist your debuffs. We got lucky that none of the demons we fought were too high in level, but there are at least three demons over level seventy out there."

"There are only two left." Silas spoke over Daniel. "We managed to kill one of their strongest. The other two are still attacking in a senseless pattern."

"That's what I mean." Orrin clenched his fist in frustration. "They don't care about taking the Wall. We have to do something drastic. I'm not going out there to die, Silas. I'll be under my [Camouflage] the entire time. Yes, Daniel. Some of the demons can still fight and move even if I hit them with five high-level [Decrease Strength] attacks. I'm pretty sure it has to do with their constitution versus mine, but if I have a hundred points in con, I think that will change."

"Why didn't you try boosting your constitution up already?" Madi pulled herself out of Brandt's grasp. He looked hurt but gave her the space she craved. "You already brought mine up and it worked fine."

Orrin knew his friends would argue against the next part of his plan. "I don't know what the consequences of fully buffing my con up will be, but there has to be a trade-off. Just like with my other buffs, you and Brandt suffered backlash from getting too powerful. I think constitution is going to do something like that, and I didn't want to push up against that wall until I knew more. But we are out of time for that. I'm going to blood cycle and use every trick I have to bring down the demons. If the main camp sees their attack fail this bad, they might pull back. If they retreat, I'll run in with them and try to find Wendigo team. I won't be able to [Teleport] them all out, but I can buff them."

Daniel had gone very still.

"I know you won't like this plan, D," Orrin started, but his friend shook his head.

"No. You almost die every time you do that."

"Not every time. I've got a little tracker now and everything. I can cycle a few times and be fine."

Daniel glowered at Orrin. "You told me that tracks how many times you can use your mana pool, including mana potions. Does that take into account a doubled amount of magic power? What about the trade-off for giving yourself what, two or three times as much health? I didn't go to a magic school and learn a bunch of magical theory, Orrin, but even I know you don't get something for nothing. Are you planning on stumbling back here and passing out at Tony's place for a week?"

Orrin planned on doing exactly that but hoped it would be more like a day or two at most. He was relatively certain he could handle a full reset of his larger mana pool at least twice. "My spells cost a point or two to cast, Daniel. I can target five demons at a time. That's ten points of mana to stop five invaders. If I pop a regen potion, I can get sixty points back every minute. That's thirty demons a minute I can stop. Almost two thousand in an hour. I might not even need to use blood cycling if they run before I reach the end of the Wall."

"And what happens when a demon sees through your camo spell and attacks you? You won't be hauled off to school again. You'll be killed or taken into their camp. I can't attack that many people. I know that even through this itch to kill all the demons. I'm not dumb enough to think I can rescue you from that."

Orrin smirked. "Then I won't get caught. I can be hard to catch when I'm not worrying about your slow ass."

Silas's wheelchair floated forward, moving between the two boys. "Orrin, you are asking to fight demons along the Wall, which I won't object to. However, you won't be able to make enough progress to turn the day with your plan. Wendigo should be on the way to their target now. Within twenty minutes, they'll be in battle."

Orrin's grin fell from his face. He could make it behind the demon camp on his own, but without the distraction of half their army returning, the more powerful demons would be able to focus their attention fully on him and the elite team.

Silas cleared his throat to pull Orrin's attention back to him. "How much damage can you do in twenty minutes without endangering yourself? I don't want you to do this thing that Daniel says is too dangerous.

I'm asking only for a number of how many demons you can slow down or drop before Wendigo starts their attack."

Orrin shrugged. "If I jumped off the Wall and started hitting the groups of demons here and moved south along the Wall . . . using a regen potion but no blood cycling . . ." He trailed off as he redid the math in his head. "I can take down five or six hundred."

Brandt whistled low.

"Sir Bennett—" Silas turned to Brandt, his voice taking on a more formal tone. "Please alert all squad leaders to reserve ten percent of their forces for night duty. Every member of the militia that can attack is to be ready in five minutes for an assault. Open the gates and let the melee fighters out, but give clear direction they should return at three horn blasts. We are going to support Orrin while he creates a distraction."

"It won't be enough," Orrin argued. Brandt was already moving away. "If I can't make the army run away, their leadership won't care enough for it to be a distraction."

"Those of us in charge agree with your assessment, Orrin. This raid isn't anything more than a probe to find our weakest areas. Your plan likely won't help Wendigo return, but if we make a push on their army, it might give them the time to succeed in their mission," Silas said. "Daniel, I won't tell you not to go with Orrin but if you do, will you slow him down?"

Daniel scowled. Orrin's [Gust] spell let him move in bursts of speed that Daniel could only keep up with if he used his own speed increase spell, [Shooting Star]. He could keep up with Orrin and even outpace him in a straight race, but only for two minutes at a time. He could cast the spell over and over but didn't have Orrin's ability to regenerate mana using [Meditate].

"If Orrin lends me a regen potion, I can keep up. I didn't use much mana in our earlier fights."

"Then good luck to the two of you. Sir Bennett and my daughter can move with the melee attack, but you two should get started now," Silas said, rolling his neck. "Madeleine, stop staring at me like you want to kill me. There is no time to argue. Go and don't waste any more time."

Orrin nodded at Daniel, tossing him a potion from his belt. The [Hero] snapped his arm out and summoned Gertrude into his open hand. Orrin used [Camouflage Ward] on his party. He teleported Daniel and himself to the other side of the Wall.

Landing on the dirt in a superhero crouch, Orrin studied the demons around them for two long seconds. Some wore robes and held staffs or wands, using spells to attack the Wall. Others lobbed magic at the defenders above or grew shields of stone to intercept the returned attacks. A few in armor and more traditional weapons tried to scale the Wall, using various ways in their attempts. One man with dark-red skin and a tail but no horns stabbed his daggers into the stone as he climbed freestyle up the side of the Wall. He made it halfway before an icy growth raced down the Wall from above, exploding into a crystalline spike right above the demon's head. He fell twenty feet but landed in a rolling tumble. Others tried to throw teammates up and over or used grappling hooks that were quickly removed or cut.

Orrin picked his first five targets and cast his spells as Daniel stood at his side, ready to defend his friend.

Chapter 25

Three of the five demons slumped to the ground, their legs unable to hold their bodies up. He'd targeted mage-like demons first, hoping to reduce the more widespread damage they would be able to muster. One stumbled but used their staff to stay upright. Lightning jumped from an outreached hand, but Orrin's shields blocked the magic. The fifth ran toward a group of twentyish more demons and humans trying to burrow a hole in the Wall.

Daniel blurred and attacked the lightning mage while Orrin highlighted another four with his [Split Spell] modifier and a strength debuff, adding the running demon as the fifth target. The man was human to all appearances and fell face forward at a dead sprint. Orrin cast [Gust] to move closer, hitting half of the entire group with his strength-sapping spells before Daniel joined the fray.

Orrin used [Identify] quickly to confirm their levels as the demons and humans died. All were between level forty and fifty. "It shouldn't be this easy. Killing them like this feels wrong somehow."

Daniel brought his massive sword down on the last crawling body. His hands were slick with blood as he stabbed Gertrude into the ground and used one of the demons' shirts to wipe his face clean. "What are you talking about? Should we fight them with our nonbuffed stats? Maybe I should only use magic against mages. If one of them drops their weapon, should I let them borrow Gerty?"

Orrin summoned a [Fire Sword] and stabbed a supine human in the chest. He twisted the sword like Brandt had taught him, ending the man's life. "I didn't say I won't do it, Daniel. I said it feels wrong."

"Of course killing feels wrong, Orrin. Is this the first time you've killed without [Mind Bastion] running? Usually you are more cold about it. It doesn't matter, though. We need to move. Try and keep up." Daniel activated [Shooting Star] and dashed out of sight.

Orrin considered his friend's words as he drank his regen potion for the day. He felt his mana bar start to fill back up as he chased after Daniel. Orrin had kept [Mind Bastion] running for much of the first months in Asmea. Only recently had he tried to use it sparingly, mostly to avoid the temptation to use blood cycling. Daniel had gone through an adjustment period after his first kill of another person, but other than some dreams that he barely remembered, Orrin's reluctance to kill was based on the scope of his powers. It was easier to knock someone out with his magic, leaving them to the authorities to deal with. It could be a holdover from his upbringing on Earth, but putting someone down permanently as an option wasn't something he considered until every other path was off the table.

"They are coming to kill everyone in Dey," Orrin reasoned with himself as he ran, casting spells and dropping demons left and right. Hidden doors were opening, letting the defenders out on the field of battle. Orrin stopped worrying about finishing each person and focused on taking down as many as possible. "The demons knew what they were marching toward. This is the natural consequence of starting a war."

Ten minutes passed in a blur. Orrin had to target each person with [Split Spell] and [Decrease Dexterity] or [Decrease Strength] depending on what he saw with [Identify]. Despite the cacophony of battle cries and screams of pain around him, Orrin focused on his task. The more demons he brought down, the greater chance they could grab the attention of the rest of the Horde. He needed to be the distraction that kept Wendigo alive long enough to complete their mission and hopefully make it back in one piece.

As they moved south along the Wall, Daniel ranged farther away from him time and time again. The [Hero] swooped into pitched battles between the stronger demons and the waning members of Asmea's meager resistance, using his sword to strike down the aggressors. Occasionally, a demon would hold him off for a few strikes. They had stopped almost four hundred demons by Orrin's informal count. He would slow them down and Daniel would end the fight with a [Gravity Strike]. More often than not, they left the cleanup to the troops fighting beside them.

Daniel also used spells that Orrin hadn't seen. Small rocks fell from the sky, mostly missing their targets but kicking up dust. The momentary distractions were enough for Daniel to slip between enemy attacks and land cuts and strikes of his own.

When they reached a level-seventy demon with thirty mages and fighters at his side, Daniel used [Gravity Well]. The ability was an upgraded version of his initial skill [Pull Attention]. It was a provoking ability that made targets focus on him at first, but the newer version allowed Daniel to physically pull his enemies closer to his swinging blade as well. That, in and of itself, wasn't new to Orrin. He'd seen his friend use it multiple times.

When only half the demons and humans tripped forward toward Daniel, he used [Shooting Star] to burst through them like a wrecking ball. He did some damage, but more than anything, most of the demons who fell for his [Gravity Well] were stunned at the sudden change of their position on the battlefield. Orrin moved to push the advantage, hitting as many of the demons with his debuffs as possible before they regained their senses.

A lull in the fight saw Daniel come to a halt before the highest-level demon they'd encountered on the field.

"I am Sir Ekakas Hiey of the Valley of Burned Whispers," the demon announced, spreading his arms wide as Daniel waited in a low crouch with his sword held over his head. "You are the [Hero]. I could feel your taint drifting closer for some time. I will be the one to end you."

Sir Ekakas Hiey held a hammer in each hand. In his left hand, the metal head was spiked on one end but looked no different than a hammer that Orrin would use at home to pound in a nail. The hammer in his right hand was larger, about as thick as a football. It had flat, heavy heads but spikes along the top and sides. The demon had tall, curved bull's horns sticking from his head. Most of his human troops wore metal helmets topped with the same design, imitating their leader's horns. These were all fighters in heavy armor. Ekakas wore armor better maintained than his men but covered in nicks and small dents that proved it wasn't ornamental in nature.

"Ekakas? Your name sounds like something I leave in the toilet. Are you in charge of this little skirmish?" Daniel asked nonchalantly, acting as if he wasn't slowly being surrounded by his enemy. "If I beat you, does that mean your men will run back home? I'm getting bored of all this running about. Today was supposed to be arms and chest day, not cardio."

Orrin continued to drop demons and humans around them as Daniel bluffed. Of the roughly thirty troops around the hammer-wielding demon, Orrin had twenty down. As he targeted the next five, he felt a wave of magic roll off Ekakas.

The demon raised his hammers above his head and slammed them together, creating a visible wave in the air that spread out from him. A few of the already-dropped demons stood up groggily while the ones that Orrin had yet to target roared as they threw back their heads. The humans remained face-first in the churned mud.

Orrin tried to catch a glimpse of the mana patterns from the skill or spell, but it went too quickly for him to see. He used [Identify] on the demons standing up and frowned.

Their stats went up but only to half what I drained. He checked a few different targets before it clicked.

"Daniel, he's buffing their strength, dex, and constitution. All the demons around him are up by about fifty percent," Orrin yelled out, targeting the humans. He cursed when only half of them fell to their knees. *They must be demons even though they look like humans.* Another [Identify] confirmed his theory.

Orrin clicked [Mind Bastion] on for a few seconds as Daniel and Ekakas exchanged barbs. *He didn't cast a buff like mine. It has to be something different.* Orrin tried to use [Identify] on Ekakas. The demon stopped midsentence and snapped his head at Orrin.

"You dare?"

"No, I'm a coward. I always pick truth," Orrin responded. *[Identify] was blocked, damn.* He dropped out of [Mind Bastion] before it convinced him to do something stupid. To Daniel, Orrin yelled, "We don't have time to fight this loser. Get close and let's go."

"You keep going," Daniel replied, a smile on his face. "I'll keep them busy."

Orrin considered knocking his friend's strength down to one and teleporting them both out. "Daniel, don't be stupid. We need to get more demons. This guy isn't worth it right now."

"Yes, [Hero]." Ekakas salivated over his words. "Run away and show my people how worthless you are. Prove that our lord's words ring true. You hide behind your mountain range and walls, hoping that we ignore your pathetic attempts to grow stronger. You could train for a hundred years and not come close to being my equal. You cannot hope to best me, so you should retreat. I'll kill you quickly. You won't even see me coming."

Daniel's hands squeezed and turned around his sword's bone handle. "I'm going to cut you down. Then I'm going to find your Demon Lord and make him eat his words."

Ekakas laughed. "Lord Niko will never meet you. You'll be dead long before he moves on this edifice to arrogance. I'll nail your body to this wall using your friend's spine."

Daniel disappeared in a plume of dust. A bell-like twang echoed loudly over the field, with a few closer members of Ekakas's guards holding their ears in pain.

Ekakas held his two hammers crossed in front of him. He'd blocked Daniel's simple overhead strike with his smaller weapons. His arms quivered for a heartbeat and a bloodthirsty smile crossed the demon's lips.

"You are strong, I'll admit," Ekakas said before taking a single step and pushing Daniel back, his feet digging into the dirt. "But for all your strength, you use it so poorly."

Ekakas attacked Daniel.

Daniel threw himself back at the demon.

Orrin groaned as he summoned his [Ice Sword]. "Why does my best friend have to be such a moron?"

Orrin went to work using his debuffs on Ekakas, who barely seemed to slow. He targeted the remaining demons with more [Decrease Strength] and [Decrease Dexterity] spells, but with Ekakas's spell, they stayed upright if a little slower than Orrin.

"Guess we do this the hard way," Orrin muttered, watching Daniel throw Gertrude at Ekakas. The giant sword was a flash of metal in the dimming sunlight. The demon knocked it off course, but that much weight couldn't be moved so easily. Gertrude left a long gouge in the metal armor of Ekakas's upper arm.

The demon advanced, swinging his hammers. He jumped back in surprise when the large sword flew back to Daniel's hand. Orrin heard a satisfying smack as the handle hit Daniel's palm.

Orrin wove his way through the demons, attacking with superheated [Gust] attacks or flash-freezing demons with his [Ice Sword] attacks. He'd learned how to combine his sword spells with the mana from [Gust] to create various effects depending on how much MP he used. [Sword Proficiency] didn't make him an expert with the swords. In fact, Orrin felt himself moving in ways that hindered his movement after the attacks. Only the quick movements of his fighting skill, [Way of the Water], saved him from ending up impaled on a spear.

He left a sword stuck in a demon's thigh, exploding it to superheat the metal around the man's body. He screamed as he tore at the armor on his leg. Orrin took his head with the [Ice Sword].

Orrin leaped in the air, turning his body to avoid a battle-ax from his right and a spiked maul from the left. He let both his newly summoned swords drop from his hands, tucking his arms close to avoid being sliced and crushed. Landing into a roll, he came up on one knee and recast the spells. Blue ice and orange flames spiraled up from his hands.

"Did you see that?" Orrin asked nobody in particular as he took deep breaths. The remaining demons had left the [Hero] to Ekakas and circled around him. "Be honest. I looked badass, didn't I?"

Chapter 26

Eight demons remained in Ekakas's retinue. Orrin wasn't particularly worried, despite their relatively high levels, ranging from midfifties to high sixties. His debuffs slowed them down a bit but didn't drop them like their unmoving compatriots. Orrin's stats gave him the edge in keeping away. He didn't need to bring them down; he just needed to distract them long enough for Daniel to join the fight.

One armored demon with the copycat horned helmet swung his weapon in circles. The thin blades on either side gave the appearance of swords mixed with spears. Orrin dubbed him Darth in his mind. The red eyes behind the helm's sockets played nicely into his nickname.

Two carried maces of vastly different sizes. One had a spiky, bowling ball–size tip at the end of a metal pole. The other demon held a shorter mace with both hands. The top half was covered in metal with flanges down the four sides. *Getting crushed by that big mace would not be fun.* Orrin shivered at the blood dripping from the spikes. Someone had already met their end to that demon today. *I'll make sure to repay the debt.* He mentally named them Biggs and Smalls.

Two demons held their spears pointed at Orrin. One had the crossguard ending that would keep Orrin at a distance if it stabbed him, while the second demon was moving his traditional spear in patterns in the air. He seemed eager to attack and pressed a few testing strikes at Orrin. Orrin decided the first one would be Spike. The overeager demon would be Stabby.

The last two wore matching armor and weapons. The front of their breastplates held an engraving of a tree. One of them, Orrin wasn't sure which, was the one who had swung at him a moment before using a battle-ax. They each carried their huge double-sided tree cutter in both hands, ready to advance. *Tweedledee and Tweedledumb,* Orrin tagged them, knowing he'd never be able to keep them straight.

The final demon was smaller than the others by a foot. He swung his spiked maul at Orrin, not waiting for his teammates to help. When Orrin landed after his acrobatic display, Shorty pressed the attack.

"Listen, if you don't like how cool I am, maybe you should run back to your camp," Orrin said, ducking under swings and letting [Way of the Water] guide his steps. More often than not, he was getting the hang of using the fighting style without activating it. His training with Styx had begun to pay off. Orrin felt [Side Steps] trigger as a spear missed his ribs by inches. "Stabby, you better wait your turn. I'll dance with you in a minute."

Orrin parried a hit from Shorty's maul with his [Ice Sword]. The moment the weapons connected, Orrin cast [Gust] and let the ice in his hand explode outward. Frost covered the demon's entire right arm and shoulder. Orrin chopped with his second sword, shattering the ice and removing the arm in the process.

With one of their own badly hurt, the demons attacked. Orrin barely noticed the other defenders moving in to help. The two spearmen turned to keep them at bay. Orrin spent every moment trying hard to avoid the strikes and slashes of the weapons around him.

Daniel was using every tool he had against Ekakas. His large sword, Gertrude, was the perfect weapon for Daniel's way of fighting. He used his strength to strike with the full weight of the metal blade, making it nearly impossible to block and harder to avoid. Except the demon kept doing just that. His crossed hammers created a shield that Daniel could not break through. The armored enemy was quick enough to avoid Daniel's attacks and learned how to counter each new threat quicker than Daniel would have liked.

He used [Meteor Shower] to kick up dust around them, trusting his other senses like he'd been taught. He activated [Momentum], a new skill that allowed him to attack in a flurry of blows. Each strike increased in speed for as long as Daniel kept his feet planted. He even activated his rune on Gertrude's bone hilt, [Crooked]. Each strike came down at a different angle, making Ekakas spend all his attention on keeping the [Hero] from hitting him.

Orrin renewed his [Ward] and [Mana Shield], targeting Daniel when he had line of sight as well. Darth, the demon with the double-sword weapon, pulled back from his barrage of attacks. Biggs took the opportunity to swing the huge, spiked mace down at Orrin from a distance. It missed but left a divot in the ground. Smalls came in with his smaller weapon, and the two Tweedles swung their axes, keeping Orrin from moving away.

One of the blades left a cut along his side deep enough that Orrin turned on [Mind Bastion] to avoid the pain response. He could still feel the burning sensation but ignored it better with the calm, cold skill running.

Daniel hammered Gerty down on Ekakas with such strength that the demon's feet sank a few inches into the ground. The demon smiled and Orrin felt his alarm bells ringing as mana gathered around the two.

"Daniel, pull back!" Orrin yelled.

Daniel's trust in Orrin was all that saved him. The [Hero] fought off the bloodlust to kill the demonic humanoids around him and he listened to his friend immediately. He used [Shooting Star] to run past Ekakas. Fractions of a second later, spikes extended up out of the ground all around the demon. One mage from their side who had been trying to get close enough to help was speared through the chest and died instantly.

Orrin's distraction cost him another two cuts across his chest and back, carving through his light leather armor. Without the numbing effects of [Mind Bastion], he would be screaming in pain. Instead, he used [Teleport] to launch himself away from the circle of demons, landing beside Daniel.

"Thanks for the heads-up," Daniel huffed as they moved together. His eyes widened. "Orrin! You're hurt."

Orrin cast [Heal Small Wounds] on himself as he checked over his friend. "Not a single scratch on you. I guess you are only fighting one demon to my eight."

Orrin didn't tell Daniel his health had been reduced by half from the attack across his back. When he landed after the [Teleport], his left leg had felt heavy and tingling. *They got my spine, I guess.* Orrin considered how lucky he was to have healing magic. The spells knit his flesh back together and he kicked out his leg, feeling it return to normal.

"I can't break through his hammers. I think they're made of Mythril, just like Gerty," Daniel admitted as the demons regrouped.

Ekakas walked to the dead mage and pulled her off the spike. He threw the body toward the group of adventurers that waited nearby. One of the two spear-wielding demons was dead, but the party had been cut to ribbons for its efforts. Orrin doubted they'd be up for another pass.

"I debuffed all of them as much as I could," Orrin said quickly. "We don't need to kill them. We need to move."

Daniel nodded toward the group. One of them knelt near the dead mage's body and glared at the demons. Orrin could feel the rage emanating from the adventurer.

"They aren't going to leave. I told you to keep going. You can go stealth and get away. I see some reinforcements running from farther north. I can keep them occupied until we can overwhelm them with numbers."

Orrin gestured to the dead bodies around them. "These are not all demons. That group is killing our people faster than anywhere else we've been. We should have everyone run."

Daniel tilted his head. "I'm not running."

Orrin made another two swords appear. He'd lost them both in the dash to get away for a moment. The demons were almost upon them again. "This is the last chance, D. We can't take these alone."

He noticed Shorty was in the group again. His right arm was cauterized from Orrin's hit with the [Fire Sword], and he held his weapon awkwardly with the other.

Daniel held his sword up, with the tip pointed at the demons. "Bring it on!"

A piercing scream crashed over the battlefield from the demon camp. The rushing demons turned their attention for a moment to the sound.

It was all Daniel needed.

The [Hero] broke Darth's sword haft in two, leaving him holding two small blades. Gertrude continued the strike through one of the Tweedles, leaving the demon cleaved in two on the ground. Daniel's [Shooting Star] made him a blur as he attacked.

Orrin was right behind him, hitting Darth with a frozen blast of

[Gust] and [Ice Sword]. He dumped more mana into the spell, keeping the demon from moving. He aimed for the head with his [Fire Sword], only to find it blocked by Ekakas's hammer.

"Little flea sucking on the blood of his betters," Ekakas chided as he knocked Orrin's sword out of his hand. The demon's weapon skills were beyond Orrin's one level in [Sword Proficiency]. "You are the one who slowed my men."

Orrin backed away, watching from the corner of his eye as the party of the killed mage moved in from behind. One shot an arrow that grew larger as it traveled. Just as Darth broke one arm from the icy encasement, the shot knocked his head clean from his shoulders.

Orrin took a deep breath. He tried something he hadn't wanted to do in the middle of battle. Testing new magic while fighting for his life wasn't high on the priority list.

One of the best spells Orrin ever bought was [Inverse]. It was actually a spell modifier that changed a spell to do the opposite of its intended result. He'd used it to great effect with his buff spells, creating his makeshift debuff spells until finally buying [Merge] and making a permanent version. Orrin pulled up [Increase Constitution] and pushed [Inverse] through the spell, hoping that he could reduce Ekakas's constitution as he'd once done to another enemy.

Nothing happened.

Orrin wasn't too surprised. [Inverse] didn't work with a lot of his spells. It was the same case with his healing abilities. He couldn't make a health-drain spell with [Inverse].

I could drain the demons using [Blood Mana]. Orrin considered it briefly.

[Blood Mana] could be used offensively. It sucked the health from a person, turning it into mana for Orrin to use. It allowed Orrin to use magic on a person, even while they suffered from mana withdrawal. He'd do it if he had to, but the thought of the elf Devdan, the only person that Orrin had used [Blood Mana] on besides himself, made the bile in his stomach rise. He'd pulled the elf's mana into [Toxic Touch], making the man's blood turn to acid within his own body.

Daniel made short work of Shorty with his one remaining arm. The demon simply did not have the strength to resist Daniel's attacks. The remaining demons, Spike, Smalls, and Tweedledumb, pressed their attack. Biggs kept the four members of the dead mage's party at bay with wild swings.

Orrin ducked under Ekakas's hammer blows and used [Teleport] again to get close to the party. Buffs flew from his hands as he increased their strength, dexterity, will, and intelligence by forty points each. "You have twenty minutes and then you'll collapse. Kill Biggs here and run to the Wall."

The archer drew his string back to his ear in fast repetition, launching several arrows at the demon. "I'm guessing Biggs is the one with the oversize mace? We can help the [Hero] with all of them. We just need a bit more time."

The remaining woman in the group held two staffs in her hands. One was planted into the ground by her feet while the other was pointed at the demon swinging the circular anvil on a stick. Lightning sparked from the outstretched staff and hit Biggs. The magic stunned the demon in place, giving the other two men time to rush in with their weapons. The added strength that Orrin gave them left the demon a squishy and diced piece of meat in seconds.

"Twenty minutes and you pass out," Orrin warned. "I'm not your boss. Do what you can."

The archer nodded, pointing at Tweedledumb. "Attack the one with the ax."

Orrin joined them, pushing combinations of fire bursts at the demons or covering them in ice when he could. He healed one of the men attacking with them when Spike left a gaping wound in the man's leg with his spear. The fighter didn't pause, pushing back into the fight.

Daniel was holding off Ekakas again but taking more and more hits. Orrin refreshed his friend's wards, but the demon was doing massive damage with each attack.

When several arrows struck Tweedledumb, followed shortly thereafter by a blast of lightning, only two demons remained. Orrin superheated the air around Spike, then slid underneath the demon. His [Ice Sword] stabbed into the demon's foot, then burst into a solid piece of ice up to his knee. The two fighters made quick work of the less mobile demon. With five-on-one odds, Smalls went down before Orrin was fully off the ground.

Ekakas roared as he swung his hammers down, creating his spiked earth growth again. Daniel grunted in pain as one scraped up his back, cutting away chunks of his armor.

"Daniel," Orrin shouted and ran with [Gust] pushing him faster than he'd ever run. He'd let the fight separate them. His friend was across the field littered with demon bodies and the party that helped them. Orrin cast every spell he had at the demon. Most spells hit, but nothing seemed to do lasting damage.

I'm not going to make it.

Ekakas spat in Orrin's direction then raised his hammers again. "Thus ends another [Hero]."

Chapter 27

The archer saved Daniel's life. His arrow flew faster than a hawk chasing a field mouse, knocking one of Ekakas's hammers into the other. The demon still struck Daniel with a glancing blow. He screamed in pain as the metal spikes dug into his shoulder and ripped him away from the stone spike in his back.

Orrin got to his friend a second later, throwing [Fire Swords] at Ekakas as fast as he could summon them. The demon deflected the first few easily until Orrin started making them explode in a heated mist. Most detonated with very little mana, but every second or third sword left a blistering smog of air that burned even Orrin's skin. He paused in his hurried throws, grabbed Daniel under the arms, and ignored the curses of pain directed at him as he dragged his friend away. More arrows and bolts of lightning hit Ekakas, keeping him at bay for the moment.

Orrin used [Identify] on Daniel and was relieved to see only a dislocated shoulder and broken clavicle. He directed the mana of his [Heal Small Wounds] into those areas worst affected. Two castings were all he had time to do before the demon strode through the last of the hot air toward them.

One of the two fighters ran in with his shield and flail. He struck the demon a direct blow, the head of the flail lodging in Ekakas's armor under his ribs. When the man pulled to release his weapon, it stuck tight. He wisely let go and lifted his shield as Ekakas retaliated. The handle swung by his feet still attached to the chain as he hit the fighter's shield with his hammers.

"Are you okay?" Orrin asked quickly, seeing the prompts on Daniel's status disappear. He still had the breaks, but they were closed and healing now. As long as he didn't overdo it for a day or two, there wouldn't be any lasting damage.

"Fine. My arm is just sore." Daniel grunted as he tried to stand up. "I can use my other arm to attack. We can't let him go. He's too strong. He'll decimate our troops."

Orrin didn't argue. He knew it was pointless. "I can [Numb] the shoulder for you, if you want."

Daniel nodded. "I feel like I'm going to dislocate it again or something."

Orrin touched Daniel and cast [Numb], removing the feeling from his shoulder. His friend rolled his arms and cracked his neck to the side.

"Much better."

"It's still healing. Don't overdo it."

"You know me. I do everything with moderation." Daniel chuckled as he summoned Gertrude back into his left hand. "Can you [Numb] that guy? Maybe he'll stumble."

Orrin frowned and shook his head. "It doesn't work like that. I might have to use [Blood Mana] and [Toxic Touch]."

"Do it. These guys are great, but they are getting murdered."

Orrin made a fist and waited for Daniel to hit his knuckles. "Back me up. I have to touch him, but he's fast."

The two young men exchanged a meaningful nod and ran back into the fight.

The second fighter had tackled his own friend just as the shield broke into pieces from Ekakas's attacks. He was pushing the dazed and weaponless man behind him as he tried to keep the demon's hammers at bay with his shortsword. A small part of Orrin's mind recognized the skill in sword fighting that was on display. It was something he could aspire to, but without regular training, his own [Sword Proficiency] would never bridge that gap.

Daniel crashed into Ekakas, using his speed skill to play battering ram against the demon. It knocked him off balance for only a moment, but that was enough for the lightning-throwing mage to help her friends pull back.

Daniel and Ekakas didn't exchange more words but went right at each other. Both were hurt, with Ekakas showing some signs of fatigue. Blood ran from the flail head in his side. One of Daniel's counterattacks struck the handle of the weapon, making it move, and Ekakas hissed in pain.

Orrin turned on [Camouflage] for the added milliseconds it might give him. He used [Way of the Water] to attack.

Orrin had received his fighting style [Way of the Water] from a skill book they'd found in the Guild's storage, long forgotten and hidden. He could enter a meditation state and train the skill with a watery teacher he'd named Styx. Orrin fell into Formless stance, the base for every part of his fighting ability. It left him ready to react but also let him move his body in the slightest of ways to enter the four fighting forms he knew.

River, Ocean, Rain, and Mist forms had their own idiosyncrasies, but Orrin used River the most. Focusing more on defense, this stance let Orrin evade and move along the battlefield. River helped Orrin move in a rapid but calm flow that never stopped and wore his opponent down. It was perfect for fighting with others, making Orrin into something of a dodge tank. Enemies would attack and miss, wasting their resources and stamina as Orrin floated like a leaf on the wind.

Orrin needed more in this fight. River was fine for evading, but he had learned to switch into Rain on occasion as well, as it let him use quick and unpredictable movements to land small attacks on the enemy while still maintaining some of the maneuverability of River. The more he practiced and fought, the better he became at changing stances midcombat.

He felt most comfortable fighting with Ocean stance, meeting attacks and throwing them to the side. It gave him better opportunities to strike back, but against someone as powerful as Ekakas, Orrin was worried he wouldn't survive trying to turn the hammer attacks.

His first strike against Ekakas missed as the demon used his hammer to block the attempt. Orrin didn't pause and moved into a different stance, skipping back.

Daniel swung Gertrude, but again, Ekakas blocked the weak attack. Their new archer friend bounced an arrow off Ekakas's head. When he turned to growl in the party's general direction, Orrin leaped forward and slapped his palm against the demon's face.

[Toxic Touch] made Orrin's fingers poison to others' skin when activated. He turned on [Blood Mana] to drain Ekakas's health, changing it to MP and filling his own mana pool. Orrin dumped the same mana into [Remetabolize] over and over, supercharging the toxins he pushed into Ekakas's blood.

Orrin kept hold for two seconds before the demon dropped a hammer and grabbed his shirt collar, throwing him away bodily.

Orrin rolled to a stop and immediately charged again. The look of fury on the enemy's face was framed with concern. The blisters on his face wept blood. Orrin moved in, attacking with Scorpion Fish Strike. Down one hammer, Ekakas couldn't avoid the strike to his arm. His veins stood up against his red skin, dark and bruised. His face darkened around Orrin's earlier slap, crisping into a flaky black rash as the poison worked into him.

The two fighters rejoined the fight a moment after a lightning blast pushed the demon forward. One now held a mace he'd scavenged from the fallen demons while the other pressed a series of stabs and slashes at Ekakas. They now surrounded the powerful demon in a changeup from minutes before.

Ekakas was harried away from his fallen hammer, using the spiked one to bounce weapons away from him. Daniel scored a direct hit on the still-implanted flail and the demon skittered back, coughing blood. He wiped his face with his sleeve. The motion scored the blacked skin, ripping some flesh from his face.

"Killing me will not save your small cities," Ekakas spat. "We will exterminate every pest we find and bring an end to your evil ways."

"Shut up and die already," Daniel responded, throwing Gertrude like a spear.

Orrin expected the attack to be deflected like it had been several times so far. Instead, Ekakas grabbed the weapon in the air. It scored deep gashes on both forearms and one bicep but the demon twirled with the sword. When he faced them again, he held Gertrude in one hand and his hammer in the other.

A soft breeze rolled across the field as Orrin scrunched his eyes and gritted his teeth for what was coming. "Oh, you fucked up now."

Daniel roared and charged at the demon. His punches carried the weight of his full strength. Ekakas tried to push him back, but Daniel used [White Dwarf], making himself immovable. Orrin didn't waste the chance and struck from behind, slapping the demon's ears. More poison flooded into his body, and he shook violently. Orrin reached and grabbed a horn as he was thrown, breaking the hard bone clean off as he continued pumping his toxins into his target.

Daniel held the arm clasping Gerty and yanked. Ekakas screamed as his limb came loose. Daniel reversed his grip and stabbed. His sword bit deep into Ekakas's chest, followed a moment later by another sword, multiple arrows, and a mace strike to the face.

"Is he dead?" the female mage asked from a distance, leaning her body up against one of her two staffs.

Daniel removed Gertrude, and blood as dark as ink poured from the wound. The demon fell limply to the ground. Daniel brought his sword up and slammed the point down. Ekakas's head rolled from its body.

"It's done," Daniel said quietly and then stumbled.

Orrin hit each of them with [Heal Small Wounds] and slipped under his friend's arm as he pointed to the Wall. He dropped [Mind Bastion] as soon as he confirmed it was safe. His mana tracker told him that he'd used a lot of mana, maybe five full mana pools' worth, but he should be okay for another six hundred points before he needed to see Tony.

"Get back and lie down. You're about to be sick. Find a [Healer] if you can. [Purify] will help you get up faster, but no spell orbs for the rest of the day. I don't know what will happen to you if you buff up again," Orrin explained.

"Thank you, [Hero]," the archer said as he pointed to their fallen comrade. One of the fighters, the swordsman, cried as he gently lifted her still body. "We would have all died if not for you."

Daniel smiled. "You saved us. Tell Lord Catanzano what happened. We need to get moving."

Orrin shook his head as the party jogged away. "I'm teleporting us back up to the Wall. You need to rest."

"We need to bring down more demons."

Orrin stopped walking and ducked out from under Daniel's arm. "Walk ten steps by yourself."

Daniel growled low and tried to move. With halting steps, he walked after Orrin. "I'm not so weak that I—"

Daniel tripped in the divot left by one of the demons' earlier attacks.

"That's what I thought." Orrin grabbed Daniel by his armor and pulled him to his feet. He ran more healing magic through his friend. "You used up all your stamina, didn't you?"

Daniel shrugged. Orrin sighed and grabbed his friend's hand. "I'm teleporting us now."

Daniel didn't argue this time.

They landed behind the Wall and Orrin looked around for anyone he recognized. "Where did they go?"

Chapter 28

People scrambled around the location where Orrin and Daniel had left Silas, Madi, and Brandt. As he checked faces, he couldn't find one person he knew. Daniel was still groggy, probably from a healed concussion. He'd suffered more concussions in this world than all American football players did in a season . . . combined.

"Daniel, will you be okay if I leave you here for a minute?" Orrin helped his friend sit down against the Wall. He pulled some jerky and a container of water out of his [Dimension Hole]. He waited for Daniel to give a lazy nod as he tore into the meat with his teeth.

Orrin pulled up his [Map]. Madi and Brandt were still in a party with him, so they should be easy enough to find. Except no blue dots lined his screen. He used [Zoom] to pull back as much as possible, but no Madi or Brandt.

Orrin started to hyperventilate. He cast [Calm Mind] on himself and checked the party page of his status screen. Both names were still there next to Daniel. They hadn't left his party. He had to trust in his friends. *They're alive,* he tried to convince himself.

He grabbed a [Knight] running by and pointed to Daniel, giving explicit instructions. The woman didn't argue, saluting Orrin and calling over a small group to set up a cot near the [Hero]. Orrin was casting one more heal on Daniel when he saw his first familiar face.

"Crius!" Orrin shouted and waved. Daniel groaned beneath him.

The Agent of Lady Timpe turned toward him immediately. He paused with a deep intake of breath at seeing Daniel with his eyes closed. Crius reached tentatively toward the sleeping boy and brushed his fingers along his forehead. He let out a sigh of relief.

"Overdrawn on both stamina and mana. What happened?" Crius asked, crossing his arms back into his white robes. The normal smile that he wore all the time was strained. "That doesn't matter right now. He'll survive. I'll have the few [Healers] we've got left come take a look, but my guess is he needs rest. I have a message for you from Lord Catanzano. The rest of your party went back to the city. There was an attack."

Orrin's brow furrowed as he glanced back at the demon camp. "Did they get around us somehow? Did the Wendigo team get to the spider monsters? I can barely make out the details of their camp."

"It wasn't the demons," Crius said. His voice was uncharacteristically angry. "The Hospital made another move. They felt the lords weren't giving in to their demands fast enough and set fire to a few locations across the city. Normally, it would be nothing the guards couldn't deal with, but with the Horde attack . . . We are stretched thin and Lord Catanzano sent his daughter and her [Knight] to help. You and the [Hero] are requested to rest for the time being. Madeleine and Sir Bennett will [Teleport] back in the morning."

Orrin felt uneasy about keeping the group separated. It was rule one of tabletop games: Don't separate the party. After the fight with the Hospital the other day, the [Healers] had gone quiet. Most did their jobs and helped with the Horde effort, but some disappeared. Silas had arrested a few and kept them locked up for their role in the attack on Orrin, but according to the lord of Dey, too many were still unaccounted for. It wasn't something they had the resources to investigate with the need to defend the Walls. In Orrin's mind, it was out of sight and out of mind. What could a few noncombatants with healing magic do?

"I would feel better if our party was together," Orrin started but shook his head. "There are too many distractions. How did Wendigo's attack go?"

Crius brushed his fingers through his thin hair, moving some strands to cover his large bald spot. "Our scouting reports state both of their monster transports were taken down. The distraction you created with Daniel caused enough chaos that every member of Hornet returned unscathed. About a thousand demons in their reserve marched a few hundred yards toward the Wall when so many demons started dying. We had our forces pull back into the Wall but we estimate at least six hundred demons were killed. Perhaps fifty of their controlled monsters died as well."

Orrin nodded. The numbers were good. He hadn't focused on killing the demons he'd dropped, hoping someone could finish the grisly work for him. "How many from our side?"

Crius hesitated, his natural smile turning down. "Eighty-seven. That includes all members from Wendigo. We've not been able to locate them, and they are being counted as killed in action."

The plan had been to create enough chaos that Wendigo team could escape. Orrin had failed. He hung his head in silence for the team he'd never even met. *I need to get stronger.*

Lady Timpe's Agent awkwardly patted Orrin's back. "You gave them the chance to break through. They ended two of the biggest monsters that Dey has ever seen in a Horde. Wendigo team knew what they were doing."

Orrin didn't have time to respond as Crius turned his head and started doing his long-distance reporting spell. To anyone watching, the man appeared to be having a mimed conversation with someone. From what little Orrin knew about the ability, Crius could mark various people and talk with them anytime they said his name.

"Orrin, the plan has changed. Lady Catanzano insists you return to Dey and bring the [Hero]. Her directions are 'Go to the coffee shop.' I hope you know what that means."

Orrin frequented one coffee shop in Dey. His friend Amir helped his father run the business. Amir had dreamed of being a [Healer] since he was a child and his mother died from a curable illness. He'd worked his way into the Hospital but was demoted and rejected for not following their strict orders without question. Orrin had met him during the last Horde attack. Amir was unconscious, having overdrawn his mana in an attempt to heal more victims of the attack. He'd covered for Orrin, helping him escape the scrutiny of the Hospital management.

Later, Orrin happened upon Amir and rescued him from some overzealous members of the Hospital. When Amir was demoted, he didn't give up on his dream to be a [Healer]. Orrin ultimately used his Administrator powers to gift his friend the class that he'd always dreamed of having.

The Hospital ran a monopoly on healing in Dey. According to a few elves, the healing community elsewhere wasn't as corrupt, but the Dey Hospital cracked down on anyone touching on their area of expertise in the city. Amir's sudden emergence threw a wrench in their machinery of control and he'd been deemed an enemy. Luckily, Orrin had introduced him to Lord Catanzano. The leader of Dey kept the hounds at bay.

Recently, the Hospital had splintered. Orrin knew some members of the Hospital attacked other members over some sort of schism. One of the leaders, Logan Viccio, had tried to warn Orrin about it, but with the Horde approaching, it wasn't high on his list of things to worry about. It appeared the Hospital was making another move and jumping higher in priority.

"I know what it means," Orrin answered Crius. "Are you staying here? Do we have enough people rested to help with the Horde?"

Initially, Crius had been hesitant around Orrin and the [Hero]. He'd heard the rumors about what went down in the hills outside Dey when his acquaintance Samara had died. She was a true fighter. Crius could hold his own, especially as an Agent of Lady Timpe. However, his skills rested more in the domain of support. He coordinated, planned, and took care of Lady Timpe's day-to-day so she could focus on bigger issues. He'd worked to make himself indispensable to her, and when he'd been pawned off on the Agent killers, he was worried that he'd offended his boss.

Now, his general upbeat demeanor was back. Crius was an optimist at heart. He believed people were inherently good and tried to live up to that standard himself. He tried to remember everyone's name and greeted others with a smile. He knew little about Orrin and Daniel beyond what he'd gleaned over the last few days, but in his mind, Dey had two heroes. Both young men had risked their lives on the chance to help the Wendigo team, no matter the outcome. Now, Orrin was asking questions that only a leader would ask before leaving his men behind. It filled Crius with respect and a little pride that he was working with a person of such character.

"A general retreat of the demons seems to be underway. I will stay and coordinate with the line commanders to get our troops rested. Rest easy. We have the relic you lent us and can call for more help at any time."

Orrin clasped the man's hand and then turned to Daniel, still lying on the cot. "D, are you up for a [Teleport] back to Dey?"

Daniel groaned.

"Madi needs us there," Orrin tried again.

Daniel turned on his side and mumbled, "Five more minutes."

"We can grab a few items from that bakery you like if you get up."

Daniel rolled off the cot and stood slowly but surely. "If you don't get me more of those cinnamon buns with a crunchy shell top, I will throw you into the middle of the demon camp."

Orrin laughed, grabbed his friend's arm, and used [Teleport]. He brought them directly to the baker's shop, knowing that Daniel was only half kidding with his threat. The bell over the door chimed when they walked in.

"Sir Daniel!" the extremely thin man behind the counter, Ruffy, exclaimed when he looked up. "If I had known you were coming, I would have baked you some of your favorites."

Ruffy ate slices of bread as they cooled all day. The man lived on a diet of mostly carbs but somehow continued to look emaciated. When Daniel had told him about the store, Orrin grew worried enough that he used [Identify] on the man to make sure he didn't have some undiagnosed disease. He was just one of those lucky folk who could eat anything and never gain weight.

Ruffy glanced at the rows of soft bread. Most contained nuts and raisins, but other, hardier breads were mixed in. "I've been drafted to make as much product for the front line as possible. I have no sweets today."

Daniel glared at Orrin.

"How long would it take to make a few boxes of those cinnamon rolls that Daniel likes?" Orrin asked. "The front line could use a treat after today. I'll do the delivery myself and pay extra."

Ruffy held up a finger as he took a spatula wider than his own body and pulled the heavy iron door of his oven open. He scooped out several loaves and set them on a rack with a practiced ease. Turning back, he rubbed the sparse hairs on his chin. "Maybe an hour, or slightly more, perhaps. I can make eighty in that time."

Orrin fished two gold pieces out and set them on the counter. "We'll be back for them."

"Sir Orrin, that is too much!" Ruffy waved his hands as he approached the counter. He pushed the gold back. "I cannot accept it."

Orrin laughed and held the man's hand over the coins. "Ruffy. I promised Daniel a treat and you're saving my life. I'm not paying you enough. Keep the gold. We'll be back in an hour."

Ruffy thanked them and then jumped in place. "The rye bread! It needs to come out."

Orrin and Daniel left before the man could argue over payment and walked the three streets over to Amir's family coffee shop.

"You did overpay him," Daniel ribbed his friend. "One copper gets you four rolls. You paid him like twice what they're worth."

Orrin shook his head. "Eighty would cost twenty copper or two silver. I overpaid by a lot more than twice, Daniel."

They turned down the street while still chatting, but Orrin's smile dropped at the sight before them.

Amir's father had opened his family coffee shop after finding an open corner store. It let the natural flow of people down the street walk in one door and out the other, keeping with traffic. The store was simple but well-loved. The chairs and small tables they left outside during the day were set out of the way of people traveling the street but gave a casual ambience to the best place to get coffee in Dey.

No longer.

Black soot marks crawled up the blown-out doorway. The wooden chairs and tables were burned to a crisp. Madi and Brandt, along with several guards, stood near one of the windows pointing in and talking.

"Oh no," Daniel murmured under his breath. "What happened?"

A small figure Orrin had missed in the group pushed his way between two burly guards and ran at them. Amir's robes were burned, the sleeves entirely gone. His forearms were hairless. *He was burned and healed himself.*

Amir slammed into Orrin and hugged him. "She said you would come."

Madi and Brandt joined them a moment later. "How did your mission go?" Madi asked.

"Later," Orrin mouthed over Amir's shoulder. "What happened here?"

Brandt's face was stone as he explained. "Approximately five men, three of whom wore the white robes of the Hospital, were seen leaving Amir's shop after setting it on fire."

"Was anybody hurt?" Daniel asked, blinking a bit. He was still suffering from overdrawing his resources.

"They took my father," Amir cried. He shook in Orrin's arms. "The Hospital took him."

Chapter 29

Orrin shot a sharp look at Brandt over Amir. "What do we know?"

Brandt shook his head. "Not much. The city guards here arrived to help put out the fire. Lord Catanzano left a man to keep an eye on Amir after the threats from the Hospital, but he's missing. A few locals volunteered information, and I have people knocking on doors right now."

Daniel's arms were crossed and he drummed his fingers on his biceps. The setting sun reflected off his metal armor, casting stray rainbows on the ground around him. "Is there some magic we can use to track them? What about asking that guy who got an arrow in the neck?"

Madi stepped forward and helped extract Amir from Orrin's chest. She spoke quietly to him as she guided him away.

"We have a [Tracker] coming in, but you two made it here first." Brandt brushed his hand through his hair and sighed. "It's a long shot. We don't have anything from the people who did this, and Amir's father essentially lives at his store. Finding his trail won't be easy. As for Principal Viccio, I've been told not to start a fight with him. He's the only reason that the front line has [Healers] right now. The other principals are restricting their aid."

Orrin knew Brandt wanted to help them, but his words still came out harsher than he meant. "And if I start a fight with him because he went after a friend? What will you do, Brandt?"

The [Knight]'s eyes remained calm and kind as he placed his hand on Orrin's shoulder. "I'll stand by my friends. Amir is a good kid."

Orrin felt foolish, but Brandt removed his hand and continued talking, letting him off the hook. "I don't think this was Viccio. He doesn't like having a [Healer] outside of the Hospital's control any more than the other principals, but he's not shortsighted. He sent an apology letter to you after he learned what happened with his messenger, the one who knocked you off the Wall. His plan was to try to convince you of the trouble you and Amir were causing within the Hospital. The attack was planned by one of his underlings who betrayed him and now works for another principal."

"Wait," Daniel said, going very still. "Someone tried to kill us, we know who it is, and he's still working at the Hospital?"

Brandt sighed. "Yes, Daniel. In the middle of a Horde attack that might end our civilization as we know it, we haven't had time or resources to go after everyone."

Daniel glanced at the sun falling over the western horizon. "Orrin, I'm going to be useless in a fight, but I'll back you up if you want to go kick down a Hospital door or two."

Orrin watched Amir sitting against the wall near his burned-out shop. Madi squatted next to him, her hand on his leg. "I'm going to find Viccio. He'll help me find Amir's dad."

Brandt asked the obvious question. "What if he refuses?"

Orrin turned to look at Brandt. The large man shivered at the look on Orrin's face.

"I'll go find out what I can."

Orrin checked on Amir as Brandt went to ask the local guards for directions. The young man was shell-shocked, barely responding as Madi talked to him in a calm but nonstop prattle.

"—back to the shop, I'm sure we can help rebuild it. I know Orrin and Daniel will have him back before . . . Here's Orrin now. Let me ask him for you." Madi turned as Orrin approached. "I was just telling Amir that we will do everything we can to help find his father. I thought it might be good to keep Amir busy until we get back. Maybe we can have him brought out to do some healing on the Wall?"

Orrin considered the option. Amir's face was blank as he stared at the cobblestones beneath him. "I think it might be better to have him rest at home. It's been a long day. Madi, will you go see that a guard waits with Amir until we get back with his dad?"

Madi nodded and squeezed Amir's leg. "I'll get you something to eat, too."

She left and Orrin sat down next to Amir. The soot from the fire hadn't reached their spot on the wall, but the wind pushed some ash along the street. Amir caught a flake in his palm and studied it with dead eyes.

"I should have accepted their offer and gone back to work for the Hospital," he whispered with lifeless words. "They said I'd regret working on my own."

"Who said that?"

"Some [Healers] I don't know came by two days ago." Amir opened his cupped hand and let the ash float away. "Before the fighting started. My da told me it wasn't my fault that others lost sight of what helping others means, but teachers and students fighting in the streets? It's madness. I'm not important enough to start a fight over, but ever since you gave me this class . . ."

Amir trailed off and clenched his fists. "I know you only wanted to help me, but sometimes I wish I'd said no. I could have worked with my da and none of this would have happened."

Orrin didn't know what to say. He'd offered to change Amir's class to [Healer] after the Hospital blacklisted him and kicked him out of their little club. Without a healing amulet, Amir had no chance at fulfilling his dream of being a [Healer]. Neither of them had known the Hospital would react the way they had. Nobody could have guessed that the different ideologies within the Hospital would lead to fighting in the streets and abductions.

"Amir, I don't regret it. I think it was the only choice."

The young man rubbed his eyes and turned to look at Orrin. "The only choice? You could have left me alone and my da wouldn't be—"

"I gave you what you wanted. You help people now and heal people the Hospital won't."

Amir pointed to the dark maw of his father's café. "That's the price? The last thing my da has of my mom was destroyed. People hate me for helping others."

Orrin closed his eyes as he focused his thoughts into words. "People don't like change or things they don't understand. You're a [Healer], just like any other member of the Hospital. They've lost a bit of power, but one person doing some good isn't going to overturn everything they've built. I'm not going to go around changing other people's classes, and without the Hospital's amulets, you can't train others to be a [Healer]. The store can be rebuilt. We'll find your dad and bring him home safely. Everything will be okay."

Amir clenched his fists and didn't respond. Orrin didn't know what to say. He'd helped his friend get his dream class. He hadn't known the consequences for it would be so steep.

Brandt approached them with Daniel and Madi behind him. "The [Scout] that was watching Amir and his family was found knocked out several streets away, but he's alive. I was able to get a current location on Viccio. We need to move now, though."

Orrin stood and held his hand out for Amir. The young man glanced at it but pushed his way to his feet on his own.

Principal Logan Viccio walked down the street outside the Hospital surrounded by no fewer than ten enforcers. The Hospital employed more than healing classes, needing rank and file for everyday jobs like cleaning up the mess left by dying patients or keeping their families from blaming them when magic didn't stop the specter of death. Logan's face was covered in sweat and his hair spread out behind him in the cool night air, his customary man-bun undone.

"I need a word with Principal Viccio," Orrin announced, dropping his [Camouflage] spell. He stood in the middle of the street alone.

Swords were drawn and mana crackled as Logan's men read the threat in Orrin's stance.

"Stand down," Logan said quickly, pushing his way to the front. His senses warned him the young man was on edge and not as alone as he appeared. "Orrin, what are you doing here? I thought you would be with the [Hero] at the new Wall."

Orrin took in the man's worn visage. "Where have you been for the last two hours, Viccio?"

Logan moved to put his hair up but dropped his hands after running his fingers through his hair. He'd momentarily forgotten he'd used his hair ribbon as part of a tourniquet. "I've been giving first aid to members of the defense at a fallback station within the Pass. We are on our way to our main hall to report and rest. Are you going to answer my question?"

Orrin stepped toward the group, completely unafraid of their weapons. Nobody in this little group was above level forty, and Orrin had killed demons today. "Members of your Hospital attacked a coffee shop today and kidnapped a friend's father."

Logan Viccio was an intelligent man. He had to be in order to reach his station in the Hospital. It wasn't hard to connect the dots and figure out who Orrin was talking about. The initiate Amir was one of the causes for the current schism in the Hospital. The other stood before him with a cold menace that made the principal's neck hairs stand on end. Viccio raised his hands above his head. "I swear to you that I had no part in this. You can ask Lord Catanzano my intentions. I have only argued for discretion and regulation in your friend's healing. I would never condone an attack."

"You'll help me find out who did it, then." Orrin didn't ask, he ordered.

"Boss, this kid can't talk to—"

"Shut up, Mallory," Viccio hissed. "I will help. What do you need?"

"We're going to go with you to the Hospital. You call all your leaders together and find out who is responsible." Orrin itched for someone to attack him. Maybe putting a few people down would loosen tongues faster. Anyone who didn't show up would be guilty until proven otherwise.

Viccio stretched his back with his hands on his hips. "I'll call whoever I can, but as you know, half our forces are helping with the Horde and the other half is running around causing problems right now."

"I'm spending tonight in Dey dealing with rogue [Healers] instead of resting to continue the fight against the Horde in the morning," Orrin replied through gritted teeth. "Anyone who doesn't show up should know I'll find them and personally throw them into the middle of the demon camp."

"You're making threats against some powerful people, son."

Orrin walked up to Principal Viccio and looked him right in the eyes. "I swear that if Amir's father isn't returned alive and well, I will burn the Hospital to the ground with all its leadership inside."

"That's the last time you—" Mallory, one of Viccio's guards, took one step toward Orrin before he toppled forward like a fallen tree. He bounced once on the street.

Orrin didn't take his eyes away from Viccio. The [Decrease Strength] spell barely moved his mana bar. "Put out your call. You have half an hour or I'll assume everyone in a white robe is a target."

Chapter 30

"Do you think it's a good idea, threatening him like that?" Madi whispered as they made their way to the Hospital's main building. Their party had grown with the addition of a small regiment of Catanzano guards. Madi herself had recruited them as a show of force. "Viccio doesn't have to be an enemy."

"I still think I should hang him from a building by his ankles and make him talk. The guy did lead you into an ambush, Orrin."

Orrin slapped Daniel on the back. "He's an asshole for sure, but he's healing people. I don't think he's in on this, but if I'm wrong, you can have the first crack at making him shit his pants in fear."

Daniel smiled at the promise. Brandt was walking a step behind them, coordinating with messengers and scouts. The [Knight] was keeping Silas informed of their movements, but the lord of Dey hadn't intervened yet.

"I can hear everything you say, you know?" Principal Viccio glared from a few feet away. Madi's men surrounded the Hospital worker and his six remaining bodyguards. "I agreed to work with you, didn't I?"

Daniel grinned. "I won't let you bounce off the ground too hard. I've got to keep you alive to answer questions."

One of Viccio's men growled, but none moved to intervene. Two of them carried Mallory, the guard who threatened Orrin. Orrin could have buffed the man back to normal but thought the sight of the big man's prone body would make the others think twice about trying something.

After giving Viccio an ultimatum, the principal sent some of the faster members of his retinue to deliver messages. Every leader of the Hospital was to meet outside on the Hospital's green fields as soon as possible.

Viccio sighed heavily. "I'm no threat to you right now. My mana is nearly dry. I've been healing the wounded all day. I've put out the call to assemble. What more do you want, [Hero]?"

"I want to know why the Hospital sucks so bad. I want to know who took Amir's father and why. I want to know why it's such a problem to have more people healing in this world." Daniel pushed his fist into his hand until his knuckles popped. "Do you know how much easier it is to fight, knowing I've got Orrin to heal me if I get hurt? Think about how much good your [Healers] could do if they were out in the field instead of hiding inside your buildings. You've monopolized an entire branch of magic and charge people for healing."

Viccio stopped walking and turned to Daniel. "I tried to have this conversation with you both, but the city leadership hid you away from me. Does the Hospital have problems? Of course it does. Every organization is run by people, who make mistakes and are fallible. What you want, though, is simply not possible. [Healers] helping in dungeons or on extermination quests for the Guild would lead to deaths. Our numbers are limited and our mana is finite. There are reasons that we have quotas and keep patients waiting. You look at the Hospital and see a monolith of power, but it is a precarious tower of cards ready to fall."

"You don't heal sick people," Daniel pressed. "You charge their families or don't heal them at all."

"Of course we charge people." Viccio held a finger up to Daniel's face. "Everyone has the right to be paid for their work. We demand our [Healers] do a limited amount of healing each day for free, but most of their mana is theirs to use as they see fit. Depleting their mana pool every day is exhausting work. Not everyone is talented in the same ways. What one can heal with ease takes another twice as long to partially stem. We do what we can with what we are given."

Daniel loomed over the man. "You could do more. Why stop Amir when all he wants to do is help?"

"He isn't helping. He heals people out of order. He sees a sick child and wastes mana fixing something that would resolve on its own with time while others die. It takes training to recognize priority. It takes wisdom and teaching to make the tough calls. He is a rogue enemy causing havoc within our own members. What we do isn't perfect, but if you know a better way to administer our limited resources across the entire city, let us know. Most of us became [Healers] to help people. It destroys our souls to turn away the sick because we have run out of mana."

Orrin listened from the sideline. He knew some of these arguments from his talks with Amir. The young man wasn't running around curing colds. He was seeing to the poor and ignored who would die without help. The help that the Hospital had failed to give.

"Initiate Fallah was reprimanded multiple times for overdrawing his mana while healing others, fighting and harming other initiates, and arguing with his teacher." Viccio glared up at Daniel. "Whatever you did to make him a [Healer] was rash and ill-advised."

"Wait." Orrin snapped out of his memories. "What do you mean, fighting other initiates? Amir couldn't hurt a fly."

Viccio spat on the ground. "After the debacle where he overdrew his mana, Amir ambushed some acolytes. He bruised up three of his classmates and knocked the teeth out of one. She had to spend the next week having them regrown, a most painful process."

"Amir didn't do that. I did. I found three people beating and kicking Amir. I dropped them with my magic."

Confusion crossed the man's face before he shrugged. "That was not what the report said. They said Amir attacked them."

"Amir did overdraw in the field that day. One of his teachers seemed very excited to punish him for helping others. Amir told me later about being shown true pain," Orrin retorted. "I don't know your rules, nor do I care about them. You claim to care about helping people but hurt your own. When someone asks questions, they get demoted. You called Amir an initiate. When I met him, he was an acolyte. Did you know that he had his class stripped from him? That he isn't even part of your Hospital because you all threw him out? I heal people, Viccio. Are you going to say that you should have a say in what I do?"

Each question and revelation hammered at the fractures in Viccio's stubborn glare. By Orrin's last words, he had paled.

"True pain? Are you a [Healer]? No, that . . . It doesn't matter. When did this happen?" Viccio asked, aghast.

"Ask your coworkers," Orrin answered, noticing Brandt talking with a man in a brown-and-green cloak.

Brandt nodded to the man, who ran off. He stepped between the two groups. Daniel, Orrin, and Madi squared off against Viccio and his remaining men. "I've got news. Four principals and two elders of the Hospital are waiting outside already, but there are two missing. Principal Mangin and Elder Phendio. One of my informants sent word that Mangin was seen heading into the tailoring district ten minutes ago with a group of young [Healers]. No word on Elder Phendio."

Viccio shook his head. "That makes no sense. Mangin oversees scheduling and policy. He doesn't interact with the trainees."

Orrin tapped his fingers on one of the regen potions on his belt. "Madi, why does that name seem familiar?"

"Principal Mangin was there when you . . . helped," Madi answered, trying to be circumspect. "He tried to strong-arm me into reporting on the incident, but my father forced him to stop harassing me."

One of the guards was quicker than the others. "It was you. You healed everyone when the Fogbinder attacked with its Fetid Canines. You're the invisible healer."

Orrin needed to work on his poker face. The blush behind his ears gave him away even as he shook his head. "That's . . . not . . . No, it wasn't me."

Principal Viccio glanced at the guard and back at Orrin. "Him?"

The man wore leather armor and carried long knives strapped at his hip. He raised his hand out to Orrin. "My name is Jonathan. You saved my son, Eli." He choked back a sob as they shook hands. "My wife is going to want to thank you in person. Our families have worked for the Hospital for generations. We knew he wasn't coming back from that wound. I was yelling at a teacher while you saved my boy."

Orrin had saved hundreds that day, including multiple children. He let the man hug him and ignored the tears the guard left on his shoulder.

"I asked around to find you, but nobody knew who you were," the man said as he stepped back, still holding Orrin's shoulders.

"As touching as this is," Daniel interjected, "what do we do about this guy leaving with some [Healers]? Is that a normal thing or did we find the baddies?"

Viccio was staring at Orrin with an appraising twinkle in his eye, not paying any attention to the conversations around him. Some of the guards were patting Jonathan on the back as he wiped his eyes.

"We need to meet with the group waiting for us," Brandt decided. "I sent a few people I trust to watch over Mangin and report back on what he's doing."

Viccio squared his shoulders and pointed to two of his men. "Go to the tailoring district and find Principal Mangin. Tell him if he doesn't report back immediately, I will move to strip him from his office."

He turned to the two men still holding Mallory. "Put him in a shop nearby and pay the storekeeper some copper to watch over him until he recovers. I need everyone ready to fight. I fear Mangin is behind the recent attacks. Go to every clinic and Hospital site. Spread the word that all initiates, acolytes, and healers within our ranks are to report to the greens. Anyone who doesn't comply will be demoted or removed from our lists."

Orrin sighed and pointed at Mallory, casting [Increase Strength] and bringing the man back up to about his normal strength. As he got to his feet, wobbling, the two guards holding him helped support him.

Viccio eyed his lieutenant with what Orrin assumed was an [Identify] of some sort. He glared at Orrin. "You could have let him recover this entire time?"

Orrin shrugged. "Some lessons require consequences."

Viccio was about to say something else when Mallory coughed politely. "Boss, the kid has a point. I don't like how he talked to you, but I've been listening the entire time. He's got reason to be angry with us."

"Are you well enough to help or do you need to rest?"

Mallory rolled his shoulders and cracked his neck. "I'll round up the clinics north of Ivory Street. The members we assign up there come from richer families. They might give some of the other men a hard time."

"Not you, though?" Daniel asked, trying to irk the man.

"I was rude to your friend and I apologize," Mallory said, bowing his head toward Orrin and then Daniel in turn. "We spent the day pushing away angry commanders and family members as we healed a select few wounded from the Horde attack. My nerves were frayed, but that is no excuse for my actions. As to your question, I have enough family connections that I can afford to rap a few heads if people don't listen. I'll gather them all. What do I tell them is the reason for the recall, though?"

Orrin watched Viccio. The man's eyes hardened at the question, and he thought an answer might not come. It might not be a good idea to have every member of the Hospital congregate anyway. They didn't need the manpower—they needed answers about where Amir's father was.

Viccio slumped in defeat and spoke low so only his guards and Orrin's friends could hear. "Rot has invaded the Hospital. We must excise the disease. It's time for a purge."

Chapter 31

As Viccio's guards left to complete their jobs, Orrin walked beside the principal. He didn't fully trust the man, but Orrin had to work with people he didn't trust all the time in this world.

Sometimes, he wondered if it wouldn't be easier if he and Daniel left it all behind. They could leave, sneak into a dungeon, and level up. The world had survived for thousands of years without them. The demons were repelled today and the elite teams of Dey worked well enough.

Why should any of this be my problem? Orrin grouched as he watched stalls shutting down for the night. *None of this is my responsibility. All I want is to find a way back home. Everything here is fighting and using others. You are only valuable to someone as long as they need something from you.*

Amir's downcast demeanor and questioning of Orrin's gift had struck a chord. He'd wanted to do something for his friend and help him achieve his dream class. Orrin had spent valuable resources in helping Amir become a [Healer]. There weren't a lot of people in this world who went that route. It surprised him somewhat that in a world of magic and monsters, healing wasn't more widespread. When his friend was kicked out of the Hospital, he'd jumped at the chance to make the world a better place.

Orrin recalled the tears in Amir's eyes after he had watched his father's café burn, the regret of trying to help others in pain etched across his face. Orrin squeezed his fists until his nails dug into his palms.

"Viccio, why did you become a [Healer]?"

The Hospital leader broke from his own thoughts with a start. "Why? My father worked with the Hospital, as did his father before him. I like to think I chose this life on my own. I spent some time in my teen years learning to fight." He chuckled. "I had plans of being an adventurer for a short while."

"What happened?"

"I grew up and realized adventurers need healing when they return from killing monsters or each other. So much pointless death and waste in the name of leveling."

Orrin checked his [Map] as they walked, looking for any ambushes. No red dots populated his screen. "Why not go with groups and heal as you go? Wouldn't it make more sense to level your [Healers] as well?"

Viccio shook his head. "This mindset of yours that we have [Healers] to spare is part of your problem. What do you know of our training?"

"Beyond the fact that you torture people? Not much," Orrin answered truthfully. He snapped his fingers. "There's an amulet that you use. I know that."

"The fact that you know the phrase *true pain* is what worries me most," Viccio responded quietly. "But that is not what you asked. You want to know why we don't send [Healers] out into the field like you suggest."

Viccio caught Daniel's eye and waved him over. "The [Hero] should hear this as well. When someone joins the Hospital, they are given the rank initiate. These members take classes on anatomy, diseases, different injuries, first aid, and so much more. It's usually a three-year program with tests to advance each term. Some complete it in two with higher marks. Once an initiate proves that they listen and learn, they are elevated to acolyte and given an amulet."

"An amulet that lets you cast [Heal Small Wounds], right?" Orrin cut in. He knew this much from Amir. His amulet had been taken away for healing people. "But acolytes are only allowed to heal when told they can."

"That is not accurate," Viccio corrected. "They can, within their own discretion, heal people every day. Further, they must work a portion of their week helping senior members heal the people of Dey. Why would you think they could not heal once given an amulet?"

"Amir lost his amulet for helping heal people against orders."

Viccio frowned. "We should have talked weeks ago. Your words contradict the reports I've received. Amir was demoted for fighting and not following direct orders, but I assumed the orders were just."

It was Orrin's turn to shake his head. "No. He was passed out in the field during the Fogbinder attack. He used all his mana healing others and distracted some [Healers] who weren't doing anything to help so I could keep working. The next time I saw him, he was being attacked by three students. He didn't even try to defend himself. I'm the one who hurt them. He'd already been demoted at that point."

"I'll open an investigation once this matter is settled. From the discussions I've had with some of the other principals, everyone thought Amir was a hotheaded rule breaker who doesn't listen to his betters."

Orrin paused walking. "Not one person in the Hospital is better than Amir."

Viccio stopped as well, grinding the entire convoy to a halt. "I didn't mean it like that. We believed he wouldn't listen to those more senior in rank."

Brandt, who constantly circled the perimeter, stepped into the loose circle of guards. "Everything okay, Orrin?"

Orrin used [Calm Mind] on himself. His anger simmered to a low boil from the raging inferno it had been a moment before. "All good, Brandt. Any news?"

The [Knight] gave a sideways look at Viccio before giving a small nod. "We just received word that the demons have pulled back from the Wall. It looks like they don't want to get stuck in the dark with us throwing spells and arrows down at them. Two small breaches were contained, but total casualties remain low."

Orrin felt relief that the fighting had stopped for now. He felt guilty enough going on this errand by himself, but Daniel and Madi had refused to let him do it on his own. Amir was their friend, too. "Thank you. Any news on Wendigo?"

Brandt gave a short shake of his head. "They should have reported in by now if anyone survived. I'm right here if you need anything."

The man gave another questioning look at Viccio before returning to the circle of guards around them all. It was overkill in Orrin's mind, but it was nice to have an escort that forced everyone in the streets to move to the side.

Orrin started walking again. He decided to let Viccio's comment go for now. "So, where do these amulets come from?"

"We don't know," Viccio said, waving at a woman in white robes. The Catanzano guards moved aside and let her join the Hospital guards. "We have lost the ability to create more. That is one reason we watch our members so closely and keep them safe. We've lost amulets over the years. Acolytes can be replaced, but the amulets cannot."

"That seems like a serious limit on how many healers you can have," Daniel said, chiming in for the first time. "I can see why you wouldn't want the amulets going into dungeons, but I've seen some elf [Healers] who don't use amulets."

"After an acolyte trains with an amulet, they unlock [Heal Small Wounds] as a purchasable spell. That is the promotion point to healer within our ranks. Being a healer, whether they receive a class upgrade to [Healer] or something else, allows them more flexibility. They can work anywhere, but most are advised to stay within our clinics or travel only safe roads to villages that request our aid. A healer is the first rank at which a member can vote in our elections for principals or apply to be a teacher."

"None of this explains why you lot would give Amir a hard time for healing. If anything, it seems he should have been promoted directly to healer," Daniel said. His eyes watched every corner, waiting for an attack.

He's overvigilant, Orrin thought with concern. His friend was constantly dealing with sneak attacks and kidnap attempts. *Not that I blame him.*

"Amir became a [Healer] without using an amulet," Viccio stated. "Nobody knows how and he isn't cooperating with us."

"Why should he?" Orrin fumed. "After all he went through, he owes the Hospital nothing."

Viccio raised a finger. "One, we fed and educated him with the understanding that he would work for us." He raised a second finger. "Two, we spent valuable resources in his development, namely an amulet." A third finger joined the others. "Three, he is still a member of the Hospital. Albeit a demoted initiate."

"I'm telling you, Amir was kicked out completely. His class was changed back to [Brewer]."

Orrin watched as Viccio wound his hair up into a bun only to let it fall again. "That was not reported. It is not common to be removed from the Hospital completely. We reserve that for people who . . . use the knowledge we teach for less savory means."

"What does that mean?" Madi asked. She'd been content to stand by most of the conversation. Growing up a Catanzano, she was already privy to most of the information given, but a few new facts had sneaked through. "What are you teaching at your schools?"

"Our classes include all our knowledge on how the human body works. In advanced classes, volunteers undergo small operations to give us visual familiarity with the inner workings of the human body. On occasion, we have found certain people who go beyond the bounds of what is acceptable in their attempt to 'learn.'" Viccio's last word was laced with derision. He looked at Madi's confused face. "We remove sadists who like to watch people suffer."

"Why wouldn't you use [Numb]? If the patient can't feel the operation, you could see the way the muscles move under the knife without worrying about someone drooling over the pain." Orrin scratched the back of his neck. *Am I ever going to get over that collar?*

"How . . . ? Who told you about [Numb]? Only a select few principals and one of our elders can use it. It isn't a common spell to unlock."

Orrin reached out and tapped the back of Viccio's left hand. The man's eyes widened as he held his limp wrist with his right. He was too stunned to speak.

"Back to what I was saying," Orrin continued. They were nearing the block where the main Hospital building stood. He could already see the green grass that surrounded the squat building. "Amir owes you nothing. Your Hospital kicked him out. If you fire someone, you don't get to demand they share their secrets with you later. He gave back the amulet."

Viccio cast something and moved his fingers as he regained control. "His class is nigh impossible to get without amulet use, or so we believed for generations. The younger initiates believe there is a secret way to be a [Healer] without going through our training. Healing magic is mana intensive and works better with a detailed understanding of what the body should be like naturally. A sickness of the blood must be removed with care, and slowly, or a [Healer] will waste their mana as the patient dies. A broken bone must be set correctly or the leg may never work properly again. Compound Amir's case with an invisible healer that brought hundreds back from death's door and our applications dropped. Rumors start that the [Hero]'s party member heals people on missions and our initiates quit. Several of our acolytes were found hoarding your new spell orbs to boost their mana pools. They wanted to speed up the process of learning [Heal Small Wounds] on their own. All these things have caused unrest in our ranks. It is what I was trying to talk with you about before the fighting began. Our members are split. Some see you as a threat to our ways. Others find Amir to be a hero in his own right. Fights between initiates and acolytes alike have escalated. Now, I'm beginning to suspect there is more at play here. Luckily, we should have some answers soon. I see Elder Kali and most of my fellow principals ahead."

As the Hospital members split from the Catanzano guards, Daniel leaned over to Orrin. "How much of his story do you buy?"

"He didn't appear to be lying," Madi whispered as they walked toward the group of Hospital leadership. Viccio was shaking hands with a few and talking animatedly. "I've only met him a few times, though. I don't know him well."

Orrin checked his [Map] again. "No enemies around that I can see, but my [Map] isn't a lie detector. If they help us find Amir's dad and promise to leave him alone, I don't care how they run their business. Even if it shouldn't be one."

Brandt ordered a few guards to sweep the block but stood as a pillar behind them. "Lord Catanzano asked me to remind you all that the Hospital is still supplying healing to our wounded. He also gave authority to his daughter, Lady Madeleine Catanzano, to find and punish anyone using this time of strife to harm citizens."

Madi smiled at the trust her father was showing them. Orrin made a note to thank Silas later—if he didn't end up putting the entire Hospital leadership into the ground.

Chapter 32

Since she had training in politics, Madi took charge as they were introduced to the various principals and Elder Kali. She shook hands with each person, usually with a comment about meeting them in the past at one event or another. Introductions with the [Hero] followed. Both sides had their guards wait at a polite distance.

In practice, the Hospital was run by the principals. The six members held their positions for a period of two years before a new vote could be called for if anyone ran against them. The elders created broad rules, leaving the actual administration to the principals. Six principals and three elders chosen from their best and most seasoned veterans. The two elders present, Kali and Seif, nodded their heads in deference to the [Hero].

Elder Seif was a tall, beefy man with dark skin and a bald head. Several scars crossed his face, neck, and arms where they showed through the long white robes.

Elder Kali walked with a short staff she used more like a cane, her hunched body curled over the stick. Her milky-white eyes turned to each person in their group before resting on Orrin. She sucked her lower lip and tutted.

"This is the other rogue [Healer] I feel, but not a [Healer] at all. What are you, child?" Her voice was grandmotherly, but with a sharp tone reserved for cookie thieves.

Orrin could tell the woman was blind without using [Identify], but her face followed him as he moved back behind Madi. "I'm a [Utility Warder], ma'am. I can do some low-level healing, but I'm not a rogue [Healer]. Neither is Amir, for that matter."

Madi raised her voice in an attempt to pacify the principals as they began arguing.

Viccio stepped in as they talked over her. "Quiet. You are not initiates. This is the [Hero]'s party. Show respect."

Of the six principals who ran the Hospital, four were present. Logan Viccio, who Orrin already knew. Salvotor Croix, a frail man with a heavy mace hanging from his belt and a shock of white hair standing nearly straight up. Carmine Morelli was a stout woman and the only one not wearing white robes. Her armor might have been painted white at one point, as Orrin noted the dents had flecks of a lighter color showing through, but the beaten plate showed only the steel at this point. Emma Vandran was the last present principal. Her blond hair and blue eyes shone with empathy and concern to the point where Orrin wouldn't meet her eyes for longer than a second.

"Where are Leora and Ark?" Logan asked after the introductions were finished.

"Principal Brack and Principal Mangin have not responded to the summons," Seif boomed in his baritone voice. "Elder Phendio has likewise been unreachable. What is this about, Logan?"

Viccio cleared his throat and began explaining the attack on the Fallah café and the kidnapping of the family patriarch. He also recited what he'd learned from Orrin about Amir's difficulties in the Hospital.

"The boy believes he was expelled from the Hospital and no longer is an initiate at all," the man finished. He'd borrowed a small ribbon from Principal Vandran and tied his hair back into his signature bun. "The reports sent to me from Mangin contradict the eyewitness statements I've collected from this young man, a member of the [Hero]'s party."

"I have a request for the [Utility Warder]," Elder Kali declared during the silence that followed. "Initiate Fallah refused us the answer to a question. How did you both learn [Heal Small Wounds]?"

Orrin scowled. "Is your control over healing magic so important that you care more about that question than where an innocent man is being held? Amir is not an initiate and you've allowed him to continue to be bullied. I'm not Amir. I don't answer to you nor owe you anything beyond the limited respect I still have for you as workers in the medical field. You heard Viccio. You know what we want. Someone in your organization kidnapped my friend's father. Who did it and where is he?"

Kali chuckled, a dry sound like leaves crackling underfoot. "Passionate, loyal, and headstrong. You would make a fine [Healer]. Do not assume every member of our Hospital is the same, friend of the [Hero]. Principal Croix is already searching for the senior Fallah. None in this circle knew of these events or the subterfuge that brought you to our door."

Daniel inclined his head toward the willowy man with his eyes closed. "He's standing right there and it looks like he's sleeping. How is he searching for anyone? And how would you know everyone here is innocent?"

The crone shuffled forward until she was uncomfortably close to Daniel. "Salvotor has a rare ability that lets him feel distress in a wide range. Usually, he helps us find survivors after natural disasters. He can read a patient's heartbeat ten miles away if he has the time to find them. He's searching Dey for someone showing signs of stress beyond the norm. He should also be looking for our missing members."

"Mangin is with Brack and Elder Phendio," the high-pitched voice of Principal Croix screeched. "Many are with them. Not all are ours. Someone is being harmed . . . tortured, maybe."

Daniel growled. "Where?"

Principal Croix opened his eyes and glanced at the elders. Seif nodded, and a moment later, Kali did as well. "Tell them. The others have made their choices."

Croix gave directions to Brandt and Madi, naming streets and crossroads to one of the Hospital's clinics. Elder Kali stayed close to Daniel but with her eyes on Orrin.

"You have a question. Ask."

Orrin was curious, but not enough to waste their time. "It doesn't matter."

"Questions matter as much as the answers. Ask." She kept her white eyes trained on him.

"The Hospital had to know—" Orrin started then shook his head. "People under your control have been making life a living hell for Amir. Even Viccio argued against helping more with the Dark Horde. Your members are fighting in the streets. You had to know who was behind it. Why didn't you do anything?"

Elder Kali tilted her head like a curious bird. "What would you have done if a small portion of your party decided it wanted control and moved behind your back to steal control from you? We can listen to our members' hearts but not know them until a crisis brings them to bear. The fighting was between members not admitted as full [Healers] and their hired help. We treat the disease where we find it, but sometimes you need a knife to cut to the root. I apologize you will have to play that role today."

Madi pushed her way between Orrin and the old lady before he got the chance to hit her.

"Elder Kali, the [Hero] and I will find and charge members of the Hospital with kidnapping, civil disobedience during a Horde attack, destruction of private property, and most likely resisting arrest. Do you have any dispute with these actions?" Madi kept her hand on Orrin's chest. He could cast a spell, but the rage at the woman's casual use and disregard for them infuriated him so much that he regressed to wanting to punch her.

The old lady turned her back and walked back to the principals and her fellow elders. "All members of the Hospital are before you, Lady Catanzano. Anyone absent is no longer welcome within our halls. Do as you see fit. We are done here."

"That's not good enough," Orrin yelled. He knew he should cast [Calm Mind] but let the heat burn. All the people who'd used him flashed through his mind. Silas, Madi's dad, before he knew them. Lord Wendeln. Guildmaster Pritus. Lord and Lady Sanerris. So many others who used people in the city for their own needs, never worrying about the consequences to others. "You could have stopped this."

The tall elder, Seif, moved in front of the smaller woman. "Back down, son. We have no quarrel with you."

Daniel's hand gripped Orrin's shoulder. "Do you trust me, O? If so, don't do anything but keep looking angry."

"It's not hard. I'm pissed off."

Daniel gave his friend a slight shake before addressing the Hospital leadership. "I heard the Hospital hasn't been sending more than a few [Healers] to the front lines of the Horde attack. Is that true?"

The principal in armor had a glowing sword in her hand that hadn't been around a moment ago. "We have sent an acceptable number of defenders per our contract with the ci—"

"When I get back from saving my friend's dad, every member of the Hospital better be traveling to the Wall. You all fucked up. You want us to do your dirty work and clean house? We are going to shake the floorboards loose, but you will stop trying to negotiate and help. You're all [Healers]. Do your job. Go heal the people fighting to let you live."

Elder Kali leaned around Seif. "Are you threatening us, [Hero]?"

"I don't have to threaten," Daniel answered, keeping his hand on Orrin. "All I have to do is let go of my friend. He stopped five hundred demons today by himself. He killed a demon at . . . what level was it we reported again, Brandt?"

"Level seventy, per multiple reports," the [Knight] answered. He, too, seemed on edge at the moment.

Not one person scoffed. The principal with the soft blue eyes paled a bit, but nobody questioned Brandt.

"And you, Lady Catanzano? We have contracts with your father. What do you have to say to your party member's words?" Elder Kali asked. Her voice still stayed a near whisper.

Madi didn't hesitate in her response. "I think Daniel was more generous than I would be. He gave you until we return. I'd let Orrin drop you all right now and send every [Healer] in that building out into the field to fight. You as much as admitted you were party to what has happened in this city. Only as a bystander, yes. But party nonetheless. I would get moving if I were you."

The old lady laughed her dry, croaking chuckle again. "Oh, to be young and so sure of everything again. Principals Morelli and Viccio. Coordinate and send our members to the Wall. Have them report to the generals in charge. Create a staggered schedule and make sure we keep enough in reserve to help with our critical care patients. Only those absolutely necessary may remain. Seif and I will join the first group. Croix, you will remain here to monitor the city. I'm sorry, Salvotor. I know it's taxing, but most Horde attacks last only a day or two at most."

At her grudging acceptance, Orrin regained enough control to cast [Calm Mind] on himself.

Elder Kali's blind eyes zeroed in on him immediately. She smiled at Orrin. "What a [Healer] you would make."

"Let's get going before Orrin kills this grandma, huh?" Daniel kept hold of Orrin and steered him away. Once they were through the guards, Daniel ducked down and stared into Orrin's eyes. "Good. Not using your mind thingy. That was actually you being pissed. You're a scary dude sometimes, O."

Orrin took a few steadying breaths. "I'm tired of getting used. How far away is this clinic?"

"Not far. I'm sure you could [Teleport] us there. It's three streets away from the Guild. We'd need to leave the guards behind, but they can catch up." Brandt reached up and pulled the straps of his chest piece tight. "It might be better that way. We can sneak in and stop them if they try to hurt Mr. Fallah. The main force can arrest any who try and escape."

Orrin felt the coals of his anger settling, but at the thought of people hurting the kind man who gave him coffee, Orrin had to cast [Calm Mind] again. "Nobody will escape. Gather up."

His friends reached out. Madi took his hand. Daniel still gripped his shoulder. Brandt placed a palm on his head. Once they were ready, Orrin cast [Teleport].

Chapter 33

Orrin landed nimbly on the cobblestone street outside the Guild of Dey. The building was larger than even the Hospital, with multiple towers. It was built like a fortress with six stories and even more in the basement storage rooms that Orrin had explored with his friends. It was where he'd found the [Way of the Water] skill book that gave him the fighting ability he used to such great effect. They'd found other interesting items as well. Finding out what they were and did was one more item on Orrin's list of never-ending projects that were put on the back burner while they raced around Asmea putting out fire after fire.

Daniel and Madi settled easily on the ground as well. Brandt grunted as his knees buckled, but he kept his feet.

"Have I mentioned how much I hate [Teleport]?" the [Knight] grumbled. "The clinic is this way. The guards are a few minutes behind us. Are you sure you don't want to wait for them, Orrin?"

Orrin didn't answer or wait to see if his friends kept up. He marched down the street that Brandt pointed at and started to jog. *We better make it on time. If they've tortured Amir's dad, he's going to need help. I'll have to ask Lyra if she's available. The elves know a bit about mind healing and trauma. I wonder if Leanthun got some help to Nina.*

"Orrin, we need to turn here," Madi shouted from the corner street he'd just crossed by. "Stop being impatient."

Orrin used [Gust] to push the air behind him. He flashed back to his party, throwing dirt up in the street. A few people cursed his way as they waved the dust cloud out of their faces. "I can move faster alone. Tell me how to get there."

"Nope, we aren't doing that." Daniel spoke first, stepping up to Orrin. "It's risky enough going in with just four of us. We should wait for the guards before moving in, but I get your frustration. Amir's dad isn't going anywhere."

"He's being tortured."

Madi crossed her arms. "These renegade [Healers] want to know where Amir is or how he got his class. Even if Amir told his father, the man will protect his child. They'll start slow, because breaking someone with that kind of resolve takes time. They'll need to ingrain some level of trust that they won't go after Amir if his father talks. I think Daniel called it good cop and bad cop."

"What?" Orrin asked, confused. "What are you talking about?"

Daniel sighed. "When we lost you, Madi stopped me from asking some questions in a hard way of a few survivors at Lady Sanerris's house. I wanted to beat this guy until he told me where you went, but she said it wouldn't work like that. People will say anything if you simply hurt them. You have to trick them into thinking they can get away, too."

"When did you become an expert on torture?"

"He isn't," Madi said with a sigh. "My training to take over as a lady of Dey involved a lot of . . . necessary but unpalatable lessons. Trust me, Orrin. These people know how to get what they want, but it takes a few days at least. If we're lucky, they will have started with only a light beating and water deprivation. We can hurry, but stay with us. Elder Phendio has one of the highest levels in the city, and Principals Mangin and Brack are not slouches, either. We don't have a full list of these rebels yet, and the Hospital has some powerful members. You might not be able to take on everyone alone. Besides, rescue is our primary mission. Let the guards and the Hospital deal with these scum."

Orrin took a few deep breaths. "Okay, I'll slow down. But I will drop everyone I can find. If some escape, so be it. We'll find them later."

Daniel lightly punched Orrin on the arm. "Good man."

They traveled closer together. After another minute down the road, Brandt stopped them on the corner. "To the left and halfway down the street. There's a single man standing outside the door."

"How do we want to do this?" Daniel asked, glancing at them. "I've never been here before. What's it look like inside?"

Brandt ducked his head back from his surveillance. "It's a large warehouse filled with cots for sick or recovering individuals. Lots of hanging curtains for privacy. They might have cleared everyone out, but we can't assume there won't be innocent bystanders inside. Along the back wall, I think I remember a few storerooms or offices, but I've never been inside those. If I wanted someone to disappear, I'd keep them in the back. The walls are thick enough that nobody could hear . . . anything. We'd need a [Stone Mage] to burrow through without collapsing part of the building."

Orrin pulled up [Map]. "The entire building is blank. No dots inside. Are you sure this is the right place?"

Brandt nodded. "Clinics are emergency shelters during Horde attacks or other events. The buildings are covered in antiscrying and antiteleport wards."

Orrin raised an eyebrow. "Why?"

Madi answered. "If someone knew where the clinics were located, they could target them. That would create chaos, because the normal people wouldn't trust going to shelter, and it would demoralize our troops with families."

Orrin felt disgusted. Between her knowledge of torture theory and strategy to harm innocents to strike at the hearts of an enemy, Madi's childhood classes must have been a nightmare.

"Rush the lookout and then move in fast?" Daniel offered. "Or should we try and talk our way in first?"

Orrin shook his head. "I'll apologize to anyone caught in the cross fire after this if I have to. You three start walking toward the guy, and when he turns, I'll tackle him out of the way. If I hit him with [Decrease Strength] right before I get to him, he shouldn't make a sound."

"I can move faster with [Shooting Star]. I'll catch him as he falls." Daniel reached over his shoulder and unstrapped Gertrude. "After I get the guard settled, we go in together?"

Madi and Brandt nodded.

Without a word, the four executed the plan. Orrin knew his friend well enough to target the single lookout with his debuff the moment they rounded the corner. The man was leaning against the doorpost with his hand on the pommel of a sword but started to slide when his limbs went slack. Daniel blurred and caught the man in a princess carry. He turned and gently laid the body down, holding a finger up to his lips at the few passersby.

Brandt hit the wooden door with his shoulder. The hinges didn't stand a chance against his armored body. The frame splintered and the door crashed to the ground inside the clinic. Brandt closed his eyes as he rushed in.

Madi was one step behind him. She threw a disco ball's worth of lights into the wide room, hopefully blinding anyone with line of sight to the door. Orrin followed behind her, and Daniel followed fourth, ducking to avoid snagging his sword.

Now that they were inside, Orrin could make out several people sitting on low beds in various states of injury. Joists along the ceiling held long poles in crisscross patterns. Long drapes hung from the poles, separating the large, open space into smaller private areas. Two [Healers] were tending to a man with burns along the side of his body. Three more surrounded a woman bleeding from a wound on her leg. Something stuck out from the center of where the blood poured.

Orrin wasted no time and cast [Decrease Strength] and [Decrease Will] several times in rapid succession. All five [Healers] were on the ground as Brandt moved forward, tearing the sheets from their frames. Orrin hit four more [Healers] working on patients.

"What are you doing? Who are you?" the burned man shouted, trying to stand. His shiny skin stretched and cracked. The movement caused too much pain and he stumbled.

Orrin caught him and slapped a [Heal Small Wounds] into the man's side, focusing on the first two layers of skin. Two more casts and the cracks smoothed out. The blood and pus were still there, but no new liquids emerged.

"You're healed. Get out of here," Orrin ordered, turning to the bleeding woman. "This is going to hurt."

He ripped the piece of . . . pottery? No, it was a clay roof shingle . . . out of the lady's leg and healed her until the wound closed. "You, too. It isn't safe in here."

Orrin cast [Identify] on the rest of the patients, checking for major injuries. Nobody else was in immediate danger, so he pointed to the door. "The clinic is closed. Time to leave."

Nobody argued. Brandt and Madi continued to pull the sheets back as they worked their way to the back of the warehouse, but it seemed as though the Hospital members stuck to the front.

"There," Brandt said, not bothering to whisper. The sounds of a few patients' screaming likely alerted anyone they were coming. He pointed with his sword at a set of double doors.

Orrin cast his wards, saving [Camouflage Ward] until last. Brandt took hold of one door handle and Daniel grabbed the other. They pulled, slightly out of time with each other, and Madi cast another blinding spell into the room beyond.

Orrin stormed in a moment later, opening his eyes. He watched three figures in white robes manhandling a taller, hooded man toward a black door in the back wall. The man fought back, but his hands were tied behind his back.

I thought there was no back door, Orrin thought with a frown as he hit the three robed Hospital members with [Decrease Strength]. One resisted and ran toward the door. The other two slumped. The hooded man swung his elbows, clocking one of the falling bodies in the head.

"Mr. Fallah?" Orrin shouted as he ran toward the man. "Amir sent me. It's Orrin from the coffee shop."

Without someone holding his arms, Mr. Fallah bent and shook his head. The hood fell off, but a gag was tied around his mouth. He shouted into the balled-up cloth and nodded toward the door. The other goon had almost gotten away.

"Don't worry," Orrin said, turning Mr. Fallah and trying to reach up to grab the gag. "There are guards coming. They won't get far. Let's get—"

"Orrin, get down!" Madi screamed.

Orrin reached his arms around Amir's dad and twisted, pulling them both to the ground. Something hit him hard in the back and against the legs, but his wards protected him from most of the damage. Before he could turn his head, the room lit up with twisting colors of light, and a scream of pain died out as quickly as it started.

"One down," Brandt yelled. "It's an illegal [Portal]. More might come through at any time. We need to regroup and retreat."

Orrin rolled away from Mr. Fallah and stood. Swords of ice and fire erupted from his hands. "Like hell, we're retreating. I'm going through."

Daniel stepped in front of Orrin and held him back. "Orrin, calm down. We need you here. Quick—"

"No, I'm tired of bad guys escaping."

Daniel reached down and yanked. An ice lance the size of a baseball bat ripped out of Orrin's thigh.

Orrin blinked.

"Where did that come from?"

"You look like a porcupine, Orrin. Mr. Fallah looks worse. You need to heal him and yourself. We'll watch the door. Are you okay? How are you still standing?"

Brandt wiped his blade against the woman who'd come out of the black doorway. The ground around her was polished and reflective like ice, but it wasn't melting. The other robed figure had escaped. Now that he had a moment, Orrin felt the magic coming off the door. It felt similar to his [Teleport] spell, but only slightly.

"Orrin, it's healing time. Half of his leg is hanging off." Daniel slapped Orrin's face gently to get his attention. He grabbed Orrin by the shoulders and turned him slowly. "You both got hit hard."

Orrin had blocked most of the ice lances with his body, but a few got through. Mr. Fallah had several smaller, railroad spike–size ice daggers stuck in his side, and one of the larger lances had gone through his leg right above the knee. There was too much blood on the floor. *Why isn't the ice melting?*

Orrin felt cold. [Mind Bastion] had triggered when he got hit, which scared him. He was better at controlling the skill, but it still sneaked through his mental barriers when he was scared or hurt enough. He glanced down. His blood was pouring out now, too. *Did that mage hit something important? I should be invincible with all my wards.*

"Orrin? Heal yourself. Now!" Daniel shouted, but to Orrin, he was whispering from the other side of a tunnel.

"Oh, it's not ice. It's glass," Orrin muttered as his leg gave out and he fell to a knee. "Shit."

Darkness crept along the edges of his vision. "This isn't good."

Chapter 34

Orrin was in shock. His health points weren't particularly low, but something about the attack left him unable to form complete thoughts as he bled out. A [Heal Small Wounds] on a couple of the bigger glass lances would make him whole, but things weren't working as they should. Daniel saved the day, like always.

"Stay with me." Daniel squatted down and examined Orrin. He touched two of the bigger shards of glass sticking out of Orrin's back before noticing a medium-size spike to the left of his spine. It was smaller than some of the other wounds but went directly into Orrin's heart, based on the length. "This might hurt."

Orrin screamed when Daniel wrenched the glass from his back. Daniel used the opportunity to pour a health potion from Orrin's belt down his open mouth. Orrin coughed and choked, but his HP refilled.

The darkness in his eyes cleared. He tried to stand. "Thanks. That's better."

Daniel raised an eyebrow and held his shoulder, keeping him down. "You have another twenty glass rods sticking out of your back and legs, Orrin. Heal yourself first. If you go down, we don't have another [Healer] nearby."

Orrin reached to his leg and pulled one of the glass lances out of his calf. The pain was dulled due to [Mind Bastion], but the sickening sucking sound was enough to turn his stomach. He cast [Heal Small Wounds], directing the mana into the gaping wound. "Help me pull them out. I have to help Mr. Fallah."

"Madi gave him a health potion. He'll be fine for now. Keep still. This is disgusting."

Orrin felt the pressure of each wound filling with blood as Daniel pulled the glass from his back. He targeted a healing spell into each laceration, but none hurt like the first had. "What was different about the one you pulled out first?"

Daniel made a heaving noise as he had to twist a smaller glass rod that was stuck between two ribs. "What? This is so gross, O. Do you mean the one I took from your leg or the one in your heart?"

Orrin contemplated. *The lance he yanked from my leg didn't hurt. It must have been the one in my heart. It doesn't make sense why that one hurt even through [Mind Bastion], though.*

"You're doing the thing where you ignore me, aren't you?" Daniel said, talking fast. His friend was nervous and scared. It had been a while since Orrin took a hit this bad. "It's okay. I get it. If I grew a bunch of spikes all over my body, I'd want to stay quiet, too. I've got most of the big ones out, so if you want to try and heal Mr. Fallah, you probably could. Let me help you walk, though. Those scars on your leg are closed, but I can still see scabs."

"Daniel. I'm fine. Calm down." Orrin got to his feet and gingerly tested his weight on the leg that had taken most of the projectiles. "I'm not overhealing myself yet. The holes were bigger than a normal cut or stab wound, so it takes more mana to close it up. I'll get to it after I see to Amir's dad."

Maybe the mage got lucky and my heart is my critical weakness. Orrin remembered the time Madi got hit in the head by a snowball-throwing ape. She'd gone down hard and fast. His foot felt fine, so Orrin walked to where Madi had dragged the unconscious man they'd come to rescue.

"How is he?" Orrin asked, even as he pulled up the man's stats. "Whoa."

Qaasim Fallah	Shadow Alchemist Level 41	Status: fatigued, dizzy
HP: 70/210	MP: 254/280	
Strength: 14	Constitution: 21	Dexterity: 16
Will: 28	Intelligence: 23	

"What's a [Shadow Alchemist]?" Orrin muttered. "Damn, he got hit hard, too. I thought I protected him with my body."

Orrin used [Diagnose] as well and sighed as the list populated: puncture wounds, perforated kidney, shattered femur, and sepsis.

Madi used her sleeve to wipe the sweat from the man's brow. "He's twice your size, Orrin. I gave him a healing potion, but he's sweating and his breath is fast and shallow. He doesn't seem to know where he is, either."

Orrin nodded and began to pull the glass shards from Mr. Fallah's side. "That's probably the sepsis. I thought it took longer than a few minutes after an injury to happen."

He alternated casting [Heal Small Wounds] and [Purify]. The fatigued and dizzy statuses disappeared. *They drugged him,* Orrin realized. He worked a long bar of glass out of Qaasim's side and pushed the mana into where he remembered the kidney should be.

"Please work," Orrin said under his breath. "Daniel, take hold of the thick rod of glass in his knee. Pull it out slowly. I think the glass is messing with the healing. I can't get rid of his sepsis."

Orrin let out a sigh of relief when the perforated kidney diagnosis went away. He followed up with another [Purify] and sepsis also disappeared. Daniel pulled once and Mr. Fallah cried out.

"Orrin, it's stuck pretty tight. I'm going to twist it." Daniel grabbed hold with both hands. "Madi, hold his shoulders down."

The glass scraped on bone, like nails on a chalkboard, as Daniel removed it. Orrin saw the floor through the hole in Qaasim's leg for a moment before blood filled the massive puncture wound. He kept healing the leg.

"Orrin, that is a big injury," Madi said with a tone in her voice that Orrin did not like. He hated the following sentence even more. "People don't survive something like this. We need to get him to the Hospital."

"He's unconscious and I can't [Teleport] him unless he wakes up," Orrin stated. He had used almost seven hundred points of mana closing the other wounds as he worked on the fist-size hole directly above Qassim's knee. "I can do it."

Brandt was guarding the black door with his sword. He turned as he heard shouting from the front room. "Back here. Send for [Healers]."

The room filled with Catanzano guards. One of them slipped in a pool of blood Orrin had left behind, but another caught him under the arms before he fell. The woman holding her colleague up glanced around. "I thought the [Healers] were the troublemakers. What happened here, sir?"

"Unsanctioned [Portal] set up in the clinic. You need to get a message to Lord Tarris. He'll know how to track this, but they could close it at any minute."

Orrin listened with half an ear as he yelled at his magic. "Come on. Work, damn it."

The femur wouldn't knit back together. Without the base, Mr. Fallah's leg muscles and skin wouldn't grow back like they normally would. The blood kept pouring out.

"Orrin, he's looking pale," Daniel said softly. "I don't think you can save his leg."

Ignoring Daniel, Orrin didn't respond. He turned on blood cycling and pushed even more mana at the problem.

"Orrin, Listen to me, Orrin. You have to stop."

"Daniel's right. Please."

Orrin focused on the wound. He'd promised Amir his father would be okay. He would not break that promise.

Blood sprayed as Daniel's blade severed Mr. Fallah's leg midthigh. The man screamed. Blood vessels in his eyes popped before he slumped back to the ground, unconscious from the pain.

"What did you do?" Orrin screamed even as he started healing the stump. The skin and muscles grew with ease, and the bleeding from the main body stopped. The missing leg still leaked. Orrin stood up and shoved Daniel hard. "Why did you do that?"

"Orrin, it was the only way to save his life. Sometimes magic isn't enough." Madi tried to get between them but Orrin used [Way of the Water] to duck under her and push Daniel again. "Mr. Fallah needs to be moved. They could still attack."

Orrin wiped blood from his face and pointed at Daniel. "This isn't over."

Daniel had a resigned look on his face. "I saved his life. You weren't healing him; you were prolonging his death."

A shout captured their attention. One of the guards near the [Portal] poked the wall with a spear. "It disappeared."

The magical black doorway was gone.

"Mewes and Dankin," Brandt snapped, and two guards saluted at attention. "Secure the prisoners up front and transport them to prison. Have a [Message] sent to leadership and tell them what happened.

Send another to Elder Kali or Seif. We're heading back to the Hospital and they better have a bed ready for the man their [Healers] captured."

The guards nodded and left the room at a fast clip. Brandt walked over to Orrin. "Deal with the present, not with the past. Mr. Fallah needs us now. Can you get him conscious?"

Orrin grimaced but nodded. "I think so. He's probably in pain. I can [Numb] his leg. Probably should have done that first anyway."

Orrin used his spell on Qaasim's leg before casting three more [Heal Small Wounds] generally over his body. A groggy groan emerged from the man's lips.

"Mr. Fallah, it's Orrin. I'm Amir's friend, remember?" Orrin said in a calm voice. "We're going to bring you to the Hospital. I need you to—"

"No Hospital. I will not betray my son." Qaasim's voice, though weak, remained calm and patient as ever.

"Neither will I," Orrin said while checking over his status again. His health was nearly full. "I'll stay with you the entire time. We need a [Healer] to check you over. I'm not trained for this."

"Amir will care for me. He's a good boy. Bring me home."

Orrin peered up at Madi, who shrugged. "How far is your home from the coffee shop?"

Brandt and Daniel stooped under Mr. Fallah's shoulder to help him walk. Despite the [Portal] working inside the clinic, Orrin's [Teleport] still remained off-line. Once they were in front of the building, Orrin jumped them to the burned-out remains of the Fallah café.

"Father!" Amir ran toward them. The sun was well and truly down now, with a few magical torches along the street giving enough light for them to be recognized. Amir halted when he saw the missing leg. "What did they do to you?"

"What did they do to our shop?" Qaasim asked in answer. He unstrung his arms from around the taller two members of Orrin's group and hopped toward the charred door frame of his store. "Did the seals in the storeroom hold?"

Tears ran down Amir's face as he grinned at his father. "The storage spells kept the fire out. The piping is melted and the side door is fused with the wall, but we only lost the hoppers, grinders, and presses. We have the backups at home. What happened to your leg?"

Qaasim wavered with each jump but made his way to the entrance on his own. He whistled at the destruction inside. "Those fools burned everything to a crumble, but we will rebuild."

"A crisp," Amir whispered. He closed the gap and hugged his father from behind. "I was worried. I'm so sorry."

Mr. Fallah pulled his son around, hugging him back and using him as a crutch at the same time. "Sorry? You did not do this. Bad men did."

"It's all my fault," Amir cried.

Orrin and his party stood quietly. Orrin felt his rage building again.

"No," Qaasim said sternly, holding Amir at a distance. "Look me in my eyes. Evil strives to lay its wickedness at your feet. You, my son, are not wicked. Helping others is noble. You have your mother's heart. Be strong like her and fight evil wherever it treads. Do not let their actions burden you."

Amir hugged his father again. Orrin's anger evaporated at the display of familial love in front of him, but a small part of him felt envy. He could barely remember his father's hugs.

Daniel coughed politely. "Amir, he didn't want to go to the Hospital. They might be able to do something about his leg."

Amir turned his head from his father's chest but didn't let go. "We'll be fine. Thank you, Daniel. Thank you all. Orrin, I'm sorry for—"

Orrin waved his hand. "Nothing to apologize for. I'll come by for some coffee in a few days once you're open again." He turned to Brandt. "Can we get some guards to watch over them for a bit?"

Brandt nodded. "I handpicked three that I trust."

"Orrin?" Amir said, catching his attention. "Friends still, right?"

Orrin gave a goofy smile. "You gave me coffee, Amir. Friends forever."

Chapter 35

Orrin watched the Fallah men close the door to their home, only a few blocks from their café. Brandt talked with three guards, some of whom Orrin recognized from their mission to save Daniel what felt like forever ago. Orrin cast a few rounds of [Heal Small Wounds] on himself, making the scabbed-over skin across his arm and leg fade.

Daniel leaned over and whispered a question to Madi, his voice low enough that Orrin couldn't hear him.

"No, Daniel. I'm not letting you and Orrin go searching for the ones that got away. We still have a Horde of demons on our doorstep. We should all be sleeping right now." Madi crossed her arms. "In fact, I'm going to tell Brandt his shift is done for tonight as well. Don't move, you two."

As she crossed the street to yell at her bodyguard, Orrin glanced awkwardly at Daniel. The [Hero] ran his fingers through his hair and acted like he didn't notice.

"Sorry I freaked out when you cut the leg off," Orrin said in a rush, tripping over his words.

"Forget it." Daniel's voice was cold.

"D?"

"Hmm?"

"I didn't know what to do and you made the right call. Seriously, dude. Sorry."

Daniel's shoulders stretched up as he took a deep breath. "I'm not stupid, but you treat me like I am. It's hurtful. You get fixated on one path and refuse to budge or see other options. You have to listen to me more."

Orrin knew that he could get hyperfocused but didn't think it was fair to say he didn't budge. He accepted Daniel's advice all the time. That wasn't the issue here, though. Daniel felt ignored. *We've been treat-*

ing him with kid gloves because of the demons and his urge to kill them, but he is still the [Hero].

"I'll do better. If I don't, you have my permission to knock some sense into me," Orrin tried with a grin.

Daniel chuckled. "That would take too much work."

Madi watched them both as she returned. "Good, you two made up. Let's go to my house. We can rest the night there and [Teleport] back to the Wall in the morning."

"Actually, I was hoping we could go to the Hospital," Orrin said timidly. "I wanted to ask a question about healing magic, and they kind of owe me one right now."

Madi rubbed her eyes with her fingers. "How did you get to that conclusion?"

Daniel answered for him. "We did just expose an entire ring of corruption within their ranks."

"If you think the elders of the Hospital will roll over and answer questions for an outsider like you, Orrin . . ."

Orrin held up his hands. "Hear me out before you say no. I want to ask if they know a way to regrow Mr. Fallah's leg. I doubt Amir would let one of them do it, but if we sold it to the Hospital as a step in mending their relationship with him, they might tell me which path to take. I could unlock it myself."

Madi's smile didn't reach her eyes. "The Hospital doesn't heal lost limbs or permanent injuries."

"There has to be a—"

"No, Orrin. If my father couldn't convince the [Healers] to fix his spine, what makes you think they know a way to regrow a leg? There are many soldiers who lost limbs today. Brandt lost his fingers and it took three [Healers] working together two full days to grow them back, but they'll never be as functional as his original digits. It's the way magic works."

Madi was tired, but the way she snapped told Orrin this issue wasn't one to pursue with her. *It makes sense. If the Hospital denies there is a way, it wouldn't be worth doing. If they said there was a spell, they'd have been lying to Lord Catanzano. Either way, Madi loses.*

"Thanks, Madi. I didn't know," Orrin said with a smile. Internally, he considered sneaking out later. If the Horde wasn't around, along with the rogue [Healers], he might have. Instead, he jumped his party back to the Catanzano manor and followed Daniel to their room.

Orrin let Daniel shower first while he healed the scars remaining on his body. He also searched the store in his blue box screen while he waited his turn, hoping to find a healing spell he'd yet to buy. The elven leader of healing, Lyra, had told him once that selecting [Heal Moderate Wounds] would lock out other options. He'd accepted her advice and bought [Diagnose], a skill like [Identify] that let him see the problems a person had from the system's perspective. He'd also purchased [Purify], [Calm], [Numb], and [Excise].

I have [Calm Mind] and [Calm], Orrin pondered as he looked over his status. *Shouldn't that be the same thing?* He pulled up each spell in turn.

> **[Calm Mind]—Negates mind magic to a degree. Calms the target, reducing stress, anger, or sadness. Increases peacefulness and allows logical thoughts. 5 MP**

One of the first spells Orrin bought upon arrival, [Calm Mind] was a lifesaver. Without it, Daniel would have taken longer to acclimate. Orrin's [Mind Bastion] helped keep him steady most of the time, but those first few days required a few castings of [Calm Mind] on his friend. He pulled up [Calm].

> **[Calm]—Calms the target. 5 MP**

Orrin read the two descriptions, back and forth. "It's the same thing."

Daniel walked into the room wearing only shorts and rubbing a towel on his wet hair. "Your turn."

"D, can I try something on you?"

Daniel covered his chest with his towel. "Orrin, I like you as a friend but . . ."

Orrin grabbed a nearby pillow and threw it at his friend. "Don't be an ass. I realized I have two spells that are the exact same thing, [Calm Mind] and [Calm]."

Daniel dodged the pillow with ease and grabbed a shirt from his dresser drawer. He pulled it over his head. "And? That's the one you always cast on someone when they're flipping out, right?"

"[Calm Mind] is," Orrin answered, gathering up some clean clothes for his shower. He made sure to grab a shirt. Daniel was muscular and vain enough to walk down the hallway topless, but Orrin felt it was disrespectful . . . and he wasn't as comfortable being half-naked where anyone could see him. "I've never used [Calm] before."

"Why'd you buy it, then?" Daniel snorted as he crawled into bed. He fluffed two pillows and pushed them against the backboard. "That's not like you."

"[Calm] is one of the healing spells Lyra, the elven healer lady, told me might open other healing spells."

Daniel's pause was slight, but Orrin caught it. "You're trying to buy something to regrow Mr. Fallah's leg, aren't you?"

Orrin ignored the obvious statement and continued. "I haven't used most of the spells she told me to get. Actually, other than trying [Numb] once or twice, I haven't used [Excise] or [Calm]. [Purify] comes in handy when I accidentally overbuff someone but it still hasn't unlocked anything else."

"What do you want, Orrin?" Daniel asked in his get-on-with-it-already voice. "I need to get to sleep."

"Can I cast [Calm] on you?" Orrin gave him a wide, fake smile. "Please?"

Daniel rolled his eyes. "Yeah, whatever. It might take this headache away—woww . . ." His voice turned drowsy.

Orrin had cast it as soon as Daniel said yes. "What happened?"

"S'like I just got a massage and drank chamomile tea while floating on a cloud. Oh, this is my new favorite spell." Daniel closed his eyes. "Can you throw a blanket over me? I don't wanna move."

Orrin tucked his friend in and collected his things. Daniel was snoring lightly before he turned off the light and left for his shower. *[Calm] must relax the body while [Calm Mind] calms the . . . mind. Duh.*

Using the spell hadn't opened up any new possibilities for Orrin. He kept a running list of possible [Merge] spells as well. If he combined [Heal Small Wounds] and [Split Spell], he would make [Healing

Hands]. The new spell would heal a few health points for every person he touched at once. Nothing that would help Qaasim's missing leg.

A few minutes later, Orrin leaned against the cold stone wall while the hot water poured over his head. The Catanzano showers made fighting the demons worth it. Orrin sighed and rubbed a stiff muscle in his shoulder from overextending a sword thrust. His fighting was getting better, but he had a long way to go before he stopped injuring himself. Luckily a pulled muscle was within his healing range. The phantom stiffness remained for a bit, though.

Orrin closed his eyes and sighed. He should go to sleep, but he needed to train, too. The shower was the perfect opportunity as well.

> **[Way of the Water] 40% 8/20 completed.**
> **Continue?**

Orrin mentally clicked and opened his eyes in Styx's training room. "Hey, my man. How are you doing?"

Styx, a figure of pure water that sloshed with each movement, inclined his head in welcome before sitting on the floor with his legs crossed under him.

"Oh, come on. This again?"

The last time Orrin trained in [Way of the Water], Styx made him turn a drop of water into a thread that stretched between his hands. It wasn't real water . . . and it wasn't mana, either, but his "sensei" refused to tell him what it was.

It might be hard for him to talk using only one-word responses, though, Orrin reflected.

Styx summoned the drop of not-water between his hands and waited.

"How does this help with fighting?" Orrin complained as he sat down. It took him about ten seconds to remember how to make the little bead appear. "Maybe if I fight a fire elemental or something. I can splash them to death."

Styx sighed. He didn't breathe and Orrin didn't know how he did it, but the nonhuman person of water sighed.

Orrin narrowed his eyes. "Don't get sassy with me, Styx. What are we doing today? Tie the water needle into a pretty bow?"

Styx moved his hands like a dancer at a rave. The water drop split into two thin cords that tied into a complex knot.

"Holy shit, I was making a joke. Is that really the lesson?" Orrin surprised himself with his genius.

Styx shook his head and concentrated. The bead of water rippled and then grew from the size of an eraser tip into a marble. The marble bulged to the size of a small orange before stopping around a soccer ball–size sphere of water.

"Styx, were you messing with me? Do I need to shout, 'Kamehameha'?"

Styx shrugged and flexed his arms like he was pushing the water together. The large ball of water compressed again into a pea. "EXPAND. CONTRACT."

Orrin's water evaporated as he lost concentration. "Did you just speak two different words? Dude, we can almost converse now. I've been dying to know. When I'm not here, what happens to you? Do you keep training or do you have a nice bucket you sleep in?"

Styx ignored him. Orrin spent some time relearning how to feel the water and stretch it out. Once he felt the drop moving like it was a part of him, he practiced stretching it. He couldn't separate it into two threads like Styx had with his mockery of Orrin's idea, but he did figure out how to inflate the water a bit. It stretched and reached almost double its size before it popped.

"I'm getting it!" Orrin exclaimed. It was rare that he got one of Styx's lessons so quickly and—

"NO."

Styx brought the bead of water up and grew it again. This time, he split the orb in two so Orrin could see inside. It was completely full, with no air or stretching of the bead. Styx simply summoned more of the water.

"Oh, that shouldn't be hard," Orrin grouched. "Just summon more of the mystery water. Not a problem."

He learned it wasn't hard to summon more of the water mana now that he knew how. The problem was controlling the increased volume. Orrin could handle up to a large marble of the stuff, maybe half a cup of liquid. Any more than that and the bubble popped, leaving Orrin to start again.

After what might have been an hour in training time, Orrin was sweating. Constantly focusing on the water calmed him like meditation at first, but soon the exhaustion sneaked in.

Orrin almost gave up and left but felt his stubbornness kick into high gear. "Today, I was supposed to create a distraction to save a bunch of people. I didn't hit my target number of demons and they are dead. I got caught in a fight with someone and he wasted our time. Then I wasn't able to save a friend. Well, I did save him, but not all of him."

Orrin continued sharing with Styx, even though the watery figure never responded. It felt nice to vent a bit. "I have to wake up tomorrow and make more spell orbs. Do you know what spell orbs are? Of course you do. You're probably some ancient being of knowledge. I need to sleep and I have a hundred things I have to do, but right now, I'm going to get this stupid . . . ball . . . of water . . . to grow."

Orrin gritted his teeth and pushed harder. He ignored the fatigue and weariness as he continued trying. When Styx started this exercise, Orrin simply had to use his energy to hold water between his hands. When the exercises upgraded, Orrin realized it wasn't water he held but some sort of mana. It was an extension of himself, and with some effort, Orrin tried to push more of his own energy into the drop. The orb grew a little bigger until it was the size of a closed fist. Orrin smiled.

The ball exploded into a rain of mana that disappeared before it touched him.

"Damn it."

Chapter 36

Orrin gave up after an hour of training with poor results. He could make the drop grow but only to half the size Styx wanted. He didn't even get to attempt compressing the water mana.

While in the training hall of [Way of the Water], time acted differently. Although he spent an hour with Styx, Orrin knew he was still standing in the shower back in his body with little time passing. He could spend another hour or two trying the exercise, but his frustration at failing over and over was hindering his concentration and he knew it.

"Styx, my buddy, I'm going to hit the hay," Orrin said as he stood and wiped his hands on his pants. "I'll practice each night from now on, I promise."

The watery form undulated, his entire body flowing into a standing position. Styx gave a formal bow to Orrin. "PRACTICE."

"Back to one-word responses, huh?"

Styx didn't respond.

Orrin rolled his eyes and waved before quitting the training session. He didn't get the level-up prompt, which sucked. However, the warm water still raining on his back made him sigh in relief. While he didn't really leave when he trained [Way of the Water], his body did get sore from sitting in that position for so long. Or maybe it was the way his body clenched up while his consciousness was elsewhere. Either way, Orrin rolled his neck in the hot water.

He turned off the magical switches in the bathroom and was toweling off when he heard the pleading screams from inside the house.

"Nooo!"

Orrin wrapped the towel around his waist and ran. His wards popped back to life as he refreshed any that had dropped off and [Camouflage] rolled over him like a fog. The bathroom was in the middle of the upper hallway of the Catanzano house, with Orrin and Daniel's room at the far end. The screams came from one of the other rooms that Orrin had never been in. Madi's door was wide-open, but he couldn't see her inside.

"PLEASE!"

That was Brandt.

Orrin cast [Gust], pushing up dust that the maids had missed as he practically flew over the wooden floors. He didn't try to slow himself and grabbed the door frame to swing into the room, both swords summoned in his hands as he dropped into a crouch ready to fight.

"Shhh. Wake up, Brandt. You're safe." Madi sat on the edge of Brandt's bed. The [Knight] was asleep, covered in sweat, and thrashing in his sheets.

A nightmare, Orrin realized, throwing his eyes over every corner of the room to make sure. Brandt's room was tidy. His armor hung on a wooden dummy, and his sword rested on a counter near his bed. A painting of a forest with a deer hiding between the trees hung opposite the door. A few dressers and a desk lined the walls. Orrin noticed a small oval frame with a picture of Madi on a cleared portion of Brandt's desk.

"Orrin?" Madi whispered, squinting in the dark. "What are you doing in here? I thought you were asleep."

"I heard screaming."

Madi whipped back around, her back straight. "Orrin . . . your towel."

He looked down. The knot he'd tied was loose. The towel hadn't fallen off yet, but there was a lot of thigh showing. He blushed furiously and dismissed his swords, grabbing the fabric and cinching it back together. "Sorry. I was in the shower."

Brandt moaned and rocked in the bed.

"What's wrong with him?" Orrin dared not enter the room more than he had. His nakedness and the intimacy of Madi wearing her silk pajamas in Brandt's room was not lost on him. "Did something happen?"

Madi kept her back to Orrin. "He's been having nightmares since we returned from Odrana . . . about the things they did to him. The [Healer] said trauma like this needs time more than anything else. There's nothing I can do to help him."

Madi held Brandt's sheets tightly in her fists. "I can't even wake him half the time. It's getting worse."

Orrin used [Identify] and [Diagnose] on Brandt, but neither gave him anything odd. He was having a nightmare, that much was obvious from his whimpers and tossing, but nothing the system thought pertinent enough to list as a status effect.

"I used the spell [Calm] on Daniel earlier and he fell asleep. I could use it on Brandt," Orrin offered.

Madi looked back, a glimmer of hope in her eyes before she turned back away. "It can't hurt. Thank you, Orrin."

Orrin cast both [Calm] and [Calm Mind] on Brandt, hoping the combination would help. Brandt's breathing slowed. He reached up and pulled Madi into his arms. She let herself get snuggled into small spoon.

"Um, Orrin. You can leave," Madi's mortified voice muttered.

He backed out and closed the door, but not before he heard Madi's low voice again. "Brandt, behave."

Orrin returned to the bathroom and got dressed. He crawled into bed as Daniel snored across the room and tried to list all the things he needed to do the following day.

Orrin woke up and spent thirty minutes creating spell orbs filled with various levels of buffs. He sat in his bed, making piles of the glass balls.

"Morning," Daniel yawned and sat back against his headboard. "Damn. How long have you been working?"

Orrin looked at the stacks of buff balls. "Not even an hour. Silas will be happy. I have about a hundred of each type."

Daniel stretched and cracked his neck. "I'll help carry them. I slept great last night. I might have you cast [Calm] every day."

Orrin began pushing the stacks into an empty pillowcase. The glass tinkled as they rolled inside. He pushed the entire makeshift bag into his [Dimension Hole]. "I've got it, don't worry."

Daniel jumped out of bed and started pulling on his armor. "Leave a few [Increase Will] and [Increase Intelligence] to the side, would you?"

"Huh? Why?" Orrin complied but looked askance at his friend. "You don't need these. I'll boost you with Madi and Brandt after we eat breakfast."

"I was thinking about what you said last night. You have all these healing spells but don't use them. You're too busy fighting to experiment, and I had an idea," Daniel explained as he tied his bracers on. "Let Amir do it."

Orrin followed Daniel's line of thought perfectly but hesitated. "He's already a [Healer] but still leveling up [Heal Small Wounds]. If I point him toward the other skills, he can purchase them as well. He already spends his days healing people, so it's a win-win. Giving him some buffs that he can use when he needs them would let him cast more spells and level them up faster. It's smart, but he should probably stay quiet for a while after yesterday."

"I disagree," Daniel said as he jogged in place and then readjusted one of his leg armor buckles. "If he doesn't go out and continue work as usual, the bad guys will think they won. He's got some guards with him now. Maybe we can have Silas set up a clinic for him. Not to compete with the Hospital, just to take care of anyone overlooked."

Orrin finished storing the majority of the orbs and began to get dressed himself. "It's a good idea, Daniel. I just don't know if Silas will go for it. He has to play both sides and keep the Hospital from going on strike."

"Leave him to me." Daniel smiled as he lifted Gertrude in the air and swung her once before slapping her on his back.

Silas wasn't at breakfast when they went downstairs five minutes later. Brandt was making two plates from the smaller array of foodstuff that lined the table. Horde rationing had been implemented.

"Hey, Brandt," Daniel said, grabbing a plate as he joined the man at the tiny buffet. "Dude, Orrin got this new spell and it makes you sleep like a baby. It's like the best flu medicine sleep of your life."

"I'm not sure I understand everything you just said." Brandt smiled as Daniel grabbed a handful of bacon. "But Madi told me I should thank you, Orrin. You did something to help me sleep?"

Orrin blushed and moved so he was standing with Daniel between them. "Yeah. [Calm] spell. I guess it helps knock you out."

Daniel studied Orrin. "Why are you red?"

"No reason. Just hot from running down the stairs," Orrin muttered. He piled food on his plate as quickly as possible and set his breakfast down. He moved to grab the coffee, but Daniel snatched it up.

"No coffee until you answer me." Daniel held the pot out of Orrin's reach.

Orrin cast [Decrease Strength] multiple times but slowly. When Daniel frowned, Orrin caught the handle of the coffeepot right before it slipped from the [Hero]'s hand.

"Not fair," Daniel slurred as he sank in his seat. "Fix me."

Orrin poured the beautiful liquid into a mug and sat back in his chair. "Whatever do you mean, sir?"

"Orrin, stop messing with Daniel," Madi ordered as she walked into the dining room. "We have our orders for the day. The demons were up at dawn building more ladders. They're going to make another push at the Wall. We'll meet the same place we did and rendezvous with Crius."

Orrin cast [Increase Strength] on Daniel until he was back to normal before asking, "Why would they do that? They didn't make any headway yesterday, right?"

Madi accepted the plate from Brandt and smiled kindly up at him. "Thank you." She sat down with the two young men and answered Orrin but didn't look him in the eyes. "I don't know how demons think. They did some damage but nothing that we couldn't fix overnight. The losses are firmly in our favor. It doesn't make sense, but we have to react to what we know."

They ate quickly and Orrin poured another cup of coffee. He would steal the mug for the day and return it later if he remembered. "Time to buff up?"

"It's so weird to hear you say something like that when you're still so scrawny," Daniel joked.

"I could say, 'It's buffing time' or—"

"No. No." Daniel waved his hands. "Time to buff up. Let's go."

Orrin increased his intelligence and wisdom a small bit before casting [Utility Ward] on his teammates. The number was slightly higher than yesterday, as neither Madi nor Brandt had shown negative effects from their buffs. He checked that the math worked right and then nodded at Daniel.

"Kick them."

Madi and Brandt were removed from their party and Orrin maxed out his spell stats. Another [Utility Ward] brought him and Daniel to one hundred. "Invite them back."

The morning routine to maximize their stats was quicker now than the first time they'd done it. Orrin also had a better idea of how much extra strength Brandt or intelligence Madi could handle. They had to leave the party so Orrin could use his all-day buff [Utility Ward] on just him and Daniel, giving them the full use of maxed-out stats.

Orrin pulled a glass ball from his pocket. "Daniel had an idea. I'm going to give a few of these to Amir so he can heal more and try a few things for me. I made more for your dad, too."

Madi's refusal to look at him was becoming more obvious. "That's fine. Do you want us to come with you or should we meet you at the Wall? I think Jack and Jillian are around."

"Neither of them can [Teleport] you more than ten miles," Orrin said. "Just come with us."

Daniel narrowed his eyes. "Madi . . . what's going on with you and Orrin?"

"Nothing," they answered at the same time. Orrin blushed again.

Brandt chuckled. "Orrin came into my room last night. Madi told me I was having a nightmare and screaming. He cast a spell and helped me sleep but I . . . sort of kept Madi there."

"Kept her where?" Daniel asked puzzled. "Why would that make Orrin blush?"

"I pulled her into my bed," Brandt said with a slight blush of his own. "I guess Orrin left after that. I'm sorry you had to see me like that, Orrin."

Orrin muttered and took a big sip of his coffee.

Madi sighed. "He's not embarrassed about that, Brandt. They know we . . . about us."

Brandt shrugged. "I've never tried to hide it."

"He's red because you screamed and he thought you were in trouble. He burst into your room, swords drawn—" Madi started.

"Super happy Madi was taking care of you already. Let's go," Orrin interrupted her. "Ready to [Teleport]?"

Madi smirked. "He was still wet from his shower. Daniel, I wouldn't call him scrawny if I were you."

"Maybe I will meet you guys at the Wall," Orrin stammered.

"Are you saying what I think you're saying?" Daniel asked gleefully.

"His towel almost fell to his knees."

"Next time I'm letting the assassins kill you all."

Chapter 37

After a quick visit to Amir's home, Orrin brought them back to the front line. Crius stood waiting for them under a small umbrella. His white robes were dirtier today, but his smile remained plastered on his face as the party approached him on the Wall.

"Good morning to you all on this hot and muggy day. I see the benefit of having a [Locationist] in your group is not wasted. I dream of my bath and a glass of brandy." Crius bowed; his spear leaned against the wall behind him.

"Good morning, Crius," Daniel replied as he advanced to the far side of the Wall. He inspected the enemy camp in the distance. "Any movement yet?"

"They are preparing for another attack, that much is certain." Crius sighed and rested back against his perch. "We don't know what they'll try this time, though."

The day before, fighters and mages had run the length of the Wall, delivering messages and bringing supplies to needed locations. Orrin realized how quiet it was today.

"Where is everybody?"

Crius yawned. "Anyone not needed is sleeping. We have tents set up behind us and a few small barracks assembled within the Wall itself. If the call is issued, the captains will have their men stationed within three minutes."

Madi joined Daniel at the Wall's edge and made a hand gesture in the air. She curled her fingers into circles and looked through an invisible spyglass.

"New spell?" Daniel asked.

"New application," Madi answered. "Do you see the south embankment where the fence is made of small trees?"

Daniel's eyes glinted as he used [Telescope]. "Where the three red smudges are pulling a dark smudge?"

Madi gave Daniel a look of such disdain that Orrin chuckled. "Can you not see that far?"

Daniel blinked and disengaged his ability. "I can see four times farther than normal, but I can't make out details that far away. Can you?"

Madi shrugged. "I guess my spells are better. Three demons are dragging a large dark sphere of some sort into place. I've found about a dozen of them up and down the line behind their fence."

Crius spoke with his eyes closed. "None of the scouts can make out what they are or where they're coming from. The demons bring them from the center of camp."

Brandt reached into a backpack of supplies he'd brought and pulled out a waterskin. He nudged Crius with it.

"I hope this is wine," Crius groaned with one eye open. He sipped daintily and smiled. "Still hot. Brandt, you dog. They refused to light any fires last night for us for fear we'd make easy targets. One [Fire Mage] tried to brew some using a heat spell and melted the metal coffee press."

Orrin's ears perked up. Brandt sighed.

"Yes, Orrin. I brought coffee. It's for the people who stood watch all night. If you wanted more, you should have brought some."

Orrin grinned and pulled a carafe out of his [Dimension Hole]. "I'm always prepared." He put it back.

Brandt grumbled something about checking on supplies and stomped down the stairs.

Crius drank and occasionally moved his lips like he was talking to someone but didn't leave his shadowy corner. Madi and Brandt pointed and talked about the demon camp. Orrin sat down and tried to summon the water droplet outside of the [Way of the Water] skill training.

It was harder with the noise and chaos around him, but in a few minutes Orrin got the water to move between his hands. It took more concentration to even start the training and he failed to make it grow. He was still at it when Daniel turned around.

"They're coming."

The second day of fighting started off the same as the first. Demons poured over the open plain separating their camp from the Wall as the defenders of Dey fired magic and arrows at the approaching Horde. Far fewer enemies fell as they approached.

"Commander, my arrows keep moving in the air," an archer nearby shouted.

Orrin waited for orders, but Crius informed them that the [Hero]'s party was being held in reserve for now. No ladder carts were spotted, and other than the troops, no attacks were sent their way.

Once the demons were almost to the Wall, Madi shouted, "One of the spheres just opened. A demon poked his head out but someone shoved him back in. They have people inside them."

"Why?" Brandt questioned with a confused and scrunched brow. "What are they doing?"

His question seemed to be the trigger, because a moment later, several dark shapes lifted up from the enemy camp and flew through the air. Orrin couldn't see what had launched the spheres, but as they curved in the air, he had a dark thought.

"Crius, are the tents behind the Wall still filled with people?" He ran up to the man.

Crius's mouth was open watching the falling projectiles. "Most of our day-rotation troops are awake and on the Wall."

"What about the people who kept watch all night?" Orrin pushed himself up on his toes to peer over the back edge. He could see a few tents below. "Those missiles might go right through the Wall."

Crius whispered to himself and shook his head. "The Wall is magically reinforced to withstand catapult shells. Our engineers are certain they can withstand the—"

"And if they're wrong? Look where those things are aiming. To me, it looks like they've aimed for sections of the Wall our men sleep behind."

Crius paled as he whispered. His magic let him talk to people all over the battlefield for real-time communication. He was essentially a human walkie-talkie. His voice, normally a whisper when using his skill, grew to full volume as he essentially shouted. ". . . care what they say. Get them away from the camps now."

Daniel drew Gertrude as he approached. "I think they are pulling a Trojan horse."

Orrin frowned. "Nobody is bringing one of those inside. Besides, anyone in one of those wouldn't survive the crash."

The first black spheres hit the ground in front of the Wall and bounced once before striking the stone exterior. The entire Wall trembled and quaked.

"Magic, Orrin." Daniel leaped to the top of the battlement and pointed. "It embedded itself in the Wall."

Orrin ran to the edge and glanced down. The dust cleared slowly and a cheer went up from the demons running their way. Several dark orbs stuck in the Wall but none had fully punched through.

"More incoming," someone shouted.

Movement caught Orrin's eye as lines carved themselves along the black embedded shells. Within moments, the perfect spheres were honeycombed with holes. A hand reached out from one cavity, and a demon pulled himself out and roared.

A yell rang out from up the Wall. "Attackers in the missiles."

Daniel gave Orrin a look. "I told you."

The next few minutes were the longest of Orrin's life. The strikes continued hitting the Wall for five minutes, giving the entire demon army time to reach their desired locations. Mages and archers waited a few hundred feet away while the fighters ran into the firing range. Some defenders focused on those running to them, while others cast spells at the pockmarked demon carriers.

Luckily, the engineers were mostly correct in their assessment. Only one ball made it through the Wall but landed nowhere near the tents. Of course, it was only a matter of luck that saved the sleeping soldiers.

Demons were falling out of an already-embedded ball when a second one struck it. The demons from the first wave exploded in a display of viscera that Orrin would not soon forget. The first ball was forced through completely while the second ricocheted away. It rolled over a few demons before coming to a stop.

[Stone Mages] rushed to fill the hole, and Orrin and Daniel helped keep the area clear of demons while they worked. Orrin dropped demons with his debuffs while Daniel cleaved more in two. Brandt followed Orrin with swift strikes and a twist of his blade to end any he could find until one of the mages turned the entire opening into a slide. The bodies poured out of the front of the Wall, and with a concentrated yell, the rest of the mages raised a temporary wall to cover the hole.

It took thirty minutes to fix the damage from that one attack.

Orrin and his friends continued to attack the demons from atop the Wall, but the attacking forces were better prepared on their second day. Several demons carried large shields that reflected spells. Orrin watched five demons run shoulder to shoulder and slam the pointed bottom of their shields into the Wall. The makeshift roof gave cover for those up front. When the fighters from Dey tried to attack, the demon archers and mages targeted them.

Orrin debuffed demons where he could. Madi sent floating balls of light that exploded. Daniel threw Gertrude like a spear, then waited for his sword to snap back to his hand. Not everyone had a long-range option. Brandt relegated himself to bringing arrows to the archers and carrying those injured that he could reach back down to the [Healers]' tent. Even with his increased strength, Brandt was soon sweating and huffing from running up and down the stairs so many times in his armor.

When the second group of shield-wielding demons jumped on top of the first shields, Orrin cursed.

"They're trying to climb the Wall one set of shields at a time," he said bitterly. He was angry because the shields blocked his debuffs, just like the firebolts and arrows.

"Crius, tell everyone to target the shield guys," Daniel yelled. "They're trying to climb up."

Not waiting for a response, Daniel grabbed Orrin's arm. "How fast can you [Teleport]?"

"What?"

Daniel's eyes widened in glee. He'd had the same look in his eyes when he convinced Orrin that building a ramp during their skateboarding phase would be fun. The ramp they'd placed at the end of a steep hill. *The bushes will cushion our landing,* he'd said.

"I'm going to pull an Orrin. [Teleport] down to the bottom and then jump me back up."

Orrin glared. "I do not like it when you do something stupid and call it 'an Orrin.' Whatever you're planning, don't do it. We can go through one of the hidden doors."

Daniel smiled. "This is going to be so fun it if works."

Madi stopped casting spells to look back. "What is he doing?"

"Stop him," Orrin shouted but Daniel was already moving.

"Geronimo!" Daniel screamed as he ran and threw himself off the edge of the Wall. He curled his feet into a cannonball position like he was diving into a pool.

"Daniel, no!" Madi reached for him but was too slow.

Orrin watched in horror. Daniel's hatred of the demons had finally made him snap. He fell normally through the air for a moment, then blurred. A concussion of air smacked up against the Wall. The wind pushed Orrin's hair back and burned his eyes.

He blinked tears free and stared.

The shields were gone.

The demons were gone, too.

Daniel sat curled in a pit filled with blood up to his chest. Pieces of floating meat bobbed up around him.

Orrin shouted at Crius to turn off the teleport ward. Two quick casts of [Teleport] and Orrin was back on the wall with his friend, shouting at a wide-eyed [Hero]. Daniel was soaked in red.

"Are you stupid? Why would you do that?"

"Now they won't try the shields again," Daniel said with a far-off look. "That worked better than I thought it would."

Madi pointed to a barrel, and Brandt tipped the entire container over Daniel. Water washed away some but not all of the blood, staining the floor around them. "What was that?" she demanded. "Don't ever do that again."

"I did what Orrin does: I had an idea and tried it." Daniel was still smiling, proud of himself. "I used [Gravity Strike] to hit harder and [Stone Skin] to protect myself. I turned on [White Dwarf] to make myself solid and [Shooting Star] to increase my speed. I made a Daniel rocket."

Madi turned on Orrin. "You are a bad influence on him. Control him better."

She stomped back to the edge and cast [Sunbeam], turning a group of charging demons into a screaming batch of bacon.

Orrin squinted at Brandt through the bright light. "I'm the bad influence?"

Chapter 38

In typical Daniel fashion, he was barely hurt. Orrin cast a few cure spells on him to be sure, but between the [Hero] ability that doubled his physical stats and the use of his skills, Daniel suffered only a few bruises from turning himself into a human wrecking ball.

After the demons' attempt at battering down the Wall, the attacks continued as they had the day before. A few demons were able to scale the stone to the top, but Dey's army stood waiting.

"I don't get it," Orrin muttered during a lull in the attacks. The demons would retreat and regroup between the camp and Wall every half hour. Only the best archers or mages with more mana to spare than sense could hit them with accuracy, so it became a welcome respite for everyone. "What are they trying to do here?"

Brandt finished drinking from his waterskin and wiped his mouth with the back of his hand. "What do you mean? They're trying to climb the Wall and kill us all."

Daniel stretched out on the ground, reaching his arms above his head as he tried to unkink his back. Throwing his massive sword down while hanging halfway over the Wall was taking a toll on him. "They're half-assing it. None of the demons trying to climb the Wall are above level fifty. Half their camp is still waiting back there away from the battle. They haven't used any of their monsters yet, either."

Orrin nodded. "I saw one demon use a pickax on the stone below us, grab the bit that fell off, and run away. I bet they did that yesterday, too. Those launcher balls they threw at us were an attempt to knock the Wall down, but they didn't know enough. We'll see more of those tomorrow, I bet."

Daniel sat up. "You think the demons are researching the best way to knock down the Wall? If they figure out something, the rest of the Walls will fall quicker than this one."

Madi and Crius had left to talk with her father. Orrin glanced around, hoping to spot her nearby. "Brandt, that kind of information might be helpful to the guys in charge. How close by are Madi and Silas?"

Brandt shrugged. "Crius said a few minutes, but they've been gone for ten minutes already. I can find out if you want."

Daniel and Orrin exchanged a long look that involved raised eyebrows and shrugs. Their long friendship allowed the entire conversation to take place with few words.

What do you think? Orrin asked by tilting his head and raising an eyebrow.

I think it can wait until Madi gets back, Daniel answered with a quizzical shrug.

What if they attack again before she does? Orrin moved his eyes toward the Horde. *The mages can start to reinforce the other Walls in different ways now.* He knocked the stone with his knuckles.

"You two know everyone hates it when you do that, right?" Brandt asked sardonically. "What should we do?"

Orrin chuckled softly. "We're wondering if it's worth the time right now. If we can have the workers building the Walls change things up at each new obstacle, the demons won't be able to figure out a one-stop solution for breaking down the Walls. I think they must be trying to find a good way to get through the Wall with these attacks, and once they find a way, they'll steamroll over us all the way to Dey."

Brandt bit his cheek and narrowed his eyes as he thought. "That's . . . a terrifying image. Don't either of you move. I'm going to find a runner or someone I can order around. I'll find out where Lord Catanzano is."

"I'm not going anywhere," Daniel complained and flopped back on the ground. "Next time I level up, I'm buying some long-range spells. My neck and back are killing me."

"You have [Meteor Shower]," Orrin pointed out. "I haven't seen you use that."

"I'm also not shooting a bow and arrow," Daniel grumbled. "It's doing about the same damage . . . nothing." He sighed and rolled to his side. "I tried with a bow yesterday and felt like it was a waste. I'd miss more often than not, and when I did hit, it barely hurt the enemy.

I used [Meteor Shower] this morning—don't look at me like that. It was when you went to heal those people hit from that fire spell—but all it did was kick up a bunch of dirt. Madi complained she couldn't see anything to hit afterward."

Orrin pulled some lunch out of his [Dimension Hole] and passed half over to Daniel. The slices of meat on bread were still hot from when he'd pilfered them from Lord Catanzano's kitchen this morning.

"Thanks," Daniel said between bites, his mouth still full of food. "I swear, they forget to feed us up here."

Orrin chewed and swallowed before answering. "They have tables set up behind the line for when your shift is over or if you need a break. Since we don't have someone telling us what to do, I guess it's up to us to monitor ourselves."

Daniel grunted and polished off his sandwich. "Got any more?"

Orrin made another appear. He knew Daniel's appetite.

"Something isn't right about the way they're attacking," Daniel said quietly. "If I was playing offense with their numbers, I'd sweep the Wall away. They're toying with us."

Orrin feared the same thing. The demons he'd identified in the camp were high levels. They'd fought one midseventies demon, and while that fight was tough, Orrin shivered at the thought of someone over level one hundred hitting the Wall.

"All we can do is be thankful for now," Orrin responded, holding up his hand as Daniel opened his mouth to argue. "Not because they're toying with us. Knocking their numbers down only helps. There hasn't been an effort to focus on one point in the Wall or to go after our stronger defenders. When they change and start fighting smart, then we should worry."

Orrin and Daniel continued talking until Brandt returned. The grim look on his face had both standing before he made it to them.

"What's wrong?" Daniel asked with his hand already on Gertrude.

"Lord Catanzano agrees with your assessment—" Brandt started to answer and stopped. His eyes moved to nearby fighters. Some rested during the small break while others were carrying more crates of arrows or even small bags of food around the top of the Wall. "Too many ears here. Let's go downstairs."

The back side of the Wall had various escape routes for the defenders. Orrin and Daniel kept returning to one with a narrow stairwell and were used to it. As they entered, Brandt nodded in content.

"This will do. I can hear anyone coming up the stairs. What I'm telling you now is need-to-know only. According to the others in the leadership tent, you do not need to know." Brandt's fingers curled around his sword hilt. "I disagree."

"Brandt," Orrin said with a warning in his voice. "Don't get yourself in trouble. We can find Silas and ask him questions if you think we should, but don't get on his bad side."

Brandt smiled and held up his hand. "Lord Catanzano likewise disagreed with excluding you. Let me finish. I found a scout who pointed me to leadership. They were discussing other matters when I told Lord Catanzano of your theory. He cursed, which is unlike him, and it alerted the others. There have been a few other developments that I don't need to get into, but suffice it to say, you were right. Everyone in command believes the demons are probing for weaknesses and intend to launch one big attack in the imminent future. Likely after they've found a way to break down the Walls."

"Did you tell them about the idea to change up the Walls?" Daniel asked. He stood a step lower than Brandt and had to look up. "Are they going to have the engineers and mages figure out different solutions?"

"Yes, I told them." Brandt nodded. "They sent directives out immediately. With strict orders to not share the changes between each Wall with anyone else. A smaller circle of shared knowledge means less chance for a leak."

Orrin applauded the lords of Dey for that. It was a good idea he'd not thought of.

"That doesn't explain the cloak and dagger act," Orrin said, waving his hand around the stairwell. "You could have told us later in our tent. What happened?"

Brandt winced. "Madi was there with Crius. They were reporting to Lord Catanzano. After hearing my report, Lord Tarris and Lady Timpe, along with the majority of the generals, voted for a nighttime assault against the demons. An attempt to reduce their numbers and sow chaos in their ranks before they learn a way to break through the Wall."

"That's stupid," Daniel said, slapping his forehead. "I specifically told them to keep the high ground. You never give up the high ground. It's the entire point of building the Walls."

"They think a few small strike teams can do a lot of damage and escape back to the Wall," the [Knight] continued. "The teams will damage provisions, release horses, set fire to tents, and destroy any weapons or supplies they can before retreating. The order is to avoid conflict."

"I think it's a dumb idea, but if it's just hit-and-run tactics . . ." Orrin trailed off as he thought about it. "That might not be so bad. I can set things on fire with my swords and run pretty quickly. Daniel can use [Shooting Star] and probably keep up."

Daniel stuck his tongue out.

"The attack is the confidential information. Lord Catanzano voted against it. He said it would antagonize the demons when waiting would allow us to continue pursuing a win through slow attrition. He was outvoted. He also lost the vote to include you two. Orrin, your spell-orb buffs are revolutionary. They are keeping our fighters up longer and our mages casting more spells. Even the [Healers] are singing your praises. Daniel, you are a beacon of hope for the men and women on the Wall. They aren't going to let you rush out there and fight again. You won't be part of this fight, and Lord Catanzano was ordered to not inform you of the attack."

Orrin stared at Brandt. The man was a sworn guard in the Catanzano house. He was one of the most trusted men in Silas's retinue and honest to a fault. Brandt's passion for his adopted family had brought him to Odrana in a misguided attempt to kill Lord Sanerris after the attack on Dey and the death of his friend Jude. If he was ordered to keep a secret, he would do it.

"Why are you telling us about the attack, Brandt?" Orrin hoped he was wrong, but the next words made his stomach drop.

"Madi was handpicked to lead one of the strike teams."

Chapter 39

Daniel growled, "That's not happening."

Brandt grinned. "I was hoping you'd say that."

Orrin felt the same fear for their friend but saw a few problems. "Did they tell Madi she's going or did they ask her?"

Daniel and Brandt were already walking back up the stairs.

"It doesn't matter. We need to go tell Silas we aren't letting our party member go off without us," Daniel said over his shoulder.

Brandt paused. "I was hoping you'd convince the leadership not to send her at all."

Orrin sighed. "Did Madi agree to go? If we walk in there and argue she should be left out, it might look like we don't trust her or think she can't handle the task."

Brandt made a fist and hit his hip. "She's strong enough to fight, but this isn't a fight. It's too dangerous."

Orrin knew that if Madi wanted to go, there was nothing they could do to stop her. She was a strong magic user and fighter. With her light magic, she could create illusions to distract demons, set fire to targeted areas, and illuminate the way for her party members. The lords' decision to exclude them sucked, but it made sense objectively.

Letting Daniel fight outside the Wall on the first day had been a calculated risk. The usefulness of Orrin's spell-orb buffs was not fully known, either. A raid at night wasn't well suited for Daniel with his big, flashy sword and demon-murder rage. Orrin assumed the lords would ask him to make more spell orbs.

Madi was a smart choice once he thought about it. She was trained in all sorts of things as the daughter of a lord. She'd be able to pinpoint important supplies or targets on the fly. Her spells were perfect for a night attack if it turned bad—she could blind the enemies while they ran.

"If Madi wants to do this, we should support her," Orrin said quietly.

While Daniel looked shocked at Orrin's seemingly casual acceptance of breaking up the party, Brandt got angry.

"She only agreed because Lady Timpe suggested it. Lord Catanzano doesn't want her out there. We have to convince her that she's needed here instead."

Orrin shook his head. "Let's talk to her, but Brandt . . . she's a big girl and can make her own decisions."

The [Knight] stared at Orrin like he was someone else. "You can't be serious. You think she should go?"

"If Madi thinks she should, why should we get to stop her?"

"Because this is what happens with this group. Somebody goes off alone and gets kidnapped or killed. Every time we split up the party, one of us needs to get rescued. Letting Madi go into the demon camp is asking for trouble," Brandt nearly shouted.

Orrin wanted to cast [Calm Mind] on Brandt but hesitated. *He's scared,* Orrin thought but dared not say it aloud to the big man.

"Don't worry about Madi," Daniel said finally. "If she thinks she can do it, I'm with Orrin. She's the most capable of any of us."

Brandt whipped his head back and forth between the two other men. "You, too? Am I the only one who sees how bad this is going to go?"

Daniel placed his hand on Brandt's shoulder but quickly withdrew it when he saw the anger in Brandt's eyes. "Dude, chill out. Orrin's right. If Madi heard the way you're talking right now, she'd be furious. Trust her a bit."

Orrin rubbed his neck. "We can trust her and still help."

"What do you mean?" Brandt asked with desperation. "If you cast [Camouflage Ward], the three of us could take one of the secret exits and shadow her group. We wouldn't even need to attack, just wait for something to go wrong."

"Not what I was thinking." Orrin grimaced. "I could buff the teams up to max stats and make a few extra spell orbs with [Purify]. That way, they could remove any side effects after the twenty minutes were up. How are they planning on getting over there?"

"The parties will go out tonight after the demons retreat to their camps. I was dismissed before the exact plans were made."

Orrin thought for a minute before clapping his hands. "They aren't going to like that you told us about the attack after you were specifically ordered not to. Here's my plan."

The flaps to the tent flared open as Daniel marched into the commander center. "Silas? Where's Madi? I want to go hunt down a few of those rogue [Healers] after the demons retreat for the day."

Before the flaps closed again, Orrin sneaked in. [Camouflage] was active, and with something else to focus on, namely Daniel, the occupants of the tent didn't catch him. They'd left Brandt standing guard outside so he wouldn't get in trouble if their plan backfired.

Silas stopped talking with the warrior woman in half plate. Lady Timpe's longsword cleared her scabbard a few inches at the sudden disturbance, but she quickly pushed the blade back down.

Three generals, a handful of lieutenants Orrin didn't know, and some messengers milled about, watching the [Hero] barge in unsummoned. Leanthun watched from a corner. His eyes flitted over Orrin, but he kept quiet.

"Daniel," Silas said in an exasperated voice. "I was going to send Brandt to tell you that she was selected for a mission today. I don't know where he went, but Madi won't be back until morning."

"What kind of mission?" Daniel asked, his voice stilted. "Should I find Orrin? We can be ready to go in twenty minutes."

Lady Timpe rubbed her eyes. "Silas, you assured me Sir Bennett could be trusted. It's obvious he told Daniel. My grandchildren lie better than he does and they're three years old."

Daniel tried to plaster a look of confusion on his face, but it only made him appear constipated. Orrin rolled his eyes. He'd hoped Daniel could keep it together for longer than this. Luckily, Daniel changed tactics quickly.

"Brandt is trustworthy," the [Hero] said in a soft voice that carried over the cramped room. "I trust him and Madi with my life. They feel the same way. That's why Madi came to me immediately when you tried to break up my party."

Silas rolled his chair around the table in the middle of the room and stopped it right in front of Daniel. "Madi didn't have time to approach you. Further, she would follow the orders given and not tell you or anyone of her mission. Whatever you are attempting here, cease immediately. I can forgive Sir Bennett's . . . enthusiasm, but we do not have time for whatever games you are playing."

Orrin finally finished his assignment and got into place. He coughed loudly a few steps from Lady Timpe against the back of the tent.

Several swords were drawn, and a wave of spells flew toward where he'd been. Orrin ducked after his fake cough and waited on the ground. He disengaged [Camouflage] and held his hands up in the air. A few guards moved toward him, but Lady Timpe ordered them to halt. Leanthun covered his mouth to hide his grin when two of the guards tripped.

"I surrender. You got us."

Daniel chuckled. "How was I?"

"Like her ladyship said. You suck at acting," Orrin poked fun at his friend.

"But I was distracting." Daniel puffed out his chest. "I did my job."

"Same."

"What is going on here?" Lady Timpe barked, glaring at her men on the floor. "General Fels, you assured me the best scouts were watching this tent. We can't group our leaders if one [Assassin] can get in this easily."

The older man with salt-and-pepper hair and a mustache that drooped down either cheek huffed and started yelling at one of his lieutenants.

"Enough. Silence," Silas ordered, filling his voice with magic.

Orrin remembered a time when Silas's infused voice could make Daniel sit with a word. Orrin didn't have [Mind Bastion] running, but it toggled itself on and off as the wave of sound magic hit him. He knew the spell would silence everyone around him for a moment.

"Huh? Nice," Daniel murmured then spoke louder. "I guess that doesn't work on me anymore."

Silas closed his eyes and took a deep breath. Orrin could see his lips moving as he silently counted.

"Daniel gets under my skin too sometimes," Orrin joked.

"Will one of you . . . please . . . explain what you are doing?" Silas said through gritted teeth.

"First off," Daniel answered and walked over to the table. He grabbed an apple from a small bowl and bit into it. "I don't like when people steal my party members without asking. You know we aren't unreasonable people."

One of the generals, Hayder, let out a huff of displeasure, but Daniel ignored him. The two fallen guards finally untangled themselves and stood.

"Second, if everyone will look down at their feet for me?" Daniel instructed, pointedly looking at Silas. "I guess not Silas, but you can't get everyone."

Orrin grinned as people started muttering expletives. While Daniel had distracted everyone with his bad attempts at lying, Orrin had sneaked around tying a small rope around everyone's left foot. He'd cheated and made a slipknot for speed, but the message was the same. For a few of the guards, he'd gone farther and crossed their shoelaces in knots.

"I understand not wanting to send me out into the demon camp," Daniel said with growing anger. "I understand picking people best suited for the job. But I don't know why you'd try to hide things from me. Especially when you know how many tricks I have up my sleeve. Orrin tied a rope around you because you were focused on me. Use that. He came up with a way to sneak in here undetected. Use that. If Madi agreed to go out there, I'm not in charge of her any more than Brandt is, or even you, Silas. Now, let's discuss a few things."

Lady Timpe pulled a knife from her side and cut the rope off her ankle. "A good distraction, but you don't get to—"

"Daniel is right." Silas spoke over her. "Orrin can cast [Camouflage]. We focused only on [Invisibility], which we know the demon guards can see through and are watching for. He can increase the selected parties' stats directly instead of relying on spell orbs. Spell orbs that he created, I'll add."

"If it's not too many people, I could buff them up to a hundred," Orrin chimed in. Muttering filled the room. "If each person carries a [Purify] spell orb, they can use it right at the end of the time limit and get rid of any negative effects."

General Hayder stepped forward. "Why didn't we know this was an option before? We could use your spell orbs to increase every member of the coalition to their strongest. We could stop the fight tonight."

Orrin shook his head. The man was dead set on attacking the demons. "Even if I had the mana to buff everyone, the timing is tricky. Each person will need to have a staggered buff. When person one runs out of strength, person two will need to use the buff ball . . . damn it, Daniel . . . the spell orb on person one. In a small group, it's doable. For an army? That's asking for chaos."

"We could still create—"

"General Hayder, we can discuss further uses of this later. Lady Timple, I admit I'm biased in this. My daughter agreed to it despite my objections. But I believe this might increase our chances of success." Silas turned his gaze back across the table. "Do you agree?"

Lady Timpe nodded slowly. "Two sources of illusion magic might give them a better chance at getting close before an alarm is raised. I have at least two scouts who use [Camouflage] as well."

"I'd like to create a distraction," Daniel said suddenly, breaking from Orrin's plan. "Orrin can [Teleport] me out to the opposite side and back. I can cast a few spells and make a scene. More eyes focused on the [Hero] would mean less people watching for an ambush."

Orrin groaned internally, but Silas was nodding already.

"That might be worth discussing. General Hayder, please recall Lord Tarris. We're changing the nighttime raid plans around and could use his magical knowledge," the lord of Dey ordered before turning back toward Daniel. "What kind of distraction are you thinking?"

Chapter 40

Fighting broke out along the Wall while the leaders of Dey, the elves, and even Finley Madvarr, the representative of the Odranan forces, discussed their plan. The occasional cry for aid broke through the air as everyone gathered.

Lady Timpe, Lord Tarris, and Lord Catanzano clumped together at one end of the table. Silas sat in his wheelchair with the other rulers of Dey at his sides. The imperial image naturally lent credence to his voice when he spoke and the rest of the tent listened. His generals waited patiently behind the trio, waiting to be called on or offer assistance.

Finley didn't stand on ceremony and pulled a chair to the table next to Orrin and Leanthun. A seasoned fighter, he used the break to rest and eat. His armor was scratched and two daggers were missing from the arsenal of knives strapped to his chest. He used one to cut into a hunk of cheese before offering some to the elf standing next to him.

Leanthun's eyes still held a glint of amusement at from Orrin's sneaky entrance. He'd quickly elicited a promise for a talk with Orrin after they hammered out the details of the nighttime raid. The elf accepted the offered snack with a shallow nod of his head. He spoke the least during the planning. He was against the plan of leaving the Wall's safety for his kinsmen and refused to aid in the actual attack. Despite his presence in the Pass, the elves were not beholden to Dey and could not be ordered into a plan they did not agree with.

Orrin raised his eyes when Elder Seif of the Hospital ducked into the tent. His gaze paused on Orrin for a moment and a grumble echoed from his chest, but he said nothing. The dark and scarred man stood opposite Daniel and Orrin across the table.

"If that is everyone"—Silas clapped his hands—"we can begin."

"Where's Madi?" Daniel coughed as he swallowed a piece of cheese too quickly. "Sorry. It went down the wrong pipe. Madi should be here."

"We don't need her for the planning stage," Lady Timpe said from Silas's side. "This is about how to integrate your distraction and young Master Orrin's spells into the attack. We must restrict the information she has in the chance she is captured before the strike is finished."

Orrin was both pleased the leadership council here was doing a good job at keeping the relevant knowledge consolidated and secret but still pissed they were excluded.

"Nah, I want Madi's input," Daniel countered like a petulant child, and Orrin sighed.

"I've found it easier to give the [Hero] what he wants," Brandt inserted from the side. Most of the Dey leaders glared at him. The [Knight] shrugged. "It's true. He's stubborn."

"All the more reason not to tell him about an attack he isn't to be part of," Lord Tarris muttered. "Will someone find Lady Catanzano and have her return to the tent?" He turned toward Daniel. "Can we begin discussions and you can inform her of anything she missed? We are at war here and there are better places I could be."

"Yeah, just one more question," Daniel said as he chewed. "Why's the [Healer] here?"

Orrin put his head in his hands on the table. *He's your best friend. Don't kill him.*

Lady Timpe raised her head. "I invited him. The Hospital has sent nearly every [Healer] to the front and Elder Seif will be waiting for the strike teams personally tonight when they return."

"I thought the plan was to avoid a fight," Daniel said. He reached forward and poured himself a glass of water from the communal pitcher. "Orrin will be there, too. I trust him to heal us more than someone we've had to fight recently."

"You have not fought a member of the Hospital." Seif's deep voice echoed in the silent room. "Traitors to our calling, yes. We will fulfill our responsibility to Dey."

Only because we threatened you, Orrin thought but didn't dare say aloud. Daniel was already playing bad cop. Instead, he tried to mend the peace. "What's the plan, Silas? You know our suggestions. What's the best way we can help?"

Madi's dad raised his chin slightly in thanks to Orrin before explaining Orrin and Daniel's plan to add a distraction and additional buffs to the strike teams. It quickly became clear that the major points of their strategy wouldn't change much, but the additional time that Daniel's commotion could buy let them pick new targets for destruction. Leanthun offered information on what the elven scouts had seen, pointing to a crude map in the middle of the table to show points of interest.

Finley leaned over and whispered to Orrin, "You mind if my team and I go out with you tomorrow? I'd love to try fighting with maxed-out stats, and I know my party would, too."

Orrin ignored Lady Timpe and Silas discussing the merits of targeting arrow caches over crates of picks and spears. "I don't see why not. I can make you a few [Purify] spell orbs, but make sure you keep a timer going. Madi and Brandt went down after I overbuffed them once and the results were not pretty."

Finley smiled eagerly but then let his face return to normal. "I spoke with Maeve by [Message] this morning. She asked if you were going back to Ceraun. She has more supplies for you and said Rae wanted to get dinner with you."

Orrin felt his collar heat up. "I'll see if we need more potions. I don't have to be the one to get them. I'm sure Silas has—"

Finley laughed and hit the table. "Oh man, you are too easy to rile up. Listen. With your abilities, I would be teleporting home every night. Find a warm bed, and if someone like Rae wants to join you . . ." Finley wiggled his eyebrows mischievously.

"Mr. Madvarr, did you have a comment to make?" Silas rattled from the end of the table. The knife in Finley's hand spun along his fingers, but he looked chastised. "Have you selected a team for this mission?"

Finley nodded and spoke formally. "I'll send some of my best [Rogues], a [Tracker], and a [Hunter]. They don't need to work as a group but can each raid a target on their own. With Orrin's buffs, I have two [Locationists] that can move them to the edge of the camp and back. We should pick a spot far enough away that the demons can't immediately spot them but close enough that the teams have time to work before Orrin's spells wear off."

Orrin and Daniel didn't add much to the conversation. After another five minutes, Leanthun tapped Orrin on the shoulder. "Come with me?"

Orrin glanced at Daniel, who shrugged. He got up from the table and moved outside.

Leanthun sucked in the air and looked into the sky above. "Tonight, there will be good cloud cover. That is good."

Orrin saw Madi jogging toward them. He glanced at the elf. Had he known Madi was coming and brought him outside to meet her?

"Hey, Madi. Everyone is inside." Orrin threw a thumb over his shoulder. "Keep Daniel in check for me for a minute?"

Madi grimaced but nodded in agreement. Her hair, which was in coiled knots on her head, barely moved. "What's this about? I was meeting with . . . some new friends when I got the order to return."

Orrin rolled his eyes. "Brandt was overprotective." He held up his hands when he saw the anger in her eyes. "No. He didn't do anything wrong. We all know you're smart and strong enough for your . . . mission. We just decided to add a little Orrin and Daniel spice to the mix."

Madi groaned. "Do I want to know?"

Leanthun laughed. "It will be helpful if all goes well. Head inside, young Catanzano. I think they await your presence to discuss a few details."

Madi pointed at Orrin. "I'm still going to yell at Brandt later. Do not get in my way." She ducked inside.

"Walk with me," Leanthun said, not looking back as he started walking the Wall. The demons were attacking again, but it was mid afternoon and most seemed tired. A few arrows hit the stone walls and a single spell flew overhead, but the attacking army was content to wait back at its rest spot.

"You humans amuse me. The way you use skills changes in cycles over the decades and everyone forgets how the last generation fought," Leanthun reflected aloud. "My mother used [Camouflage], much like you. There are ways to see around it, but [Invisibility] became prevalent over the last hundred years. It takes specific skills to see through [Invisibility], but that is what humans train for now. Not one person in that room knew you were among them. I wonder if that's how the demons are as well."

"Leanthun, you didn't ask me out here to talk about my skills," Orrin said when the man went quiet. "What do you want?"

"So direct. You used to be patient."

"We're at war."

"This isn't a war."

Orrin glanced at the elf from the corner of his eye. "What do you mean?" he asked experimentally.

Leanthun stopped and placed his arms on two separate crenellations. He stared at the camp in the distance. "Why are they here, Orrin? The demands for the [Hero] and retreating from the Pass were bluster. There were no structures in the Pass until after we knew the Dark Horde was on its way. Demons do not show up in large numbers every time a [Hero] appears. There is something going on. The council of elders is worried."

He flicked a small stone off the edge. "If the demons begin to march over these Walls, the elves that I command will have to return to the forest. Arandir wants to speak with you when you have a moment. He's researching something but won't tell the rest of the council. He won't tell me."

Orrin didn't know Leanthun to be vulnerable, but the pain in his voice at the end was obvious even to him. "Arandir trusts you. I wouldn't worry about him. He'll tell you when he's ready."

Leanthun smiled a sad smile. "You are young and full of hope. I hope that does not ever leave you." He straightened and nodded to himself. "I apologize. I have to relay a request from the council."

"Sure. What do they need?" An arrow struck the Wall right under their feet and Orrin backed away from the edge. "Maybe we should talk away from the kill zone."

"If the Walls fall and the demons overrun Dey, they want you to retreat to the forest with your party," Leanthun said. "Before you say no, this is a formal invitation. We will supply you with dungeons to level yourself and whatever you need. With your spell orbs, our archers can hold off even the Dark Horde from fully encroaching on our lands. I think it is a good worst-case scenario to have in place, but . . ."

Orrin stared at Leanthun. "You think we'll abandon everyone in Dey? Why even ask me? Daniel is the [Hero]."

"A [Hero] isn't what the council needs . . . what we need. Daniel is proud and will fight a losing battle. You may be brave enough to retreat and win another day."

Orrin understood the council's worry. The elves were here to help push back the Horde, but if Dey fell, it wasn't the end for them. They didn't have to die here. Their forest had remained relatively unscathed through the millennia. If the demons attacked, they could leave the humans to their fate.

Arandir was part Administrator as well. He was the most knowledgeable source of information in the world regarding Orrin's secondary powers. Asking Orrin to bring his party to the elves would let them work together and maybe revive the Administrators. He'd be able to strike back at the demons eventually.

"All the people of Dey," Orrin whispered. "They would die."

"The council would say humans repopulate quickly," Leanthun said as he placed his hand on Orrin's shoulder. "They would likely take in any refugees that they could, but they would not be allowed to stay long. I've grown to like some of the humans around here. While I am bound to tell you of the request, I don't believe you will need to accept it. I found it is not a smart thing to underestimate your party."

Orrin hated that the elves even put the thought of running in his head. The doubt that normally sat quietly in his mind began to get louder and he was forced to cast [Calm Mind] on himself. "Next time you talk to the council, tell them thank you for the offer." Orrin clenched his fists. "Between you and me, I'm going to burn that camp to the ground before I return to your forest."

Leanthun's grin was bright and fierce. "Good. I will let my kind decide their own fate, but know many will return to the forest if Dey falls. I will stay and help to the end."

Orrin took Leanthun's outstretched hand and squeezed. "Let's make sure it doesn't happen, then."

Chapter 41

Night fell and Orrin watched his friends be whisked away by a team of [Locationists]. A small area had been removed from the [Teleport] wards with clear markers and a rope to avoid any accidents. Finley stood by his side and slapped his back when Madi waved from the middle of her new team before disappearing with a silent pop. Daniel had left with the Hornet team a few minutes prior. He was going to throw a few of his space spells at the demon camp, attacking them from the north while the strike teams hit from the west. The attempt to sneak up behind the camp would be dangerous, but hopefully Daniel's presence would cause the demons to react in haste.

"It's a good plan and they're all survivors. Don't think about it too much," Finley said jovially. "Let's find something to distract ourselves. Want to spar a bit?"

Orrin and Finley had met at magic school in a course called Battle Class. Finley was a battle junkie, fixated on the fight. He'd taken Battle Class multiple times and come out on top each year. He'd even fought with Daniel to test his skills against the [Hero]. Orrin had no doubt he could take Finley down with his debuffs, but in a "fair" fight, he still gave the trained man a run for his money. Fighting against Orrin wasn't a straightforward thing. His opponent had to catch him first. Orrin's [Gust] let him slide around a battlefield with speeds that rivaled dexterity builds like [Scout], while his variety of spell options gave him choices beyond most mages.

If Finley could get close, Orrin also had [Way of the Water]. With it, Orrin was hard to pin down even with Finley's air magic. Finley had the experience, but Orrin knew it was good practice fighting someone so skilled.

Now was not the time, though.

"I won't be able to concentrate until they get back," Orrin answered, shaking his head.

"Brandt, what about you? Care for a round?" Finley turned to the [Knight].

Brandt sighed. "No. They shouldn't be gone more than half an hour. I'll wait here."

Orrin took a satchel of cookies out of his [Dimension Hole] and offered one to the comrades. Brandt declined, but Finley took two.

"I'm going to train for a bit," Finley said when only crumbs remained. He licked his fingers. "I wish killing those demons gave more experience. I'm close to the next level."

"There are a few monsters left in the Pass," Brandt said absentmindedly. "You can take a team out and help clear some."

Finley shrugged. "You'll never clear the Pass of monsters. I'm positive some of those caves go deeper into the mountains than we know. Besides, I don't have time. I have to send a report to my father. I'll ask him again for more troops, but Vas is still sending raids into Odrana, even now." He sighed and tossed one of his daggers in the air. It landed point down on his finger. Finley continued to balance it as he talked. "Maybe Dey can help with that after the demons are taken care of. A reciprocal relationship where we keep everyone in line."

Brandt harrumphed. "Above my level."

Finley spun the blade on his fingers before strapping it back to his chest. "Have someone send for me when they get back?" He slapped Orrin on the back before he walked away.

Orrin checked his own notifications. He'd avoided killing, focusing more on reducing the enemy's stats, but he'd killed a few demons. If only his debuffs counted as participation in a kill, he and Daniel would have gotten a lot more experience.

Experience Gained: 250 XP (100 XP x 2; 50 XP x 1)

A hundred points per demon? That seems low.

Brandt stood nearby without talking for a few minutes. Orrin checked the position of the moon. Madi had taught them how to approximate time based on the sky, but it looked to have barely moved from when he let them go on this stupid mission.

I get why Brandt hates this. It sucks. Orrin looked around, searching for anything or anyone to distract him.

The rows of small triangular shelters were high enough to crouch in. As long as one was unoccupied, anyone could use it. A small bedroll and an extra blanket were in each one. Orrin usually would [Teleport] back to Dey at night, but they'd all spent some time sleeping here.

Most of the guards stuck together, sleeping near the Wall in tents lined up in rigid lines. There was no rule that the volunteers without an offensive class couldn't stay there but the militia had trained with the elves in groups. Those groups grew close and made up their own smaller parties. Although most slept, Orrin noticed a few clusters of people huddled around each other. No fires were lit on orders from on high. The demons hadn't attacked at night yet, but they would after this night.

Orrin sighed and checked through his stats and skills. "Brandt, I'm going to train my fighting skill. Shake me if they come back."

The [Knight] grunted.

Orrin sat, finding a comfortable position on the grass, and activated his fighting skill.

> **[Way of the Water] 40% 8/20 completed.**
> **Continue?**

Styx rested on the ground, his feet crossed underneath him. A barely perceptible nod of welcome sloshed the water of his body around.

"Styx, can we just fight a bit? I'm too worried about my friends to focus on the water exercise." Orrin explained what was going on in the real world as Styx failed to respond. "They're out there doing something and I have to wait behind. It's frustrating. I just want to hit something."

The watery figure held his hands out and summoned a bead of water. It grew to the size of a cantaloupe and shrunk back. Styx looked up expectantly at Orrin as the water oscillated in size.

"Ahh." Orrin darted forward and kicked at the man's hands. His foot caught the ball midgrowth and he punted the water into Styx's chest. It splashed and covered his teacher's torso, absorbing into the liquid body.

Styx didn't move as Orrin's foot continued its trajectory. Instead of connecting, Orrin felt his foot miss completely. The force of his kick was too much and Orrin spun like a top before landing hard on his ass.

He had time to see Styx's shoulder reform. The entire right side was distorted like the water had moved to avoid Orrin's attack. He blinked and Styx was whole again.

"Stupid water teacher man," Orrin grumbled as he got to his feet. "Be that way."

Orrin tried to train, but he couldn't get the orb to grow as big as Styx. His teacher kept his ball at the correct size for reference.

"I need a tip or hint," Orrin complained as the ball of water splashed over him again. It didn't leave him wet, but it was annoying finding the trigger in his mind to resummon the bead of water. "This is never going to work if I'm trying blind."

"EXPAND."

"Expand what?" Orrin all but shouted.

Styx leaned forward faster than a whip and flicked a finger against Orrin's forehead.

"Asshole, don't hit me." Orrin's bead fell from his hands and he rolled, trying to kick Styx again. If the man of water wanted to fight, Orrin would gladly oblige right now. Sitting with his thoughts wasn't helping with the training. He wanted to hit something.

Unfortunately, Styx let the hit flow right through him. Orrin ended up sitting in an awkward crouch, breathing heavily.

"EXPAND."

Orrin huffed and tried again. He focused and cut off all thoughts about Madi fighting her way through the demon camp to set fire to their food and burn their tents. He ignored the fear in his gut for Daniel, who would fuck it up somehow and end up fighting demons. Letting all his thoughts go, he focused on this little dot of water between his hands.

When Styx first summoned the bead, it had taken Orrin a while to learn to make the water hover between his hands. His own energy kept it suspended. Styx had made him learn to keep the water protected and even draw it into different shapes. Well . . . one shape, a long needle. But now Orrin could make it grow in size.

During the last successful training, Orrin remembered, he'd even made the ball grow a little. He tried to recall what he'd done. Staring at the bead in its smallest state, Orrin searched it for mana. It looked like water, felt like mana, but wasn't, and could be shaped by his mind.

Is it my mind? Styx flicked my head. Was that him being angry at me or a sign? Orrin imagined the water growing. *Use the Force!* He chuckled to himself.

He was getting frustrated again when nothing worked. He could make the water rapidly expand but not to the right size. He'd achieved something close once, but he still needed to control it and return it to a bead. Orrin stared at the water and grew angry.

The water rippled.

The small movement clicked thoughts together in his head, and Orrin cast [Calm Mind]. As soon as he felt the peace come over him, the bead became serene as well.

"The water is me," Orrin whispered. "It's water but also my mana." He glanced up at Styx. "Right?"

Styx waffled his head back and forth. "NEARLY. BECOME. EXPAND."

Orrin fell into meditation as he reached his thoughts toward the water. The connection he'd used to turn it into a long thread, once a fragile thing, strengthened. While before, Orrin felt his connection with the water as a small conduit of willpower, now he smiled as Styx's directions made sense.

"Expand." He wanted to laugh. It wasn't the water he needed to expand. It was the connection with it. Orrin opened himself up and felt that small drip become a flood. The water in his hand ballooned larger than a basketball, and with a thought, Orrin sucked the same energy back inside. The bead grew and shrank in his hands a dozen times and Orrin's smile grew wide.

"FINALLY."

Orrin raised an eyebrow. "Is that sass? Are you sassing me?"

Styx nodded as the notification filled Orrin's view.

[Way of the Water] 45% 9/20 completed. Test your progress and unlock the second gate?
Warning: Failure three (3) times will result in all progress being lost.

Orrin whooped and jumped into the air. "You see that? I did it."

Styx watched Orrin cheering. He'd swear the water around the figure's face waved in delight. However, a moment later, Orrin felt someone shaking his body.

"I'll be back for that gate," Orrin promised and bowed to Styx. "Thank you."

He exited the training skill and Brandt held his shoulders. "Orrin!"

"I'm back. Where are they?"

Brandt pointed toward the roped-off [Teleport] area. People were appearing in groups of five every few seconds. The [Locationists] stopped only long enough to make sure people arrived before popping back out of existence.

"I don't see Madi. Where's Daniel?"

Brandt marched across the field, but two guards stopped him at the ropes. One stepped forward and blocked his path. "Nobody allowed inside except [Healers]," she said, planting a glaive in the dirt in front of them.

"He can heal," Brandt said, pushing Orrin forward. "Find her."

The female guard raised an eyebrow. "What kind of [Healer] doesn't wear the white robes?"

"I'm Orrin. I'm in the [Hero]'s party. I can cast [Heal Small Wounds], but I'm not a full [Healer]." Orrin hoped for once his reputation would be enough. Brandt was nearly beside himself with anxiety over Madi. "Come watch, and if I can't heal, throw me over the Wall, okay?"

The guard leaned closer in the dark, trying to see Orrin better. "You'd better not be lying. I hear the [Hero] is protective of his party."

"Protective enough to leave half of us behind," Orrin mumbled as they let him past the ropes.

He started using [Identify] to check people's health, but near the edge, everyone was healed already. White-robed [Healers] were moving around.

"Madi? Daniel?" Orrin hissed into the darkness. "Has anyone seen the [Hero] or Lady Catanzano?"

"Orrin?" A dark smudge in the distance stood up. "What are you doing in here? You didn't go out there, did you?"

Orrin sighed at seeing Daniel on his feet. He realized he was already hugging his friend. "I'm glad you're back."

Daniel gently peeled Orrin off and smirked. "You're going to need a shower now. I got hit with some sort of pus attack. It's sticky and won't come off."

"Goddamn it, Daniel." Orrin rubbed his hands over his chest and arms, feeling the slime all over him. "Have you seen Madi? Brandt is over there freaking out."

Another figure turned and approached as he spoke. "Why is Brandt freaking out, Orrin?"

Madi stepped closer and held her hand over her face. "What is that smell?"

"It's Orrin," Daniel answered first. "Who knows what he gets up to while we're doing all the hard work."

Madi backed away a bit. "Maybe we should go find a [Water Mage]."

"Are you both okay? Either of you need a heal?" Orrin checked both over with [Identify] and sighed in relief. Both had full health. Madi's mana was low—like, ten points of MP left low—but she seemed fine.

"I'm going to need a full night of rest," Madi said. "I'm exhausted but fine. We hit two of our ten targets before they realized we'd broken through their fence line. My squad took out nine total targets before we had to retreat. Only one got hit with a spell, but we carried him back. Thankfully, he was awake enough to accept the [Teleport]."

"I can heal him. I came through to heal," Orrin said lamely. "I can't see anything, though."

"No lanterns until everyone is accounted for. We don't want to give the demons a landing zone if they try to retaliate," a voice Orrin recognized said from nearby.

"Sof?" Orrin squinted into the dark.

The leader of team Dragoon stepped close and shook Orrin's hand. He looked down in disgust and shook something free that splatted on the dirt below. "I'm not going to ask what that was. Daniel, good to see you. Lady Catanzano, we saw your team in there. Well done."

"Dragoon made up two of the parties in the attack," Madi explained. "Let's get out of here and talk. I hear someone has been worrying when they should have been working."

The tone in her voice made Orrin cringe. He might have gotten Brandt in trouble.

Chapter 42

Moving away from the landing zone for the returning strike teams, Orrin and his party were joined by Sof's teammates, the Dragoon team.

Sof was a [Tree Druid] and leader of one of the best parties in Dey. His calm demeanor and quick thinking during the Fogbinder attack endeared him to Orrin and Daniel. And Orrin had buffed Sof's team before Dragoon faced the demon, earning them a modicum of trust from the man in return. Dragoon team was made up of ten members split into two parties, but Orrin hadn't seen them all since they'd rushed off to kill some demons back when he was still a new adventurer.

Examining the faces in the glittering torchlight as they approached the Wall, Orrin counted only nine others.

"Where's Ira?" Orrin asked, missing the [Metal Mage]. Orrin had saved his life after a run-in with the Fogbinder's monster companions left him missing a limb and slowly dying. If Orrin could watch Ira cast a few spells, maybe he could get a metal-based ward.

"Ira retired after losing his foot," Maya, their wind-magic user, said as she darted up to Orrin. "When Sofy told us you were fighting outside the Wall, I almost didn't believe him. You've grown in level. Good for you."

Orrin chuckled nervously at the way she examined him. "Thanks, I guess. How did the attack go?"

"It was successful." Sof spoke softly and sat down against the inner Wall. He pulled a small satchel from behind him and started rummaging through it. "We planted the seeds of doubt in their camp."

Farah, a petite woman wearing all black and carrying an oversize scythe, laughed darkly. "Sof is being modest. We destroyed most of their food. Bin broke their anvils to pieces, so they'll have trouble fixing their weapons. Al and Gustaf found a tent filled with chests of potions. We didn't have time to steal any, but the boys smashed them up."

Madi whispered something in Brandt's ear. Even in the flickering light, Orrin saw him go pale and start stuttering a response. Madi gently patted his arm, but Orrin felt his fear from across their little circle.

"What about you? Did you drop a bunch of demons? We've been hearing more and more about your little adventures." Farah, who'd been standoffish at first, suddenly scooted closer to Orrin. "I didn't get to thank you properly for healing me last time we met."

Orrin waved his hand. "It was nothing. We're all on the same team, right?"

Bin, their large bruiser, growled.

"That's Bin's way of asking if you want to join our team," Farah said sweetly. "Having a [Healer] around is much better than pulling someone through the woods for hours. Plus you make those amazing buff balls."

Orrin groaned. Daniel was calling his spell orbs "buff balls" to anyone who would listen. He'd really hoped it wouldn't catch on.

"He is not yet ready to join Dragoon," Sof whispered in his soft voice. It still carried across the small area as though he sat next to Orrin. He found what he was looking for and pulled a small flask from his bag. "We do owe Orrin a drink."

Other than Sof, Farah, Bin, and Maya, the Dragoon team was comprised of Noah, a fighter who used shields; Al, a thrown melee specialist; Gustaf, a [Sword Dancer]; Clifford or Cliff, an archer; and Gracie, a woman who might have had orc blood in her past based on her size. Her club was the size of a small tree, and resting against the Wall was taller than Orrin.

Gustaf languidly made his way around the circle and handed out small, mismatched cups. Once the last was handed to Bin, Gustaf accepted Sof's flask and gave a healthy pour of a clear liquid to everyone. Noah downed his immediately and held the cup up for seconds.

"Noah . . ." Sof said in a warning tone. Gustaf waited for Sof's nod before pouring the man another shot.

Sof held his cup in the air. "To friends lost and friends found. To help in the dark. To healers and heroes."

Dragoon team whispered the last line and everyone drank.

Orrin sniffed the alcohol and politely sipped it. It didn't burn at all. It was sweet like flat soda, but once it went down his throat, the flavor changed to something citrusy.

"That was delicious," Daniel said, sitting forward. "Where can I get some of that?"

"Sof makes it. Some old family recipe," Maya said, her voice on the edge of singing. "He lets us have it so rarely, and I'm convinced it's the only reason Noah stays with us."

"Not completely wrong," Noah slurred and fell over backward. His snores started almost immediately.

"Is he all right?" Orrin asked, quickly sitting forward. He readied [Identify].

Gustaf and Al laughed. Maya shook her head like an annoyed older sister.

"Noah is a [Pain Drinker]. His class is . . ." Sof searched for the word. "—unique. He drinks alcohol to reduce the damage he takes. It has been a long day for us all."

Gracie nodded and leaned her giant head back against the Wall. Orrin wondered how loud her snores would be.

Sof and Madi took turns describing their raid on the demon camp. Daniel had used [Gravity Well] and [Meteor Shower] over and over, creating a huge dust storm that could be seen even in the darkness.

"The way the moonlight bouncing off the sand and rocks above me was like my own mini universe," Daniel bragged. "Once the first demons came to investigate, I shouted a challenge for the Demon Lord. We had about one . . . two hundred demons running our way when the [Locationist] pissed himself and made us [Teleport] away."

The circle closed and shuffled as some of the Dragoon team fell asleep. They were a hard bunch, used to long forays into the Pass and dungeons. They slept where and when they could. Orrin ended up next to Madi.

"One to two hundred," he whispered to her. "I'll bet you a gold piece he changes it to three hundred the next time he tells this story."

Madi shook her head. "No bet. That's all but a certainty."

Brandt laughed at something Daniel said. His eyes moved over Madi then quickly flicked away again.

"Are you going to keep Brandt on eggshells? He was worried about you, but it's not like he thought you couldn't handle the task." Orrin scuffed his foot against the ground. "I feel like I got him in trouble."

"I'm raking him over the coals a bit so he won't protest the next time I do something risky that he doesn't like," Madi confided. "But we're fine. It's hard to watch our friends run into danger. I get it."

She stared at Orrin. "I mean, I'm friends with you and Daniel. I think I put up with that more than anyone."

Orrin covered his heart with his hand. "I'm wounded. I am the epitome of safety and caution. Never do I run into— Ouch."

Madi chopped him on the head.

Orrin rubbed at his hair and rolled his eyes. "Next time I'll side with Brandt and convince your dad to keep you locked away in a tower like the princess you are."

Madi chopped him again.

"Damn it, that hurts."

Madi smirked and threw her arm over his shoulders. "Heal yourself then and prove that I'm strong enough to hurt you with my weakest taps. Show the world I am a warrior mage to be feared."

Orrin stared at her, then shrugged. He cast [Heal Small Wounds]. "That feels better. Now I have to tell everyone you are stronger than me, though."

Madi's laughter cut through the others' conversation, and Brandt looked up hopefully.

"I've always been stronger, Orrin. You just cheat."

"What's so funny?" Daniel asked, looking a little miffed that his story had been interrupted.

"Madi is the strongest of us all. A warrior mage to be afraid of," Orrin joked. [Side Steps] activated when she tried to hit him again.

Daniel rolled his eyes. "Anyways, like I was saying . . ."

The next morning, Dragoon team dispersed from their makeshift camp with quick goodbyes. Orrin rolled over and groaned.

"Sleeping on the ground was a mistake."

"You didn't want to find a tent," Daniel countered, already up and fully armored.

"You wouldn't stop talking."

"Coffee?" Madi sang like an angel. Orrin would gladly preach of the woman's magical prowess.

Five minutes and two cups later, Orrin was ready. "What's the plan?"

"You're supposed to make more spell orbs until Brandt gets back," Madi said while setting a few dried foods out for breakfast. "He left to find command and see how we could help."

Orrin made a few stacks of the orbs between bites of food. Brandt came down the stairs nearby and looked the wrong way before spotting them. He jogged to their side. "We pissed them off. The demons are coming in fast."

Orrin stopped casting his spell and stretched his arms over his head. "Are we on ladder duty again or what?"

Brandt shook his head. "All the demons are coming. This isn't a probing attack. It's beginning for real today. Our orders are to attack from the Wall. Some teams are being jumped out to hit them from behind. Be careful of your attacks. Let's go."

Orrin threw his buffs on his party faster than ever before. He left the spell orbs on the ground, yelling at a nearby soldier to handle them. He was finishing up his wards as he ran up the stairs behind Daniel. They cleared the small door and hit the ledge at the same time. Madi and Brandt stared with them.

The Dark Horde approached like a shadow. One of the giant spider transports crawled behind them. Monsters flew above and slithered on the ground in front of the demons. Some demons rode horses, but Orrin saw tigers with multiple tails, a crocodile the size of a car, and a small cavalry riding what looked like ostriches but with too many legs.

"Ready your attacks." Silas's voice echoed from down the Wall. Orrin couldn't even see him but felt calm and sure of himself after hearing the words.

Orrin picked a target. His debuffs worked once they were closer, but at this range, he could only use [Lightstrikes]. *Note to self, long-range options needed. Maybe combine [Lightstrike] and a debuff?*

Spells started pouring off the Wall, followed a moment later by thousands of arrows. The demons kept coming. Those that fell in the rush toward Dey rolled and picked themselves up before continuing on.

Madi burned an early cast of [Sunbeam], shredding apart two demons in a fiery death, but a demon mage cast a barrier of ice overhead. Her spell winked out as she realized the waste of mana burning through the ice would be.

Orrin threw spells in clusters, trying to hit the same monsters. He picked targets that might be able to scale the wall. The smaller monsters used by the demons usually ran alongside their summoner or [Ranger] friend, but Orrin went after the larger groups. He couldn't see the [Fogbinder] but knew the small monster pack within the Horde had to be from that class. Over forty lizard-like, waist-tall monsters standing upright and holding daggers in each hand rushed in his direction.

"One. Two. Three." Orrin counted off as Daniel chucked Gertrude into the distance, hoping the massive grouping would give him some luck hitting an enemy.

"What are you doing?" Daniel asked as he called his sword back to his hand. "This isn't *Lord of the Rings*. You don't need to count how many you kill."

"Seven. Eight," Orrin finished. "Eight casts of [Lightstrikes] and I can kill one of those lizard guys. I'm targeting five of them at a time with each cast. I can handle that group."

Madi pointed toward the demons riding the avian monsters with the long, bent legs. Orrin shivered at the multilimbed birds. "I'm going to explode some [Shimmersight] spells in their way. Brandt and Daniel, target the ones up front. If we can trip them up, the ones behind might fall."

Madi didn't wait for an answer but threw two dazzling streaks of light from her hands. Her upgraded class let her change the spell from the slow-moving ball of light that acted like a flash-bang grenade into bullets. The streaks moved faster, but the status effect lasted for a shorter duration. In this case, she used it right.

One demon was slightly ahead of the others in the small pack of bird-riding cavalry. Both of Madi's spells went off by his face. His bird monster crowed and bucked just before an arrow struck the demon in the arm.

"Damn, I was aiming for his chest." Brandt cursed and pulled another arrow back before releasing it.

Daniel's sword sounded like a helicopter as it flew through the air in a twirling dervish of death. It missed the lead demon but unseated two behind him. Orrin winced as the birds kept going, crushing one of the demons underfoot.

Orrin kept up his [Lightstrikes], ignoring the small dings of experience popping up on his blue screen. The monsters gave good XP, which he would use to his advantage. Maybe he could level from this.

He didn't have time to check his status or run numbers before the Dark Horde hit the Wall. The real fight had begun.

Chapter 43

The demons slammed against the Wall like a tidal wave, pressing against it with such strength that Orrin felt a slight shift in the stone beneath his feet. The mages around him hurled blasts of fire and lances of ice, along with a dozen other spells Orrin didn't have time to identify.

"Daniel, don't you dare," Brandt shouted, grabbing the [Hero]'s belt and pulling him back from the ledge. "You are melee and this is still a ranged fight."

Daniel cursed and argued, but Orrin ignored it. Brandt had him under control. He leaned over the edge and began casting [Decrease Strength] and [Split Spell]. The combination let him debuff multiple targets at the same time. Most of the demons dropped after a few castings, digging their fingers into the mud and trying to crawl away from the Wall.

Madi didn't let that happen. Her spells were more varied now with her upgraded class. She was learning new depths to her power every day.

"[Vivid Lightshow]." Madi clutched her collapsible spear in one hand and held her free hand pointed toward the weakened demons, palm out. Butterflies larger than her normal spell funneled from between her fingers in a stunning array of bright colors. Winged creatures of light in shades of red, orange, and yellow drifted slowly among the demons below. When one of the butterflies touched a demon, the skin hissed and spat like water on hot oil. The reds burst into flares of fire, while the oranges melted into the demons' armor like lava. The yellow butterflies traveled toward faces and disappeared in a flash of bright light that temporarily blinded all the enemies within five feet.

Orrin continued to cast his debuffs and risked a glance over his shoulder at Daniel. He was grinning wide as he pulled flasks out of a box. "Brandt, what is Daniel doing?" Orrin asked.

Hearing the alarm in his voice, Madi took her eyes away from the battle. "Daniel, be careful with those."

Daniel ran up to the ledge, holding six clay flasks between his fingers. "I've got them. Don't worry so much. Brandt said you can light these up?"

"Will somebody tell me what is going on?" Orrin asked. "Daniel, you should be throwing spears or Gerty at the demons."

Daniel laughed. "Watch this."

He set down half the bottles and raised one over his head before throwing it into a cluster of monsters under the demons' control. The clay shattered over a six-legged wolf with two heads. It burst like a water balloon, covering another four of the wolves and two demons with the substance inside.

"Now, Madi."

Madi dropped her spear into her hip holster and sent a small [Lightbeam] at the demon in the middle. Normally, her most basic attack spell jumped from her finger like a powerful flashlight, but this time she cupped her right hand into her left like steadying a gun. The blast that came out from her pointer finger was bright red. Orrin felt the heat from a few feet away.

The [Lightbeam] struck the demon and he went up in flames. The inferno caught on the liquid Daniel threw and set a small part of the battlefield on fire. Wolves howled and demons screamed. The Horde was still rushing in, and while some tried to slow or change their direction, the press of bodies pushed more into the flames. It took only ten seconds before the fire was trampled out, but close to twenty more demons suffered burns in that time.

"That was badass," Daniel cheered and pointed toward another group with a few monsters spread in. "There next."

Orrin rolled his eyes. Daniel was trying to level himself as well.

They continued to defend against the demons in what became a well-honed machine. If the demons were close enough, Orrin threw a few debuffs to slow them down. Daniel threw oil and Madi set them on fire. Brandt restocked Daniel with the bottles of oil, as his higher stats allowed him to throw harder and with more accuracy.

All around them, mages rotated out as they ran out of mana. A few archers went down as the demons' own ranged fighters found targets. One arrow hit Madi in the shoulder, but Orrin's [Ward] kept it from doing damage. He made sure to check over his friends from time to time and even spent a minute healing a nearby mage who took an arrow to the knee. The idiot had stood on the ledge trying to summon what could have been a tornado but fell back when the demons saw a prime target.

"Breach to the south!" Cries came down the line as the defenders played the longest game of telephone ever conceived. "Demons through the Wall."

Orrin cursed and plucked a bottle from Daniel's fingers right before he threw it. "Let's go help. I'm going to [Teleport] us a mile down the Wall. Ready?"

Orrin didn't wait for an answer and ran down the stairs. One of the first things Orrin had done when the Wall was complete was walk the entire length of the thing. He could pick a specific spot he remembered clearly to travel to or move along it with a distance in mind. Now that the Dark Horde was here, the powers that be had activated the teleport wards on the Wall. The demons couldn't simply jump by the Wall if they couldn't [Teleport]; however, that meant traveling up and down the Wall for the defenders was just as hard. He needed to get down the stairs before he could pop his party to the breach.

Orrin barely had time to tap his foot twice before Daniel and Madi reached the bottom of the stairs, followed shortly thereafter by Brandt.

He activated his spell and felt the familiar tumble of magic before they landed in a loose circle in a different part of the Pass. Several people were running about, and Orrin reached out to grab the closest one.

"How far to the breach?" he demanded as the poor woman dropped a stack of pots. He used [Identify]. The lady was a [Cook].

"T-the soldiers said to r-run." She shivered in fear, her eyes darting to every corner. "The demons got through one of the doorways."

Brandt stepped in front and took Orrin's hand off the woman's shoulder. "If it's a doorway, I know where the nearest one is. There should only be two or three total this far south anyway. Let her escape, Orrin."

Orrin realized his mistake and released her with a quiet "sorry." She ran like he was a demon himself. His adrenaline was spiking from the shouting and screams from the Wall.

"Lead the way, Brandt."

They ran until Brandt slowed with a hand up. Jagged rocks were strewn about the ground inside the Wall, with a fifteen-foot hole blasted into the side. Forty or fifty men fought to hold back the tide, but more demons poured into the opening every second they watched.

"Orrin, you need to [Teleport] back to command and bring a [Earth Mage] or [Stone Mage] back here," Brandt started ordering them as he drew his longsword. "Madi, I want lights inside that hole so bright nobody can see. Daniel, come with me and let's kill a few demons."

Orrin started forward. "I can help drop them. We can—"

"Go now," Brandt yelled over his shoulder as he ran to help the soldiers. "More will come through until we close the gap."

Orrin watched a woman swing a pickax at a demon who side-stepped and stabbed her through the chest. *I can heal her. I can stop the demons.* Orrin warred with himself and closed his eyes. He cast [Teleport].

The screaming in his head didn't stop as he ran to the tent and threw himself in. Two guards had weapons leveled at him, but Orrin ignored the sharp blades as he found someone he knew. Lord Tarris stood in the back with his smudged glasses and thin hair. He glanced up for a moment before dismissing Orrin from his thoughts.

"Lord Tarris, there is a breach along the southern Wall. We need a stone or earth mage to help close it," Orrin explained in a rush. "I can [Teleport] them back. Who do you have?"

Lord Tarris snapped his attention back to Orrin and spun the map he was studying on the table around. "Point where it is."

Orrin dragged his finger along and gave his best guess. "About here? I think it was one of the hidden rooms where we could attack from. It's a huge gateway now."

Lord Tarris spoke quickly to an aide at his side and pointed toward the door. "Someone will be outside shortly. Go."

Orrin shifted from foot to foot, tapping his fingers on his crossed arms as he waited. Only a minute passed, but to Orrin, it felt like days.

Daniel and Brandt were fighting with others from Dey. They would be fine. Madi would stay in the back and cast spells. Nobody would get hurt. Orrin kept telling himself the same comforting lies until a man in black-and-gray robes walked up to him.

"Are you the [Locationist]? I was told someone would bring me to a crack in our Wall. I'm Everet Gemillia, [Earth Mage] and protégé of—"

"I don't give a fuck." Orrin shuffled the man into his party, grabbed his arm, and jumped them both to the hole.

His entire trip lasted three minutes. Three minutes was a long time for the defenders.

Daniel was a blur in the middle of a hundred demons. A group of dirty-white monsters that Orrin could have mistaken for infants scurried along the ground as well. The baby monsters had four hands with long nails instead of feet and tumbled like little acrobats as they flipped over demons and defenders alike. Their teeth stuck out of their mouths like a shark's and blood gushed wherever they bit down.

Orrin started casting debuffs on the demons. In between, he threw heals on the wounded and tried to buff any soldier still fighting.

"This is not safe," Everet screeched as he backed up slowly. "You were only supposed to bring me places that are safe."

Orrin growled and grabbed the man's shirt collar before he could run. "You are going to close that hole up. If you run, I will [Teleport] you into the middle of the Horde. Do you understand?"

Everet paled and then threw up on Orrin's shoes. Orrin shook him once and grabbed his face. "Everet, if you close that up, I'll keep you safe. This is nothing. That's the [Hero] fighting in there."

The [Earth Mage] didn't answer, but neither did he run when Orrin turned his attention back to his friends. Madi was a disco ball of lights. The spells bounced off her in what Orrin was sure would make the greatest EDM party of all time. Brandt was a dervish with his blade, moving through demons and the creepy monster babies with a fire in his eyes. Blood covered half of his face, and Orrin cast [Heal Small Wounds].

Orrin used [Identify] on the monsters, learning they were Snarlclutches. He summoned two [Ice Swords] and cast [Gust]. Each one he hit froze solid. Usually, Orrin's attack with the combination of [Gust] and ice magic left a limb stuck in ice. The smaller size of the monsters let him become a human ice-cube maker.

"Orrin, over here," Madi shouted. The demons kept coming through, but Everet was finally working on the breach. The rough edges were filling in and slowly moving down.

At this rate, he can close it in another two or three minutes, Orrin guessed as he sprinted through the demons. "What do you need, Madi?"

Her face was covered with sweat despite being stationary and away from the main fighting force. She'd gathered the few mages to create a ranged attack squad, but the extensive mana use was still exhausting. She pulled him behind the front line of mages and pointed to a few people lying down. Some didn't move, but others cried in pain.

"Some of our mages got hit with a fire attack. The damage won't heal," she answered even as she cast another group of butterflies. A [Sunbeam] followed shortly after, ceasing the rush of another ten demons into the hole. "Can you take a look?"

Orrin used [Diagnose] on one of the grimacing mages. "Fire chilled. I haven't seen that before. Does anyone know what that does?"

One of the defenders used a spell that threw a flamethrower's worth of fire magic into the middle of the incoming demons before sucking in through his teeth. "That's an outlawed spell, then. Fire chill is an effect of [Funeral Fire] or the like. It sucks in any healing mana until the damage over time is complete."

Orrin rolled his eyes at someone complaining about an illegal spell while fighting demons. "[Purify]."

The red splotch on the mage's leg faded. Orrin cast [Heal Small Wounds] to be sure. The female mage stopped writhing in pain and sat up, shaking her head. She didn't even thank Orrin before standing and rushing back into the line of magic users.

"You're welcome," Orrin shouted and then went back to work fixing up the rest. It took one minute to get the rest on their feet, and Orrin sighed in relief as the stone finally grew back into the ground.

Daniel finished mopping up the last of the demons, using his [Gravity Well] to pull a few that tried to run back into his sword's path. Orrin tossed Madi a mana potion before slapping Everet on the back.

"Good job, Everet. I'll call for you next time they break through. Very nice work."

The [Earth Mage] was red in the face from pushing the large amount of mana required for his spells so quickly. At Orrin's words, his eyebrows raised up in terror and he promptly fainted.

"Should we leave him here?" the flamethrower mage asked, kicking at Everet's side with his foot.

Orrin sighed and picked up the man with ease. His smaller frame holding the man over his shoulder gave a few of the mages pause. "I'll bring him back when he wakes up. Everybody back up the Wall. This isn't over."

Daniel sat on the ground in the middle of the bodies of nearly a hundred demons. Gertrude stood upright in the ground next to him, covered in blood. Orrin carried Everet to his friend and kicked a few bodies to make space for the mage's limp body.

"You doing good? You look tired," Orrin ribbed Daniel. "If you have time to take a break, we must not be using you hard enough. Aren't you supposed to be the [Hero] or something?"

Daniel held up his fists with a single finger outstretched in Orrin's direction.

Chapter 44

The momentum of the demon attack changed after another two hours. Orrin and his party were back on top of the Wall, filling in the gaps wherever they could. Daniel continued to throw his Gertrude, along with a few other choice surprises that the people of Dey cooked up, including flammable oil, a bag of powder that blinded anyone who got caught in the wind, and a few spears with ice blades that exploded into a crystalline growth of spikes. Madi tried to be judicious in her mana consumption, but like the rest of the mages, she began to run low.

When the spells from the Wall flagged, the high-level demons struck. The push from the stronger demons gave the workers more time to implant themselves a hundred yards from the Wall. Shovels and earth magic threw dirt up as the demon army made foxholes. They connected a few, but it would take time to finish a long embankment.

"There's another level-ninety demon over there," Orrin shouted. The defenders around them focused their attacks on the one Orrin pointed out. It was becoming a common strategy for the humans and elves. Orrin had even seen an orc mage carrying two staffs throwing magic around in a flurry. Everyone targeted the high-level demon.

Levels and stats were important in Asmea, but the people had a saying: "Even a [Farmer] can take down a [Hero]."

Even with his own prodigious stats, a targeted hit would take Orrin down. He saw it firsthand when five arrows hit the demon, barely slowing her. Her thin tail moved sinuously in time with her body as she ducked under an [Ice Lance], but she came to a stop in front of a pit of fire that appeared without warning. Another few arrows hit her, with one sticking deep into her thigh. The female demon hissed and cut the arrows with a single strike from her shortsword, leaving the barbs inside.

Two spears hit her. One went through the same leg as the arrow, sticking through her and planting its point in the ground. While the demon tried to pull the weapon from the dirt, a hail of different magic hit her in an explosion of colors. Within seconds, the demon was shredded to pieces.

Orrin kept throwing out [Decrease Strength] on the demons until Madi sat down to rest. "Are you okay?"

Madi closed her eyes and breathed through her nose in short, fast puffs. "I'm almost at zero mana. I need a minute. I feel dizzy."

Orrin offered a regen potion to her, but she shook her head. "I'll save that for later. They just keep coming. If all the mages run out of magic, we might have to open part of the Wall to fight them head-on."

Orrin put the glass vial in her hand for safekeeping. He tried to tell her to use it now, but a cheer went up from the northern part of the Wall.

"Phoenix team is back."

"They took out twenty demons in a minute."

Whispers of praise made their way down the pipeline of fighters, happy to gossip about something positive.

"What is going on?" Daniel popped back from chucking random items at the demons. "What is Phoenix team? Is it like Dragoon team?"

Madi's eyes, a moment ago so tired, lit up with joy. "Phoenix team is the strongest five adventurers in Asmea. They're the best of the best. I didn't think they'd get here in time."

Orrin cast another [Decrease Dexterity] on a group of demons. The higher level kept them from falling over, but at least he slowed them enough for others to hit them. "Why weren't they here from the beginning? If they're the best, we could have used them from the start."

"They delve the dungeons and keep them from overflowing. They've been in Mistwater Lanterns for the last year." Madi pushed herself to her feet and paused, glancing at the potion in her hand. She threw her head back and drank it down. "I was able to meet two of them once when my father awarded them a medal. They turned an entire Horde back at the Wall of Dey. Not even the entire team. Just two of them."

Daniel glanced at Orrin and raised an eyebrow. Madi was fangirling hard.

Brandt threw another javelin at a demon but missed. They were running low and he cursed. "If you have time to talk, you should be calling out your target. Get back over to the edge and attack."

A few of the soldiers gave sheepish grins and resumed the fight.

The sun crested in the sky. The tuffs of grass that remained from the heavy boots and claws of the Dark Horde reflected brightly among the puddles of blood. A horn echoed from farther north and most of the demons turned to the sound. A few began backing away from the small entrenchment they'd finally finished. The trickle became a rushing flood as the demons fought each other to get out of the trench they'd dug.

"What's going on?" Daniel asked even as he threw his giant sword again. With his Return rune on Gertrude and the twin rune on his dragon bone ring, his weapon worked like a boomerang. A boomerang made of a hunk of metal weighing more than most humans and large enough to cleave through running demons like they were butter. His sword slapped back into his hand when he recalled it. "Why are they running?"

A rod of flames shot from the north. It filled the ditch but the head of the fire rose into the air from time to time, tossing burning demons to either side.

"That's [Blaze Serpent]," Madi whispered in awe. "June the [Pyrocaster]'s famous spell . . . right in front of me."

Orrin watched as the snake consumed demons by the dozens. Depending on how far it had traveled, it might have already killed a thousand of the invaders. "I'm getting that spell."

He ignored the incredulous expressions from everyone around him as he quickly pulled up his system store. "[Blaze Serpent]? Did you say it right?"

Madi simply nodded as she watched the spell rush the line in front of them. The demons were in full retreat mode now.

"Damn. I can't find it. I'll have to ask what spells unlock it." Orrin cast a few [Lightstrikes] on stragglers, but they all were able to move out of range. "Did we win?"

The demons retreated to lick their wounds and Dey's defenders celebrated. Orders to conserve mana and rest were ignored, with many people claiming the Phoenix team would eradicate the demons for them.

Orrin brought an early dinner out from his [Dimension Hole] and poured another cup of coffee as they ate. Daniel tore into his beef stew with gusto and asked Madi questions about the powerful party they'd yet to meet.

Orrin checked his notifications. He'd killed a few monsters in the fight. The demons didn't give him much experience individually, but some of the creatures they commanded did.

Experience Gained: 400 XP (80 XP x 5)

Level 32 Obtained!
+10 AP

Experience Gained: 600 XP (40 XP x 15)
Experience Gained: 1,600 XP (100 XP x 8; 50 XP x 11; 25 XP x 10)
Experience Gained: 375 XP (375 XP x 1)
Experience Gained: 30 XP (10 XP x 3)

A good start toward the next level, too. Orrin grinned at the new ability points. He could probably buy something if he wanted to. Madi's voice broke into his reverie.

"Phoenix spends a lot of time dungeon diving," Madi explained as she ate from the bowl Orrin provided. His ability to keep food in storage fresh let them eat better than most on the Wall. "My father sent runners into the dungeon as soon as we knew about the demon threat, but it was a long shot to find them. They're gone for up to a year at a time, trying to find the end of the larger dungeons."

Daniel tilted his head. "But I thought the big dungeons were farmed for resources. Wouldn't it be a bad thing if they destroyed one?"

Madi waved a spoon around as she answered. "They don't defeat a dungeon unless it's requested. They map it out for other adventurers. They reduce the number of monsters so there isn't a dungeon break."

Brandt, on his back, groaned. He'd collapsed almost immediately upon sitting down. His job as a [Knight] meant a lot of running around the top, giving orders, and making sure consumables stayed ready for use. "They are a headache and a half. Whenever they roll into Dey, they drink too much, get into fights, and destroy buildings."

"Brandt doesn't like them because Henrick was my first crush," Madi confided. "He's a [Paragon Knight]."

"You know him well?" Orrin asked. "What's the difference between a [Knight] and a [Paragon Knight]?"

Madi kept her face pointed down toward her food. "I've never met him. He's a bit older than me."

"He's almost twice her age and a dick," Brandt answered. "A [Paragon Knight] isn't like a [Knight] at all. He takes damage. That's his entire arsenal."

"[Paragon Knights] are tanks," Madi said, throwing shade at Brandt. "They stay in front of their teammates and soak up hits from monsters. They might not be huge damage machines, but they rarely get knocked down."

Brandt grunted and pushed his way up to a seated position. "Orrin, can I have some coffee? I have some things to do before I turn in."

"It's four in the afternoon," Madi chided. "What do you need to do and why would you go to bed this early?"

Brandt accepted the cup from Orrin and stood slowly. "I have reports to give and need to make sure a few people are doing their jobs. I have night shift tonight. That means I have to sleep when I can to be able to stay fresh for the morning."

"Knight shift." Daniel chuckled at his own pun. Orrin rolled his eyes and hit him with the back of his hand.

"Do you need me to [Teleport] you back to Dey?" Orrin offered, but Brandt shook his head.

"I'll be on the Wall all night. We can meet at the usual spot in the morning. Keep her out of trouble." Brandt nodded his head toward Madi. "Good job today, all of you."

Brandt left and Daniel chatted with Madi, teasing her about her celebrity crush. Once their early dinner was finished, Daniel fulfilled a promise he'd made to Silas by walking around and talking with random soldiers. Orrin's charismatic friend easily chummed it up with the lower-class volunteers and the lifetime soldiers, joking with them and giving a little hope to the defenders of Dey.

"Do you think the demons will attack again today or wait until tomorrow?" Orrin asked Madi. They sat in folding chairs in the back of the tent city that had popped up behind the Wall.

Madi shuffled around a few paper reports that she'd been reading through. Even now, Silas trained his daughter by having her double-check intelligence letters and field reports. "I would assume the demons keep their mages and spellcasters on rotation like us. War is a game of Kala where you must save your red marbles for greatest effect." She held a finger to a report and glanced at Orrin. "Mages are the red marbles of war. Limited use but of great importance. We can't simply throw our melee fighters against theirs. One mage could massacre them all like June did today. We keep a strict schedule for most of our forces, regulating how many mana potions some use and assigning conflicting magic types far from each other. It doesn't help to have an [Ice Mage] make the ground slick and difficult to traverse, only for a [Fire Mage] to melt everything a moment later."

She held a stack of papers toward Orrin. "These are reports by our [Analysts] and the Guild assessor. It gives suggestions on the best use of our people based on what we know of their abilities. Not everyone shares their entire spell list, but even a general idea lets us streamline our attacks better. This is the reason we can hold off the demons. They're still sending people in haphazardly to attack. Today was a little more organized, but scout reports note that a few troops waited in the camp. Our best guess is that their leaders are holding back and reorganizing their own troops. Did you notice how many of the demons fight in small groups instead of working together? One of the [Analysts] wrote . . . here it is, he wrote that the demons are acting like clans from Veskar. They fight independently from the rest of the groups, almost as if the demons are from a bunch of different countries. We keep calling them all demons, too, but most of them appear to be human. The dwarves and orcs are easier to spot, but we have reports of orcs with horns and dwarves with tails as well."

Daniel returned and slumped into a chair. "I'm drained. What are you guys reading?"

Madi sighed and began to recount all the things she'd just told Orrin. The sun began to set, and with no imminent warning of attack, Orrin closed his eyes in the chair. His sleep schedule was off due to the Hospital and Horde working in concert to keep him running around. A quick catnap would be nice.

Madi smirked at Daniel as Orrin started to snore.

Chapter 45

Orrin woke a few hours later to a small chime. His neck was sore from sleeping in a chair, but a quick healing spell relieved his stiffness. Madi and Daniel spoke in whispers, still going over the reports from Silas.

"Did you have a nice nap?" Daniel asked playfully upon seeing Orrin was awake.

"What was that sound?" Orrin asked, half-asleep still. "Are the demons attacking?"

Madi frowned and raised her head, cocking an ear to the sky. "I didn't hear anything."

Orrin blinked and noticed a blinking marker in his vision. "Oh, it's a system thing."

He opened the box and read. The words woke him up fast.

"Um, guys . . ." Orrin tried to turn the blue box and share it, but it resisted. "Listen to this." Orrin read the notification aloud.

Administrator Access Engaged:
Amir Fallah [Healer] synchronization complete.
Reward: Two (2) administrator points.

"When did you see Amir?" Daniel asked in confusion. He turned his head to look over his shoulder. "Is he around here?"

"I have no idea," Orrin responded, checking his status and seeing the extra points already added. "I don't know what happened."

Madi's brow furrowed in thought. "Orrin, how many points did you spend to change our classes?"

"One," Orrin answered while running prices for Administrator skills through his head. "I have twenty-five now."

"What does 'synchronization' mean?" Madi asked. "Do you think Amir is safe?"

Orrin mentally prodded the notification, but no more information was available. "I need to find him. I'm going to [Teleport] into the city. You guys want to come or stay here?"

Daniel shrugged and waved a hand at the paper around them. "Go ahead. We'll be here. This is actually fascinating. They have information on how people's spells might interact. I'm trying to make combinations that might be useful. What do you think would happen if we had a [Wind Mage] use . . ." Daniel shuffled a few papers and read aloud. "[Fog Cloud], and then have an [Ice Mage] cast some ice magic into it?"

Orrin gave Madi a long-suffering look before answering. "The mana from two different mages wouldn't mix unless it was also an area effect. From what I learned in school—"

"Magic school," Daniel interrupted with a grin.

"From what I learned in magic school, the mana of each individual is slightly different. If the spell leaves residuals, like fire or ice on the ground, there's a chance the two can interact, but those are all mostly known." Orrin stood up and stretched his arms above his head. "I'm sure Madi told you this."

Madi nodded. "I did. The things we know work are already being used, just like we keep some mages separated so their spells don't negate each other. There might be some combination that we don't know, but it's highly unlikely."

Daniel pointed at Orrin. "He mixes his spells."

"Using my own mana." Orrin sighed. "If some caster has two spells and can figure out how to combine them, good for them. I'm off to talk with Amir."

Madi waved as Daniel grumbled. Two [Teleports] brought Orrin to the front of the Fallah coffee shop.

Someone had taken the time to cover the windows with boards, and a few planks of wood lay in a pile near the door. Small clouds of soot drifted out from inside. Two guards that Orrin recognized from Brandt's command sat at one of the less destroyed tables playing cards.

"Hello?" Orrin walked up to peek inside. "Amir? Mr. Fallah? Is anyone home?"

"Orrin?" Amir's father lurched out. He held a crutch in one arm and a broom in the other. "What brings you to my shop? Is Amir safe? Did something happen?"

Orrin couldn't believe Mr. Fallah was cleaning up his café. It had been less than a day since he'd lost his leg and he was sweeping the ash from his business with one arm. "What are you doing here, Mr. Fallah? We can come help you clean after we drive the Horde away. Where's Amir?"

"Something happened, yes? I pushed too hard on him. He was not ready." The tall, dark man leaned against the door jam and dropped his broom. His dirty palm left a smear of soot across his forehead and nose as he rubbed down his face. "Is Amir alive?"

Orrin picked up the fallen broom and leaned it against the inside of the store. "What are you talking about? I thought Amir was with you."

"He thought this was his fault." Mr. Fallah waved a hand at his missing leg. "Amir is a good boy. Passionate and smart, but timid at times. I talked sense at him. Told him he needed to use his powers for helping others, even at the dark times. He went to ask Lord Catanzano for orders, like a soldier. He's been gone all day."

Orrin thought he understood but clarified, "You mean, Amir went to heal people and help with the Horde?"

"Yes. One of the watcher men went with him. You arrived and I feared for my boy."

"Mr. Fallah, I don't think Amir is in trouble. I just wanted to find him . . . for something," Orrin finished lamely. He didn't want to get into Administrator powers and how he'd given Amir the class that resulted in his father's missing leg. "I'll find him and have him send a message to you. You shouldn't be on your feet, though. Take a day off and rest."

Mr. Fallah grinned and Orrin saw the family resemblance in the smile. "I am not on feet. Just one foot." He laughed and hopped to the broom. "If Orrin is watching my son, he will be safe. I will make coffee for you when I reopen, yes?"

Orrin assured the man he would return and waited for him to go back into his store. He walked up to the two guards. One of the guards, a mage named Lethe, Orrin recognized. They'd fought Sproits together. "You let Amir run off? What if the Hospital comes after him?"

Lethe didn't take her eyes off the cards in front of her but raised an eyebrow. "We brought him to Lord Catanzano, who gave him permission to help. He's not a prisoner."

Orrin steadied his breathing. "Can you at least help him clean up in there? You use water magic, right? How hard would it be to clean the place?"

Lethe shook her head and played a card, resting it on the other guard's card. The other man cursed. "My orders are to keep him safe. I need to conserve mana in case we're attacked or I get reassigned to the Wall."

Orrin counted out two gold pieces from his pocket and yanked a mana potion off his belt. He slammed the items on the table, disrupting the card game. "Here. This should cover your services. Don't let the man with one leg work harder than you."

Orrin didn't wait for an answer and teleported back to camp.

"Back already?" Daniel asked absently. He stared into space like he was reading something on his status screen. "Amir was fine?"

"Amir wasn't there," Orrin spat, disgusted at the guard's attitude. He explained about the missing [Healer] before turning to Madi. "Do you mind coming with me to ask your dad about Amir? He likes you better than me for some reason."

Madi snorted but stood from her chair. "I wouldn't be so sure, Orrin. If he could adopt you at this point, I think he would. Did I tell you how many guards from the Catanzano house or adventurers from the Guild have taken [Side Steps] because of you in the last few months? From the reports I read, no less than ten people are alive today because of that skill. A skill that we were underutilizing until you. That doesn't even begin to cover the lives saved because of the buff balls you made."

Orrin groaned. "Not you, too. *Spell orbs.* Please don't say 'buff balls.'"

Madi laughed. "Come on. They moved the command tent. I'll go with you."

Daniel joined them and Madi led the way to the back of the troop tents. She pointed to a nondescript pavilion with heavy canvas sides. "I'll talk to the guard first. We don't need to scare them every time you want to talk, right?"

A few minutes later, a guard announced Orrin and Daniel. Instead of them being ushered into the tent, Silas wheeled himself out.

"Orrin. Daniel." Silas nodded at each in turn before smiling at his daughter. "I appreciate you waiting. What brings you three my way this time?"

Orrin went on the attack. "Where is Amir Fallah?"

Silas remained calm and gave nothing away on his face. "The young [Healer] requested to join the defense and help with injuries. I have talked with the Hospital, and they are staying out of his way. I believe he is at one of the secondary locations a few miles from here, but I can find out for sure if you give me a moment."

"Yes, please." Orrin scowled. He'd halfway hoped for more of a fight. Amir shouldn't be out here. He couldn't fight, and half the Hospital wanted him dead. If anything happened to him because Silas had allowed his friend to come out into danger . . .

Silas opened the tent flap and gave a quiet order for someone to find Amir. The inside bustled with activity, and Madi covered her mouth when she recognized faces.

"Phoenix team is inside?" Madi whispered to her father. "You weren't going to introduce me?"

Silas sighed. "They appeared in the middle of the last attack and only now deemed it prudent to report in. High-level adventurers don't follow the same rules as the rest of us, Madeleine. They aren't answering our questions and I don't want to bother them. We can use their help."

Daniel leaned over and waved. "Hello in there. That fire-snake spell was badass. My friend wants to get it, too. Any advice?" His voice rang out and a moment of stunned silence followed from inside.

"Daniel, what are you doing?" Madi chastised and kicked him in the leg.

The flap pulled back farther as a shield larger than Orrin exited the tent. Behind the massive tower shield, a man pushing seven feet tall in full plate armor stepped out. His helmet flared to a point but left his eyes and face unprotected. The longsword on his back rested higher than his head but still barely cleared the ground at his feet. White scars marked his tanned skin and his dark-brown hair fell to his shoulders, covering half his face. A fresh, jagged cut marred one cheek, crusty and still covered in blood.

"Lord Catanzano, is there a problem with the discipline of your men?" the man asked softly; however, Orrin felt the threat behind the words. This man was powerful in the don't-fuck-about type of way.

"Not at all, Sir Henrick." Silas yanked on a wheel to spin himself around. "This is my daughter, Madeleine, and some of her party. This is the [Hero], Daniel. That is Orrin. He makes the spell orbs we discussed."

Orrin gaped. Silas was speaking with respect and sounded nervous, something he'd never seen in the man before.

"The [Hero] is the one asking about June's spells?" the [Paragon Knight] asked slowly with the same soft but threatening tone. "Has he not been taught how rude that is?"

Orrin readied [Teleport], because he knew Daniel was about to open his stupid mouth and get them killed. *Please don't be an idiot. Please don't be an idiot,* Orrin chanted, trying to send his thoughts into Daniel's mind telepathically.

"Hi, Sir Henrick. I'm Daniel." Daniel held out his hand. "Sorry if I asked something improperly, I didn't mean to offend anyone. Thank you for the help today. It was awesome to see your party member's spell."

Orrin felt Madi and Silas holding their breath.

Henrick nodded once, and a smile caught a corner of his mouth. "Good. You have decorum. Lord Catanzano, please invite these three into the discussions. I believe [Heroes] have a skill to help with Demon Lords. It could be beneficial." He ducked back into the tent without waiting for an answer.

Silas blinked twice before grabbing Madi and practically shoving her into the tent. He paused and stared at Orrin. "Behave yourself around Sir Henrick, please."

"Why are you worried about me?" Orrin asked, pointing at Daniel. "He's the one you should be warning."

Daniel sauntered into the tent behind Madi. Everyone ignored Orrin.

"Seriously?" Orrin rubbed his hands down his sides, smoothing out his shirt before stomping inside.

Chapter 46

Orrin entered a packed tent. Leanthun stood to one side with the other lords of Dey. A few generals that Orrin recognized also waited behind them, but the table was covered in food and large mugs filled with beer. Four people he didn't recognize were tearing into the meal with a speed that spoke to hunger but also high stats.

The four adventurers could not be more different. While Henrick continued to stand at the head of the table in his gleaming metal armor and both hands clasped on the tiny chair in front of him, another man tipped his chair back on two legs. His feet rested on the table, and he was dropping strips of meat directly down his throat.

"Henrick, this lamb is tasty. You should pick some up for our next run." The thin, pale man moaned as he chewed. A red bandanna was tied around his head, covering his ears, but his golden hair hung long down his back. It clashed with his green-and-brown leather cuirass. Two serrated blades hung at his hips. "Who are the kids?"

Madi bowed. "My name is Madeleine Catanzano, daughter of Lord Silas Catanzano. This is the [Hero] Daniel and [Utility Warder] Orrin. It's an honor to meet you, Sir Vulwin."

The man waved a strip of meat back and forth in front of Madi. "Don't go calling me 'sir.' I don't care for the fancy titles. The [Hero], you say? Didn't I hear the [Hero] stayed up on the Wall, out of the fight?"

Orrin's foot moved on its own, stepping forward to challenge the man, but Daniel's hand fell heavy on his shoulder. "I did stay on the Wall today. I've got this problem that once I start fighting demons, it's a bit hard to stop me. I thought I'd let everyone else have a go at it for once."

The wisp of a man laughed so hard his chair tipped and he fell backward with a thud. He was on his feet and sitting again in a flash of movement, banging the table. "Henrick, this one has spunk. I like him."

The knight grunted what could have been a laugh before pointing to the other members in turn. "That is Vulwin. He runs point and keeps us appraised of the beasts in our path. Watch your pockets around him. Tell me if things go missing and I'll turn him over and shake your items loose."

Vulwin held his hands up in surrender. "I don't know what he's talking about."

"Hey, that's my ring," Daniel cried and pointed to the man's finger. His Return dragon-bone ring was on Vulwin's pinky.

Henrick growled and the man tossed the ring to Daniel.

"June is our mage," Henrick resumed, pointing to a stocky woman with messy brown hair and wearing a baggy gray sweater. She waved to them and Orrin half raised a hand in return. "Don't be rude." Henrick glared at Daniel for a moment before continuing.

Orrin expected red robes from someone with a class called [Pyrocaster], but June would have fit in as a mom in the car pickup lane at school. She appeared to be in her thirties or forties. Vulwin was harder to figure out. Orrin would have thought late twenties or early thirties, but something about his eyes gave him pause from picking a number.

"Rasha is a spellsword and Thram is our dwarf," Henrick finished up, pointing out a woman who couldn't be much older than Madi and a short, stout dwarven man with his beard tucked into his shirt. He had three empty tankards of beer in front of him and was nursing a fourth.

"A dwarf?" Thram barked. "That's how you introduce me now? You even shorten my mighty name in an attempt to mock me. Henrick, I swear on your mother's tits, I will let the next monster bite your liver if you don't introduce me right."

Henrick's small smile peeked out again. "Be honored, fair mortals, for you are in the presence of Thramnaek Hillguard, our resourceful [Earth Mage] and faithful friend. Woe to the monster or maiden that gets in his way."

Rasha slapped Thram on the back playfully as she piled meat on her plate. "Thram is bluffing. He'd never let a monster get to us." She turned her deep-brown eyes on Orrin. "Are you the one who made the spell orbs with stat-increase spells?"

Rasha wore a mix of armor that showed off a lot of her light-brown skin. Both her shoulders were bare and her chest piece ended well above her stomach. Although Henrick called her a spellsword, Orrin saw no weapon on her. He tried not to ogle, as he'd seen some swimsuits that covered more in the past.

"Yes, I am. Did you get to use one?" Orrin answered, keeping his eyes on her face.

Rasha smiled as she chewed. "Not yet. We heard about the commotion out here in the Pass when we came up from the dungeon and headed straight in to fight. It's not every day we get to mix it up with high-level demons, is it, Vulwin?"

"Astoundingly rare for something so fun," Vulwin responded, slicing a loaf of bread with his knife. His hand blurred as he worked. "We must do it more often. If only they were worth more experience."

Silas coughed. "We are grateful for your assistance. Your timely arrival surprised the Horde and forced them into an early retreat. You saved many lives today."

June blushed and busied herself with the food. Orrin realized she was making extra plates and passing them to her teammates. Madi couldn't tear her eyes away from Henrick. He didn't look twice her age like Brandt criticized. Orrin would guess early thirties at most.

"I invited them into these discussions because of Daniel. From what I've read, a [Hero] has the power to stop a Demon Lord. That is what we are facing here, right, Vulwin?" Henrick remained standing.

Vulwin started cutting strips of lamb and making sandwiches as he answered. "I poked around the demons' camp a bit after we routed them. There's a few powerful demons for sure, and even a human or two that I'd not want to meet alone, but the Demon Lord might give Phoenix a run for our gold." He glanced up quickly at Henrick and spoke quicker. "Not that we wouldn't get him in the end. Just would be a hard fight if it was five on one."

"With all the horned brutes fighting at once, we wouldn't be able to take them?" Thram asked.

Vulwin shrugged. "If it was just us and we fought our way? We could take them down in a few months. I don't think they'll wait around for us, though. Nor do I want to spend that much time away from the dungeon. We still need to ask about that, Henrick."

"Later," the knight said, dismissing the issue. "Daniel, if you would be so kind as to describe how a [Hero] stops a Demon Lord, we can prepare a plan to end this threat quickly."

Orrin thought it ironic that Henrick wanted to know the particulars of one of Daniel's skills shortly after chastising him for asking about June's spell. For some reason, Daniel was being on his best behavior and answered, though.

"I don't have it yet." Daniel prefaced his answer with the bad news first. "But it's called [Demon Seal]. I can seal the Demon Lord one time when he's at low health. I'm not even sure what it means, but it costs more ability points than anything else I've seen."

June perked up at the last few words he spoke. Her voice was soft and soothing. "How many points is it and how many do you have?"

"It costs three hundred and I'm halfway there," Daniel answered her. "I didn't know about it until I'd spent a lot of points already. I got a notification that I get it free at level fifty, but I'm still over a dozen levels away."

Vulwin whistled. "Three hundred is a lot for a one-time-use skill."

Henrick nodded slowly, rubbing the inflamed skin around his facial wound. "That might be out of reach."

Orrin winced as the cut wept blood. "Do you need a heal? That's going to leave a nasty scar."

Vulwin chuckled and teetered on his chair again. "The Hospital already tried. Two [Healers] fainted trying to stop the bleeding. Henrick is a monster in his own right."

Orrin knew healing magic had a reduced effect on those with higher constitution. He'd healed a dwarf once who was dumbstruck at being saved due to his racially enhanced con. He guessed if someone reached Henrick's level, he'd need a lot of constitution. Still, the idea of not trying to help the man didn't even cross Orrin's mind.

"Let me try?" Orrin stepped around the table but found a spear floating in his way. "Or not."

"Rasha, he's not attacking," Henrick said without taking his eyes off Orrin. "Dismiss your weapon."

Rasha grumbled, but the glowing spear disappeared in a flurry of sparks.

"I heard rumors that you could heal, but that is not your class, correct?" Henrick released the back of the chair and stepped closer to Orrin. "Why would you succeed where others failed?"

Orrin glanced at Madi for help. He didn't want to have these people asking questions about his powers, but the damage was done. Madi moved to stand behind Orrin and put her hands on his shoulders. "Orrin works with buffs. That's what he calls his spells that increase stats. He has more mana than most." Orrin noticed June's head twitch, but he kept looking forward as Madi continued. "I watched him heal an entire crowd of people in less than an hour. I trust him with my life. Besides, what's the worst that can happen? He can't stop the bleeding?"

Henrick waved a hand at Orrin. "If you have mana, I would appreciate what you can spare."

Orrin wiggled out from under Madi's grip before starting to cast [Heal Small Wound]. He watched his mana bar slip down as he kept casting. His high intelligence and will made the cost negligible while maximizing the healing power, but the skin barely began to stitch itself back together. Orrin wanted to use [Diagnose] to make sure the inflamed skin wasn't infected but figured a [Purify] spell would do the trick. He spun the other spell up, only to find June holding a wand to his eye.

"What are you doing?" she asked in the same tone his mother would use when he was caught doing something bad. "That is not [Heal Small Wounds]."

Orrin blinked as the thin tip of her wand brushed his eyelashes. He hadn't even seen her move around the table. "Um. I was going to use [Purify] in case the skin is infected. I didn't want to use [Diagnose], since you're all high level and it's rude to use identification spells on others. Can you maybe lower the stabby stick from my eyeball?"

"June?" Henrick said from outside Orrin's vision. Everything was focused on the eye-putter-outer hovering over his nose. "It's fine. Let him continue. I can feel his healing mana work."

June's weapon disappeared and her docile smile returned, making Orrin doubt if he'd seen the intense, murdery glint in her eyes before. "I'm sorry, dear. Please restrict yourself to those two spells or let me know before you cast something different. The mana signatures were different."

Orrin felt sweat trickle down his back. "Yes, ma'am."

June ruffled Orrin's hair. "I'm not old enough for you to 'ma'am' me. Go ahead and fix up Henrick. I want to see your stat spells later if you don't waste all your mana pool."

Orrin swallowed hard and continued to heal Henrick. Although he'd taken a nap, it wasn't enough sleep to reset his stats to normal. His stats peaked at one hundred due to his buffs. The normal eleven hundred points of mana dipped quickly. Five hundred points of mana used and the cut was moving in the right direction.

"Has the bleeding stopped?" Henrick asked as he wiped under his cheek. "You may stop if you need to. It was a valiant effort."

"No." Orrin shook his head and pushed more mana. He started spamming [Heal Small Wounds]. *I'll bring my MP down to a hundred then stop. I can always go to sleep and try again tomorrow.* "I've got this."

June kept close and looked impressed. "He has more mana than I do."

Henrick's face snapped to her at the words.

"It's closing." Orrin smirked. "I think another minute and it'll be all closed up."

Henrick turned back to Orrin. "You may stop now. It is healed enough. I do not fear a scar."

Orrin cast another five times before he sighed and stopped. A thin line remained, but it could have been from a bad paper cut instead of the bite of a blade. He'd reached his mana limit without blood cycling. "I can—"

"He can stop now," Daniel interrupted and stepped up next to Orrin. "He's always outdoing himself."

Henrick touched the wound and examined his fingers. "Thank you for the assistance. I will not forget this."

Silas was all smiles as he rolled up and patted Orrin on the back. "Now, I believe you wanted to discuss next steps?"

Chapter 47

Henrick touched his cheek again while studying Orrin before he answered. "Yes. Tomorrow, Phoenix team will go on the offensive. I want to target high-level demons while your people deal with the remnants. From Vulwin's scouting, we should worry less about the rank and file and more about the fifty to sixty demons above level one hundred."

Silas fidgeted in his chair. "Orrin confirmed some demons were above the level cap. Do you know how the demons accomplished this?"

Henrick nodded toward June.

The mage still had eyes on Orrin when she realized the conversation had shifted to her. "What? Oh, the demons. No magic can break the level cap that I know of. That doesn't mean it couldn't exist . . . I mean, we know it has to. The proof is in the pudding. I also have never heard of targeted multistat increases from a spell, but this rascal has twisted that up in my head, too. I'll need to study the body of one. A demon, not Orrin. Although, I would quite like to see the spell . . . if you don't mind."

Orrin sighed. He'd met the scholarly type before. June wasn't going to stop until she saw him in action. "[Increase Strength]," he said, targeting Madi. "[Increase Dexterity], [Increase Will], and [Increase Intelligence]. Madi, let me know when the twenty minutes are up and I'll [Purify] you if that was too much."

"Fascinating," June said as she scribbled in a notebook that appeared in her hands. "Why [Purify]? What is too much?"

Orrin began explaining the side effects of using more stats than a person could handle, and June caught on.

"Yes. Yes. The level of the body dictates how many stats a person can handle. Like how a melee class won't be able to handle the same level of intelligence as a mage. Not that it happens often. What kind of melee fighter overextends their spell stats?" June spoke excitedly, much at odds with her motherly appearance.

"Hey, that sounds targeted," Rasha protested and threw a small roll at June. It disappeared when it got close to her.

"Your spell temporarily swells the matrices for the body's individual channels, allowing the mana to artificially increase the power structure behind each stat. For example, Lady Catanzano's musculoskeletal structure ballooned up with your strength spell . . . you called it a buff, right? Lady Catanzano, when the spell subsides, please let me know. I need to see what happens to the mana in your system. It sounds like your body returns to its normal mana channels, but that would leave diluted mana from a different source in your body. Does [Purify] take care of that for you? I guess it would. Leftover mana would cause abnormal statuses based on the channels targeted. Purging the leftover mana once it leads to an abnormal status. That's clever. Would it be acceptable to suffer the effects for a moment so I can see?"

"June, they are children, not experiments," Henrick scolded with a small smile. Turning to Orrin, he clenched his hand into a fist, which began to turn bright red. "What does your strength spell do if someone is using a strengthening ability of their own?"

Orrin felt a pressure building around Henrick. "I don't know."

Henrick nodded at his hand. "[Might] increases my strength temporarily so I can knock a monster away from my team. Would you allow me the honor? I did not want to waste one of the strength orbs floating around camp for a test."

Orrin knew that thousands of his spell orbs were being passed around by now. He'd purposefully left the planning to others. It wasn't something he had an interest in getting bogged down with. Letting Henrick try a buff spell wasn't going to hurt anything, though.

"[Increase Strength]." Orrin cast the spell and watched Henrick as the knight's eyes grew wide. "How's that?"

"Thram, give me your best hold," Henrick ordered, and the dwarf grumbled as he pointed at his leader. An earthen fist sprouted from the ground and gripped Henrick's arm around the wrist. Henrick's face clenched as he heaved and the simulacrum arm was torn from the floor.

"That was terrifying," Thram said in his deep voice. "You're not supposed to get out of that one."

Henrick broke the stone fingers from around his arm one by one. His small smile had blossomed into a toothy grin. "That was one hundred strength."

Orrin wasn't impressed. He kept his own strength that high most of the time now. Silas, on the other hand, shook in his wheelchair. Henrick's team seemed suitably impressed.

"Want to arm wrestle?" Daniel plopped his elbow down on the corner of the table. "Orrin tried to explain to me once about how my normal strength isn't the same as my buffed strength, but all I heard was blah, blah, blah. I learn more by doing."

Phoenix team was stunned quiet until Rasha slapped the table and roared in laughter. "He's feisty. I like this guy. Henrick, crush him."

Orrin, Madi, and Silas found themselves pushed back as Phoenix team surrounded their captain and cheered him on as Daniel and Henrick set up to test their strength against each other.

"Is this the best use of their time?" Madi whispered to her father.

Silas sighed. "We don't give orders to Phoenix team. We asked Guildmaster Pritus to help with them, but she sent a message that just said, 'No.' Once adventurers break past level sixty, normal rules don't apply anymore. They showed up and fought demons. That's all we could ask for. If we can get them to help more, it would be a miracle."

A guard poked his head in and found Silas with his eyes before marching inside. His shaggy hair covered part of his face, and he pushed it aside to report. "Sir, I've located the man you wanted. He is at healing tent five and is still being guarded by your soldiers."

Silas nodded and pointed to Orrin. "Show this man to him. He's to be given every courtesy and has the final say over whether Fallah continues working at the front line or is to be sent back to Dey. Understood?"

Orrin felt awkward hearing Silas give orders like that. He shouldn't be in charge of whether Amir was allowed to help or not. That wasn't what he was doing here . . . was it?

Orrin caught Madi and waved a hand at Daniel. She nodded and rolled her eyes. Madi would make sure he stayed out of trouble. He cast

[Spell Orb] and [Purify], tossing the ball to Madi. "In case I don't get back in time and you need it."

"Leaving so soon?" June held up the tent flap as Orrin moved toward the exit. "Mind if I come along? I have a few more questions, if you don't mind."

Orrin hesitated but shrugged in acceptance. "I'm going to see a friend. I should be right back, but you can come, too."

June smiled and waited for Orrin and his guard escort to leave the tent before falling in behind them. The nervous man glanced back at both of them, his hair shaking with each movement, but he kept walking. He led them down a series of paths between tents before stopping at one that looked no different than any other. He gestured inside.

"The healing stations are set up on a different map to keep them safer. I'll point out where it is and can get a [Locationist] for us, unless you wanted to [Teleport] yourself, sir." The man must have known about Orrin's abilities, or more likely, Orrin had briefly met him in the past. It was getting hard to keep all the guards' names straight.

"I can do it," Orrin offered. "What's your name? You look familiar," he lied.

The man straightened up a bit. "I'm Ryan, sir. We met during the [Hero]'s and your procession through the town after you defeated Lord Wendeln. I was part of the honor guard that protected you through the crowds."

"Yes. Ryan. How have you been?" Orrin asked. He didn't remember the man at all.

"Can't complain." The man shrugged and held the tent flap open for June and Orrin to enter. "I've been mostly running missions for the higher-ups. I wasn't lucky enough to be picked for Wall duty yet, but I'm going to show everyone the strength of Dey. I can't wait to kill a few demons."

June paused and looked the man over. A sad smile stole across her face so quickly that Orrin thought he was mistaken.

Ryan answered a coded response to the other two guards inside before one lifted a platter of fruit off the table. Underneath was another map with markings closer to the next fallback Wall location than the front line. "This is the spot," Ryan said as he pointed to an X near the middle. "Your friend is stationed there and should be healing a few of the ones who got themselves hurt today."

Orrin didn't like the way Ryan implied in that short sentence how he wouldn't have been injured. "Thanks, Ryan. June and I can take it from here."

"But, sir, I'm supposed to—"

Orrin waved Ryan off and turned to June. "You said you wanted to come along. This will be a quick trip. I'll be back in a few minutes if you want to wait."

June's smile turned from kindly to predatory. "Not until I've asked my questions. I didn't know you could [Teleport], as well. Are you still stuck at the first distance parameters, or have you broken through yet?"

Orrin took a deep breath. "I'm at level two. Want to come with me?"

June nodded in delight and Orrin accepted her into his party before jumping them away.

Orrin landed on his foot with a bit more weight than he meant and nearly stumbled before righting himself. June walked ahead and turned her head quizzically.

"You have to step halfway through the casting." She demonstrated with a heavy stomp. "You won't lose your footing and can use the spell during a fight."

Orrin blushed a bit at her gentle reprimand and nodded in thanks. "I've never tried that. Thanks." He usually stood still and let himself fall the few inches, although a few times he realized he had taken a slight run up and walked off the teleportation spell pretty easily.

Orrin's spell could only bring him where he'd been before. He'd needed to pop in toward the next Wall center and head north a bit along the stone edifice. The tree line a few hundred yards from the next Wall was cleared, but tree trunks were piled in small pyramids closer to the Wall. The second Wall into the Pass covered a larger distance than the gap they currently defended. If they fell back here, the melee fighters would need to help secure the length of the Wall.

A small cluster of tents around a larger pavilion was set up fifty feet from the Wall and a quarter of a mile north of Orrin's [Teleport] location. Several of the fallen trees had been used to make a short fence perimeter.

A voice called out as they approached a few minutes later.

"Who's there?"

"Um. I'm Orrin," he replied weakly, realizing why he should have brought Ryan. "Lord Catanzano sent me."

There was a pause and scrape of leather barely heard over the whispers in the distance.

June sighed. "Phoenix team, June, also reporting for inspection. Stand ready but don't fire. We are approaching. I don't want to kill anyone else today." She patted Orrin on the head and whispered, "A little fire in the honey makes it taste better."

Orrin walked behind her as she wandered in without a care in the world. Three soldiers, two with pikes and one with a crossbow, backed away slowly as they rounded the stack of wood.

"Hi, I'm looking for Amir Fallah, a [Healer]," Orrin said with a small wave. The man with the crossbow was shaking and Orrin refreshed his wards.

"Whatever that was, I want to know more," June whispered. "Such wonderful spells."

"Orrin?" A familiar voice sounded from between two tents. Amir, his hands and light-brown tunic covered in blood, rounded the corner and smiled. His head swiveled between the soldiers and Orrin. "They're fine, Intavius. That's Orrin. He's part of the [Hero]'s party and a friend."

The shorter pikeman lowered his weapon and inclined his head respectfully toward Amir. "Yes, [Healer]. I'll release them to you."

June chuckled under her breath but didn't say anything aloud.

"Orrin, what brings you here?" Amir closed the distance to grab Orrin's hand but then saw his dirty state. "Oh, my. Sorry. I was just stitching up someone who had a nasty cut across her back. Let me find some water."

Orrin grabbed a pail nearby and cast [Water Reservoir], filling the bucket. "Here. Amir, what are you doing here? I saw your father and—"

"Is he all right?" Amir's head shot up. "I thought he would be safe with the guards. What happened?"

Orrin held his hands up. "Nothing. He's fine. I was more worried about you. I . . ." Orrin trailed off and looked at June out of the corner of his eye. ". . . thought something might have happened to you."

"Why?" Amir squinted his eyes as he rubbed his hands together in the bucket. "There haven't been any demons this far back. Lord Catanzano refused to let me help on the front line. He said it would be a distraction to you, but he still allowed me to help here. Orrin, as terrible as the injuries are, I've gained so much experience in the last two days. My spells are getting easier to cast. I took your recommendation and have been staggering points into will, intelligence, and constitution. I reached level ten just a few hours ago."

Amir squared his shoulders in pride. A low moaning came from one of the tents nearby. The [Healer] blinked and gestured for Orrin to join him. "I've been pacing myself, but I can heal another two or three people today. If you have time, I wouldn't say no to some help."

Chapter 48

June trailed behind Orrin as he helped Amir heal the injured soldiers. Orrin called them soldiers, but the men and women they treated were almost exclusively the untrained commonfolk of Dey who'd responded to the call for help.

Orrin drank a mana potion instead of blood cycling, afraid of what June would do or say if she caught him using another type of magic. He knew his class was an oddball mix of skills, but June's eyes watched him with the same intensity as some past enemies. Anabella Sanerris came to mind prominently.

Amir chatted with Orrin but kept his topics vague and broad. They didn't bring up in front of June the Hospital, his father, or how Orrin had granted him the healing class. Instead, they offered pointers on the best way to heal different wounds on their patients. Amir confirmed he'd reached level ten a few hours ago, roughly about the time Orrin got his Administrator message.

Maybe he had to reach level ten? Was that the moment he reached synchronization?

"Did anything else happen when you reached level ten?" Orrin whispered as they wrapped a bandage around a man's broken fingers.

"Like what?" Amir glanced up from cutting the gauze down to size.

"I don't know. No new spells or anything?"

Amir shook his head. "No, but I was able to reach level two of [Heal Small Wounds] shortly after. I increased my mana like you suggested for quicker growth."

That must be it, Orrin reasoned. *If Amir synchronized with his new class by leveling up his healing spell, that is the trigger for the Administrator reward. But if he reached it by hitting level ten, why hasn't Madi synchronized with her class yet?*

Orrin's thoughts drifted as they moved to another tent. He looked around and realized they were mostly alone in the camp.

"Are there any other [Healers] here helping you?" Orrin asked after they finished closing a gaping hole in the side of an archer. She'd gotten hit in the gut after a lucky spear throw by a demon.

Amir shrugged. "I haven't seen any. Lord Catanzano set this up for me and left a few guards to . . . help with my problem. It's working out well. Using my healing spell gives me experience for my class at a greater pace than fighting monsters ever did."

"Nonoffensive classes most often have noncombat-related paths to leveling," June commented. From time to time, she would add a bit of knowledge to their conversation but mostly kept to herself.

"Um, yeah." Amir scratched his head. "Like I said, I hit level ten a few hours ago. There's a notification that some new spells are available, but you promised I could go talk with your elf friend, remember? I wanted to make the best choices, and since I don't have . . . anyone else to ask . . ." He trailed off hopefully.

Orrin grabbed his friend's shoulder and squeezed playfully. "Of course. I need to head back and let Daniel and the others know where I'm off to, but I could make a round trip to the forest tonight. It might be better for you to hang out there for a day or two and study with Lyra."

Amir ducked his arm out of Orrin's grip. "I'm not leaving now."

Orrin raised an eyebrow. "I thought you wanted to buy the new spells?"

"I can wait to do that until after the Horde is pushed back."

"It's not safe for you to be here at all," Orrin snapped. "You should be caring for your father."

Amir blinked rapidly but kept his back straight. "I have every right to be here. Lots of people are risking their lives, and my father agrees with my choices."

"What if something happens to him again?"

Amir's chest rose and fell as he answered, "Nothing will happen to him. He's guarded. Mangin and the others were stripped of their titles and thrown from the Hospital. Nobody has seen them, and the rumor is they have escaped to Veskar. Elder Seif came by personally to apologize and tell me the news."

Orrin threw his hands in the air. "I'm just trying to keep you safe. You barely hit level ten today, Amir."

Amir pointed toward the tent they'd just left. His bloody sleeve fell over his finger. "That girl in there is our age and a [Merchant Apprentice]. She's only level twenty, but compared to a melee class, she might as well be level one. There are hundreds of people like her doing the work and you want me to hide? I'm a [Healer], Orrin. You gave me this chance, and I will not lose it because you think I'm weak. I'm sorry I questioned your choice before. That was wrong of me. But class or not, this is who I am. [Brewer], [Healer], or unclassed beggar, I would be here helping, and I don't need anyone telling me otherwise."

Orrin growled in frustration. He didn't mean to upset Amir or make his friend think that he didn't believe in him. His words were getting all twisted up inside. *A [Calm Mind] would help me right now,* he thought before risking a glance at his new shadow.

"Amir, you can do whatever you want. I'm just worried about you. You are still a target and I can't help you out here," Orrin tried to explain.

"I appreciate your concern, but I don't need you watching over me. You are my friend, Orrin. Not my parent."

June chose that moment to intervene. "What did you mean when you said Orrin gave you this chance? Who is targeting you?"

Orrin waved a hand in her face. "June, not now. Leave us alone for a minute."

The pressure of doom that rolled off her like waves froze Orrin to the spot.

"Please do not assume to give me orders." The sweet middle-aged woman from down the street radiated power and pure mana into the air in a visible aura. Her smile was the same, but there was a glint of steel in her eyes.

Amir fell to the ground, wide-eyed, as he stared at June.

Orrin had faced two power-hungry rulers of countries, countless monsters, and Daniel's mom when he accidentally knocked over her favorite lamp. June's display didn't faze him for more than a moment. "June, that's enough. I'm not ordering you. I'm asking you to be polite. We are having an important conversation that would take too long to explain right now."

June blinked twice at Orrin, then, in an instant, she wrapped her hands back around her center and smiled. "Of course. That was rude of me. You'll explain later."

Orrin swallowed at the implied threat and helped Amir stand back up. He slapped the dirt off the back of Amir's robe. "You're right. I'm hovering. I feel like this target on your back is my fault, though. I can't help keep you safe if I don't know you're about to run off and fight the Horde."

Amir waited until Orrin stopped moving and looked him in the eye. He smiled and threw his arms around Orrin, pulling him into a hug. "You are a good friend, but, like Daniel says, a little slow at times. I am not looking to fight demons, Orrin. I will do my part and return to Dey. We can talk about visiting your friend after you find a way to defeat the Horde, yes?"

Orrin studied his friend and realized he wasn't going to change his mind. If he kept pushing, he might drive a wedge between himself and Amir. "I'll see you back at the coffee shop, then." He held up his fist and Amir fist-bumped him.

Orrin saw his friend back to his tent, waving at the guards who'd shadowed them for the last thirty minutes. The men stationed themselves around Amir's tent and saluted Orrin. He turned to June. "Let's go back. I should make sure Daniel doesn't try to spar with Henrick."

"Not quite yet," June said with a smile. "I have questions."

He sighed. It was always questions but never answers. "I'll answer one question today, but I need to get back and sleep. I'm running lower on mana than I like."

June bit her bottom lip in thought. "One question isn't enough. You have too many peculiarities. I will answer questions as well. One for one."

Orrin rubbed his face. "June, you seem like a wonderful person, but I don't have any questions for you. Your fire snake spell is awesome, but I don't think it fits with the way I fight. Madi might want to try it, but I'm too tired to . . ."

"This is not something I do often," June cut him off. "I have studied in every school in Asmea, written new spells with [Archmage] Genou, and reached depths of the dungeons you will never see. I'm level seventy-nine and forged my path to power with the manipulation of mana, but I've never seen some of the things you've done. Individually, your buff spells are intriguing, groundbreaking even, but not enough to pull me from my own pursuits. Your class is unique, with several spells across different disciplines. If I heard of you, I might even have hired a researcher to interview you. You walk with the [Hero] as a friend and equal but command the lord of Dey's ear. My interest is piqued and you should not squander this opportunity. I can count on one hand the number of times I've made this offer. I will keep your confidence, if that is your worry. I can offer you knowledge, Orrin. I know more spells than [Blaze Serpent]."

Orrin considered teleporting away but figured she'd just show up in an hour or so anyway. "Ask your question," he said in a monotone voice.

June smiled. "I'll start simple. What spells and skills do you have?"

"That's a big list . . . and quite personal." Orrin paused. He checked over his status and made sure [Obscure] was still blocking some of his more esoteric spells and skills. He made sure to add [Increase Constitution] to the blacked-out list. [Obscure] would keep the prying eye of [Identify] from seeing all his power.

"You just used [Obscure]. I would not be so rude as to use [Identify] without your consent." June frowned in consternation. "As I said, anything you tell me is held in strictest confidence. I enjoy learning new ways to use mana. That is all."

"I can't very well say no to you, can I?" Orrin grumbled. "You're more powerful than me and could turn me into a smear if I say no."

"I wouldn't do that," June said softly. "I might annoy you a bit, but I would not threaten you."

Orrin let out a breath. "You already know about my buffs. I can do the opposite and steal stats from a person for a time. I can heal and use [Teleport]. I have a few different spells in the healing area like [Purify], [Diagnose], and the like. I have [Map], [Meditate], and [Camouflage]. I can summon swords made of fire and ice, use [Gust] to run fast or explode my swords, and have a bunch of different wards that block different magic types from damaging a person. I also can make spell orbs of any spells I have. That's about what you could find out if you hired someone to stalk me for a week. Are you satisfied? Can we go back now?"

June shook her head. "You didn't give me a complete list, but that isn't what I wanted. You don't specialize in anything, do you?"

"Is that another question?"

The fiery mage laughed. "Yes. Let it be counted as question two."

"I thought it was one for one," Orrin countered, not really wanting to have this conversation at all. He should have brought Madi.

"Ask your question then."

Orrin didn't care enough to ask anything, but her [Blaze Serpent] spell was powerful. Maybe he could find something in that area to make his own. With [Merge], he could even have an elemental summon that raced around and debuffed people. "What spells would I need to learn to cast [Blaze Serpent]?"

June's eyes twinkled. "You go right for my prized spell, huh? Let me think. I unlocked that spell at level sixty. You aren't a [Fire Mage], which is where I started, by the way. I needed [Fireball], [Firewall], and [Flame Snake], which is a waste of points, to be honest. The snake is no bigger than your arm and costs way too much mana. Then [Far] and [Boost]. You have to cast [Flame Snake] several times with both [Far] and [Boost] while making it crawl through a [Firewall]. Once it catches fire, which took me about a month of casting the spells in combination to do, you bombard it with [Fireball] until you pass out from mana exhaustion. You have [Meditate], which will make that hard to do, but I'm not sure you have to go that far. It could be a simple matter of a set mana cost per day or an overall spent mana amount. After that, [Blaze Serpent] should be offered by the system if it feels you are worthy."

Orrin stared at her as she rattled off the instructions like a grocery list. It was the most insane thing he'd heard in a few days. "How do you even figure that out?"

June smiled. "By asking questions. If you haven't learned a summon yet, it's tricky to learn how to peel a piece of your mana off from the whole."

"How—" Orrin caught himself and smirked. "Nice try. What's your next question?"

Chapter 49

June spoke slowly, picking her words with care. "Who is targeting your friend and why?"

"That's two questions again," Orrin said as they walked to the edge of the healing camp. "Do I get two in return?"

"Only if that counts as a question as well." June smiled patiently.

Orrin shook his head. "Amir is a [Healer] outside of the Hospital's control. Some of the people in charge didn't like that and we had to knock a few heads together."

June paused and leaned against one of the stacks of felled trees. "The Hospital of Dey is controlling, but they don't let people obtain a [Healer] class without extensive training. I know a few kings and nobles who paid to keep their own [Healer] on retainer, but even then, it's more of a lending situation."

Orrin almost explained but kept his mouth shut. If June was going to make him answer questions, he would play her game. "What did you mean about peeling a piece of mana from the whole and how do you do it?"

June smiled and put her hands together in front of herself. "When you cast a spell, you are using your mana to shape the world around you. The saying 'no two mages are the same' is true for this single reason. No two people's magic is the same." She pulled her hands apart and a beam of fire spread between her palms. It grew until it was the size of a small garden snake, and then she twisted her hands. A serpent made entirely of fire dropped to the ground and hissed at Orrin. "As you gain levels, your body changes to accommodate your new potential. Stats don't make you stronger or faster; they only give you the chance to become stronger or faster."

"But will and intelligence give you immediate results. I don't have to work harder to cast my spells for a cheaper price," Orrin countered. *Maybe I can get more information from her.*

June reached out and tapped Orrin on the forehead. "That's only half the answer." She pulled a cup of tea out of the air and sipped it. "Once your body is strong enough, you become your mana. That is a poor explanation, but without giving you three years of classes on the topic, it is enough for our discussion. You can learn to take some of the mana within you"—she paused and made a fist with her free hand—"and separate it to give a spell life."

Her fist opened and a smaller snake no longer than her pinky wiggled on her palm.

"Learning to separate your mana is advanced magic that is usually relegated to spells unlocked at level fifty or beyond. Now, my question. What did the young [Healer] mean when he said you gave him this chance?"

Orrin didn't want to talk about his Administrator powers. He also felt that telling a lie to June would be a mistake. "Pass. I'm not answering that."

June's smile split her face in two. "You did anyway."

Orrin flinched in frustration. He thought he'd gotten better at playing these games with powerful people, but they still seemed to run circles around him. "Then it's my question. Explain what you meant about will and intelligence not reducing the price of spells immediately."

June put her cup to her lips. She sighed in contentment. "Where are my manners? Would you care for a cup of tea? I find it soothing before bed."

"No, thank you. I'm a coffee guy," Orrin said, pulling his own cup from his [Dimension Hole]. "It helps me keep going when people keep me prisoner with twenty questions."

"You are no prisoner. You can leave and go back to your friends. I will simply send my questions through Lord Catanzano and let him know that I will not help with the Horde until a response is satisfactorily received."

Orrin glared at the mage in front of him. She didn't even do him the courtesy of looking ashamed.

"I'll pass on that question. You aren't ready for that knowledge at your level."

"I'm level thirty-two. That's plenty high."

June loudly sipped her tea.

Orrin turned to the store on his blue box display and pulled up [Fireball], [Firewall], and [Flame Snake]. He already had [Far] and [Boost].

> **[Fireball]—cast a ball of fiery death that explodes among your enemies. 30 MP. -20 AP**

> **[Firewall]—create a wall of fire up to twenty feet long and two feet thick between two points. 50 MP. -25 AP**

> **[Flame Snake]—summon a snake of fire with your mana. 80 MP summon + 10 MP per minute. -50 AP**

"Dang, that costs a lot of AP," Orrin muttered to himself.

June narrowed her eyes. "Which spell?"

Orrin smirked. "Is that a question?"

"Yes. What spell are you looking up?"

Orrin shrugged. "The requirements for your [Blaze Serpent] spell. Just the big three alone cost almost a hundred ability points."

The teacup disappeared back into whatever magical storage June had and she was upon him before he blinked. "You can see [Fireball] and [Flame Snake] at level thirty-two? And you are not a [Fire Mage]?"

Orrin realized their little game was suddenly over. She wasn't just interested anymore. June was unsettled. He tried to pull her hand off his arm. "I can see a lot of spells once I get a ward for that magic type. I have [Fire Ward]. It lets me protect against fire magic. Maybe that's why? June, you're squeezing my arm pretty hard."

She realized she was holding him tight and let go. "I know that your class is called [Utility Warder], but I have never heard of that class before. I'm sure you received it after some sort of extreme struggle, as new classes are rare but not unheard-of. Skills or spells that increase a person's individual stats are also uncommon. These wards are not unique, either. However, nobody below level fifty should be able to see [Flame Snake]. Part of the requirement is practical application in throwing your mana into a spell. What other abilities do you have where you can split your mana?"

Orrin rubbed his arm. "I have [Split Spell]. Maybe that?"

June paced. "No. That wouldn't be enough. Where did you study? Who taught you these spells?"

"I kind of learned them on my own," Orrin answered slowly. "I mean, I did study at the Sanerris School for a bit under weird circumstances. I learned to see mana signatures pretty easily. Maybe it's a class thing."

June muttered to herself and shook her head as she started casting spells. Shimmering geometric shapes began to appear around Orrin. He started and put his hands up. "What are you doing?"

"Don't move. I'm using an enhanced version of [Identify]." She continued muttering and the mana around Orrin began to solidify.

"I'm not sure that I like this, June. Please stop." Orrin tried to ask nicely, but he kept his finger on the mental trigger of [Decrease Intelligence]. "I don't want to fight you."

June stopped pacing and the spells fell apart around her. "It won't hurt. Think of how many people could benefit from knowing how to get around locks on spell levels. I only want to use a scrying spell to figure out which spell or skill you have that lets you bypass twenty levels of requirements." The fervor in her eyes disappeared as June's motherly persona came crashing back in full force. She turned her wide, pleading gaze on him. "Please, Orrin."

Orrin took a moment to decide. June's curiosity scared him a little, but a bigger part of him wanted to know what was so special about his class. She wasn't outright hostile, and despite the level difference, she did seem to be asking for his consent. Maybe she could help him figure out a way to get back home. She was the highest-leveled mage he'd met. "I'll let you cast the spell, but under a few conditions."

June crossed her arms and pursed her lips. "What conditions?"

"You have to promise that you'll help push the Horde back and answer my questions about spells and magic. You can't tell anyone about my class or spells. I have a few that are . . . questionable."

June's smile was bashful. "You want me to be your mentor? How sweet."

"I'm serious, June. Agree or I'll [Teleport] out of here." Orrin tried to sound sure of himself. He put a little Daniel bravado in his voice.

She tapped a finger to her lips. "I promise to keep your secrets and convince my team to help with the demons. We were going to anyway. The dungeon is acting weird, and until it settles down, this is the most fun we can have without having to pay for another inn when Vulwin sets something on fire. I'll give you one day to ask any questions you want. I won't hold back on my answers, but you have to be forthcoming as well."

Orrin felt like he was making a deal with the devil. A devil that would fit in at a neighborhood bake sale, but a devil nonetheless. The opportunity to ask more questions about spell combinations was too tempting, though. "Agreed."

Orrin closed his eyes and waited. He felt a foreign mana tentatively touch his chest. [Mind Bastion] clamped down and activated. *I don't know anything about June. This is dangerous and stupid.*

"You promised not to fight the skill," June complained. "Whatever skill that is, turn it off."

She might be casting something other than an [Identify] spell. I should have let Madi or Daniel come along with us. Orrin kicked himself, but it was too late. He wasn't going to go back on his deal and doubted he would be able to anyway. He would have to trust June.

[Mind Bastion] came down and Orrin felt a light flow through his body. He shivered and goose bumps crawled along his arms. Orrin felt naked to the world. Directly in front of him, his stat sheet appeared like it did on his blue box, but without the missing bits usually restricted by [Obscure].

He'd been busy lately and missed the few notifications that some new spells were ready to level up. He'd finally reached ten thousand experience in [Camouflage], as well as maxing out his debuffs on intelligence and will. Some of his other spells, like [Remetabolize] and [Heal Small Wounds], he'd reached the ability to level a while ago; however, he'd not done so for different reasons. [Remetabolize] wasn't something he felt like he needed to progress, and the elven [Healer], Lyra, had warned him not to level [Heal Small Wounds] to [Heal Moderate Wounds] until he'd branched out his healing spells. Orrin was happy to see his Administrator Points didn't appear. At least one secret was safe.

"You have spells from multiple practice areas. This isn't normal," June muttered as she read his stat screen. She tsked. "Did you buy spells simply to get different wards?"

"Yes," Orrin answered. He rubbed his elbows. The night chill cut deeper than normal and he felt no protection from his cloak. "Is it supposed to feel cold?"

June ignored him. "I've never heard of some of these abilities. [Mind Bastion] and [Way of the Water]. Tell me what they—" June paused as her eyebrows shot up, trying to hide in her hair. "You unlocked [Merge]? How? Do you know what this means?"

Orrin shivered harder. "June, turn off your spell."

June made a few more gestures and frowned. "What are you doing? You stopped your spell, but you're fighting my mana still. You are draining yourself—stop it."

"I'm not doing anything," Orrin said, his teeth chattering. He held his fingers up. They felt like ice and the nails were turning blue. "Turn it off."

June yanked hard to the side, and Orrin gasped as warmth spread back over his body. [Mind Bastion] snapped on immediately.

June touched his head gently and rubbed his hair off his forehead. "I'm sorry. I don't know what happened. I've never seen my spell do that before."

Orrin's breathing steadied as he studied his body's reaction. [Mind Bastion] prowled his mind like a wild animal, bristling at the intrusion. Orrin tried to turn it off again, but the skill slipped through his grip like a slimy pumpkin seed. His control over [Mind Bastion] was perfect—or so he'd thought—but now he realized the skill had activated on its own again.

"Orrin? Are you okay? Do you need anything from me?"

Orrin held up a finger and started meditating. The skill was useful for more than just mana regeneration. It helped him find calm and examine [Mind Bastion].

I'm in control, Orrin chanted, feeling the cold anger inside fading. *You are my skill. When I turn you off, you stay off.*

[Mind Bastion] stopped circling and Orrin subdued it. He felt the last influence of the skill dissipate and opened his eyes. "One of my skills can activate on its own when it feels I'm in danger. I thought I had it under better control."

June's curiosity was absent from her face. "I'm sorry, Orrin. I should have stopped when you asked. Your class is unlike anything I've seen and I lost myself. I apologize."

Orrin smiled, pulling up his status again to check his abilities. "I've survived worse. I get to ask questions now, right?"

Orrin	Utility Warder Level 32 (2,860/25,000)	Ability Points: 31
HP: 300/300	MP: 97/1,100	
Strength: 9 (100)	Constitution: 30	Dexterity: 11 (100)
Will: 40 (100)	Intelligence: 11 (100)	
Abilities: [Analyze] [Blood Mana] [Create Poison] [Create Corrosive] [Diagnose] [Dimension Hole] [Identify] [Mana Pool] [Map]—[Party View]; [Monster View]; [Trap View]; [Zoom] [Meditate] [Merge] [Mind Bastion] [Obscure] [Side Steps] Level 3 (119/300) [Spell Orb]	Healing Spells: [Calm] (75/100) [Calm Mind] [Excise] (0/100) [Heal Small Wounds] Level 3 (10,000/10,000) [Numb] (20/100) [Purify] Spell Modifiers: [Boost]—(Spell Modifier) [Far]—(Spell Modifier) [Increase Durational Spell]—(Spell Modifier) [Split Spell]—(Spell Modifier)	Buff/Debuff Spells: [Increase Constitution] [Increase Strength] Level 3 [Increase Dexterity] Level 3 [Increase Will] Level 3 [Increase Intelligence] Level 3 [Decrease Strength] Level 2 (330/5,000) [Decrease Dexterity] Level 2 (590/5,000) [Decrease Will] Level 1 (1,000/1,000)

[Storage]	Ward Spells:	Other Spells:
[Through the Ages]	[Ward]	[Camouflage] Level
[Way of the Water]	[Utility Ward]	2 (10,000/10,000)
	[Mana Shield]	[Fire Sword]
	[Camouflage Ward]	[Gust]
	[Earth Ward]	[Ice Sword]
	[Fire Ward]	[Inverse]
	[Ice Ward]	[Lightstrike]
	[Light Ward]	[Lightstrikes]
	[Plant Ward]	[Remetabolize]
	[Poison Ward]	(1,000/1,000)
	[Space Ward]	[Teleport] Level 2
	[Time Ward]	(5,525/10,000)
	[Water Ward]	[Tilth]
	[Wind Ward]	[Toxic Touch]
		[Water Reservoir]

Chapter 50

June laughed. "Yes, you more than earned a few questions. But we are coming back to a few things later."

Orrin tried again. "When I increase my intelligence, the base cost of a spell goes down. You said it doesn't really reduce the price of spells immediately. Why?"

June glanced up at the darkening sky and paused before answering. "If I answer this, you cannot tell your friends. Spellcasters have to find this out on their own. It can squash your growth or kill you."

Orrin shrugged noncommittally. "I think they could handle it, but I promise not to tell them unless I think they're ready."

June narrowed her eyes and stared at Orrin. "I'm only entertaining the idea of teaching you because you already understand how to split your mana. You already know that intelligence reduces the base cost of a spell and will increases the base damage, correct?"

Orrin nodded. This was something he'd figured out on day one.

June continued. "Have you ever overdrawn your mana?"

Orrin remembered the first few days after he and Daniel arrived in Asmea. He'd spent his entire mana pool fighting bandits and healing Brandt at their first encounter. After he finished, he'd passed out. "Yes," he answered, feeling a phantom headache appear.

"Please understand, what I'm trying to explain to you is the equivalent of teaching a baby to read. I can only give you the broad strokes."

Orrin rolled his hand for her to continue.

"Will increases your mana pool directly but also allows growth into the negative. You can use your mana beyond your limits. Intelligence makes spells cost less, but it also creates a synergy between you and the magic. The higher your intelligence, the better you are able to tweak the mana as it leaves your body to create new spells. It isn't as straightforward as strength. For your strength stat, if you increase the number by ten points, you can spend the next few months working out to find the exact weight difference you could lift. Intelligence and will are more esoteric. You have to feel the changes. Most mages don't ever try to overdraw once in the twenties or thirties. You began to pull from your own self." June hesitated again. "Do you remember how I said once you gain enough levels, you become your mana?"

"Yeah." Orrin elongated the word. "Are you saying the mental stats allow you to play with mana better? Like create more spells and go harder with them?"

June smiled, and Orrin felt a burst of pride from her happy expression. "That is a sufficient picture of the idea. Once your body has a high enough level of mana flowing through it, which usually happens around level fifty or above, you can go beyond what the status screen says is possible. But it is risky and usually leaves you weak for days."

Orrin thought about what she was saying. The ability to use extra mana would be a game changer for most mages, but he already had blood cycling. [Meditate] also kept him topped off with more mana than a normal person. The ability to play with mana to create better spells was something he'd heard of a few times as well. Anabella Sanerris had bragged she had a system-granted spell. June had also just mentioned using spells in a new way. It brought up his next question.

"You said create new spells," Orrin started slowly. "I know someone who said her spell was system-granted. Is that what you mean?"

June's nose scrunched up. "Ugh, no. People who worship the system are simply ignorant. I believe all spells are there behind the store but we haven't unlocked them yet. When you use your magic in a different way, you have the chance to find that perfect note of music in the mana that reveals the hidden spell behind it."

Orrin had used [Gust] and [Ice Sword] in combination several times, but he'd never unlocked a new spell. "How do you know the spells work together?"

June clapped. "You've tried it? Oh, I knew you were special. Tell me, please."

This woman is too observant. Orrin kicked himself. He found a bush nearby and summoned an [Ice Sword]. "I use [Gust] and throw the mana through my [Ice Sword] like this."

Orrin swung the sword and struck a small branch. The wind mana pushed through the frozen sword in a flash. In an instant, the mana covered the entire growth in a fine layer of ice.

"Not bad." June reached out and snapped a leaf off. "You're relying too much on the wind spell to carry the ice mana. There are two different spells that I can think of that might populate from that combination. For one, you need to direct the ice mana to strike a specific target. For the other, you must work on snapping the wind mana over the target without losing more than five to ten percent of the initial spell."

Orrin listened but had no idea what she meant. "I just push the wind mana at the sword. It explodes over something when I hit it. I can do the same thing with a [Fire Sword], but it creates a little explosion of heated air."

June's smile grew wider. "How much sleep do you need tonight?"

Orrin teleported them both back and collapsed outside the command tent.

"Orrin?" Madi rushed forward and checked him over for injuries. "Where are you hurt?"

"Let me die," Orrin grumbled into the dirt.

June rolled her eyes. "He's fine. We practiced some magic exercises, but he ran low on mana after a few attempts." She knelt down next to Orrin. "Don't think you got away easily. I have more questions for you, but you can sleep for now."

Orrin wrestled himself into a sitting position. His mouth hung open. "A few attempts? I don't think there is a tree or bush left in the entire Pass that I didn't freeze."

Madi watched the exchange and shook her head. "I can't with you, Orrin. Did you convince the [Pyrocaster] to teach you magic? And now you're complaining?" Madi turned her back to Orrin and bowed her head to June. "Please teach me. I work harder than Orrin."

June chewed on her lip. "I'm not teaching him so much as exchanging information. His class is unique and he's been answering questions in exchange for some light training."

"Light training? You made me run from your fire snake. It almost killed me." Orrin got to his feet unsteadily and Madi caught him before he fell. "All while peppering me with questions."

Orrin shivered as he remembered. June had seemed to float next to him as he pumped his legs. Even using [Gust] and with maxed-out dexterity, he still could feel the flames licking his heels. All the while, June threw out question after question.

She'd assumed he stole a [Healer]'s amulet and figured out how to train healing magic into his repertoire. June had asked if he could replicate the ability for more than just Amir, but Orrin kept his answers vague.

"It takes a lot out of me and the other person."

Orrin told no lies, but he didn't go out of his way to disabuse her conclusion. June's questions about [Way of the Water] were unhelpful as well.

"A fighting ability? Why not focus on magic? The things people waste their ability points on . . ." June had trailed off in thought. "You should train with Rasha. She is a spellsword like you. She fights with magic and weapons."

[Mind Bastion] was likewise a dead end for questions as June helped him focus his mana in a precise manner. "It allows you to bypass the effects of mana exhaustion but you pay for it later? That doesn't sound like something you should be using. If it turns on by itself as well, you might have an incomplete skill. I've no recollection of that skill name, though."

Of all Orrin's abilities, [Merge] was the one June was most interested in. She was momentarily put off that he could only use spells he'd already bought. June wanted him to run through a dozen combinations of her own spells, but she sighed and said, "We'll have to train you up then."

That's when she started chasing him with her fire snake. June had pushed Orrin to focus the wind in small points around his body. Usually, Orrin cast [Gust] and let the wind push him from behind like a wall. June's suggestion that he focused on the center of his back with smaller areas hitting his feet as he ran paid dividends . . . after he stopped tripping himself.

Orrin's speed doubled under ten minutes of June's tutelage. She spurred him on by making her summoned pet snap at his heels until he ran out of mana.

Orrin glanced around outside the command tent but didn't see Daniel. "Where is everyone?"

"Brandt went to keep Daniel in line. My father asked them to take their strength contests into the Pass after Daniel threw Henrick through a few tents. They're playing like children," Madi sighed.

June tilted her head and stared into the distance. "They'll be back in ten minutes. Lady Catanzano, it was a pleasure to meet you. Orrin, I'll see you in the morning."

"You're still going to help with the Horde, right?" Orrin asked as he clomped his way to Madi. He was going to sleep like the dead tonight. "I can't train like that every day. I have to make spell orbs and fight demons."

June smiled gently. "I'll give you easy homework tomorrow, but Phoenix will assist Dey. You have my word."

Madi stared at the unassuming woman as she walked away before whipping her head toward Orrin. "How did you make friends with the [Pyrocaster], and will you ask her to train me, too? I swear, Orrin. It's not fair how much luck you have."

Orrin spent the next few minutes fending off Madi's questions until Brandt and Daniel returned. His friend was covered in dirt and his armor had grass stains, but he was smiling ear to ear.

"Brandt, Orrin is getting special training from June the [Pyrocaster]," Madi complained as soon as they were close. She pulled back a moment later. "Daniel, you need a shower. What is that smell?"

"Henrick's class is awesome." Daniel grinned with wide eyes. "He's a tank, O. He's got all kinds of abilities to make monsters focus on him or to drive them away like my [Gravity Well]. The guy has some serious strength, too."

Orrin sniffed and took a big step back. "Did you get in a fight with a skunk?"

Brandt, looking haggard, joined Orrin. Madi stepped away a moment later. "Daniel had Henrick pinned and he set off a deterrent spell. Most people would have backed away . . ."

"He skunk sprayed Daniel?" Orrin asked incredulously. "That's a real spell?"

Daniel shrugged. "You get used to the smell. It was effective, though. He got around me while I was gagging." Daniel frowned. "I can't believe you just left again. We wanted to come see Amir, too."

"Yes," Brandt said as he held up a hand and blocked Daniel from getting closer. "How is he doing? Lord Catanzano told us he was healing the injured."

Orrin scratched the back of his neck. "He's helping at a [Healer]'s camp by the next Wall. I tried to convince him to go wait in Dey with his father, but he wasn't listening. Your dad is keeping guards on him, at least. Tell him thanks for me, Madi."

Brandt's forehead furrowed. "You asked him to go back to Dey and not help?" When Orrin nodded, Brandt scowled at him. "You realize how hypocritical that is?"

"What?"

"I didn't want Madi to help with that mission, but you told me to trust in her. Do you not trust in Amir?"

Orrin was exhausted and took a second to catch up on what Brandt was saying. "Of course I trust Amir, but he's a [Healer], not a fighter. Madi can make her own decisions and watch out for herself. Amir hit level ten today. Does that seem like someone who should be on the front line?"

To his dismay, Madi sided with Brandt. "Amir can make his own choices, Orrin. If he wants to help, why wouldn't you support him?"

Daniel threw his hands in the air when Orrin glanced at him. "Don't look at me. I'm not dumb enough to take your side."

Orrin scowled. "Anyway, Amir hit level ten and reached the first level-up for [Heal Small Wounds] today. I think that's what triggered my new points. Madi blew by level ten and I didn't get any achievement, so it must have to do with a spell you haven't leveled up yet. Any ideas?"

Brandt appeared to want to continue his admonishment but kept quiet when the topic turned to Madi. He was always protective of her.

"I agree it's likely a spell, but I have a lot of spells it could be. The few illusion spells I use are moving up slowly. [Sunbeam] is only about a third of the way to the second level, which is insanely fast thanks to the buffs you give me daily. It could be my reflection ability . . . you know, the one I used to absorb some of your mana during our duel the other day? I could focus on one spell tomorrow. If you get more administrator points, it could be worth it."

Daniel yawned pointedly. "Can we figure it out tomorrow morning? I'm exhausted."

"You went ten rounds with the strongest man in the world. You're lucky to be alive," Brandt said, shaking his head. "But he has a good point. We should sleep in our tents near the Wall tonight and get up early. Orrin can take a look at those special abilities again. If we find some volunteers, he can turn a bunch of them into [Healers]. With some intelligence buffs, they could reach level two of [Heal Small Wounds] in a day or two and you could double your administrator points."

Orrin was hesitant to advertise his ability to change classes, but getting more points was nearly impossible. He would need to find a dungeon and destroy the core. There was no time for that with the demons at the door. From his experience with Madi and Amir, he knew he needed the person's permission to change their class. Maybe he could convince people he knew a secret way around the amulet training. A few of the Hospital initiates would jump at the chance to bypass the months of grueling hazing. "I'll think about it. It's not the worst idea you've had, Brandt."

Daniel tried to keep a straight face, but a snort slipped through. "Sorry, Brandt. Lead the way to our tents. It's late."

Chapter 51

Orrin woke up early and stretched on his cot. Each of their tents was nothing more than a small triangular canvas frame sitting low to the ground. A simple, thick blanket was provided, but the straps that made up the bed were uncomfortable without an actual mattress. Orrin luckily had enough extra blankets in his [Dimension Hole] to fold into something resembling a comfy bed.

He checked over his stats before starting the day. There were no horns in the distance signaling a demon attack, so he took his time. He was getting better at running the numbers for maximum efficiency with his buffs. His new spell, [Increase Constitution], reset after a full night's rest, giving him back his spent mana. Orrin's plan was to start adding five more points to his party's constitution each day. From the current numbers, he figured Madi and Brandt could handle an extra ten points over the normal buff into their other stats after he gave them the con boost.

Now that he had a minute, Orrin also checked over the exclamation points near some of his spells.

[Decrease Will] and [Decrease Intelligence] both had topped off at a thousand and were ready to be leveled to the second tier.

> **Would you like to Upgrade [Decrease Will] for 2 AP?**
> **Yes or No?**
>
> **Would you like to Upgrade [Decrease Intelligence] for 2 AP?**
> **Yes or No?**

Orrin hesitated and checked his other blinking spell first.

> **Unlocked [Camouflage III]—melt into your surroundings. Increase ability to remain undetected and avoid detection magic. 30 minutes. 10 MP. -4 AP**

A straight upgrade again to [Camouflage]. Orrin had thirty-one ability points. He didn't need the decrease-spell upgrades—with his increased will, even the level-one version of the spell would knock most people down. The main reason to purchase the second level was the eventual [Decrease Constitution] ability, if it existed. Orrin cracked his knuckles before he decided and spent the eight points for all three purchases.

When he bought the new [Camouflage], another notification blinked.

> **Unlocked [Invisibility]—disguise yourself from the senses of others. 5 minutes. 50 MP. -10 AP**

"That's the same thing as camo," Orrin complained and minimized the box. Rolling out of the tent, he hauled himself to the small campfire nearby. The tents were set in rows, with a partially covered pit to bank a fire every thirty yards. Two soldiers were sitting near the closest one, chatting softly. The dim light of the sun cresting the horizon gave Orrin enough to see as he made his way closer.

"Mind if I boil some water?" Orrin asked the two, pulling his small kettle from his pocket. "I'll share some coffee."

The man and woman glanced up as he approached. She was dressed in leather armor and had a longbow resting across her legs. He wore a robe and Orrin spotted a staff on the ground within reach. They were sitting on the ground but scooched themselves back to give Orrin room.

He tried to make conversation with the two, but an air of despair hung between them. They didn't introduce themselves, and the woman left without a word before Orrin's water was hot.

"Sorry," the mage whispered, trying to keep quiet for those still sleeping. "Her brother took a spray of acid to his face yesterday. He was rushed to the [Healers] and we haven't heard if he made it or not. I'm Fred. [Fire Mage]. I'm working up on the fourteenth tower between healing station two and the mess tents. Where do they have you assigned?"

Orrin noticed the small valve flapping on his kettle indicating the water was boiling and poured some coffee grounds into the top. "I'm Orrin. Um, my group goes all over. Sorry about her brother."

Fred gave a tight-lipped smile in thanks and stared into the fire. Orrin offered some coffee, but Fred declined. The silence of the camp was interrupted from time to time by people waking and making their way to the latrines. Some staggered north toward the nearest mess tent for some of their daily rations. Fred's empty plate sat in the grass behind him.

"Orrin?" Madi's voice rang out from where he'd slept. "Where'd you go?"

"Over here," Orrin called softly and waved a hand. Madi caught the movement and picked her way between tents as she approached.

"Coffee?"

Madi dropped to the ground and nodded, taking the cup after he poured it. "I slept like the dead. Brandt said I snored . . . I do not snore."

Orrin chuckled at the indignant look on her face. "Madi, this is Fred. Fred, Madi."

Fred's eyes were wide and he bowed his head. "Lady Catanzano. It's a pleasure."

"'Madi' is fine out here, Fred. We're all protecting Dey together."

Fred glanced back and forth between Madi and Orrin nervously. Orrin watched him grab his staff as if to leave, but two more figures stepped up.

"I knew if we followed the smell of coffee, we'd find you," Daniel said groggily, rubbing his hair down. He had terrible bed head this morning. "Brandt thought you might have gone to kidnap Amir."

"I did not. I merely said that Orrin could be anywhere," the knight grunted as he sat heavily on the ground. His metal armor jangled a bit. "Daniel is grumpy this morning and starting fights."

"Oh, hello," Daniel said as he sat in the spot Fred's partner had vacated. "I'm Daniel. Did Orrin offer some coffee?" He leaned toward the mage conspiratorially. "He saves the best stuff for himself and doesn't bring enough cream, but it's still delicious."

Orrin shook his head and pulled a pitcher of milk and a small container of sugar from his dimensional storage. "Fred didn't want any coffee. Leave him alone, Daniel."

"Daniel? The [Hero]?" Fred chanced, his voice barely audible. "Sir Bennett. Lady Catanzano." He turned back to Orrin. "You're the [Healer] who makes the stat-increase spell orbs?"

Orrin swallowed his coffee with a gulp. "Not a [Healer], but yeah, I make the orbs."

"Buff balls," Daniel corrected as he spooned half of Orrin's sugar into his coffee. "We call them buff balls."

"We do not." Orrin reached over and swiped the sugar container before Daniel used it all.

"My group received a handful of them, but I only used one. My will increased so much I nearly doubled my spell length." Fred beamed with pride. "I took down three of the demons myself."

Orrin smiled encouragingly to the man before turning to his party. "I'm going to spin up the buffs and take care of Silas's daily orb tax, then we can go grab some food."

He cast the spells in the normal sequence before fulfilling his quota of spell orbs for Silas to hand out. Fred stared in awe at the growing pile.

"He has so much mana," Fred muttered to himself, but Daniel heard him. He chuckled.

"Orrin's not even breaking a sweat. That Demon Lord better watch his ass." Orrin's friend reached out and snagged a handful of the orbs. "Here. Have a few."

"Those are dex," Orrin said, rolling his eyes. He nudged his foot against another of the four piles. "These are will."

Daniel tossed the three he'd taken back and scooped up several of the correct type. "Here you go, Fred. Courtesy of the [Hero]."

"You know people are selling those for five silver an orb?" Brandt asked as he pulled a strap on his chest piece. "Orrin is going to be rich after this Horde is dealt with. Mages are lining up at the chance to use more mana each day and increase their spell experience. A few melee fighters realize how much use training with higher stats will be as well. Practicing today for the stats you'll have tomorrow means quicker growth."

Orrin groaned. "I'm not going to keep making spell orbs indefinitely. This is to help people with the Horde."

Fred heard Orrin's complaint and swiftly gathered the offered orbs from Daniel. "Thank you, sir. I'm honored." He glanced at the dexterity balls that Daniel had rolled back to the pile. "Would it be presumptuous to request a few of the dexterity type for my friend? She doesn't have a fighting class but trained with the elves. She's an archer and doing well, but I know she'd appreciate dealing more damage to the bastards. Her kid brother was injured yesterday. Just seventeen and classed as a [Fire Mage]. I was showing him the basics."

Orrin cast his spells a few more times and poured a dozen orbs at the man's feet. "There's a mix of all four. Try and be safe."

Fred beamed as he folded the end of his robe into a basket, exposing his knees. "Thank you. I will. My summon does most of the work. He can fly in and stab a few demons with his horn before he explodes. Veera is going to be a terror today. I bet she kills six demons at least."

Orrin held his tongue. They'd taken out hundreds of the demons, but it was still progress. Fred and his friends weren't warriors or adventurers. The robes the man wore were the same Orrin saw on some of the mages who spent their time keeping the streetlamps burning or heating the giant baths that he'd heard about. Fred wasn't the type of mage that fought monsters or delved into dungeons, but he was here fighting and helping now.

Orrin waved to the man as he scampered away with the orbs. He pushed the piles into a bag, keeping them safe in his [Dimension Hole] for later delivery to Silas. "Breakfast?"

After eating, they visited the Wall. No alarms blared and the demons remained in their camp. They listened to the complaints of the watch on duty, pissed that they had to stand and wait while some of their comrades still slept.

"Do they not realize the alternative is fighting and death?" Daniel spat as two soldiers walked by them. "This could be a good thing. Maybe they lost so many people yesterday, the demons will leave."

"People will complain about any inconvenience and when they are content, they'll make something up to bitch about," Brandt answered Daniel's question. "The Horde did not pull up camp. They won't be going anywhere. If I had to guess, their leaders are trying to figure out a strategy to deal with Phoenix team. It's the unknown variable they hadn't planned for."

"Very astute, Sir Bennett."

Orrin jumped at the soft voice from behind them. He turned to find June standing next to Henrick. She waved to Orrin.

"Would you four come with us? Your father demanded your presence," Henrick said with a slight glower at being ordered around. "I don't know why we should listen, but—"

"But I convinced him you four deserve more respect than your levels warrant." June spoke over Henrick, her gentle voice tinged with a little steel. The large man nodded his head in her direction and turned on his heels. June raised her hands and gestured for them to follow.

"Orrin, what did you do?" Daniel whispered as they walked back down the stairs. June led them in a different direction from yesterday's command tent. It was being rotated around frequently, sometimes as much as three times a day. "Why is Henrick mad at us?"

"Why would he be mad at me? You're the one who fought him yesterday."

"Enough," Madi hissed at them both. "Let's see what they want."

June held back the tent flap for them as they entered. The rest of Phoenix team waited inside, with Henrick glowering in the corner. Silas, Leanthun, Lady Timpe, Lord Tarris, Finley Madvarr, and even Elder Kali sat or stood on one side while the professional adventurers lined the other canvas wall. Sof, the leader of Dragoon team, stood close to the door with Maya, one of his teammates.

"Hey, Sof," Orrin greeted the man. "Good to see you here."

Sof took Orrin's offered hand and squeezed gently but didn't say anything. He appeared nervous and inclined his head ever so slightly.

"Is everyone satisfied now?" Henrick asked in a surlier voice than Orrin had ever heard him use. "We could have attacked by now."

Silas nervously rolled his chair forward and back a few inches at a time but answered in a confident tone, "I believe this represents our best available forces."

Henrick didn't argue and waved a hand at Vulwin. The man dropped his feet from the table and let his chair rock back to the ground.

"The Demon Lord is here," Vulwin said and tapped on the southwest side of the Horde camp outline drawn on the map.

Daniel straightened. "Are you sure?"

"Got close enough to see the hairs in his nose." Vulwin smirked and began spinning a small knife between his fingers. "Would have stuck him, but he's got about twenty soldiers above level one hundred around him at all times. There are maybe another thirty that they send out with the bigger groups to keep them in line. I thought to take a few down but didn't like my odds of getting out without ruining my shirt." The man lifted his silk collar and let it drop back on his shoulder.

"What's the plan?" Daniel's eyes sparked and his hand reached to touch the handle of Gertrude on his shoulder.

"We could have used the spell orbs and left by now, but the 'leadership' of Dey"—Henrick fixed on the word like it was stuck in his mouth—"wouldn't hand over what we need. Lord Catanzano says you can make the buffs last all day instead of twenty minutes?"

Daniel deflated but nodded at Orrin to step forward.

"I can, but I have to cycle you through my party. It costs a bunch of mana, but I can get you all in two—"

"Good, then do it and we can go," Henrick ordered. "We're going to kill the Demon Lord."

Chapter 52

Daniel ducked in front of Orrin and raised his hand in the air. "Um, hi. Excuse me. Daniel the [Hero] here. How do you think you'll take out the Demon Lord without my spell?"

Vulwin speared a sausage off his plate with his knife and took a bite. "Likely the same way we take down every other threat we've ever encountered."

Henrick glowered at the thief and Vulwin ducked his head. The large knight took a breath before turning to Daniel.

"You won't be able to help us in this fight. Your level is a liability. You are strong, there is no question, but in a real fight against the power of these demons, it wouldn't be enough. Your ability to lock the Demon Lord's power isn't ready, and we will have to hope none of the demons assembled have the ability to secure the title after we kill the current one." Henrick paused and looked at Silas. "Our hope is the current Demon Lord is using his abilities to keep the demons in check. It's likely the high levels are a by-product of his as well. In the chaos after his death, the Horde should break up and retreat."

"I have a lot of questions about what you just said," Daniel said, not letting Henrick have the last word. "I thought Demon Lord was a class. What do you mean, someone else could take the title?"

June, still standing behind them, put her fingers on Daniel's back. "We can talk after the battle. The demons are not attacking right now, likely due to their fear of us. We must strike quickly before they plan around our presence."

"I think we have time for answers right now," Daniel said stubbornly and crossed his arms in front of his chest. "How would someone secure the Demon Lord title?"

June glanced at Henrick, who gave a slight nod. The mage tapped a finger on her chin before she spoke. "Do you know much about demons?"

Daniel shrugged. "I know how to kill them and I know they get experience from killing people. Some look all red and shit, but a lot of them just seem like normal people."

June nodded. "They are the same as you and me in most ways, but demons spread their genetic quirk to all children. Everyone on the other side of that Wall will be getting experience for killing us. It's why we don't travel past the Pass. It's a dangerous land that only the most foolhardy explore. Rarely do those return. The demons have classes just like us, but they all get more powerful from killing other sentient races. We don't know why. We don't know how one of them becomes a Demon Lord, either. When a demon gains the title, though, a [Hero] always appears. If you die, another will show within a month or two. If the Demon Lord dies, that is sometimes the end, but other stories say the Demon Lord can pass its powers to another. We don't know how. That's why we cannot wait. We will kill this one today. He is too powerful. If another picks up the mantle, we will have bought time for you to grow."

Orrin listened to June's words, but they felt wrong. Daniel needed to kill the Demon Lord. He knew it somehow in his bones, but he'd thought they'd had more time. He'd planned on using his Administrator powers later, but the more he thought about it, the better the Assign Quests option looked. Resetting Daniel's class came with all sorts of complications and as his friends had pointed out, unlocking the spell wouldn't necessarily give Daniel the [Demon Seal] spell. He ignored Silas as the man tried to argue some point or another. Every time Orrin thought he had a grip on the knowledge of this world, someone inevitably dropped a bomb on them. Administrators, mana signatures, the Accords, whatever they were. Now Demon Lord wasn't a class but a title?

He looked at his administrator point total. Twenty-five. Assign Quests cost ten points and Edit Reward cost another ten. That would leave him with five administrator points.

Orrin had hesitated over his points for weeks because he didn't know if he could get more. Finding a dungeon to defeat was nearly impossible, but with the knowledge that he could use Assign Class to get more, he found the courage to take the leap.

Unlock the Administrator Skill Assign Quests for 10 administrator points?
Yes or No?

Orrin mentally slapped the Yes button and then added the Edit Reward option as well.

"—find a way for Dragoon team to help," Silas said as Orrin blinked away from the blue screens. "They've been instrumental in our—"

"Daniel, I need to talk with you real quick," Orrin leaned back and whispered. "I did it."

His friend ran his fingers through the hair around his ear, a trait that Orrin knew meant he was irritated by the continued talks. "What did you do?"

"It's time for a Quest," Orrin said and winked.

Daniel stared at him. "Huh?"

Orrin rolled his eyes. "I spent some points. You're about to get a Quest that will unlock your [Demon Seal] spell."

Understanding flooded the [Hero]'s eyes, and a smile blossomed across his annoyed face. "Let's go! That's what I'm talking about."

Silas stopped talking and everyone turned to Daniel.

"I'm sorry." Daniel brought his eyes to the ground and tried to look apologetic. "Please continue."

Orrin opened his status back up and searched for the mark next to Assign Class. The new blinking words "Assign Quests" scrolled down into a complicated grid of options, but the top button, Select Target, caught his eye immediately. Orrin selected the drop-down and a list of names appeared. Everyone in the small tent was registered. He selected Daniel and sighed in relief as half the grids farther down grayed out.

Daniel. Check. Monster domination? Dungeon exploration? Collection? Orrin started going through the first drop-down. None of the selections were labeled, but this one was obviously the Quest type. After reading through the options, Orrin left it on "monster domination." More of the squares farther down turned gray. The next option was monster types, followed by selected numbers. The monster choices spun by in an unending scroll.

Orrin moved back and flicked the first box through the choices until he found Attack and Defend. Playing with the boxes, he found a set of options he thought might work. He tugged on Daniel's sleeve. "Attack selected sentient creatures or defend a location from damage for a selected time?"

"What?" Daniel whispered. "What does that mean?"

"Do you want to kill a bunch of demons or play king of the hill?"

Daniel's smile was murderous. "Kill some demons."

Orrin continued down the selections with each pull-down bar. Attack, sentient creatures, hostile, within ten miles, and one. The bar at the bottom that read "Create" turned white.

Quest Creation:
Kill a Spy (1)
Assault a Deserter (1)
Kill a Demon (1)
More . . .

Orrin smiled and selected "Kill a Demon." The smile slipped away at the next screen.

Kill a Demon—Demons are attacking the Wall of Dey in a Horde. Kill a demon.
Reward: 100 XP
Target: Daniel Kayson
Cost: 1 administrator point

"Damn," Orrin muttered but didn't give up hope. He tried to use Edit Reward. The ability wouldn't target the Quest. He flipped it over to the available options. "Defeat the Demon Lord" populated, but Orrin didn't want that to be the trigger Quest.

I have to buy it first, don't I?

Orrin sucked in air and gritted his teeth as he spent the point to confirm the Quest.

"Orrin? I just—"

"Shut up for a second." Orrin tried Edit Reward again and found "Kill a Demon."

Edit Reward:
Experience
Spell
Skill
Stats
More . . .

Orrin's heart beat so loud that he was surprised everyone else in the tent didn't stop talking to stare at him. The moment of truth was here, and Orrin's palms grew slick. He clicked "spell" and typed in "[Demon Seal]."

He almost puked when the search revealed nothing. His fingers moving along with his eyes in a typing motion, Orrin backed up and searched "skill."

"It's a skill," he sighed out in relief. Silas stopped and turned to look at him again.

"Orrin? What's going on?" the man asked, turning his wheelchair toward the young party. Henrick's back was to them as he hunched over the table pointing at something with his group.

"One minute, Silas." Orrin kept reading to make sure everything was correct and hit "accept."

Reward Customization:
Quest Selected: Kill a Demon
Target: Daniel Kayson
Old Reward: 100 XP
New Reward: [Demon Seal]
Cost: 30 administrator points
Approve?

"Fuck!" Orrin spat and looked up at everyone staring at him. "I'll cast your spells when you want. I need some air."

Orrin hit the tent flap and moved out of the enclosure. Everything around him was red as he raged. He'd spent the points for nothing. Thirty points might as well be a hundred when he only had four left. He wasn't going to be able to get Daniel the skill. They'd have to hope the Phoenix team could defeat the Demon Lord and then pray that whatever happened when the guy died didn't bring another one back to the gates of Dey.

"Orrin?" Daniel was right on his heels. Madi and Brandt followed close behind. "What's wrong?"

"Not here. Not now," Orrin said, shaking his head. He'd made a scene but didn't care. Everyone in there could think he was a dick and it wouldn't change a thing. "I need to . . . I don't know. I need to hit something."

Madi nodded at Brandt, and the man went back into the tent. She stepped close and put her hand on Orrin's chest. "Use your spell. Cast [Calm Mind]."

"I don't want to be calm," Orrin snapped. He clenched his fists and moved away from her. "This is a war. It isn't some monsters or escaping a few bad guys. I thought . . . maybe if the Demon Lord was stopped . . ." He shook his head and rubbed his neck. The collar was long gone, but he still chafed from time to time where the metal ring had been. "You heard them, Madi. Twenty demons above level one hundred. That's insane odds. Even buffed out, what if they fail?"

Brandt stepped back out with one of the guards who stood behind Silas in most meetings. Orrin had never learned his name and always assumed he was one of the generals. "Cast [Sound Seal] on the four of us," Brandt ordered. "Then leave us."

The man didn't ask questions, and Orrin felt a familiar bubble surround him. One of the teachers at the Sanerris School for Spells, Graem, had used the same magic a few times. The guard nodded at Brandt and returned to the tent.

"What happened?" Brandt asked, standing behind Madi. Her hand moved back to grab the [Knight]'s fingers. "You don't usually lose it like that, Orrin."

"He said, later," Daniel whispered with a look at the door. "I think he bought a new ability and it didn't work like he wanted it to." Daniel put extra emphasis on *ability* and wagged his eyebrows to indicate he meant Administrator powers.

"That's obvious enough to us," Madi said. "We're in a [Sound Seal]. Nobody can hear us in here. Orrin, talk to us."

Orrin explained what he'd done in terse, clipped words. He'd been stupid to put so much hope in the plan, but they'd had no other choice. He blinked hard, trying not to let his anger bring tears to his eyes as he finished telling them how he'd messed up. "So, now Daniel has a pointless Quest and I have four points left. I can't even try Unlock Skill. Not much help I am."

Brandt snapped his fingers in front of Orrin's face. "That's enough. You found a tree in your path. That doesn't mean you give up. Listen to Madi and calm yourself. Tell us again, in detail, what the options said."

Orrin blinked at Brandt taking charge like that. It had been a while since the man stepped back to let Daniel lead, and the authority in his voice made Orrin jump a little. He clicked [Calm Mind] and felt the growing panic at screwing up fade into a distant roar.

"I was able to pick what kind of Quest it would be," Orrin started, going into more detail. He even pulled the ability back up to read a few entries to them. He finished with the cost of the unpurchased upgrade.

"Can you change the Quest?" Daniel asked. "Like maybe if it was more demons, the cost would be lower?"

Orrin shook his head. "I can't pull the Quest I gave you back into Assign Quests. Edit Reward doesn't give me an option to change the Quest, either."

"You could try making a new, harder Quest," Brandt offered and quickly followed up as Orrin seemed about to argue. "It's better to know for sure. We already agreed that Unlock Skill wouldn't help Daniel, and we don't have time for you to reset his class to one."

"Technically, I would be able to buy the spell if I got my original three hundred points back."

Brandt mumbled something unkind about [Heroes] and their luck.

"That wouldn't work," Madi countered. "You told me once that [Demon Seal] didn't appear on your list until you leveled up. Even if Orrin got more points and used them all to reset your class, we still would need to raise your level. I agree with Brandt. Try another

Quest. If it doesn't work, we'll figure it out. Don't worry, Orrin. We believe in you."

Orrin looked at his three friends and felt the last of his anxiety lift from his shoulders. He nodded in agreement and pulled the screen up. "Daniel can probably kill five demons, right? He's not totally useless."

Daniel knocked his fist on Orrin's head. "Make it fifty. If I bring you along to drop a few of them, we could even do a hundred."

Orrin rubbed his head but smiled as he started working.

Chapter 53

Orrin created the same Quest but rolled the number up to fifty. After a moment of thought, he moved the ticker to an even hundred. *Better overshot than sorry.* He moved to accept the Quest, and a new button generated as he selected Daniel as the target.

"I might have freaked out for nothing," Orrin said slowly, reading the notification aloud. "'Replace Quest' popped up as an option when I made the new Quest. I'm going to try it."

Before anyone could respond, Orrin hit the button. Daniel's eyes crossed a bit as he read his own blue screen.

"Accept upgraded Quest?" Daniel read aloud. "Yes, please. The reward changed by a lot. This makes killing the demons worth it."

Orrin grinned. "It didn't even cost a thing. I guess making the same Quest and changing the parameters is like editing a Quest. The reward experience went up, but everything else stayed the same."

Daniel gave a sigh of relief. "Did the cost to change the reward go down?"

Orrin tried Edit Reward again.

Reward Customization:
Quest Selected: Kill a Demon
Target: Daniel Kayson
Old Reward: 10,000 XP
New Reward: [Demon Seal]
Cost: 3 administrator points
Approve?

"I'm glad I changed it to a hundred demons. It costs three administrator points. That's worth it."

Brandt clapped Orrin on the back. "You did good, Orrin."

Daniel grinned, bouncing on the balls of his feet. "Do it. I can't wait to see the look on Henrick's face. That asshole . . . trying to sideline us."

Orrin clicked the button and watched his administrator points roll down to one. He could assign the [Healer] class to someone and get more points in the future, at least. "We need to come up with a cover story. You could say the system gave you a new Quest."

"It's worked before." Daniel shrugged before turning slowly to Brandt and Madi. "We kind of lied to you guys about the elf war Quest. Sometimes Orrin gets Quests."

"And uses other abilities that are outside his class description," Madi said slowly. "I wonder if you are using Administrator powers when you are in extreme situations. You took a few points off Samara's constitution, which sounds like Edit Stats."

"Not to mention you always find the weirdest skills," Daniel added. "You have a handful of spells that nobody has ever heard of."

"I don't know," Orrin started but remembered that June and Tony had both been stumped by [Mind Bastion]. It wasn't a skill he'd found in any book or class description. *Maybe I unlocked it with my rare class?*

"I wish I had this yesterday," Daniel grouched but with a smile on his face. "All those demons I finished off after you debuffed them would have covered the Quest already."

Orrin shrugged. His job wasn't to kill the demons but to make them easier for everyone else to stop. They'd discussed how little experience the demons gave. Their level didn't even matter. Every demon killed gave only a hundred experience. That was if you took one down by yourself. In a team, the experience was split across a few people. Even worse, if someone outside your party dealt the killing blow, all your work was for nothing. Doubly unfortunate for Orrin, his decrease-stat spells didn't count as damage, so he'd missed out on more XP than anyone. Daniel, on the other hand, had leveled once from the demon kills alone.

"We should request a delay in Phoenix's attack so Daniel can get this skill," Brandt said, glancing at the nearby tent. "I'm sure both teams would accept helping the [Hero] complete a Quest."

"If you share the Quest, more people can get the [Demon Seal] as well," Madi said excitedly. "That will convince them more than anything else."

Orrin had doubts the system would allow a [Hero]-specific skill to be shared but didn't want to ruin the mood. In any scenario, he could bypass the system with his reward list patch. In the past, he'd been able to change Quest rewards that were unavailable to something helpful.

"What are we waiting for?" Daniel was smiling. "I wish we had a camera. I want to see Henrick's face when I tell him."

Madi mouthed, "Camera?" to Orrin, and he shook his head. The party stepped through the [Sound Seal] and entered the tent again.

"Welcome back to the adult table," Henrick said, frowning and crossing his arms. "Is there something you want to add before we leave?"

Daniel bowed his head contritely. "I apologize for our departure, Sir Henrick. It seems the system wants us to succeed in defeating the Demon Lord and granted me a new Quest. Since Lord Catanzano is one of those in charge of Dey's defense, I think he should see this first. If you'd be so kind as to accept this gesture . . ."

Daniel winked at Silas as he flicked the Quest to the man. Madi's dad straightened in his wheelchair, and the avarice on his face was apparent to everyone in the room. "The [Hero] once again finds a way to help Dey in its time of need. Sir Henrick, I formally request you delay your attack. We have much to do."

June's eyes bounced from Silas to Daniel before she tilted her head toward Orrin. He kept his face neutral and tried to ignore the sweat sliding down his back.

"You've already accepted we are your best chance at . . . What? A Quest?" Henrick's stern rebuke died on his lips as Silas shared a blue box with the large knight. His eyes read quickly and he turned to his team. "June, take a look."

As Phoenix read over the list, Leanthun drew near to Orrin. "Was this you?"

Orrin didn't spare the elf a glance but tightened his shoulders in response. Leanthun was Arandir's number two. Arandir had a limited Administrator power list but couldn't create Quests. He was something of an unofficial mentor to Orrin. *I'm getting a bunch of mentors lately.*

"He'll want to talk with you," Leanthun pressed.

"When we're not fighting a war and waiting for the elves to abandon us, I'll visit," Orrin said with a scowl. At the pained look on the man's face, he quickly changed his tone. "I'm sorry, Leanthun. That was uncalled-for. I'm stressed, but you can tell Arandir that I'll visit when I can to talk with him."

Lady Timpe and Lord Tarris sided with Silas over delaying the Phoenix team strike. Henrick and Vulwin argued their team was ready now. Thram, their dwarven mage, sighed and pulled out a small flask that he began to take increasingly longer sips from. Finally, June interrupted Henrick.

"Calm down, Henrick. We'll support the [Hero] in his Quest and then attack together."

The large man huffed but didn't argue with her, showing Orrin once and for all who was really in charge of the Phoenix team. Logistics of fighting demons during their next raid were discussed and approved. Orrin would cycle between the two parties to buff all nine members of his own team and Phoenix. Vulwin made snide remarks about fighting alongside weaker teams, but June shushed him. Orrin thought they were finally done when Henrick agreed to only incapacitate demons so Daniel could get kill credit for his Quest, but Silas wasn't done with them yet.

"As some of you know, part of Dragoon team has been tracking the former members of the Hospital that attacked citizens of Dey during this Horde." The dark-skinned man rolled his chair around the table and stopped in front of Sof. "This is Sof, the leader of Dragoon. He'll report on what they've found."

"What does this have to do with us?" Vulwin interrupted. He was admiring a long golden necklace that Rasha snatched from his hands. He glared at her before turning back to Silas. "Phoenix is here to take out demons, not babysit—"

"Vulwin, I have all the respect for you and your high level, but if you don't shut up, we are never going to get out of here," Daniel said with a heavy sigh. "We all get it. You're better than all of us. Prove it and listen, dude."

The man was out of his seat and in front of Daniel before Orrin could blink. A long dagger pressed against Daniel's neck and a single drop of blood pooled at the tip.

"You might be the [Hero], but if you can't back up your—" Vulwin started to threaten Daniel but stopped and watched his hand.

The rogue's knife dipped and slid along Daniel's armor, leaving a small scratch before his arm fell to his side. "That's new," Vulwin mumbled before he fell into a heap at Daniel's feet.

Daniel raised an eyebrow at Henrick and Rasha. Both stood with their weapons out, but June was sipping at her drink. "You mentioned manners and keeping your party in control, Henrick. If Vulwin is going to be a liability, maybe he shouldn't be in this next battle."

Orrin rolled his eyes at Daniel taking advantage of his spells. The five [Decrease Strength] and [Decrease Dexterity] spells at the second level had worked better than he'd hoped. Vulwin was level seventy-five at least, and while he was still able to crawl, the rogue was distinctly moving away from the [Hero].

Rasha's laughter broke the tense mood in the tent. "He's got your number, Henry. Vulwin, stand up. Whatever the [Hero]'s teammate did to you can't be that bad."

Vulwin tried to say something, but only drool slipped from his mouth. Orrin spammed a few regular buffs on the man. Just enough to get him up again.

Vulwin sucked the spit into his mouth and stretched his jaw as he slowly got up with one palm up toward Daniel. "That was more effective than I thought it would be. That was you or Orrin?"

Orrin waggled his fingers. "Please try not to hurt my friends. I'm a little trigger-happy when they're threatened."

Rasha laughed again and clapped Vulwin on the back. "Come on, sit down and shut up like the [Hero] said or we'll let Orrin turn you into a pile of cow droppings again."

June was mouthing something but didn't cast a spell. A moment of silence across the tent made the air awkward until Sof coughed politely.

"As Lord Catanzano requested, members of my team tracked the group of [Healers] from the Hospital in Dey—"

"Former members but with no current affiliation with us," Elder Kali, the wizened old crone [Healer], interjected. When she didn't add anything more, Sof nodded and continued.

"Former members, yes. We found an abandoned village they've been living at near the Untamed Forest. The village is nothing more than forty-odd houses built of stone and rotting timber, but they've been refortifying it for some time, it seems. They have at least an [Earth Mage] on hand. The best count my team could make was thirty [Healers] or trainees, twice that number in melee or magic classes for protection, and another two hundred people in support roles or family members. They've been using a barn as a safe house of sorts, and we believe they've created underground tunnels around town. Maya counted their numbers with the wind and believes that with another two teams, we could apprehend these criminals with ease. She did overhear something troubling, though."

Maya was a [Wind Singer], Orrin recalled. It was a sort of [Wind Mage] offshoot that he didn't know much about.

Maya stretched her hands overhead as she pushed away from the tent wall. "A few of the more powerful fighters had the beginning of a plan to attack the Wall during a demon raid. They want to take out Orrin, his party, and the [Healer] who disrupted what they call the natural order of things."

Silas held up his hand as Orrin stepped forward. "We've already sent for Mr. Fallah. He's in a tent nearby and understands the danger. You can visit him after we finish this."

"Finish what?" Daniel asked. "That's like three hundred people plotting against my friends."

"Yes," Elder Kali crowed. "Three hundred people who once helped bring healing to the people and now must be purged thanks to your actions. [Healers] led astray by the greed of a few and their families that will never know peace and now must be dealt with."

Orrin balled his hands into fists. Elder Kali was climbing higher on his shit list with every word she spoke. He couldn't do anything about the woman's attitude, but he'd watch her for sure.

Daniel took a different approach. "Will somebody get this bitch out of here before I decide the entire Hospital is rotten? I can't fight everybody, but I'm not above beating her up because she's old."

The lords of Dey exchanged wide-eyed looks with each other. Sof's normal passive persona perked up at the sudden tension around him. Henrick's hand rested on the hilt of his sword.

Goddamn it, Daniel.

Chapter 54

Rasha's nervous laughter broke the silence. Henrick glared at Daniel again.

"The Hospital is not something you threaten, boy." A single step brought the [Paragon Knight] in front of Daniel. "Everyone protects the [Healers]. They help us back up after we take the fight to the monsters."

"In case you missed this while off playing in the dungeons, the Hospital around here tries to kill people, kidnaps parents, and generally pisses in my direction everywhere I go," Daniel said calmly, counting off items on his fingers. "We've explained to those that matter what happened . . . multiple times. I'm tired of being told what a bad boy I've been. I'm here to help fight demons, but the next time somebody gets in my face with a knife or questions the actions of my friends, I'll leave. You can fight the Demon Lord and do what you want. I'll level up and get the hell off this planet, because I'm done being pushed around by people who think they're better than me. This isn't my fight or my city. I'm not demanding gold like the [Healers] you love so much. I'm not starting fights with old grandmas, but you better bet your ass, the next time she talks to me like that, I will show you how far someone can fly."

Henrick's anger flickered to confusion. "You can fly? What does that have to do with—"

"No." Daniel blinked. "I mean, I'll throw her far away."

"Then why say fly?"

"Because she'll look like she's flying?" Daniel turned his statement into a question at the last second. "That doesn't matter. I'm tired of the insults. Sof, what's the plan for the excommunicated [Healers] or whatever?"

The druid watched the interplay between the two men without comment, but when Daniel turned the attention his way, he gave no indication of the thoughts in his head. "There are only a few members that are above level forty in the entire encampment. Elder Phendio is in the low seventies. Principal Brack is level fifty or thereabouts. There are a handful of their fighters in the lower-forties range, no more than five by our count. With surprise, we can take out most of them before they know we're there. No offense to the elder, but the Hospital rests mostly on its reputation and later consequences for harming members of its organization. Elder Phendio is the only member I'm worried about. The rumors about her class . . ." He trailed off with an askance glance at Kali.

The woman ignored him and picked at something on her staff.

"Elder Kali, it would help us tremendously if you told us what you know about Elder Phendio," Silas said diplomatically. "You claim she is no longer a member of your Hospital, but protecting her does not do you any favors."

Kali spat on the floor and continued polishing the wood on her staff.

"We could ask Tony to come help," Madi offered. "He's very good at getting answers from people."

Orrin was shocked at Madi's declaration. Tony was a white-hat [Mind Mage] who worked to keep the darker side of Dey's mage populace, those interested in mind magic, contained. Madi's reference to the man's illusion torture of a man who'd attacked them and helped kidnap Daniel was the closest thing to a compliment she'd ever given him. Madi was terrified of Quiet Anthony, the boogeyman of Dey. She'd spent some time with him lately with Orrin, but there was a history between her father and Tony that nobody broached. To hear her suggest bringing him in to help speed up Kali's cooperation was interesting, to say the least.

"Quiet Anthony need not be involved," Silas said darkly. "I'm sure that the elders will remember that we are in a time of crisis and interfering with a matter of security of this level is a capital offense, no matter your station."

Kali sighed heavily and shook her head at Madi. "You were once such a sweet child with promise. Such a pity. You will end up just like your mother."

Daniel's heavy step toward the little old lady was a moment too late. Orrin used [Gust] and held the woman by her throat in the air. Her staff fell as she grabbed at his fingers. Dark shadows pulled his vision into a tunnel as he stared into Kali's eyes.

Henrick's sword was already at his neck, but June's hand stayed his strike.

"You've been given too many chances to cooperate, but I draw the line at you insulting my friend's family. Your authority ends now. Tell us what we need to know to end this threat from your Hospital or else." Orrin's voice came out cold and he realized [Mind Bastion] was running.

Kali stared into his eyes and smirked, a smug grin that showed no fear at her current predicament. "You are surrounded by people who won't allow you to harm me, young man. You've already cut my family in two. What could you possibly think you could do to hurt me more? I won't betray my friend even if she has strayed."

"I could use [Toxic Touch] to burn through your throat, but I won't," Orrin whispered. June pushed Henrick back at the words, and Orrin filed her trust away for later perusal. "I can respect you protecting a friend. That doesn't mean you're a good guy."

Orrin used [Numb] on the woman's spine. Her hands fell limp to her sides, and her eyes widened. "If you aren't part of the solution, you're part of the problem. Sir Henrick, please bring this traitor to . . . wherever you guys take prisoners."

The lords of Dey were wide-eyed at Orrin's display of power. Sof's eyebrow was raised in surprise. June let out a sigh of relief as Orrin handed the woman over to the large knight. She got close to Orrin. "That was very dangerous. We are going to need to talk about that spell you almost used."

Henrick glanced around awkwardly, holding the paralyzed woman in his arms like a doll. "Lord Catanzano?"

Silas was the first of the rulers of Dey to recover. "Put her in the prison and inform Elder Seif that his presence is requested immediately. We'll reconvene in ten minutes."

Orrin shivered as [Mind Bastion] rolled down and Daniel clapped a hand on his back. "You beat me to the punch. I was going to punt the hag into next week."

Brandt said nothing, but his smile was encouragement enough. Madi's face was flat.

"Are you okay, Madi? I'm sorry you had to hear her talk about your mom." Orrin approached her like she was a stray cat. He couldn't get a read on her emotions. "I think somebody was going to throw her arrogant ass out anyway. She has been no help since she arrived."

Madi's arms moved faster than Orrin could stop. He winced, waiting for the strike, but her elbows locked around him in a tight hug. "Thank you, Orrin. I didn't need you to defend my mom or me but . . . thank you."

"I was half worried you or Daniel would kill her outright," he laughed as she let go. "How somebody like that gets put in charge of something as big as the Hospital, I'll never understand."

Silas pushed into their little circle and took Madi's hand in his. "Are you all right?"

Madi nodded and held her head high.

Silas squeezed her fingers and turned to Orrin. "What you did was brash, broke half a dozen laws, and will have consequences I can't even imagine . . . but thank you. When she mentioned my wife . . ." He scowled and shook himself. "Let us hope that Elder Seif is more forthcoming. If not, more members of the Hospital will fill the prison cells tonight. To play such games with the demons right outside—"

Leanthun and Dragoon team kept out of the way and Henrick returned within the ten minutes allotted. Elder Seif walked in behind the knight.

"Why is Elder Kali in a cell?" the deep baritone voice of the elder spoke without preamble. "After all we've done during this—"

Silas used his skill and spoke a single word. "Quiet."

Elder Seif's mouth bobbled like a fish, but no words came out.

Silas rolled close to the man. Elder Seif towered over him in his chair, but Silas's authority made the tall healer shrink. "You are the last elder of the Hospital of Dey. We are about to strike at those who killed during a Horde and kidnapped or attempted the same with multiple people instrumental to the defense of Dey. This is no longer a request but an order from the rulers of Dey. You will tell us everything you know about Elder Phendio, Principal Brack, and any high-level members of your group that have gone missing. They will be apprehended or killed depending on their ability to surrender. Elder Kali will have her trial, but as you know, the lords of Dey are judge and jury during a Horde. She will be banished from these lands and never allowed to return. This is your only warning, Seif. Speak."

The last word carried the weight of his magic again. Between the two elders, Orrin had thought Seif was the strong, silent type, but he was quickly disabused of that notion when the man began spilling secrets. The Hospital had been holding back. They had a full list of who was missing, what with their meticulous records.

"Principal Brack is a [Fire Medic]. He started as a [Fire Mage] but learned to heal fire damage better than anyone we've ever trained. Elder Phendio is a [Mind Caster]. She talks with patients and helps calm them from trauma, but nobody goes into a room with her alone. There were . . . incidents. People behaving strangely after sessions with her. Elder Kali has known her since she was a child and spoiled the girl. She touches on the magic we've outlawed in Dey, but no formal charges were ever brought."

Sof's shoulders sagged. "That was our fear. She's a [Mind Mage]."

Elder Seif shook his head, the scars along his body shining in the lantern light of the tent. Although it was still daytime, the entire pavilion was darkened and closed down against any listening ears. "There is no reason to call her that. She cannot read another's mind, as far as I know. Her magic allows her to help guide a person's thoughts and face their fears or past with a comforting presence at their side."

"Sure," Daniel muttered to Orrin. "The scary lady who tries to kill everyone who doesn't follow her orders totally doesn't fuck with people's minds."

Sof asked a few more questions about certain targets, but the main threats seemed to be Brack and Phendio. "Dragoon can take two teams and arrest anyone who surrenders within the hour. At your command, sirs and lady."

Lady Timpe, Lord Tarris, and Lord Catanzano nodded and the mission was set. The Hospital would be cleansed of the filth that hurt Amir's father.

"I should point out," Brandt interrupted. "They have the ability to use [Portal]. Lord Tarris, you might be needed."

The leader of Dey pushed his glasses up his nose before putting his arms into his robe sleeves. "When can you leave, Dragoon team? I am needed on the Wall."

As Sof and Lord Tarris discussed their schedules, Henrick moved toward Daniel and Orrin. Madi quietly moved herself to stand beside them.

"June has decided that she, Rasha, and Thram will accompany you to help complete your Quest. Vulwin and I will remain behind to help the defenders." The knight's jaw barely moved as he ground the words out. "I apologize for my harsh words earlier. I hope we can fight together in the future."

Something told Orrin that June's words—through Henrick—were not completely sincere. However, Madi, ever the politician, bowed her head slightly and graciously spoke to the man before he dragged his rogue friend from the room.

"You make friends everywhere you go," Daniel joked and poked Orrin in the side. "If the demons don't attack us soon, can we rush them for once? I haven't fought anyone today."

Orrin and Madi sighed in exasperation at the same time. Brandt laughed, and the occupants of the tent glanced as one at the party.

"Ignore us." Orrin waved. "Just Daniel being Daniel."

Chapter 55

Orrin hadn't realized that Dragoon meant to head out immediately for the ex–Hospital member capture mission. Lord Tarris was needed to stop the use of [Portal] and wanted to be back on the Wall as soon as possible. Henrick and Vulwin would accompany Dragoon as well, at June's direction. Orrin noticed the woman giving stern orders to the knight and rogue outside the tent.

"Be safe, Sof," Orrin said as the druid stood by waiting. "We're getting used to having Dragoon around to help us out."

Maya's soft titter drew both their gazes to her. "What? I can't wait to tell the others that we're the [Hero]'s go-to squad. That should get us a few extra drinks at the bar, don't you think?"

Sof shook his head. "We should be fine. These buffs of yours are incredible." He flexed his arm and smiled the tiniest bit. "The [Purify] spell orbs for tomorrow are welcome, too. Some of our team could not handle the full one hundred points last time and were sick for a day."

Orrin winced, but there was nothing he could do. The decision to give Dragoon a boost from his [Utility Ward] against the last demon attack had been a Hail Mary attempt to save their lives. That they'd all survived meant it worked. He'd cycled Sof, Maya, Henrick, Vulwin, and even Lord Tarris through his party already and was waiting for the other seven members of Dragoon to answer their summons. Once everyone was buffed, the team would move out.

"Not that any of them complained for more than a week or two," Maya said with her impish grin still in place. "Having a mana pool twice the size of normal saved our lives. Finding Daniel in that forest was a blessing."

Sof's grunt spoke to only partial disagreement. "You should be careful as well. The Horde will respond with force when they attack.

Keep your party together and have an escape plan ready for when things go wrong."

Orrin stretched his arms above his head as he answered, "Hopefully, nothing goes wrong. We'll have June there to get us out of trouble, too."

Sof tapped his fingers on his leg in agitation. "Do not trust Phoenix with your lives. They value only strength and do not fight for Dey. They seek glory and power in the dungeons. I will fight beside Sir Henrick and his light-fingered friend, but I would not expect them to come to my rescue."

Orrin felt the same about Henrick and Vulwin after their earlier displays, but June was cool. She'd helped him train a bit. Rasha appeared to be good in a fight, and Orrin looked forward to seeing the dwarf in action. Still, he appreciated Sof's worry. "Thanks, Sof. We'll be careful."

As the rest of Dragoon team arrived, Orrin partied up with them in spurts, making sure to give everyone a full set of buffs. He handed out the [Purify] orbs as well, explaining how to use them.

Lord Tarris took command, with Henrick standing at his side. "You have been briefed on the plan, but the important thing to remember is this is not an execution. Capture, not kill, is the command for the day. Incapacitate if you must, accept surrender when you can, and kill only if forced. Most of these criminals are still citizens of Dey, and we do not know the level of complicity in their numbers. Strike fast, but remember some of the people we are about to take in are children following orders."

Henrick shuffled his feet, and when Lord Tarris turned, the knight spoke as well. "That order applies only toward the lower-ranked members. If you encounter Elder Phendio, Principal Brack, Principal Mangin, or anyone above level fifty, point them out to me and Vulwin. Elder Phendio may not come quietly, but we will subdue the principals at Elder Seif's request. If the leadership here wants a trial for these criminals, we will do our best not to kill them outright."

Elder Seif, the last official elder of the Hospital, raised his arm. He didn't wait for Henrick to acknowledge him. "We have several members that would like to go with you. Some can fight, but we can also heal any injuri—"

"No," Lord Tarris cut the man off. "No members of the Hospital will be involved in this matter. You can wait at the target field to heal those that return."

Seif didn't look happy, but he kept his response to a subtle shake of his head.

Daniel bumped against Orrin as he watched the assembled fighters split into groups of four. Each would party with a [Locationist] or [Teleport]-class specialist for a single strike at the snake. "You don't want to go with them?"

Orrin chewed his lip. "They don't need me. I don't know when the demons are going to attack, but I want to be there for you. We need that skill, and I'm not letting you out of my sight again until the Demon Lord is dead."

Madi put her hand on his shoulder. "That's the smartest thing you've said all day. Delegating tasks to others is one of the hardest choices a leader can make. Picking battles and where to focus my attention was the keystone of my education growing up. I'm proud of you, O."

Orrin smiled, but it didn't reach his eyes. If he could, he'd [Teleport] to the Hospital camp and debuff every single one into a crawling invalid. Buffing the attack group was the least he could do, and every minute that Amir and Daniel were still in danger was another minute that Orrin felt the need to end the threat.

"Why haven't the demons attacked?" Daniel complained as he touched Gerty's handle over his shoulder. "It's midmorning. I need to kill some demons."

Madi rolled her eyes. "If I was in charge of directing the Horde, I'd wait for Phoenix to attack. After they've used up their stamina and mana, I'd throw my best at them. The reason the fighting has been so sporadic and short is simple resource management. Without knowing where our best resources are, they have to wait. If it reaches midday and they haven't attacked, I'd bet they try a night raid. Demons can't see much better in the dark than humans on their own, but the ones that look like elves or dwarves will have better night vision."

Orrin didn't think that was fair. From the experience the defenders were getting, it was clear everyone in the Horde was a demon, whether they looked elven, human, or had big spiky horns. The ones that looked more like a traditional race were still demons and gave experience when killed, but from the limited records they had about demons, they kept the bonus perk of better vision from their ancestors' race.

"We could [Teleport] into the middle of the camp and I could cannonball my body on them. A few random attacks would kill a lot," Daniel offered.

"They have [Teleport] wards set up," Orrin said, watching as Henrick and Vulwin teamed up with Maya and Clifford the archer from Dragoon. "Our Wall keeps them from trying a physical push and limits the number of demons that can [Teleport] past us. Not that they haven't tried that. We have teams waiting for them in the spots we keep open around the back side of the Wall. That was smart thinking, whoever came up with that idea."

"Lady Timpe called them 'appetizing traps,'" Madi said with a smile. "She's ruthless and cunning."

"We can't wait for night," Daniel whined. "If I go stand on the Wall, a few might attack."

Orrin felt Daniel's frustration but tried to keep his own in check. "Skirmishes throughout the day wouldn't help. All the casters have a finite amount of mana to use. We need to save it for the real fight."

"You could teach them all [Meditate]," Daniel offered in response. "Get a few more points and find a way to unlock that for— Ouch. What was that for?"

Madi's elbow dug into Daniel's side. "There are too many people around. Shut up."

Orrin had considered using his last point to turn someone into a [Healer]. Even without a demon attack, injuries happened on a regular basis out in the field. Dropped weapons, jumpy scouts, and barely trained recruits meant the [Healers] were seeing action even on a slow day. The problem was he didn't have anyone he trusted enough to keep the class change quiet. If he could double the points every week or so, he might be able to purchase Unlock Skill. Getting [Meditate] into a mage's hand would give them sixty extra mana an hour to spend. It irked him to no end that it wasn't already available to anyone with mana, but Madi said it was normally used by classes that required long days of concentration and slow mana use. A [Cleanser] might unlock [Meditate] if they worked in a big enough city. It was a noncombat class that spent the days using low-level purifying spells on the town water supply, keeping it safe for consumption.

"They're leaving," Orrin interrupted Daniel and Madi's playful shoving. "I feel weird watching them go off."

"You don't have to be the center of every battle," Brandt said, surprising Orrin. He'd left to retrieve Amir after the meeting ended. Amir waved at Madi, a smile on his face.

"Hey, Amir." Daniel caught the smaller man's hand in his own and pulled him in for a side hug. "I heard you've been helping out and healing the injured. Good for you."

Amir's ears reddened and he ducked his head. "I'm simply doing my part for Dey."

"Dey appreciates it," Madi responded with a smile at Amir. Turning to Brandt, she grabbed his hands. "We need to figure out a game plan for when the demons attack. Daniel will be down below fighting, and I want us to join him."

"Absolutely not," Brandt argued. "He can get kills from above." Orrin smiled and tuned them out as another figure approached.

"Orrin, walk with me," June said curtly. The normal warmth of her voice was gone, and she snapped her fingers when he didn't move fast enough. "Now."

A frown creased his brow, but Orrin waved off his friends. Daniel in particular seemed about to follow, but Madi grabbed his arm. Orrin followed the fire mage as she walked away from the Wall. He struggled to keep up as she strode deeper into the Pass. After a few minutes, he started to fall behind. "June, wait up."

June swooped down on Orrin with intense fury, and for the first time, Orrin was truly afraid of the mage. He forgot his spells and put his hands up to push her away but found his body moving slowly like the air had turned to mud.

"You told me [Blood Mana] was for your blood cycling. You lied. How many times have you used the spell to kill?" Her calm, motherly persona was gone and Orrin caught a glimpse of the hard will of the [Pyrocaster] behind the facade. "Think carefully before you answer. Do not lie again."

Orrin stumbled over his words as he tried to think. June was supposed to be a friend. This wasn't right. His thoughts couldn't keep up with the changeup and he felt [Mind Bastion] snap into place.

"No," June snarled. A light mist of fire surrounded her and she stepped back. "Do not attack me or it will be the last thing you do. I like you, Orrin, but I will not let you go down the path of a [Vampire]."

The cold hug of [Mind Bastion] helped him bring his defenses up. His wards snapped into place, but Orrin knew he wouldn't survive an attack from June. During their training, she'd asked questions about his skills and spells. She probably knew more ways he could attack her than he'd dreamed of yet. "June, I don't know what is going on. You're scaring me."

"In the tent, when Henrick moved to kill you," June explained. "You were using [Blood Mana]. It was primed and ready to destroy. In close quarters like that, it felt alive. A single draw from you and everyone in that tent could have died."

Orrin remembered June pulling Henrick back, but he'd thought it was because she trusted him. *She was afraid of me*, Orrin realized and the thought was enough to make [Mind Bastion] pause. Orrin raised his hands and dropped the skill. His mana calmed and he waited for June to notice.

"I did not use [Blood Mana] in there. I have used it offensively in the past, but only when I had no choice. I used it against an elf in their forest when Lord Sanerris tried to get the council to turn on Daniel. I did it again when we fought that high-level demon the other day. I use their health to fuel my [Toxic Touch]. It's disgusting and I feel gross after using it so I don't—"

June's hand swiped through the air, cutting her fire spell into pieces. "Don't use it like that again in the future until you have control of the skill. If you had told me, I could have warned you." She took a few deep breaths and closed her eyes, muttering something about idiot children. When she opened them again, June's calm-teacher mode was back on. "Orrin, when I saw [Blood Mana] on your status screen, I asked what you used it for. It is not an inherently bad ability, but using it as a boost for your own spells using others' health . . . it changes you. It is one of the main ways that people gain the [Vampire] class or unlock [Blood Mage]. When you held Kali, you touched every person around you with your [Blood Mana]. Just for a moment, you could have sucked every bit of health from my body and everyone in that tent. You have no control over it. I felt like I was watching a toddler with [Fireball] playing in a house made of hay."

Orrin wiped the sweat from his forehead and let his hands drop. "I didn't do that . . . on purpose."

June sighed. "I'm sorry I scared you. I was worried you'd lied and were changing your class."

"I don't want to change my class," Orrin answered honestly. He'd turned down the opportunity to be a [Hero] once. He loved his wacky utility class. "I won't ever use it like that again."

"No. It is a tool, but a dangerous one. I only know of it in theory, but with practice, you should be able to use it without the changes. You said you know mana signatures? Good. Once you understand a mana signature, you can change it upon casting. You should be able to control the negative effects and purge them before the target's mana enters you."

"What does that mean?"

June held her arms around her middle and tilted her head. "It means we have a lot more training to do."

Chapter 56

Daniel came to check on Orrin but left again when he found June and Orrin sitting cross-legged on the ground, touching palms. He'd backed away from the boring-looking training, but not before whispering that the Hospital team was leaving.

"I'll speak with you later, [Hero]," June promised, opening one eye to make sure he left. "Orrin needs to do his homework or he might kill us all by accident."

Realizing homework was still a thing across dimensions, Orrin's respect for this world dropped a bit more.

"Focus and change a single point of your health into mana while feeling the skill manifest inside." June spoke slowly and in a calm, meditative tone that lulled Orrin into peacefulness. "Stretch that moment out and watch it activate. Notice how the health changes into mana?"

Orrin thought he was good at this. Anabella and Wren, two teachers of a sort, had praised his quick pickup of mana signatures. [Blood Mana] didn't activate the same way, as it was a skill that he simply willed into being, but June wanted him to watch the process. She explained that skills worked mostly the same way, especially if there was a cost to activate them.

He'd tried forty-seven times over the last half an hour and the closest he got to figuring out what happened was making the change from health to mana take an extra second.

"This is a waste of time," Orrin muttered after the latest failure. Sweat covered his forehead and his damp shirt was stuck to his chest. "I should be watching the Wall with the others."

June tilted her head. "Would you be of extra help watching the Wall for demons? How long would it take you to run to your party? A minute? Two minutes? I think you could [Teleport] closer, right?" She sighed and put her hand on Orrin's knee. "You are frustrated, but this is important. Your friends will tell you when the others return."

"Aren't you worried about Henrick and Vulwin?" Orrin tried to change the subject. The constant calm insistence on watching the interplay of health and mana changes was grating. "They have to fight some pretty strong people."

June held her hand over her mouth. Her eyes twinkled. "Please, say that again in front of Henrick when they get back. He needs a good laugh."

Orrin glared at her. "Elder Phendio has almost as many levels as them. I've taken down people at twice my current level before."

June held her hand up and snorted. "Oh, Orrin. She's still only a healer type. She'll have a few tricks, but Vulwin . . . He won't attack her where she can see him. You've felt Henrick's resistance to your buffs. His constitution is high enough to throw off most spells with minimal damage. He once found a [Mind Mage] in Odrana . . . about to be executed . . . and bartered with the woman to attack him to gain resistance. This was twenty levels ago and she barely could get him to twitch."

"What do you pay someone on death row?" Orrin wondered aloud but shook his head. June's head tilted again, like a curious bird.

"Death row?" she asked. "What's that?"

Orrin shrugged and answered hurriedly. "That's what Daniel said criminals to be executed are called where he's from. What did Henrick give her? You can't spend gold once you're dead."

June's eyes kept their focus on him for a moment. "A convicted [Mind Mage] in Odrana is killed in an excruciating and protracted manner that I don't wish to discuss. He took her head in return when he felt he'd gained enough from the interaction."

Orrin shivered.

"When you watch for a spell's mana signature, what do you do?" June changed topics abruptly, as she normally did. "Are you waiting for the spell to coalesce or inspecting it from the mana reservoir inside?"

"Um . . . I see it moving through me and gathering before it shoots out, I guess."

June narrowed her eyes in thought but then clapped and put her palms up. "Do it again, but feel the trigger. If you have to think about turning on [Blood Mana], focus your thoughts into your head. If you use it instinctively, like breathing, find the motion in your body. Don't try to follow the thread this time."

Orrin sighed and touched his hands to hers. He didn't know why she wanted him to take this position but didn't want to fight about it. His folded legs were sweating, and his knees were starting to hurt from being stuck against his shoes. "It's mental, not automatic. I just think and it happens."

June didn't respond, and Orrin followed her direction. Closing his eyes, he activated another exchange of health to mana. He kept his attention in his head, but his thoughts slipped back to his friends waiting on the Wall.

"Did you feel it?"

Orrin blushed at his failure and tried again. This time, he pushed everything else away and imagined the blue box of [Blood Mana] in his head. He read the description and moved the single health point to more mana, watching the . . . There!

A flutter of something moved in his mind, like movement in the corner of his eye. His head twitched.

"Good," June mewled. "The rest will be difficult, but the first step is the hardest."

Orrin tried three more times. He could see the flicker of . . . something but couldn't stare at it directly, like a spell's mana. He opened his eyes. "It's too hard to see."

June smiled. "You don't see a skill's mana signature. You'll need to feel it. Some descriptions I've read call it finding peace with the skill. Once you can follow it from beginning to end, you will learn the way it moves. Those motions are the signature."

Orrin's head hurt. He was supposed to watch something that he couldn't see and map out the shape it traveled . . . how, exactly? "That makes no sense."

"It will with time. This is better than I would have expected today to go. Do not use [Blood Mana] on another person until you see the way the health becomes mana within you. Once you know the signature, you should be able to use it on others safely—" June paused. "Safe for you, that is. The target will still lose their life."

"How?"

"Once you've learned the signature, you can change the spell. You need to find a way to dilute their health into pure mana before it enters your body for use. I don't know if you can find a way to power a spell with the mana before it enters your own reserve or if it would be better to absorb the pure mana directly. You'll have to experiment and learn."

Orrin stared at her aghast. "You don't know? You've been training me all this time and don't know the next step?"

June raised an eyebrow that both scolded and warned him at once. "You are taking dirty mana into your body, and it will either change you or kill you. I'm suggesting an alternative that theoretically should exist, but to answer your question, I do not know. You are playing with a skill that is not well documented."

Orrin knew he was being ungrateful, but he was annoyed. "Now I have to practice until I get the signature down? Is this enough homework for today? Can I return to my friends?"

June tsked, sucking her tongue between her teeth. "You may go. We'll pick this up again tomorrow."

Orrin didn't storm off. He used [Teleport]. The jump location wasn't far away, but he knew himself—if he stayed near June and her composed-teacher act one more minute, he was going to get himself into trouble.

"Orrin!" Amir spotted him first and waved him over. Daniel and Madi sat in the grass next to the teleportation field.

"Are you done with more magic training?" Daniel asked with a slight edge in his voice.

"You can go sit with June and try and find your inner chi next time," Orrin responded in kind. "I'm not out having fun, D."

Madi pushed Daniel over and then stood. "He's cranky because they haven't returned. They're still within the accepted time window, but another ten minutes or so . . ."

"Silas didn't have a backup team ready," Daniel complained, standing up and brushing some stray grass from his shirt. "He said it would be disrespectful to Phoenix team."

"Couldn't he ask Rasha, Thram, and June to go?" Orrin asked, looking around for the other two members of Phoenix. "Where are they?"

"Rasha and Thram are in the tent with my father," Madi explained, waving back toward the field of tents. "They are the backup, but until the time runs out or the demons attack, we're stuck waiting. How was training with the [Pyrocaster]?"

Orrin glanced at Amir but answered. "She's helping me with a skill I thought was under control. I might be able to fix it, but I shouldn't be using it against high-level demons like I did against E-ka-ka or whatever his name was."

Madi rolled her eyes. "Did she show you any cool spells or teach you how to control fire better?"

"Nope."

Madi's shoulders drooped.

"I can ask her to teach you," Orrin offered, but Madi backed away, shaking her hands.

"No, I wouldn't want to impose. She's got better things to do than teach me."

Orrin mentally noted Madi's respect for this team was borderline hero worship. "I'll still ask."

They continued to talk for another minute or two until the first team returned. One of the [Teleport] crew dropped to the ground with Gustaf, Al, Gracie, and Farah—members of Dragoon team sent to help subdue the renegade Hospital members. Gracie's side was red, but Orrin couldn't tell if it was her blood or someone else's.

"Are you four all right?" Orrin asked as he ran toward the group.

The [Locationist] flicked Orrin off. "Damn fighters not even caring about the support." He stomped off before Orrin could apologize. More groups started appearing around them.

"The mission was successful," Farah said, twirling in her black dress. "We were barely needed."

Orrin pointed at Gracie's side. "Do you need any healing?"

The large woman glanced down and blushed at the blood on her shirt. "I fell and landed on one of their fighters. Broke his leg. I'm fine."

Madi, Amir, and Daniel arrived, and Orrin realized he'd used [Gust] to cross the field before his friends. Madi jerked her head in a quick bow of respect before blabbering, "How did it go? Did you get to watch Sir Henrick fight?"

Gustaf laughed and hit Al on the chest. "Fight? That's a funny word for what he did."

Farah moved her scythe from one shoulder to the other, almost hitting Gustaf in the process. "There was some resistance at first, but nothing serious. Some of the lower-level targets tried to make a run for one of the houses, but Lord Tarris appeared on top of it. I think they had a [Portal] ready there, but he shut it down. A few heavy hitters started fighting back and Sir Henrick . . . let them whale on him. Their attacks didn't do a thing. Two threw down their weapons before he drew his sword."

"They got everyone?" Orrin asked. If Phendio or Mangin escaped, he couldn't be sure of Amir's safety. Or his own, for that matter.

Gustaf lightly touched Farah's blade and moved it away from his face. "There were more people in the houses than we accounted for, but I think so. We should report in."

Amir's sigh of relief turned into heavy breaths. Orrin caught him as he fell on his butt and hyperventilated.

"Amir?" Orrin used [Identify], but nothing was wrong on the surface. "I'm going to use [Calm Mind], okay?"

"No, Orrin." Amir looked up and grabbed Orrin's arms. "I want to feel this. My father is safe. I am safe. Thank you." Amir's face turned toward the members of Dragoon team staring at him. "Thank you all."

Chapter 57

Orrin and Daniel stood side by side as Lord Tarris debriefed the others on their successful mission. The liberation team had struck the ex–Hospital members unawares and subdued most key targets swiftly. When it was apparent they'd lost, some tried to run, but Lord Tarris was able to turn off the [Portal] before it was activated.

"They found a teenager with space magic. [Portal] is the only spell he knows. I'll work on reforming him, as I believe the Hospital was using him as a slave," Lord Tarris explained.

"What about Phendio, Mangin, and Brack?" Lady Timpe asked from her chair. She had to sit straight up due to her armor, but Orrin appreciated the ambience of feminine power she exuded throughout the room. "Did we get all the leaders?"

Lord Tarris choked a bit and looked at Sir Henrick. The knight stood to the side, speaking with June in furtive whispers. "Elder Phendio was found headless in a small room after the battle. Principals Mangin and Brack surrendered after their fighters . . . failed to harm Sir Henrick."

Vulwin raised a dagger in the air. "I got the top lady. She never knew I was there."

Henrick snorted in frustration and left the tent.

"Thank you, Lord Tarris," Silas said after a moment of silence rippled through the remaining parties. "Thank you to both Dragoon and Phoenix teams as well. This was not an easy quest to issue or fulfill, and you have the gratitude of the people of Dey."

"Mine as well," Daniel added, turning heads. "Those assholes came after my friends. I owe you all one."

The conversation turned back to when the demons might attack, and Orrin sighed as June beckoned him with a curled finger.

"Yes, June?" he drawled as he crossed the tent toward her. Madi, Brandt, and Daniel clapped Amir on the back. Sof was speaking with Thram while Maya and Rasha took turns summoning elemental weapons to one-up each other. "What is it?"

"Henrick is restless. If the demons don't attack in another hour, we will bombard their camp with or without your buffs."

Orrin hated the way people with higher levels decided what they would do without consequence. "That's not what you agreed to. Daniel needs to complete his Quest before we fight the Demon Lord."

The fire mage nodded, her hair falling around her face before she pushed it back like it had offended her. "I can control him only so far. I will try to keep it to small engagements with retreats toward the Wall. You should have the chance to take some out."

Orrin glared. "And if the Demon Lord comes to attack? You'll just run away?"

June hugged herself and shrugged. "You'll have to have the [Hero] work fast."

Orrin wanted to be mad but knew June was doing the best she could. He'd seen her arguing with Henrick. He knew what it was like dealing with a hardheaded teammate. He sighed. "Thank you for keeping him back as long as you have."

June smiled. "I'll delay him as long as I can. If they attack first, he may burn enough energy to wait another day."

"How do you get him to do anything?" Orrin joked. "I've got a Henrick, too. He barely listens."

June's smile split her face as she laughed. "Knowing what motivates him helps. Henrick needs to feel challenged. However, it must be doing something worthwhile. The last decade has been spent mapping out the dungeons and trying to clear the built-up lower levels. I convinced him that waiting until this political mess was taken care of would allow more adventurers to get experience in the inevitable backlash of our attack. Also, waiting would allow those going to deal with the Hospital to return and help. More power on the Wall means fewer lives lost."

"But now that everyone is back . . ." Orrin trailed off.

"Yes. He's ready to attack. He wants to get back to Mistwater Lanterns."

Orrin heard a shiver of uncertainty in her voice. "What is it?"

"Hmm?" June turned to look at him. "What is what?"

"You said the dungeon name weird. Don't you all spend months in there at a time?"

June hesitated and her eyes drifted to tag everyone in the tent. It wasn't spacious by any means, but nobody was paying attention to their conversation. "We were deep in the Mistwater Lanterns dungeon when something happened. Nobody else should have been as deep as we were. Vulwin thought he felt a presence on the eighty-ninth floor, but we searched for two days and found nothing. Just as we went to defeat the ninetieth-floor boss, someone triggered a dungeon break." She raised an eyebrow at Orrin's shrug. "When a party fails to defeat a floor boss on the ten-interval floors, the dungeon swarms monsters toward the entrance. We were in that dungeon for three months. We killed hundreds if not thousands of monsters, but we were pushed back. We had to escape out to the entrance and help the Odranan forces kill anything that came through for twenty-four hours. At that point, it stopped. Going back in would be starting from floor one, so we went to resupply and found out about the demon problem. This is a vacation for us, but I'm worried about what started that dungeon break."

"When did that happen? I didn't hear about this," Orrin asked, glancing at Madi. Her mom had died repelling a dungeon break.

"Odrana doesn't report dungeon breaks to the world. They contained it with our help. It was lucky some of their leaders were in Mistlight dealing with some council business—it isn't the small monsters that escape. Together, we were able to keep things from getting out of control," June said, tapping her finger to her lips. "I guess it was a day or two before the Horde reached the Wall. It took us a day to close the break, and then we came straight here to help. The timing was fortuitous."

Orrin frowned, but if the break was contained, he wouldn't mention it to Madi right now. She'd want to help. "Do random dungeon breaks happen often? It was lucky you were all there."

June picked a ball of fuzz off her sleeve. "They only happen when someone starts a fight with a floor boss and dies or runs away. Once the boss is triggered, it has to be put down or the dungeon responds with a dungeon break. Vulwin believes whoever snuck by us died or tried to run through the boss room. Henrick thinks we might have gotten too close to the boss room. Rarely, a floor boss will wait near the doorway and begin its frenzy before a group goes through."

"What do you believe?" Orrin asked, trying to figure out how anyone could have gotten by the strongest team in Asmea undetected. Henrick's theory made more sense.

"We have fought the floor boss on level ninety before, and it waits for you to approach," June said, avoiding Orrin's gaze. "But I did not sense a presence. We will investigate more when we return."

He waited to see if she would say more, but June was done with the topic. Orrin sighed and gave it one more try. "Is there anything we could do to convince Henrick not to attack? Getting that Quest and it going to waste would suck."

June shook her head. "I'm sorry, Orrin. Henrick's interests are narrow: dungeon diving, high-level adventurer subjugation, crazed monster hunts. Once you reach our level, it gets harder to gain meaningful experience or challenges."

The thought of hiring Phoenix to kill Anabella for him crossed his mind, but if June refused, that would be one more person who might warn the former leader that Orrin planned on coming for her. Instead, he thanked June for the warning. "I should let Daniel know so we can do our best to plan around your party going rogue."

"We're saving lives, not going rogue." June's posture went defensive again, but Orrin held his hands up in surrender.

"I'm not going to argue with someone who can turn me into ash. Can you hold him back for two hours at least?"

June didn't relax and narrowed her eyes. "I told you he won't attack for an hour. That's the best I can do. What are you planning?"

"Nothing," Orrin responded too quickly. "My party needs time to prepare, that's all."

Orrin glanced over at Daniel. Brandt wasn't by Madi and Daniel; his friends were still talking with Amir. His eyes skipped across the tent and found their knight talking with Silas. "Thank you for everything, June. Will you stick around after the Horde is pushed back or go back to the dungeon?"

June ruffled Orrin's hair, which made him turn his attention back to her.

"What was that for?"

"Are you worried your mentor would leave you behind?" A small smile fluttered on her lips. "The rest of Phoenix may return to the Lanterns, but I will stay until you have your skill under better control."

Orrin groaned internally. She'd decided to adopt him as her student, and based on the fire in her eyes, he had no say in the matter. "I'll work hard after we take care of the Demon Lord. I'll see you later, June."

He skipped away before she could stop him and gestured to Brandt as he moved through the room. He tapped Daniel on the shoulder and interrupted whatever he was saying. "We need to get ready. Phoenix team is going to attack the demons in an hour."

Madi's good mood fell at his words. "They agreed to wait for the Quest to be complete."

Orrin shook his head. "They agreed to wait and help with the Quest, but Henrick is impatient, like someone else we know. I think that in his mind, attacking the demons will jump-start their push to the Wall."

Daniel's lips pulled tight. "Are you calling me impatient?"

"Never," Orrin said, putting his hand over his heart. "Why would you think I meant you? You've never jumped over the Wall to attack demons . . . twice. You don't get grumpy when things don't go your way and try to hit me."

Orrin ducked back as Daniel swung.

Madi covered her mouth to hide her smile. Amir waved his arms and stepped between them. "Why are you fighting? You are friends, yes?"

Daniel grumbled but stepped back. "Jerk."

"Loser." Orrin stuck out his tongue.

Amir gawked at the two before stomping his foot. "No. You will not speak like that to each other."

Daniel grinned sheepishly, turning his back to Orrin and facing the smaller healer. "It's fine, Amir. It's how we show our love."

Orrin nodded and darted forward, slapping his hand on the back of Daniel's head. "Yep. Daniel's like a brother I never wanted."

"It's the brother you never had," Daniel corrected, rubbing the spot Orrin hit. He tried to poke Orrin, but he ducked behind Madi.

"I said it right." Orrin shrugged.

Amir looked at Madi for help. She took his arm in hers and pulled him away from the two slap-happy idiots. "They're just excited that the Hospital won't come after you or Orrin anymore. They do this sometimes."

Brandt caught Daniel's arm from behind as he reached to jab Orrin. "You two know that some of the most powerful people in the world are watching you behave like children, right?"

Daniel twisted from Brandt's grip. "Orrin started it."

Orrin rolled his eyes and explained the Phoenix problem to Brandt. The [Knight] nodded. "Sir Henrick told Lord Catanzano about the same. I recommended a few feints against the demon camp to draw them out, but Lord Tarris used over half his mana in the Hospital attack. Stopping the [Portal] drained him more than he thought it would. They've decided to wait."

Orrin smiled. "Maybe we should do it, then."

Brandt held his hand out in caution and bent his head toward the tent door. "Maybe we should get an early lunch and leave the other teams to their debrief."

Amir followed. He'd been teleported in from his healing station and would have to wait for a [Locationist] to bring him back. "What is Orrin planning now?"

"It's never anything good," Daniel answered as he threw his arm around the [Healer]'s neck. "Have I ever told you about the time—"

Daniel tilted forward and landed on the grass face-first.

"Orrin, stop casting spells on Daniel," Madi sighed in exasperation.

Chapter 58

"What's the plan?" Daniel asked as he made his giant sword disappear. It was simply too big and unwieldy when he wanted to sit on the ground. He made himself comfortable and held a hand out toward Orrin. "Food?"

Orrin frowned but pulled a few things from his [Dimension Hole]. The camp's mess served a meaty stew and chunks of bread that was filling enough, but the distance to Dey and lack of people with storage abilities and [Teleport] meant most soldiers were already groaning about the foodstuffs.

Fresh fruit, warm bread, three small chickens covered in a spicy red sauce that Orrin didn't remember the name of, and a pitcher of lemonade swiped from Lord Catanzano's kitchen spread out on a blanket as Orrin arranged their lunch.

Amir's eyes widened more with each item. "I can't take your food. I'll be back in a few minutes. I saw the others with bowls from—"

Brandt clapped Amir on the back. "This is nothing. Orrin brought Veskarian game hen into a dungeon. Eat up."

Still not completely convinced, Amir nibbled at some bread until Madi cut a leg off and handed it to him. Within seconds, everyone tore into the food. It had been a long morning.

Orrin was sinking his teeth into his own drumstick when Brandt sighed. "Orrin, you aren't going to attack the Horde on your own, are you?"

Coughing up spicy chicken made Orrin's eyes water, and he downed an entire glass of lemonade before answering. "I'm not suicidal, Brandt."

Madi reached over and rubbed Orrin's back as he huffed out deep breaths, trying to cool his throat. "I'm sure that Orrin would bring us along. I think we all know what happens when one of us goes off alone. Isn't that right, Brandt?"

The knight had the good sense to look abashed. At this point, only Madi hadn't rushed headfirst into danger on her own. The men were chastised.

Amir reached for some bread but hesitated. Daniel ripped a loaf in half and handed it to the young man. "Amir should go back to the healing camp now that the Hospital is dealt with. Or even back home, if he wants."

Amir's dark hair swung in the wind as he shook his head. "I can be helpful here. Lord Catanzano requested that I talk with Elder Seif. He said Principal Mangin lied to the elders about what happened to me, and I'm owed an apology." His chin touched his chest as he looked down. "I cannot thank you four enough for all you have done for me. I owe you my life."

Madi's hand left Orrin's back as she leaned forward. She pulled Amir's face up. "Friends don't owe each other. Keep helping others and being yourself. That is thanks enough."

Orrin smiled at the infatuation on Amir's face at Madi's kind words. *The poor guy has it bad. Brandt better watch his back.*

"Amir can stay here and heal people if they're hurt. The four of us need to [Teleport] into the middle of the Horde and create a little chaos. I'm thinking Orrin can drop a few demons with his debuffs, and I'll finish them off like we've been doing. If we keep this up, I might not even need the Quest with all the experience I'm gaining," Daniel finished with a grin.

Orrin grimaced. His strategy of leaving the demons immobile for others to finish off wasn't his favorite. He was used to his role by now and didn't object to his non-damage-dealing tactics, however, others profited off his loss. Without spending the extra mana to snap off a bunch of [Lightstrikes] at the downed demons, Orrin was leaving experience on the field. Experience that others had been happy to soak up.

It wasn't that he balked at killing demons. He knew with each spell he cast, one was going to die. He simply wanted to fully embrace his role in the battle. The extra seconds spent targeting and killing the demons were better spent dropping other attackers before someone on his side got hurt. He sacrificed his own level growth to sow more worry into the demon ranks. That didn't mean he had to continue handing over experience to everyone on a silver platter, though.

"D, we can't [Teleport] into their camp. Silas and the others won't like it if we attack the demons outright like that anyway. I was thinking more along the lines of following Henrick and his crew, mopping up anyone we can. If they start fighting the Demon Lord, we can try a quick assault, but if it's just the four of us, I don't want to try that first." Orrin smiled as he held up his hand to forestall Daniel's argument. "I think you might like my idea better after you read this."

Orrin tossed out a blue box.

> **[Camouflage Ward]—creates a ward around yourself and your party within fifty feet that mimics [Camouflage II]. 50 MP.**

"Yes, Orrin. I know you can make us . . . Wait." Daniel paused. "This is version two point oh?"

Orrin's grin turned hungry. "It cost five ability points, but I think it was worth it. You'll all be harder to hit and see. It won't go away after you attack like normal, either. That is if it works like the regular upgrade."

"You completed [Camouflage II]'s experience grind?" Brandt asked in surprise. "That's a lot of mana use, Orrin."

He shrugged in response, but Madi held up a finger. "Wait. Did anything else unlock? What's the third-level variant?"

"[Invisibility]," Orrin answered with a shrug. "It doesn't matter. The demons can see through it."

Brandt rolled his eyes. "He unlocks [Invisibility] and moves along. Why would that be cause for concern?" The knight stood up and walked off, muttering to himself.

Madi laughed quietly. "Let Sir Bennett burn off some energy. He's always complaining about thieves who unlock [Invisibility]. He'll be back in a minute."

Amir watched the man clang away in his heavy armor and frowned. "Why would he care? It's not much different than what Orrin already does, yes?"

Madi snatched the last piece of bread before Daniel could and took a bite. "It's not that Orrin could buy it. He's worried about what else Orrin could do. Every time Orrin updates his powers, Brandt has to reconfigure his view of Orrin in his mind. A [Knight] protects those under his charge. His training is about assessing threats, and even though we all know Orrin is not a threat," she answered quickly, staring Daniel's glare down with one of her own, "Brandt has contingencies in place for even me if I were to go against orders and become a threat. Orrin might be the first person I've ever heard of to have [Camouflage] at level two and [Invisibility]."

"Someone's leveled [Camouflage] to the maximum before," Orrin countered, certain in his belief. "I'm sure it's the natural progression of the spell."

Madi's head was shaking so fast, her braids whished in the air. "How much mana experience was it to complete level two?"

Orrin mumbled the answer under his breath, then repeated it aloud when Madi held her hand up to her ear. "Ten thousand."

Amir whistled. "That must have taken years. I thought it would take me a year or two to level [Heal Small Wounds]. Thanks to your spell orbs, it took only a few days."

Orrin considered what Madi was getting at. A normal mage spending two or three hundred mana a day on a single spell was rare. His higher-than-normal mana pool, along with his regeneration, was unheard-of. The prodigious growth over the last week with his spell orbs was a jump in the local power that would not be duplicated, maybe ever. For a normal person to use ten thousand points of mana on a spell that made them slightly harder to hit . . . "Yeah, you've got a point, Madi. He still has nothing to worry about. I'm not going to turn into a demon and kill everyone."

Daniel tried to ruffle Orrin's hair but missed when [Side Steps] activated. "We know . . . Damn it, stay still. We know you won't. Brandt's just feeling normal in a group of weirdos."

Amir smiled ear to ear at being included in the [Hero]'s praise.

"The plan is to wait for the demons to attack, and if they don't, follow Phoenix team into battle?" Madi summarized. "Maybe we should have waited near the tent. We can't hope to keep up with Sir Henrick or the [Pyrocaster] if they strike out."

"Maybe Orrin can ask his new friend to bring us along?" Daniel raised an eyebrow. "You two have been chummy."

"She's helping me keep control over some of my skills, but that's not a terrible idea for once, D." Orrin rubbed the back of his neck and thought it over. June's promise to stay and tutor him more after the Dark Horde was defeated ran through his head. *If I asked her to help train my entire team, we could stay close. They'll have to run to the demon camp since none of Phoenix can [Teleport]. That would give us time to follow quietly with a jump or two.* "Madi, go grab Brandt. We should go ask June a few magic questions or something."

Madi clambered to her feet with such excitement that one of her feet slipped out from under her. She didn't let that stop her and took off after the knight at a run. He was walking in circles and pulling at his hair.

"Someone is excited," Daniel chuckled.

"She's getting the chance to ask an expert questions about something that means a lot to her," Orrin responded as he got up a bit slower. "How fast would you be if you got to ask someone from your favorite soccer team a question about . . . shooting goals?"

"It's club and scoring," Daniel groaned. "You know that. Don't be an ass. What should we do with Amir? He can't come with us. Sorry, man."

Amir raised his hands in the air. "I wouldn't want to. I'll head back to Lord Catanzano and ask where I can help. Maybe I will see if Elder Seif needs a hand somewhere."

Orrin didn't know how he felt about his friend working with the leader of the Hospital—the same group that had tried to kill him and kidnapped his father just days ago. However, if Amir could see the difference between the group as it currently was and the group as it had been, he'd let it go.

Five minutes later, Orrin stood in front of June with his party behind him. Amir was waiting on a stool outside Silas's tent for his turn to talk with the busy man. He could feel Madi drooling behind him.

"June, I was wondering—"

"You want me to teach your team mana skills while you wait for the demons to attack but also to keep an eye on my party in case we run off to kill the Demon Lord." June crossed her arms and gave such a surprisingly good mom glare that Orrin felt the hairs on his neck stand up.

"Was she watching us?" Daniel whispered a touch too loudly behind him. A grunt a moment later satisfied Orrin. That would be Madi's elbow in Daniel's side.

"I didn't need to spy," June said with the same bored voice. "You are all predictable. I might be willing to give you some pointers, but only if I'm satisfied in return."

Madi's voice came out in a rush. "Whatever you need, we will supply. I can ask my—"

"I want Orrin to tell me the truth. Who are you? You are not from Asmea. No one knows your origin and you appeared with the [Hero]. You are not from this world, are you?" June's eyes held Orrin in place.

Chapter 59

Madi lied for Orrin. "I'm not sure who your sources are, Lady June, but I can assure you that my father and I investigated Orrin when he first arrived at our doorstep. We found everything to be in order."

June turned her gaze on Madi and smiled like a cat who found a wounded bird on the ground. "What is 'death row,' Lady Catanzano?"

Orrin felt his stomach drop and opened his mouth, but a finger held in his direction with a jumping ball of fire kept him from talking.

Daniel, on the other hand, stepped in front of Orrin. His giant sword popped into existence in his hand. "Please do not point spells at my team, Ms. June. Whatever you think—"

"You are the [Hero], and as such, most people you encounter will give you leeway, but if you point that sword in my direction again, I will burn the skin from your body," June threatened. "I respect Lady Catanzano and Sir Bennett. I was growing to like Orrin. You are a necessity that I tolerate. Do not assume to give me orders. I asked a question, and if you intervene again, I won't give a warning."

Orrin placed his hand on Daniel's shaking arm and pulled him back. He thought back and hoped that Daniel had mentioned the phrase in front of Madi but doubted it had come up. His single slipup with Earth language and phrases wouldn't be the end of his ruse. Orrin and Daniel had spent time without Madi. It would be believable that Orrin would know phrases she wouldn't. One such hint at his other-worldly origin wasn't enough.

"I don't know that phrase, Lady June. Where did you hear it?" Madi answered, her own hand slowly moving toward her spear. She didn't know what was going on, either, but the tension was enough that soldiers were moving away and giving them a wide berth.

"What about 'jump-start'?"

Orrin started sweating.

Madi shook her head.

June turned to Orrin. "You use phrases naturally that are not of this world. Are you a summoned [Hero]? Are you from another world?"

While Orrin floundered in how to reject her assumption, Madi moved quicker.

"Lady June, may I create a [Sound Seal]?" Madi asked, nodding her head toward the troops watching their interaction. "Your questions could be overheard and misunderstood."

June blinked and gave a sheepish grimace at the attention she'd garnered. She nodded but didn't take her eyes off Madi as she drew a circle of sapphire light around them and Orrin's ears popped.

"Well?" June stared at Orrin.

The few seconds that it took Madi to cast her spell gave Orrin time to think. June was intelligent, and Orrin had messed up. He'd been careful when they first arrived in Dey to not use Earth phrases but was able to excuse them away from time to time as having learned it from Daniel. However, the way June asked her questions to Madi had shown she didn't trust him for some reason. He'd done something beyond repeat a few words he could have picked up from Daniel.

"You already asked me the same question, and I told you I learned it from Daniel." Orrin wasn't completely lying. Daniel had made Orrin sit through his presentation for debate club. The topic was the death penalty, and death row came up more than once. "You know my class. You used [Identify] on me."

June chewed her bottom lip. "You avoid my question every time." She seemed to be debating something with herself and finally nodded. "Answer my questions yes or no, or else I will turn you over as a [Blood Mage]."

"What?" Madi gasped, turning toward Orrin and back toward June. "He's not a [Blood Mage]. We all know his class. What—"

"Lady Catanzano, this is now between me and Orrin. I accepted his request to mentor him, and he has lied to me. As I told the [Hero], do not speak again."

Brandt, who normally stood at their back, placed himself between the fire mage and Madi. "Lady June, you go too far. This is the [Hero]'s party, and Madeleine is the daughter of a lord of Dey."

June ignored him and kept watching Orrin. "Will you answer my questions?"

Orrin thought he'd done a good job keeping the focus off himself as another otherworlder. Standing near Daniel was normally enough, but with June, he'd slipped. Shaking his head, he waved off his friends. "It's fine, guys. I fucked up. Yes, June. I'm not from around here. Stop threatening my friends, please."

The smile on June's face turned positively childish in her glee. She clapped her hands and hugged him. "I knew it. When were you summoned? How did you change your class from [Hero]? What was your summoned Quest?"

Orrin extracted himself from her hug and risked a look at Brandt. He'd told the [Knight] about his Admin powers, but only Madi knew he was from Earth. He mouthed "Sorry" before turning to answer June.

"I hitched a ride with Daniel but was never a [Hero]. He's the one with the Quests," Orrin answered with a half-truth. She didn't need to know about his Administrator abilities.

"That's not possible," June answered, pulling a book from her inner sleeves. She turned the pages with such force that Orrin was worried she'd rip the paper. "You said you both awoke in our world together? Where was this?"

Daniel slashed his hand in the air. "What does that matter? You don't get to demand answers from us like this. You might have a higher level but—"

"But nothing," June snorted, holding her finger to the pages she was on. "Power rules on this world, tiny [Hero]. I've warned you."

Orrin put himself in front of Daniel. "June, I answered your question. What are you going to do now? You don't need to attack Daniel or tell anyone about me. It would just make things too complicated."

June's head bent to the side in confusion. "Why would I tell anyone? I asked because I don't appreciate lies. Your secret is safe with me, but your friend's manners need readjusting."

Orrin took June's outstretched hand in his before she could cast a spell. "Were you serious about being my mentor? Because Daniel's an ass, but he's also my best friend."

June's hand was hot against his fingers, but he didn't let go.

". . . If he apologizes and you promise to answer my questions about your world, fine."

Orrin's head snapped back to stare at Daniel.

Do I have to? Daniel's eyebrow raised up.

Only if you don't want to be burned to a crisp. Don't be stupid. Orrin pressed his lips together.

Daniel rolled his eyes up until he was staring at the sky, but he tried to keep the insincerity out of his voice. "I'm sorry, Ms. June. I was trying to protect my friend."

June clicked her tongue but squeezed Orrin's hands tighter as she stared at him. "Where did you arrive on Asmea?"

Orrin recounted their arrival in the Untamed Forest for not only June but also Brandt. The man wouldn't meet Orrin's gaze but did smile at Orrin's retelling of them waking up without clothes.

"The forest wasn't lifeless around you? No monster bodies or flaking dead trees? You're sure?" June asked, gently pulling her hand from his grip and turning a page in her book.

Orrin looked to Daniel for assurance before answering. "We were attacked by something pretty soon after we woke up, and the trees were fine."

"Oh." June started and frowned. "You were summoned, then."

"I thought that was obvious since we're here," Daniel muttered. Orrin kicked his friend in the shin. "Ouch. What the hell?"

"Summoned by someone, not by Asmea," June clarified with a satisfied smile on her face. "The summoning requirements are very specific. For natural world-summoned [Heroes], the land pays the price. Someone sacrificed summoning ingredients to bring Daniel here. I would need to see the area you arrived at to say for sure whether two were intended. One [Hero] summoning is a princely cost. The cost for two would bankrupt a country. I don't know how you both are here."

Orrin didn't know how he felt about knowing someone had brought them here, but before he had the chance to fully think it through, Brandt spoke for the first time. "How did you know Orrin was like Daniel? He had me fooled."

The betrayal in Brandt's voice stung. Madi took his arm in her hands, holding herself to him . . . or holding him back.

"It was the little things," June answered while flipping through her notebook. Orrin glanced over and saw it was all handwritten. "Improper training on multiple magical norms, strange word choices, his connection with the [Hero], his class, the way he seems to intuitively move mana in a way I've never seen anyone do before. Don't feel a fool, Sir Bennett. I had only the inkling of a theory. I pressed a few resources I have and found no prior mention of him in the Guild, nor any family name to search. His supposed village that was razed was not reported to either Dey or Odrana. I'm surprised that Lady Catanzano knew. Her lack of reaction to my questions solidified my theory."

Brandt's face finally broke as he brushed Madi away. He whispered, "You knew, too?"

"It wasn't my secret to tell," Madi half sobbed as he stepped away from her. "Brandt, please."

"Be mad at me, Brandt," Orrin said, taking the [Knight]'s attention away from Madi as she wiped at her eyes. "I told her while you were away and never found the right time to come clean. Why does it matter? I'm still the same guy."

"I wouldn't care if you were from the demon lands, Orrin," Brandt said, his voice still quiet. "After I came back, I promised Madi no more secrets. I thought she agreed that meant for both of us."

"This will change a few things with our training," June said, ignoring the drama going on in front of her. "Lady Catanzano, can I assume that Orrin has tried to teach you mana signatures? What previous schools of magic have you studied in the past? If we are to—"

"June, not now," Orrin muttered.

"Brandt, it wasn't my secret. It doesn't change anything between us, and there isn't any way Orrin's origin could have hurt us. You know there are things I would have to keep from you as the daughter of a lord of Dey. How is this different?"

Brandt's knuckles tightened around the hilt of his sword. "I know, Madi. I simply need a moment to myself. Please continue, Lady June."

Orrin listened with half an ear as June and Madi discussed her training. Madi's frequent peeks in Brandt's direction didn't go unnoticed.

"Lady Catanzano, if I am going to teach you along with Orrin, you must pay attention," June chastised.

"What about me?" Daniel grunted. "Don't I get my Yoda training moment?"

"I don't know what a Yoda is, but you swing a sword," June said without judgment but complete disinterest. "Do you use any magic?"

Daniel grinned. "I can use [Black Hole] to create a [Space Domain] where no other magic works. I can push and pull monsters or other people around me as I hit them with my sword. I can shoot fire from my hands and—"

"You can?" Orrin interrupted. "When have you ever done that?"

Daniel's foot dragged on the dirt. "I . . . um . . . always forget to cast it. [Starfire]. Remember? I used it in the dungeon to kill that copy monster thing?"

Orrin did remember it but realized for the first time how much Daniel had pulled away from casting spells in combat. "You always do that. You focus on the moves you like and ignore the rest. You should use your magic more. You have that one where you create a dirt cloud, too."

"It's not a dirt cloud. [Meteor Shower] makes rocks fall on my target. It's not worth using from the Wall because it does kick up lots of dust, and then others can't see the demons."

"This is just like when you—"

As they continued to argue back and forth, Madi crept closer to Brandt.

"How did I not realize?" Brandt sighed. "Orrin and Daniel are closer than brothers. That doesn't develop over a few days. If I can't notice something like that, how clueless am I?"

Madi took his hand in hers and rested her head on his shoulder. The metal of his armor was cool in the shade of the Wall. "You can be oblivious, but it's part of your charm. Remember how long it took you to notice I liked you?"

Brandt turned red and wrapped his arm around Madi. "I'm sorry I acted like that. I . . ." He trailed off. "I have no excuse."

"Forgiven, but you'll have to make it up to me."

Orrin threw his hands in the air. "Madi. Brandt. Tell him that I'm right? If he spent half as much time working on his magic as he does polishing Gertrude . . . a sword that doesn't need polishing or sharpening . . . he might be worth—"

Brandt's laughter cut Orrin off, but he didn't mind the interruption.

Chapter 60

The party followed the [Pyrocaster] deeper into the Pass. June started Madi and Daniel on some mana-sensing exercises. Her explanation was along the same lines as what Orrin had learned from Anabella Sanerris and at her magic school.

I hope Rhys and Maeve are safe. Orrin's concern for his former classmates moved to the forefront as he thought of the Sanerris School. With Anabella alive, both their lives became more complicated.

Brandt, with his all-melee class, practiced his sword-fighting stances. Orrin was temporarily worried about the man, but their quick exchange during June's instructions to their friends set his mind at ease.

"Don't hold it against Madi. I wanted to tell you, too, but in my own time," Orrin whispered while June tried to beat some knowledge into Daniel's thick skull. "She kept my secret, and now I hope you will, too."

Brandt held out his hand, and Orrin took it. "It was the shock of it. Once Lady June said it aloud, I felt stupid for missing it. I'm used to being an afterthought in this group." He squeezed Orrin's hand tightly before dropping it. "It's not a negative thing, it just is. The [Hero] would outshine anyone, and Madi . . . I always knew she would be amazing. You started slow and quiet, but you've changed Dey and probably the world in ways I can't even begin to understand. I'm not a complex person, Orrin. I like protecting people, and I trust the leaders we have to make the hard decisions. I don't need to know the why of every order, but I do need to trust those fighting at my side. I needed a moment to shuffle my thoughts, but you are still the same frustrating, kindhearted, pestering fool. I know you will be there for me when I need you. Where you come from doesn't matter. I would die to protect any one of you, and no one will learn of your secret from my lips."

Orrin's blush caught Daniel's eye, but his teasing remark earned him a burning glare from June. "Focus or I will set you on fire until you see your own mana."

For twenty minutes, they practiced. June watched Orrin using his magic sword and [Gust] combo until she snorted. "Grow the sword as you push the wind mana through it. You'll have better control of its direction."

Simple comments that June said as if they were obvious battered all three of them as Brandt moved through forms. Sweat beaded his brow, but his sword arm didn't waver. Orrin knew he could make his [Ice Sword] or [Fire Sword] extend, but the base summon length was perfect for him. He'd grown an [Ice Sword] until it resembled a famous video game odachi blade, but the weight made it unwieldy and slow to swing. Daniel's comments that he should dye his hair white and buy a black trench coat kept him from trying it again.

As Orrin felt the mana of [Gust] travel down his arm, he made the [Fire Sword] in his right hand grow longer. The mana that normally pushed down the middle of his [Fire Sword] began to twist and curl around the fiery blade. Orrin kept the sword pointed at the large rock he was using as a target.

Normally, this combination created a superheated blast of air that he could target at will. The result changed sporadically, from pinpoint accuracy that left a burning hole through a monster to a widespread scorching wind that knocked back his enemies with burns on their bodies. When Orrin changed the shape of his sword, the fire mana didn't break like normal but twinned with the air magic breaking from his body.

A looping burst of fire jumped from Orrin's hand and pushed the cart-size stone a few inches back. Circular black scorch were etched in the rock.

June clapped. "Good job, Orrin. That was almost perfect. Find the right frequency and cast it again until the system thinks it's perfect."

Orrin tried again, but the blade in his hand grew too much. He knew immediately as the wind that farted away from him felt muggy. No fire jumped from his hands.

"Ms. June, I think I see something?" Daniel raised a hand in the distance. "Does mana have a . . . temperature? Because I think I feel it in mine."

June skipped over to Daniel as she answered. Madi sat near him with her eyebrows furrowed and her eyes nearly crossed as she concentrated on sensing her own mana. "Everybody senses their mana differently. There is no wrong way. What do you feel?"

As Daniel described his chilly mana running through his chest, Orrin kept practicing. They all kept it up until a booming voice echoed through the forest.

"June? Where are you?"

The fire mage sighed and sent a serpent of fire racing away. A few moments later, Henrick jogged into the middle of their training scene.

"What is this?" the [Paragon Knight] asked in surprise. The large rock Orrin had been practicing on was flaming slightly.

"I'm helping the [Hero] and his party," June answered without fear. "They are halfway decent. What do you need, Henry?"

His pet name broke his stare, and the man shook his head at June. "You don't have time for this. We go now."

June ignored him for a moment, talking to Madi in a quiet voice before standing up fully. "Would you like Orrin to cast his buff spells on us all? I believe we will need them. The high levels will allow the demons to have increased resistance against our—"

"I know, June. You have been over this before." Henrick looked over and pointed at Orrin. "Come with me."

June tutted and walked to Henrick with her hands on her hips. "You do not get to talk with my protégé like that. Ask nicely, Henry, or you can be left behind while the rest of Phoenix takes care of the demon problem."

Orrin froze midstep. This did not seem like the type of conversation to get in the middle of.

Henrick growled but asked again, "Orrin, would you please cast your spell on my team so we can save the lives of everyone in Dey and get back to what's important?"

Orrin's eyes jumped to June. She nodded, and he sighed in relief. "Of course, Sir Henrick."

The knight turned and walked away without responding. Orrin's shoulders slumped as he shook his head at June. "Are you trying to get me killed?" he complained.

"The rest of you, come along as well. I believe you have a Quest to complete."

Rasha and the dwarf, Thram, were surprised to see the [Hero]'s party walking toward them, but Vulwin held out his hand.

"Pay up, Rasha. I told you June would bring them along. She can't help taking care of those less fortunate." The rogue jumped and started hitting his ankles. "Damn it, June. Get your little snakes off me."

June snapped her fingers, and wisps of smoke floated up from Vulwin's legs. "I've told you before, Vulwin. I don't appreciate being part of your bets."

Rasha's hand froze with a small bag that made clinking noises halfway to Vulwin. "What's the matter? Don't you want your money?"

Vulwin cursed and moved away as Rasha laughed and stuck her coins back in a pocket. Thram joined June, Daniel, and his party as Henrick and Vulwin spoke.

"We only need the boy to cast his spells, June," Thram said, nodding at Orrin. "Why do I get the feeling you're bringing them all along?"

June crossed her arms and smiled down at the dwarf. "Thram, do you know what happens to people that come between a [Hero] and his Quest? History is littered with fools who thought they knew better. I won't risk myself or the party over Henry's ego. They are acceptable for their level and might even surprise us. If we drive a few demons their way, it won't matter to Henry. The experience from these demons is horrendous."

The dwarf snorted. "I'll not spend a moment saving their lives if the worst happens."

"We won't need the help," Daniel promised before grinning wickedly. "But if I see you having trouble, I'll make sure to save your life."

Thram barked a laugh and clapped his hand on Daniel's shoulder, almost knocking him to the side. "Good. Good. You'll need that fire. Rasha, get over here. How well does your spell work on dwarves? Our constitution is higher than humans, so your spells don't work as well on us."

Orrin surreptitiously cast a [Heal Small Wounds] on Daniel before answering, "I healed a dwarf with a mangled arm once. I guess we'll find out how well the buffs work on you."

Thram grunted again. "[Healers] won't normally attempt that. Did you pass out from the attempt or was it a small cut?"

Orrin thought back to the piece of meat attached to a shoulder that he'd spent a few mana pools fixing. "I didn't pass out. It must have been a paper cut."

Thram's bushy eyebrows drew together. "You truly healed a dwarf?"

"He closed the man's wounds when the Hospital would have amputated it," Madi chimed in from behind Orrin.

Thram looked anew at Orrin. "Did you catch the child's name?"

Orrin shook his head. "He told me, but I forgot it. It was . . . a few adventures ago. I do remember he was about level twenty or so, I think. And eighty-two years old. He was the first dwarf I ever met."

Thram grumbled something and held out his hand to Orrin. "I'll try your buffs."

Orrin shook the man's hand and waited for June to move their parties around. Orrin needed to be in Phoenix's party to cast [Utility Ward]. Unfortunately, that meant he had to cast it twice. June let her four other members go first, then waved Henrick off.

"I will join their party for the fight." June patted down her robes and took out a small wand. "Henry, you are in charge of Phoenix for the remainder of the day, but I would advise you to route demons in our direction first. If you kill about four hundred of them, someone in charge will have to react. Let the weaker ones through to us. I'll keep myself in reserve."

Sir Henrick bristled at the first part of her statement but preened at being given charge. "You are sure about them?"

June smiled and patted Daniel's head. "He's brash but coming into his power. By the time he gets to level fifty, I would take Vulwin's bet in a fight between you two."

Vulwin perked up. "What odds?"

"Fifty to one that the [Hero] wins."

Henrick's lip curled, but he kept himself in check. "I'll simply have to get stronger before that happens."

Rasha slipped up beside Madi and touched her spear handle. "This is marvelous. Would you mind if I copy it?"

"What?" Madi swiftly grabbed her weapon as Henrick and June

discussed tactics and whether they would let the defenders on the Wall know where they would attack. "Copy my spear?"

Rasha threw her arm out and held a spear of lightning. "I need a design to base my summoned weapons on. The dragon-bone growth rune is a nice touch. Quickly changing the size of the weapon midstrike must confuse your enemies. I won't hurt it in any way."

Rasha held her hands out like a child begging for candy. Madi hesitantly handed over the footlong spear. Rasha giggled as she ran small electric charges over the length of the wood and blade.

"Is everyone ready?" June clapped. "Orrin has [Teleport], so no need to wait. Vulwin and Rasha, you will hit the camp. Lead them into your respective positions. Henrick and Thram will set up a quarter mile from their border fence. The [Hero]'s team and I will strike from the south with those two." She turned to Orrin and Daniel. "You will retreat if overwhelmed." June's smile took a slightly unhinged look. "Good luck, everyone, and don't forget to have fun."

Chapter 61

Orrin nudged Brandt as they walked out of the small castle located on the southernmost part of the Wall. It was old and used as the base support for the entire structure the people of Dey built so quickly to repel this Horde, but Orrin had never given it a second thought.

"Do you know how old that castle is? Who built it?" Orrin asked.

Brandt glanced over his shoulder at the crumbling stones that had not been absorbed into the new Wall. "Honestly, I don't know. It's been here for so long, I'm not sure anyone does."

"It was a watchtower, not a castle," Madi explained, jogging for a few steps to keep up with June's long strides. Vulwin and Rasha were gone already, having disappeared in diametrically opposite ways. Vulwin simply faded into nothing, while Rasha exploded into a flash of lightning. They were supposed to move toward the demon camp and attack, leading anyone they could back toward the waiting trap.

The lords of Dey had sighed in relief when June announced they were allowed to participate in Phoenix's attack. Lord Silas had been under the impression Sir Henrick would leave on his own whim, and the extra time they were given to set up for retaliation was very welcome. That relief was tempered by the discovery that Madi, Daniel, Brandt, and Orrin would be joining Phoenix team on the field.

June slowed from her forward march and smiled at Madi. "It is good to hear that history is still being taught in Dey. You are correct. This watchtower was part of the original battlements the people of Asmea built after the Calamity."

Orrin frowned and looked at the old tower again. "I thought the leaders of Dey built the Wall. Why come all the way through the Pass to build something here?"

June's eyes twinkled. "Why, indeed. The records we have of that time come mostly from one historian who lived over a thousand years after the relevant period. There are gaps in the story that people fight wars over still. All we know is that there were raids through the Pass almost immediately after the Sundering, or Calamity, whichever you call it. This tower is the only part that survived."

"If you can't keep them close, June, I won't wait around," Henrick shouted back from forty yards ahead. Thram's legs moved in a run to keep up with Henrick's longer strides, but the dwarf moved with the grace of a long-distance runner. He'd been going for ten minutes and hadn't broken a sweat.

"Let us hurry, or I fear Henrick will do something foolish," June sighed. Her robes whipped behind her as she began moving faster again.

The spot that Henrick had picked was thirty minutes from the Wall. A rocky formation shaped like an ocean wave jutted from the earth, cutting through the plains. Orrin could make out the start of forests in the distance. He turned when Daniel tapped his shoulder.

"The demons know we're here," his friend said quietly. "They built little towers toward the front of their camp, and a few of them are pointing our way."

"Good," Henrick grunted as he slammed his shield into the ground and drew his sword. "Thram, please set it up."

Orrin felt the rumblings around him. He knew the dwarf was an earthen magic user, but the sheer amount of mana pouring from the shorter man was more than he'd seen in one spell before.

The rocks behind him melted, fused, and braided themselves into a firm wall that split out and ran down either side of the two parties. In twenty seconds, the area was transformed into a mini fortification with an overhung backing, stairs, a raised dais, and walls ten feet tall and three feet thick that winged out into an open embrace.

Thram fell to one knee and pulled a mana potion from under his tunic. "Might have overdone that one a bit, but she'll hold through a few hundred axes. Send out the signal, June."

As the dwarf slammed back the murky liquid, June raised a finger, and a tiny flare of fire drifted up into the sky.

Orrin watched the distant Horde, but he didn't have Daniel's [Telescope] or Madi's rings of light to see details. When nothing happened, he elbowed Daniel. "See anything?"

"Nope," Daniel answered through squinted eyes. "Nobody is moving, but a few demons are pointing at the fire in the sky."

"Vulwin moves silently, and Rasha will wait for her moment," June said from the side, not taking her eyes off the camp. "She'll only strike when . . . There it is."

Over the past few days, Orrin had seen impressive magic. Madi's [Sunbeam] created a scalding ray of fire from the sky that could incinerate her enemies. June's summoned [Blaze Serpent] brought to life a snake made of fire big enough to rival a small train on Earth. Orrin's experiences on Asmea were filled with time magic, space magic, and various elemental spells that still awed him.

Rasha's display topped everything and left Orrin filled with dread. Hundreds of weapons made of lightning appeared over the demon camp. Most were located around the southeastern border, but a few giant spears and a sword that looked like Gertrude but thirty feet long dropped from the sky farther inside the perimeter. The weapons dropped as one, creating thunderclaps and flashes of light as they hit their targets.

"What the fuck was that?" Daniel sputtered. "That was Rasha? Why didn't she do that before?"

June smiled and held her wand pointed toward the camp. "She has to tag a target up close to use her [Lightning Fall] spell, but she can target as many people as she can get to in a minute. She won't be casting much else today, though. Watch yourselves. Here they come."

As the dust settled, Orrin saw a dim flicker moving their way. Rasha came to a stop directly in front of Henrick and saluted.

"Demons should be heading our way in a moment, Henry. Vulwin had some trouble with his last target but retreated to the Wall. He made sure to let them see him." Rasha's report was choppy as she took deep breaths between sentences.

Orrin noticed the mana from her spells still swirled around her body, and he tried to take a second to watch the signature of her spells. He was pleasantly surprised to see it was very similar to light and fire, with a touch of something else he couldn't pinpoint, however, his study was enough to trigger a ding from the system. Orrin quickly opened the store and found a new cursor on the spells tab.

> **[Lightning Ward]—Creates a ward around yourself and your party within fifty feet that protects against lightning magic. 20 MP. -1 AP**

Orrin hit the buy button and cast the new ward across his party. June's head snapped toward him for a moment, then she laughed.

"We are going to have fun when this mess is cleaned up."

Daniel raised an eyebrow at Orrin but kept his sword pointed forward in a ready stance. "What is she talking about, O?"

"I got a new ward and cast it on us. It should help against any lightning magic," Orrin explained as his eyes narrowed against the sun. "I think I see them. A lot of demons are breaking from the group and running at us."

"That's what happens when you piss off an army," Thram grumbled from behind them. "Stir up the bees' nest and give them a target to rush. If they had any discipline, this wouldn't work, but by all reports, this Horde is nothing more than a collection of smaller groups. Stand ready and call out your spells. I can make a few walls to slow down or redirect the demons, but I need to know what you plan to do."

Daniel raised his sword to his head and saluted the dwarf. "I was planning on killing them all. That work for you?"

Orrin heard Henrick's snort of air through his nose before the man began to glow faintly. "Try not to get in the way. I'll be watching for the demons over level one hundred." A ferocious grin split his face. "Rasha, I want you with a trident directly behind me. Thram, try and funnel them into my shield. June—"

"I'll be fighting with the [Hero]'s team, Henrick." June sat down on the grass and dug her fingers into the ground. "Daniel, I will focus my magic at the demons that attack you from the sides. If that is acceptable?"

Daniel glanced at the angry face of the knight and the calm, unconcerned look that June returned. "Um . . . I guess?"

Brandt's sword slid from its sheath. "If we set up against Thram's stone wall, Daniel and I can be the bulwark while Madi blinds them from behind or hits the demons with spells if they get close together. Orrin, I'm assuming you're going to debuff them?"

Orrin summoned two swords, one of ice and one of fire. "I will, but I have a few more tricks up my sleeve."

"Should we strike before they get to us?" Madi asked June, nervously twisting her spear in her hands. "I can't use [Sunbeam] with the accuracy that's needed around others."

"Let them get in close," Henrick shouted as the thunder of thousands of running feet got louder. The demons that left the camp's safety had split almost evenly into two groups. About a thousand weapons were raised as they charged toward the Wall. A small contingent of several hundred followed the lightning blur toward their group. "We don't want to scare them off before we get a chance to fight."

Orrin's skin felt too tight, and his breathing picked up. He made sure to keep near Madi. If things went badly, he could drag her closer to his friends and [Teleport] them away. This was a real fight.

What the hell are we doing?

Orrin cast the first spell. As a collection of the fastest forty demons slowed to make their way toward the waiting parties, he split a round of [Decrease Dexterity] spells among them. Several more castings and none fell. He used [Identify] but winced at the stab of pain as a hiding skill activated against him. Orrin cast [Heal Small Wounds] and tried another demon.

"Level sixty up front with the spear," Orrin shouted. He continued using [Identify] and pointing targets. "Seventy-one with the staff. Forty-three with the swords . . ." His shouts disappeared under a war cry from Henrick.

[Mind Bastion] clicked on without warning, which made Orrin the only person in his party not to turn toward the knight, except June. The demons split into smaller bands, with most pushing their way over each other toward Henrick. Three demons seemed unaffected and rushed Daniel. His friend tore his eyes off Sir Henrick in time to deflect the first attack, but the second's spell splashed liquid fire across his chest.

Orrin's debuffs hadn't slowed these three down, so he stepped forward to try freezing them in place with his [Ice Sword]/[Gust] combination. June's left hand left the dirt and scooped toward Daniel. The fire gathered off his armor and swirled in her hand before she shifted. Her right hand dug deeper into the soil, and a hand of fire burst from the ground under the demon mage, burning him with his own fire.

Orrin spent the next five minutes yelling out targets and hitting demons with his exploding swords when he could. He threw out a few [Lightstrikes] as well. Once, a new group of ten demons pushed through the others to harass Brandt, and Orrin pushed two hundred points of mana into [Gust]. Eight demons flew through the air, hitting upraised weapons and landing among another charging band of demons. Five didn't get up, and the three that did were bleeding from multiple wounds and broken bones.

"Do that more often," Brandt yelled over his shoulder before jumping back into the fray.

The [Knight] held his own, but rarely were his attacks strong enough to end an enemy. From Orrin's use of [Identify], he'd yet to find anyone below level forty. He shouted and pointed when he found the first demon that was over level one hundred.

"The elf in blue robes is level one oh eight."

Henrick battered away four demons well above Orrin's level with a wave of his shield and dashed in a straight line toward the demon/elf mage. Demons fell to the ground like bowling pins, and Orrin took the opportunity to hit more of them with debuffs. He was getting better at hitting mages with [Decrease Will] and fighters with strength or dexterity debuffs. At least two mages simply fainted when their mana zeroed out. These knocked-over targets were able to get up, but with a slowness to their recovery that let Orrin know it was working.

Daniel was a flying monster of blood and iron. His oversize sword cut through weapons and flesh with every swing, and he used spells from time to time to set up other attacks. He kicked up dust toward the right before darting left. He trusted Orrin to heal him and took several hits he could have avoided in order to end fights quicker. Orrin could see his mouth moving under the explosions around them but couldn't hear what he said. Focusing more, he realized Daniel was counting his kills.

Madi blinded demons, which took them out of the fight and moved behind June from time to time to sear the ground with her [Sunbeam]. June's own attacks killed swaths of demons, and despite her threat to

Henrick, she sent snakes of flame after him occasionally to end threats he'd missed.

"They're sending more from the camp," Thram yelled from above them. The demons quickly learned to avoid the walls when spikes of stone bit into the sides of those going too close. "This new group has banners . . . maybe another two or three hundred."

"Good," Rasha shouted with a smile as she danced between two large sword fighters. Her spear of lightning burst from her hands in a staccato rhythm, finding necks, thighs, and hearts with each attack. "These are boring."

Orrin used [Gust] on the bodies in front of Daniel. The dead rolled back, tripping up the next wave. "Madi, how are you doing on mana?"

"I'm about to take a potion. Do you have one of those regeneration potions to spare?" Madi's spear was stabbed into the ground behind her as she threw her hands out left, then right. Balls of light drifted toward the incoming demons, blinding the ones they hit. With so many funneling into their little battleground, she barely had to aim.

Orrin tossed her one of his potions, then stepped closer to June. "Want one?"

June smiled and took the gift. "What is this?" She was completely calm even as demons screamed around them.

"Potion that makes you recover mana. You can take one a day. I'll tell you about it later. We can't do this all day. How long until Henrick is satisfied and we can leave?"

A dark blob vaulted over Thram's wall and hit a demon close to Brandt. Vulwin materialized on top of the body with a knife stuck in the demon's back. "The [Hero] is still alive? Damn it, I owe Rasha ten gold."

Brandt reached over the rogue and stabbed one of the slower, debuffed demons that was swinging an ax at the man's head. The knight's sword turned before he withdrew it from the dead demon's chest, flicking blood over Vulwin.

"Oh, that's going to stain," Vulwin complained with a frown. He assessed the field quickly, then threw June a smile. "I'm going to help Henrick. These demons aren't as tough as we feared."

Orrin knew. The moment Vulwin spoke, he felt a moment of déjà vu. Like a dream where he couldn't move fast enough, Orrin reached toward the annoying man and tried to use [Gust] to push him back, but he was too late.

Dozens of arrows sprouted from Vulwin's back. Each one glowed with a different mana signature. Orrin counted four different types of magic before they disappeared as one, and the mana flew back to a demon standing at the entrance of Thram's enclosure.

"Vulwin!" June's calm voice broke into a scream. Even as the man toppled over and dropped his daggers, he had a disbelieving grin on his face. Light flickered behind Orrin, and heat beyond anything he'd ever felt scorched his back.

Chapter 62

Orrin dived toward Madi and shouted to Brandt and Daniel. "Get down!"

It was only due to their training and his party's trust in him that they survived. June summoned her [Blaze Serpent], and the monster ate everything in its path. Brandt pushed Daniel out of the way before diving to the side. Orrin rolled with Madi to the side, ignoring the demons still charging them. The heat was intense, and Orrin spammed [Fire Ward] on his team.

"Orrin, up," Madi ordered, pushing him away after a few seconds. They stood and found a ten-foot divot of burning dirt in front of them. Even the few demons that had moved out of the way were staring at the total destruction June's spell had wrought. "Go heal him, O. I'll help Brandt and Daniel."

Orrin blinked twice before shaking his head and rushing toward June, who held the body of her party member against her. Her head twisted in his direction, and Orrin slowed his run, holding his hands in the air. "I'm going to heal him, June. Are you okay?"

A tear went down her cheek. "It's too late, Orrin. He took arrows to his lungs. It was his critical area. Vulwin is gone."

Orrin refused to accept what she was saying and used [Identify]. Vulwin was a klepto asshole, but he was still part of Phoenix team. There was no way . . .

Vulwin was dead. Orrin was surprised that his health was so low for his level. The man had dumped nearly all his points into dexterity.

June checked his pockets and moved a few things into her own. She lowered the man's body to the ground and kissed his forehead. "I will leave your party for a bit. I suggest you bring your friends back to the Wall."

Daniel, Brandt, and Madi slid to a stop behind Orrin. Madi let out a small gasp as June incinerated Vulwin's body. No ash drifted away, as everything, including the dirt below, was burned into a small divot in the field.

"Guys, we should head back to the Wall," Orrin said, repeating June's order.

"Orrin, I didn't see what happened," Daniel said, glancing around at the dead around them. "I'm at ninety-three demons. How did Vulwin die?"

Orrin stared at the human-shaped burn on the ground. "He took a critical hit from a lucky arrow. I'm not sure sticking around here is good for anyone right now."

Madi's fingers were gripping Brandt's arm tightly. "Daniel, you can get another seven demons on the Wall. This was too dangerous. We should go."

Daniel nodded and turned to watch June for a moment. She was throwing bursts of fire out to either side as she walked toward Henrick and Rasha. The bow-wielding demon fired arrow after arrow at Henrick, then June, but nothing got through his shield or her flames. Each arrow split into multiple different projectiles in the air. When an arrow made of water hit June's fire, it hissed, and she slowed her hurried walk.

"It was that one, wasn't it?" Daniel said, squeezing Gertrude's bone handle. "I get that we're in over our head here, but Orrin, can you reach her with your debuffs? It might help them avenge Vulwin."

Orrin tried, but the magic didn't activate. "The demon is just out of range. We could double jump. I use [Teleport] to land behind her, I cast the spell, and then we get back over the Wall?"

"Are you sure you can be quick enough?" Brandt probed. "Thram said there were more coming. We shouldn't risk getting caught in the middle."

Daniel turned and waved at the dwarf. "Thram? How long before the next wave of demons hits? Orrin is going to slow the bow bitch down."

Thram gave them a cursory glance and went back to casting his spells. "Less than a minute. Hurry and get out of here."

"Should we try?" Daniel asked his friends. Orrin thought it was a sign of growth that he didn't simply rush in. "It leaves a bad taste in my mouth to leave them, but I at least want to take down the demon that killed Vulwin."

"I'm against it," Brandt volunteered first. "This is Phoenix team. They'll finish the archer. We've done what we came to do and should retreat now."

Madi hung her head. "I agree with Brandt. That could have been one of you. Daniel, you can finish your Quest behind the Wall."

"That's at least a tie, Daniel. We go back." Orrin reached over and grabbed hold of his friend. "They're professionals. We need to go."

Daniel watched for another second before sighing and nodding at Orrin. "[Teleport] us out."

Behind the Wall, Orrin landed easier than ever from the [Teleport]. June's advice to step with the spell was a godsend. He was already cataloging everyone around the secluded area, free from teleport wards, when Daniel and Madi got their balance. "Brandt, take Daniel up to the Wall and help him kill a few demons. Madi, how are you for mana?"

"What are you planning, Orrin?" Daniel pulled his arm out from Brandt's grip and got in front of Orrin. "You can't go back out there."

"We have less than a minute. You're the [Hero] and need to complete your Quest. Trust me, Daniel. I won't be in any danger." Orrin dropped [Mind Bastion] and grabbed his friend by the shoulders. "I'm in control. This isn't [Mind Bastion]. I have a good plan. Go finish your Quest."

Daniel hesitated but finally held his finger pointed up at Orrin. "If you die or do something dumb, I swear to God, I will kill you."

Orrin didn't point out that if he was dead, Daniel could never fulfill that promise. Instead, he tossed a cocksure grin on his face and tried to emulate his friend. "Didn't you hear? I'm part of the [Hero]'s party. We don't die. We do the killing."

"I'm going to steal that because it's good, but my threat stands." Daniel turned and slapped Brandt on the stomach. His metal armor clanged with the contact. "Let's go kill some demons, Brandt."

"Orrin, you can't think going back there is a good idea," Madi started as soon as Daniel was out of earshot. "Phoenix killed nearly three hundred demons, and we took out half that. Daniel did most of the killing. If they're sending another three hundred, there is nothing we can do."

"How much mana do you have?" Orrin asked again. "I don't plan on getting close. I really do have a plan."

"With the extra constitution you gave me and the regen potion, I'm at about one hundred and fifty points left," she answered with a huff.

"I tried to be as judicious with my spells as I could, but there were so many of them."

Orrin used [Identify] to catch her numbers and run the math. With the extra fifteen points of constitution that Orrin had given all three of his friends, he'd felt comfortable bringing Madi and Brandt's other stats up to sixty. They'd yet to show any side effects from the jump from his previous limit on buffs for them, and no one complained about feeling bad the next morning when their constitution returned to normal.

"If I increase your constitution another fifteen points, I'll risk boosting your will and intelligence to one hundred. That will give you an extra four hundred points of mana and make [Sunbeam] a lot more destructive. What do you think?" Orrin said quickly. They had maybe thirty seconds before the new demons got to Phoenix team's location.

"Do it, but land us far away. I need to see them, but we don't need to be so close." Madi caught on quickly and nodded in determination.

"Keep your spell going as long as you can without passing out," Orrin ordered. "I'll need to [Teleport] us back, but you can't ever tell Brandt we went back out there. You cast this from the Wall, do you understand?"

She nodded again, and Orrin unleashed his buffs. [Increase Constitution] scaled up depending on how much of his own mana he sacrificed. His mana pool dropped slightly. The buff increased the target's constitution by one for every ten mana points Orrin invested. Of course, with his intelligence and will at one hundred already, those numbers were inverted. For every point of mana that Orrin gave up for the day, Madi's constitution increased by ten.

Orrin finished up the spell and then increased Madi's other stats as well. Her eyes fluttered, and she groaned.

"Are you okay? What's the matter?" Orrin jumped forward and shook her. Madi's eyes snapped back, and she wore the biggest grin Orrin had ever seen.

"I feel so powerful. Like I could take on the entire Horde by myself," Madi announced as she spun her spear in one hand. "Orrin, this feels amazing."

Orrin frowned, but it was too late. He couldn't pull the [Increase Constitution] buff if he wanted to. "I was thinking we [Teleport] back out and you cast [Sunbeam] on the demons until you're out of mana. I'm going to watch your back and get you over the Wall as soon as you're done. Sound good?"

Madi nodded enthusiastically. "We could go back to where Phoenix team is, even. I want June to see me decimate the Horde."

Orrin started to worry more. "Madi, if you're going to pull a Daniel and charge the demons, I'm going to make you stay on the Wall. We aren't going to show off. I just want you to kill some demons near the middle of the group."

"Yes, yes. I get it, Orrin. Hurry up before Sir Henrick kills them all."

Orrin's plan was starting to seem like a bad idea. *I can just [Teleport] us back. It's okay.*

He grabbed Madi's hand and pictured a spot between the southern castle remnants and Thram's temporary structure. That should give them enough space to see the attacking demons but beat a hasty retreat if needed. With a thought, he teleported them to the location.

Luckily, nobody was in their immediate vicinity. Unfortunately, a group of demons attacking the Wall were retreating and heading their way. One shouted and pointed as Orrin and Madi landed in the grass. The knot of demons was made up of only about twenty or thirty souls, but fighting wasn't Orrin's plan here.

"Madi, you've got one minute. Do you have a target? Are we close enough? Should we [Teleport] closer?" Orrin asked in a rapid-fire succession. He risked a glance over his shoulder and saw Thram's walls in the distance. Most of the demons were at the entrance to his little murder alley.

Madi didn't answer, but a frightening amount of mana coalesced around her. It wasn't on par with Thram's earth spell or even June's [Blaze Serpent], but any doubts Orrin ever had about Madi being in their party dissipated as the woman moved her hands in circles. Her spell solidified, and she brought a finger from the heavens down to point at the demons attacking Phoenix team. Before, her spell [Sunbeam] had oscillated between a fist-size beam to something the size of a small table, depending on her mana output. With the increased constitution, intelligence, and will backing her up, Madi's spell dropped from the sky like a missile of fire.

The air around them was sucked toward the demons still outside Thram's walls, along with all sound. The sonic boom that echoed back popped Orrin's ears before he cast [Heal Small Wounds] on himself and Madi for good measure. The flames were wide enough to engulf five demons standing close to each other, and as Madi moved her hand and eyes, the pillar of fire swallowed demons up by the dozens. Her spell lasted for ten seconds before she staggered and fell to her knees. The flames continued to fall, but the top of the column in the sky shrank until all that was left was a burning line of light in Orrin's vision.

Orrin checked on the running demons, but they'd slowed to a hesitant advance at the display of magic in front of them. He didn't know how effective Madi's flames of light would be against higher-level demons, but any damage that slowed or distracted the demons fighting Phoenix team was worth it in his opinion. He grabbed Madi's arm again and used [Teleport].

Orrin's step forward as they landed back behind the Wall was arrested by Madi toppling over. He caught her before she hit the ground and used [Identify] right away.

"You idiot," Orrin muttered. "You zeroed out your mana. You are going to feel that in the morning." Orrin cast his smallest [Increase Will] on his friend and grinned as she groaned her way back to consciousness. "Welcome back, sleepyhead. You got lucky that you didn't pass out until after we teleported back. Brandt would have murdered me if I ran back carrying you."

Madi pushed away from Orrin, knocking him over. He opened his mouth to protest but saw his friend start to vomit on the grass.

"Good job, I guess, and thanks for not puking on me."

Chapter 63

The Demon Lord did not appear, and Phoenix team, minus Vulwin, returned to the Wall riding on a shield of lightning. The demons retreated from their frenzied attack, and everyone, including Phoenix team, was removed from the command tent while the lords of Dey and other military leaders discussed their next steps.

June and Henrick were relatively unharmed from their fight, but Thram had been hit with a fire spell that burned his left side. Rasha collapsed outside the Wall from mana exhaustion. If Orrin hadn't been nearby checking everyone's health, they might have missed the stab wound in her thigh. He spent a lot of mana closing up her wound.

The defenders on the Wall had suffered more casualties than expected. It turned out that the majority of higher-level demons had targeted Vulwin and followed him toward the Wall. When their target disappeared, they took it out on the ones left behind. Without the powerful Phoenix team, Dragoon, Lily, and Hornet teams took up the defense but were spread thin against the multiple skirmishes that took place as powerful spells blasted holes through the Wall.

Daniel's return had bolstered the beleaguered defenders, and the [Hero] spent most of his time using his speedy run spell to shoot up and down the Wall, plugging gaps where he could. He'd left Brandt behind too many times to count, but his need to protect others outweighed his demon-killing urges. In the end, he completed his Quest.

> **[Demon Seal] (Hero Specific)—Seal the Demon Lord. Only usable one time. The Demon Lord must be at low health when used.**

Orrin found a spot for them to camp away from the rest of the army. Too many people were walking up to thank Daniel for his help, and they needed their rest. Orrin started dinner and checked over his notifications. He was surprised to see he'd killed over thirty demons.

Experience Gained: 1,815 XP (100 XP x 5; 50 XP x 23; 33 XP x 5)

"Why won't they let us in the command tent?" Daniel grumbled as Orrin stirred ingredients into the big pot over a fire. He was making potato soup for their party after seeing the mushy meat and stale bread being served in the mess tents. "Nobody even asked for our debrief."

Brandt chopped the thick slab of bacon Orrin assigned him, the blade flying across the cutting board he'd borrowed from Orrin's never-ending pile of supplies. "They'll have June or Sir Henrick give a report. We aren't needed right now. From what I've been able to gather, this Wall took more damage in this half-hour assault than the rest of the days that we spent fighting the Horde combined. There are rumors we might pull back to the next Wall if the [Earth Mages] can't stop up the holes."

"I can make more spell orbs," Orrin volunteered. "That might give them an edge."

Brandt frowned and shook his head. "The demons that attacked the Wall were better organized than the ones that went after Phoenix team. It was like they were waiting for the assault and sent their best to the Wall. [Earth Mages] were targeted, as well as any [Healers]. No, Orrin—I checked already, and Amir is fine. He was sent back to his station. We lost three [Healers] from the Hospital and would have lost another, but Daniel shoved a health potion in her mouth."

Orrin raised a fist toward Daniel, who promptly tapped his own knuckles to his friend. "Good job, D."

"To be fair, I didn't know what her class was until after. I saw lots of blood from a neck wound, ripped some bloody rags from her robe and pressed them to her cut, and then poured a potion down her throat. It was only when she stopped gurgling blood that I realized her mud-stained robes were originally white." Daniel lounged in a camp chair, with his sword stabbed into the ground behind him like a backrest. "I'm not saying I wouldn't have helped if I'd known, but I might have saved the potion."

Madi stretched a foot out and tipped Daniel's chair a bit. He caught his balance before toppling but glared at her anyway. "What was that for?"

"For lying. You wouldn't withhold a health potion just because she was from the Hospital," Madi said as a snide grin crept across her face. "She was pretty, wasn't she, Brandt?"

Brandt coughed and focused on a thick piece of bacon. Orrin had requested strips that would cook well over a stick. He wanted to add the bacon to the soup at the end. "I didn't get a good look, but I wouldn't have an opinion either way."

Madi tilted her head and glanced at Orrin with a wink. "Correct answer, Brandt."

The four friends joked a bit more, letting off some steam from the day. The intense fighting periods followed by the endless waiting created a different type of exhaustion, and Orrin was glad to see his party had enough in them to rib each other. The last of the milk added to his soup, Orrin moved the pot off the direct flame and set it on the arranged stones to heat slowly, just as June entered their small camp area.

"Lady Catanzano, was that your [Sunbeam] spell that killed the demons near my party?" June asked, wasting no time and giving no pleasantries. "It felt like your mana but was stronger than you should be able to do."

Madi jumped up from her seat and bowed her head toward June. "It was me, Lady June. Orrin increased my constitution and will. I was able to funnel more mana into the spell than I've ever dreamed of. I hope Phoenix team was not harmed."

June waved a hand. "It got close to Henrick, but he's spent enough time around my flames to get out of the way. You turned over twenty demons to ash and injured another forty. We should focus on that spell in the future."

"In the future?" Daniel asked as he stretched and crossed his legs. "The demons are about to push us back to the next Wall because you guys wanted to fight. You lost a member of your party, and all you think about is training?"

Orrin saw the fire flicker in June's eyes and swiftly bopped Daniel on the head. "Everyone grieves in their own way, Daniel. Apologize."

Daniel rubbed his head and frowned at Orrin but did as he was told. "I'm sorry, June. That was rude of me. I'm exhausted from fighting the demons that went right over the Wall. They sent their better troops out today. I'm sorry about Vulwin. He . . . was a good fighter."

June's temper faded back down, and she nodded toward the [Hero]. "Vulwin was a pain in the ass, but he deserved more than an arrow to the back in death. He used to brag that he would loot all our bodies in the dungeon after we died. Now I have to send his things to his family."

"Vulwin had a family?" Orrin asked before his brain caught up with his mouth. "Sorry, he didn't seem like a family man."

June smiled. "He has a sister who lives in Veskar. She's not an adventurer, but his gold will let her live comfortably for years." She patted her pockets and reached into one, stretching her arm until her elbow disappeared inside. She pulled out a dagger. "This was his favorite blade. It's cold iron, so he didn't need to sharpen it, but he would oil the metal every day. He slept with it under his pillow." June's smile deepened as crinkles grew along her eyes. "He woke up every morning swinging this at whatever bad dreams he had. Henrick swore we would tie him up before bed if it wasn't for his ability to sense ambushes even in his sleep."

She sighed and put the knife back in her pocket. "He was a complicated man, and I will miss him. That doesn't stop the world from moving forward, though. We will train after dinner. Once the lords of Dey decide their next move, I may join your party for the time being."

Madi couldn't hide her excitement and moved her chair around the fire, offering it to June. "What about Phoenix? Sir Henrick won't leave before the Horde is defeated, right? We need everyone we can get to push back—"

June held up her hand as she sat, and Madi's teeth clicked shut. "Henrick is down a scout and damage dealer. The four of us are not enough for the lower levels of the larger dungeons, and he knows it. Until I'm satisfied with Orrin's progress, I will relinquish my role on

Phoenix team. Henrick is angry that Vulwin was killed. He takes it as a personal insult and won't leave until the Demon Lord is dead."

Brandt let out a sigh of relief, and everyone looked his way. He sheepishly raised his shoulders to his ears. "Having Sir Henrick fighting will help, but his loss would take more than firepower from our men. If he left, morale would drop."

Orrin grabbed the bacon from Brandt and draped the thin slices over two sticks. He positioned the meat over the flames before stirring his soup again. "Would you like some soup, June?"

June nodded, then pulled a beautiful glazed bowl from her pocket. She handed it around to Orrin, who set it next to the wooden bowls the rest of the party used.

She's got [Dimension Hole] or something like it. He smiled, knowing one of the strongest mages in the world used the same skill he did. Once the bacon was crisped up, Orrin dropped the meat back on the freshly cleaned cutting board. *Thank you, [Water Reservoir].* He chopped the meat into smaller pieces, tossed the bacon into the soup, and pulled a bag of cheese from his own storage space.

"Where do you get cheese like this?" June reached out and took a pinch of the small spirals of yellow from Orrin's bag. "Why not cut it into blocks?"

"I asked a metalsmith to make a cheese grater for me," Orrin answered, pulling the small handheld tool from a pocket and handing it over to June. "It helps the cheese melt better in soup. Plus, it tastes good on other food."

Daniel rubbed his eyes. "You invented the cheese grater? Seriously?"

Orrin shook his head. "No, I saw someone using one to grate butter in a bakery. It's just not a household item. Special order only."

Orrin tossed a handful of cheese into his soup and tasted it. "Dinner's ready."

After eating their fill and receiving more praise from June about his cooking, June trained them on mana sensing and signatures. Orrin continued to experiment with growing his summoned sword into other spells using [Gust]. June ordered Madi to start casting [Sunbeam] with the smallest mana expenditure she could pull off, but not activating the spell. She needed to find the core of the spell, which would supposedly let her cast [Sunbeam] faster and with more power using the same amount of mana.

Daniel and Brandt sparred until June moved between them. She pointed to Brandt. "Why don't you use any magic?"

Brandt sheathed his sword before wiping the sweat from his brow. "I'm a [Knight]. I use weapons to defend. I don't need magic."

June shook her head. "You don't need to cast spells at enemies, but there are spells that could help you move faster, take more damage, or even increase your weapon damage. I will have Henrick make a list. How do you fight?"

Brandt searched for Madi, needing her help, but June snapped her fingers. "I will not make you do something against your wishes, Sir Bennett, but that does not mean I offer this advice without thought. You walk in the shadow of strong party members. I do not want to see you left behind. How do you fight?"

Brandt explained his [Defensive Fighting] skill, talking about his approach to battle. June patiently waited for him to finish before asking pointed questions about his tactics in different situations. Orrin listened as he made his [Ice Sword] and [Fire Sword] grow and shrink, casting shadows of blue and red light like a strobe effect around him. It was amazing how June could take a simple skill like [Power Strike] and point out ten ways that Brandt could use it in battle. The more she talked, the more animated Brandt was in responding.

"What's in it for her?" Daniel whispered to Orrin as he moved closer to his friend. "Why is she helping us?"

Orrin dropped his swords and threw his hand around Daniel's neck, trying to pull him down. A hand to his ribs kept him from getting Daniel all the way down, and they both laughed as they split apart. Orrin smirked at Daniel. "I think she's good people. She's got her quirks, but she's a teacher at heart. Look at how she's got Brandt half convinced to buy some magic. I thought Brandt had his skills plotted out at age ten and never changed his plan."

"Daniel, what are you doing? You should be focusing on your space spells and finding the signature. Orrin, pick those swords up before someone hurts themselves." June pointed at the weapons on the ground.

Orrin saluted and jumped to grab the swords. "Yes, ma'am."

"Don't ma'am me. I'm not that old."

Chapter 64

For three days, the demons didn't attack, and June drilled the four of them with different exercises. Brandt relented after talking with Madi and spent two saved ability points on a magic spell. [Stagger] was an interesting spell that had Orrin reading the description after Brandt's explanation.

"It triggers on a parry if I want it to. There's a high chance to throw an attacker off balance or make them follow through on an attack more than they meant to. It's classified as a lightning magic because it has a shocking effect that spasms their arm muscles into overcommitting on the swing. Lady June said it was one of the best options for my style of fighting," Brandt explained, puffing up at the end. They were all starting to crave her praise. June had a way of being kind but harsh at the same time. Orrin thought it had to do with her genuine desire for them to do better—with a touch of frustration that they were a lower level than she was.

Orrin read the description of [Stagger] in his store interface. He thought about getting it himself but decided to save his points for now. Orrin's fighting style, [Way of the Water], focused more on avoiding attacks altogether. He'd watch Brandt and see if it was worth it, but Orrin doubted he'd buy the spell anytime soon.

"How are the other members of Phoenix team doing, Lady June?" Madi asked as she sparked small drifting lights from between her fingers. Madi's assignment from June was to send out as many minuscule butterflies of light as she could in one minute before finding each through her mana connection. It was supposed to help her sense her own mana signatures better, and Madi had been at it for twenty minutes. "With Vulwin's death, I mean."

June glanced up from a book she was reading. She kept a notebook out on her other leg, in which she occasionally made notes. "Rasha and

Thram held a wake and drank a brewery dry in the city. Henrick blames himself and has taken it upon himself to clear out more of the Pass. The Walls that were constructed are a good step, but if the people of Dey plan to keep their hold on the Pass, they will need to work to eradicate some of the more entrenched monsters and wildlife that live in the caves."

"What about you?" Daniel asked with a huff as he dropped Gertrude's point into the ground. Daniel's break from magic training meant more swinging of his sword. He made sure to tell them loudly and often how much he missed sparring with Brandt. The [Knight] was casting his spell, trying to sense the magic in his body, without much progress. "How are you holding up?"

June closed her book fully and recrossed her legs in the opposite direction. "Vulwin was a difficult person to work with, but he was a friend. I have lost people before, and I suppose I will again in the future, however, that does not make it any easier." She turned her head in the direction of the Wall. The forest she was training them in was only a few hundred yards away, but the usual sounds of an army going about its day were muffled by the trees. "I still see the surprise on his face in my dreams. He was unwavering in his belief that he was invincible. That he died so quickly is something I will need to remember. I believe Henrick blames himself for pushing us to attack. It's silly, really. We all agreed to it. Vulwin, most of all. Once you reach our level, you forget how close death can be."

June didn't speak for a few seconds, and Orrin continued with his practice. He tried to keep an ear out for any shouts from the Wall, but the demons kept their quiet watch on the defenders of Dey. The respite gave the [Earth Mages] the extra time they needed to reinforce the holes made by the last battle.

Orrin felt like he was getting somewhere with his spells. His control of [Blood Mana] was slowly improving. He could see his health drain from his body, near his heart, with every cast now. The single point of HP that he changed underwent a strange process, flowing up to his head and back to his mana pool, where it became a mana point. He didn't fully understand what happened, but he could watch it each time. June was beyond ecstatic for him.

There was also a definite sweet spot in his [Ice Sword]. If he grew the sword just an inch or two longer than he felt comfortable with before casting [Gust], the mana surged in a new way. He still had to strike a target to activate the effect, but the coating of ice over the dummies June set up in their small clearing was thick enough that he had to use a [Fire Sword] to melt it.

"Good job, Orrin," June shouted from her seat after he cut the ice from the human-shaped dummy. Someone had added a little crown with two horns at the sides to make it more "demon-like."

"Be sure to hold the wind mana in until the last moment. You're activating it too soon."

Orrin mumbled in reproach but dared not say anything aloud to his mentor. He did stop cutting through the ice, though, when two scouts entered from different directions.

"Orders for Lady Catanzano?" the scout from the north announced, glancing around before spotting Madi.

Madi tore open her letter and sighed. "My father wants me to report my progress. This should only take ten minutes, and I'll be back."

"Message for Lady June." The scout from the east was covered in dirt and sweating profusely. "From Sir Henrick, ma'am."

June sighed. They'd all learned she was touchy about being called *ma'am*. "What does Sir Henrick want?"

The scout handed a sealed scroll to her, and June ran a hand over the paper before opening it.

"Do you have a response, ma'am?" the dirtier man asked, clearly hoping to be dismissed and grab a bath or nap. "He said to get to you with all haste, and I made the run in six hours. He's in the middle of the Pass at Wall Stamford."

Orrin groaned. Daniel's naming of the Walls had stuck. His friend had come up with the idea of the Walls and helped with the building plans. His traps and designs were integrated into the building of the Walls, meaning he got to help name them. The original Walls of Dey were called Dey One and Dey Two, with another Wall every ten to fifteen miles out.

"I can't believe they went with your names for the Walls," Orrin complained. "Paper company branches from your favorite TV show? Really?"

Daniel raised an eyebrow. "Orrin, we have people named Jason and Carl in our little army. Nobody wants to have a Wall named after them."

"It isn't supposed to be named after real people in . . . do you not read anything I recommend? Why not name the Walls after an interdimensional kung fu wizard or a guy with a cat?"

Daniel's eyebrow went higher. "A guy with a cat?"

"She's a cool cat . . . with lasers."

"No response needed. I'll answer him myself," June replied, speaking over them and burning the note in her hands. "Orrin, can I trouble you for a [Teleport] into the Pass? You can return here and continue your training afterward. I expect five perfect casts before nightfall."

Orrin groaned before stabbing his summoned [Fire Sword] into the ground. "Sure. Orrin's shuttle ride, at your service."

June gave him a dead look and shook her head. "How did you keep your charade up for so long?"

Finding Henrick, Rasha, and Thram wasn't hard. Orrin landed near the middle Wall of the Pass, which he refused to call by its name, and listened for the shouting. The rest of Phoenix team worked with a skeleton crew, away from the front line, to kill the local monsters left by the mad dash to build more Walls.

Orrin and June found Thram sitting atop an eight-foot-tall stone tower, eating a turkey leg. Fat dripped into his beard as the dwarf's teeth ripped the meat down to the bone. "Good morrow, June. I see you got Henry's letter. The beasties aren't powerful, but they number in the hundreds and keep retreating into a cavern that goes too deep for me to feel what else is down inside."

Flashes of lightning brightened up the morning ahead of them.

"Rasha is going to use up her mana for the day again at this rate," Thram complained as he cracked, then sucked, the bone in his hand. Orrin blinked. He'd looked away for less than a second.

"Thram, can you help push them back to this cave? I'll clear it once they're packed in," June asked, but it was clearly an order, as she didn't wait for a response and swept away with her muted robes swirling behind her.

Thram hopped off his perch and nodded toward Orrin before following. Orrin wasn't sure if he was supposed to return right away or maybe stick around and watch. He decided that seeing Phoenix in action for a few minutes wouldn't hurt anyone and jogged to keep up.

Henrick stood in front of three dozen fighters and mages, glowing red and with what seemed to be hundreds of spiky balls the size of basketballs bouncing around him. Several were stuck to the man's armor, but he continued to move and strike multiple monsters down with each swing, seeming to have no trouble with the extra weight. His shield was stuck in the ground, with another thirty of the beasts stuck through the metal.

Some of the monsters stood up and ran toward a target before folding back into their bowling ball shape. The spikes threw up grass and dirt behind them as they plunged into their chosen victim. The screaming from the weaker fighters didn't help Orrin's concentration.

He used [Identify] from a distance.

[Crackle Spike] HP 55/80

It had been some time since he used his monster encyclopedia, but he flipped through the pages with practiced ease as Thram began building walls of stone on either side of the battlefield. A few trees were uprooted and fell to the side as the dwarf's magic took hold.

Crackle Spikes are found exclusively in the mountain caves of the Great Mountain Line. These humanoid creatures are clever, using pack tactics and quick retreats to overwhelm their targets. They curl their bodies into spheres that are nearly impenetrable to standard weapons and do not unfurl themselves once stuck in a target unless drowned in water or burned with fire. (****)

Orrin reached out toward one of the monsters and tried to use [Decrease Dexterity]. The Crackle was rolling toward Rasha's back as she used whips of electricity to stun the creatures, her head thrown back in laughter.

Orrin's spell hit, and the ball unfurled in an instant. The Crackle Spike came to a quick stop, with the spikes that ran down its spine and arms stuck in the ground. Rasha finally noticed it and snapped her whip's edge down on the exposed underbelly. Its life winked out.

Orrin began chaining [Decrease Dexterity] and [Split] across as many of the monsters nearby as possible. The thirty or forty defenders of the local Wall cheered as they began ending the threat with easy chops of their axes or spells. Orrin winced as some of the Crackles screamed a retreat.

The spiked balls turned and ran, but Thram's walls were magically reinforced. The monsters failed to penetrate his walls and were forced down a single direction, moving as one. Orrin realized just how many Crackle Spikes they'd been fighting. The trees hid more monsters that were waiting in reserve. Almost three hundred of the black-and-brown-mottled fiends moved like cars on a highway, trying to escape from the sudden turn of the battle behind them.

June's [Blaze Serpent] jumped out of her hand, growing comically large before rushing down the path left behind. A harsh snap sounded, like an oversize kernel of popcorn popping. Then, like gunfire, the Crackles began to explode. Small spikes whistled through the air and pelted the trees and people around him. Orrin covered his ears and ducked behind one of the few remaining trees.

"You can come out," Henrick said a few moments later, tapping Orrin on the shoulder. "It's over."

Orrin skittishly stood and peered around the tree's edge. The fighting force was finishing off a few stragglers that hadn't run as quickly as their brethren. A [Healer] in a white robe moved through the downed allies, healing any immediate injuries. June and Rasha were talking, and Thram was eating another turkey leg.

"That sound was unnerving. It was so loud," Orrin tried to explain, feeling goose bumps on his arms.

Henrick smirked. "The fire heats up the insides to a boil before the shell cracks. That area will smell terrible for the foreseeable future. You did well up until the end, though. Your spells saved a few lives as well. Good job."

The knight shook Orrin's entire body with his hand on his shoulder before walking off. He started yelling at Thram, who promptly gestured rudely back at the larger man.

Orrin groaned when he realized he hadn't used [Lightstrikes]. He'd missed out on a lot of free experience, again.

Chapter 65

Orrin joined Phoenix team's party in order to [Teleport] them back to the outer Wall. Henrick wanted to wait to report, but June overruled him, telling him not to waste the resource in front of him. The resource being Orrin.

As soon as they landed in the designated teleportation area, Orrin was dropped from the team without a word. Henrick left to investigate the situation at the front line. His march faltered a few steps away, and the large man turned back to June.

"That quickly? You are truly leaving Phoenix?"

Orrin realized that June must have left the party as well. Her inclusion in Daniel's party over the last few days was a boon to them, but he'd expected her to go off with her friends after rushing to help them in the Pass.

"I have more training to do, Henry. Perhaps you will join us? Sir Bennett could use some pointers from a fellow [Knight]," June answered, with a spark of hope in her voice.

Henrick grunted and turned his back on June. His giant shield was on his back, the holes from the recent Crackle Spikes already filling in.

"I'll talk to him," Thram said with a smile. "He's still beating himself up over Vulwin. Where are you hiding with the [Hero]?"

June sighed and told Thram their camp location. She exchanged a few more words with Rasha as well before the lightning mage turned to Orrin.

"Thanks for the assist back there," Rasha said. Her weapons were gone, stored in whatever skill she used to keep them around. "I might swing by for a practice match or two. Vulwin was the only one who could keep up with me. Think the [Hero] might want some pointers?"

Orrin felt giddy at the chance before him. "Daniel would love it. Don't hold back, though. He likes to fight dirty, and I'm not sure your electric powers could stun him for long."

Rasha grinned hungrily and pushed Orrin's shoulder playfully. "That's what I'm talking about. I've got to go make sure Henry doesn't piss off too many people. With June training you all, I'm suddenly the responsible one in this party. It sucks."

Rasha waved and ran off after her two party members. Orrin felt June's eyes on him, judging.

"What?"

"You set Daniel up. Rasha will knock him unconscious if she goes all out. She has significant levels on him and has trained her entire life, while your friend never touched a weapon before being summoned," June said, crossing her arms. "Why?"

Orrin grinned. "It's fun knocking him down a peg from time to time. He's good at everything and gets lazy if you don't remind him that he has to keep trying. I'll put a [Lightning Ward] on him before their fight so he doesn't die."

June shook her head and walked back toward their camp. Orrin distinctly heard her mutter, "Children."

Rasha and Daniel's spar went well, despite Orrin's hope. His spell [Shooting Star], which allowed him to move quickly in straight lines, kept Daniel from being put down for the first two minutes of the fight. Rasha changed weapons often, starting with a spear, trying to keep Daniel at a distance with a whip, and even getting close with two swords of lightning. Her wild grin turned into laughter when he continued to deflect her strikes through gritted teeth and push her away.

"Orrin was right," the spellsword said as she disengaged from a flurry of attacks and parries between their blades. "You are fun. Let's go all out."

Orrin saw the confusion cross Daniel's face and turn to resignation as Rasha picked up speed. Even Daniel's [Shooting Star] movement couldn't outpace her when she turned into a bolt of lightning that flickered around him. Ten seconds later, Daniel tapped out.

"Aw, but it was just getting fun," Rasha complained, throwing her swords into the dirt. They disappeared as they hit the ground.

"Daniel needs to focus more on his mana training, anyway." June stepped forward, pacifying the woman. "Perhaps a slower fight with Sir

Bennett? He fights defensively, so you can work on finding his weaknesses."

Rasha perked up and turned toward Brandt. His light skin flushed as she sauntered toward him. "How about it? Want to take me on?"

Madi made a small sound as the two started circling each other. Brandt drew his sword, and Rasha summoned a small dagger.

"How many weapons does she have?" Daniel complained as he joined them to watch. "She's too quick, and I swear I hit her a few times."

June glanced at Madi before answering Daniel's question. "Rasha spent too many points on a skill that lets her absorb weapon types for later use. She has an arsenal but can only use one at a time unless she finds a set of matching weapons. And you did strike her multiple times, Daniel. Rasha wears armor that exposes areas of her body that she has strengthened with an ability to absorb the force of your hits and transform it into energy for her to use in bursts. Watch her before a battle. She hits her shoulders and stomach to build her own stores."

Orrin glanced back at her too-small chest piece with new admiration. "She gives openings in her attacks to those areas, too. Daniel attacked where his eyes were . . . drawn."

Madi made the noise again. A definite grunt of annoyance.

June laughed. "Don't worry, Madi. Rasha has no interest in your man. You should be careful around her, though."

Madi's confused look only made June laugh harder.

The fight inevitably went to Rasha, but the lightning mage was happy and bouncing between them all after her beatdown on Brandt.

"He's so rigid, but in a good way. I had to work to find an opening, and even then, I only won because of my speed. He's a solid fighter," Rasha gushed as they sat down for lunch. "If Henry comes to train, they should spend some time together."

Orrin set up the pan for some stir-fry. Before long, sizzling meat and veggies were dancing in a brown sauce he'd bought from a store in Dey. Madi waited near another pot for the rice to be done. Plates were handed out, along with another piece of glazed porcelain from June, and they all sat back to eat.

"This is good," Rasha mumbled around a full mouth. "June, I want Orrin on Phoenix. He can cook for us and give us those buffs. We'll break through floor one ten in a week."

"Is that how far in the dungeon you've gone?" Madi asked, sitting forward and nearly dropping her plate. Her interest was evident in her eyes. "Floor one hundred and ten?"

Rasha chewed and swallowed, glancing at June before continuing. "Don't talk about it to anyone else, but yes. That was as far as we got on our second-to-last run down Mistwater Lanterns. We were going to go farther in this time, but . . . turned back."

"I've discussed it with Orrin. It's fine," June said as she took a dainty bite. "There was a dungeon break."

Madi froze. Orrin hadn't told her about June's conversation with him and now regretted it. He gestured to her quietly and leaned close. "I didn't tell you because it was contained. Phoenix had some trouble in Odrana's dungeon and left early. That's why they're here. June made it sound like it wasn't a big deal."

Madi nodded slowly but turned to June. "I thought Phoenix team cleared Odrana's dungeons to avoid dungeon breaks. What happened?"

As June and Rasha gave their sides of the story, Orrin watched Madi for a reaction. She kept her cool, but he thought it was mostly due to June's boredom in describing the response. Rasha, on the other hand, talked about the scene with gusto.

". . . we get out of the Lanterns and find almost the entire Odranan council about to throw Lady Sanerris into the dungeon without equipment. Don't ask me why, I don't know. We got them to set up some traps, and between June, Lady Sanerris, and Lady Tonsa, the monsters died before they got too far out of the entrance. It was brutal and fun." Rasha waved her hands around to demonstrate the spells whooshing in. "The melee folks barely got to play, but I was able to make a barrier of electricity that zapped a few of the stronger monsters back into the kill zone."

"Why was Anabella alive?" Daniel asked, a scowl darkening his face. "Last we were told, she was to be executed."

June snapped her fingers. "That must be the reason. Sometimes in Odrana, a condemned adventurer can request death by dungeon. If they survive and destroy the dungeon, they get a commuted sentence and live a wealthy but captive life. I bet Lady Sanerris was going to enter that way. I remember hearing her argue that she had technically survived the dungeon."

Orrin bumped against Daniel and shook his head. *Don't go there.*

Daniel dipped his head sharply. *They might know more.*

Orrin kept his hand low and slashed it down. *Drop it. We don't know where their loyalty lies.*

Brandt ruined Orrin's warning. "Lady Sanerris was supposed to die for treason against Odrana, conspiring with her son to kill the other lords' children, kidnapping Orrin, attempting to kidnap Daniel, and holding me prisoner. If she was freed under a technicality, that does not bode well for the future of Odrana."

June studied Orrin, then Daniel. "I taught her once. She's clever, but her drive to find the perfect magic slows her growth. If she can't commit to one field of magic, she'll never be a real threat."

Orrin frowned, pausing with his fork halfway to his mouth. "She used ice magic when I first met her, but somehow, she had my spells when we took her down."

Rasha's plate fell from her lap. "You fought Lady Sanerris? The Anabella Sanerris of Mistlight? Are we talking about the same person?"

Daniel nodded. "Yeah, we fought her and her son with the other rulers of Odrana." He paused. "That's being nice. They all almost died. I stopped her and her son. I guess I stole Orrin's kill. He blew up Anabella's spell, and she was so surprised, I had no trouble knocking her ass out."

Orrin ducked his head, dropping his fork on his plate and rubbing his temples.

"After the mom was down, the son went psycho and stabbed a bunch of them while he froze time. Lucky for everyone, I'm not only incredibly handsome, but smart and powerful as well."

"Humble, too," Brandt muttered.

Daniel ignored him and continued. "I killed the idiot who tried and failed to kidnap me twice, Orrin healed up the other lords, and we got out of Dodge."

"Dodge?" June probed. "Is that a place?"

"It's a saying. It sort of means we got out of Odrana quick," Daniel answered before scooping up the last of his food. "This was good, O. Put it on the rotation."

Rasha sat quietly for once, her head turning to each member of Daniel's party as if waiting for one of them to yell, "Kidding!"

June sat back, balancing her food on one knee. "That explains much, but you said she had your spells, Orrin? Which ones?"

Orrin left his fork forgotten on his plate. "She knocked Lady Tonsa's dexterity to zero. I was Anabella's prisoner for a few days, but she never told me she knew [Decrease Dexterity]."

"I doubt she did," June responded more to herself than to Orrin. "She was always good at reading mana signatures. Perhaps she was able to recreate your spell. That would explain how we handled the dungeon break so easily. Thinking back now, some of the monsters went down faster than I thought they would."

"How is that possible? Those are Orrin's spells," Daniel said, indignant for his friend.

June spread her hands. "I won't discuss her class, because that would be rude, however, Anabella is known to change her magical repertoire regularly. That is all I will say."

"But what if she comes at—"

"I hope I'm not interrupting." Henrick's voice cut over Daniel as he stepped from between the trees. "Rasha. June. Good to see you both in one place."

Rasha bounced to her feet, nearly stepping on her fallen food. "Henry, you came! You should spar with Brandt. He fights like you when you were younger, and you could give him so—"

"The demons are moving. I came for my party, not to train others. June, this is a full assault. Are you joining with us or abandoning your duty?" Henrick interrupted Rasha, speaking to June as if none of the rest of them were there.

Orrin bristled. The way Henrick asked his question was unfair.

June took her time in standing up. She ran her hand over her plate, burning the remnant food away, before returning it to her pocket. She smoothed her robes and held out her hand to Daniel. "Would you invite me back to your party, Daniel? I would like to see you kill a Demon Lord today."

Chapter 66

Orrin accepted Henrick's invite to Phoenix team. His stats were already increased, so a cast of [Utility Ward] on Henrick, Rasha, and Thram had a negligible cost on his mana pool. Rasha sighed in relief and rolled her shoulders as the stats settled on her.

"That's the good stuff," she moaned sensuously and flexed. "I could kick Henry's ass with these buffs. Tell me again. Why should we collect the spell orbs when we could have the real thing?"

Orrin started but kept his mouth shut at the revelation that Phoenix team was "collecting" his spell orbs. His stat-increase spells were stored in the glass spheres and were supposed to be strictly controlled by Dey. *At least they aren't calling them buff balls.*

Henrick ignored Rasha's comment and shook Orrin's hand. "Be safe on the field. The demons over level one hundred hit twice as hard as they should and require more damage than you would believe to take down. If you find the Demon Lord, please have June send a message. We will do the same. Perhaps the [Hero]'s new ability will be of help."

Orrin's hand disappeared into Henrick's fist, and he momentarily felt like a child. He shook himself and tried to put a Daniel-like grin on his face. "You be safe, too. We could work together. It might be the best option."

Henrick dropped his hand and nodded at Rasha, who was jumping up and touching her knees. "Keeping her contained is going to take all of Thram's attention. Once I begin drawing their awareness, the field around us will be indiscriminate death. I would avoid being too close."

Orrin didn't argue. June gave each of her teammates a hug as Orrin moved back to Daniel's team and topped off every ward and buff he could. He handed a regeneration potion to Madi, then walked up to Rasha and Thram. June was speaking quietly with Henrick.

"These are regeneration potions. They let you recover your mana at one MP a minute for one hour, so use it wisely," Orrin explained, handing one to each of the members of Phoenix team. "You can't use more than one a day, so don't ask for more. You'll get sixty points back over the hour. It's not a lot, but it's something."

Rasha pulled Orrin into a side hug. "I'm not quitting until you're on my team. You are the [Iron Bear] that bleeds gold."

Orrin stared. "Huh?"

"You don't know that story?" Rasha frowned. "It's one of my favorites. There is this [Iron Bear], and he's attacking a village—"

"Rasha, we are leaving," Henrick shouted. "Good luck to you [Hero]. Keep Lady June alive."

Rasha waved and skipped after Henrick and Thram. Brandt moved one hand to the hilt of his sword and the other to cover his eyes from the setting sun beaming through the trees. "With the sun in our eyes, it will be harder to pick targets from the Wall. I'll find Lord Catanzano and see where they want us."

Madi grabbed his elbow before he took a step. "We'll go together. If this is a full assault, we stick together."

She spoke to Brandt but kept her eyes on Daniel and Orrin.

"Why is she looking at us like that, O?"

"Maybe because she knows you?"

"I don't have any idea what you mean."

"You know—" Orrin gestured broadly to the world. "The way you always rush in without thought for survival?"

Daniel crossed his arms over his chest and raised his nose in the air, giving a haughty sniff. "Why, I never."

As Orrin and Daniel did their two-man routine, June only watched. Orrin caught her eye as he smiled. She snapped her fingers in front of them both.

"This is not a game. People are about to die. Do you care so little for your party members' worry?"

Daniel deflated. June's presence over the past few days as a teacher made him regress to the people-pleasing high school boy he once was.

"We know it isn't a game, June. We joke to keep the fear away." Orrin was surprised to find himself standing between June and Daniel. "If Daniel stops telling jokes, that's when we should all worry."

"He's right, Lady June," Madi squeaked before coughing to clear her throat. "They use humor to deflect, but I trust them both with my life."

June's eyes moved between each member of the party before settling on Daniel. "You are the [Hero]. Lead your party."

Orrin moved to argue, but Daniel's hand fell on him. "Orrin, she's right. This is what I'm here for. We need to get up the Wall and see what's coming."

Orrin followed behind Daniel as they left the tree line, climbing the stairs to the top of the Wall. The guards and volunteer fighters were tense, watching the slow advance of the entire Horde below. Brandt spoke with a captain nearby and returned quickly with an update.

The demon camp had been abandoned. Wagons filled with supplies were parked outside their fence, but Orrin couldn't see any demons waiting with them. Three lines of demons were advancing at a crawl, with the front line holding shields. They could just make out one from their position.

The Horde's past behavior of moving in small groups was gone. This looked like a trained army, compact and moving in close step. From their perch, the nearest group of demons would encounter the Wall two miles north of them. The other two battalions would hit farther up the Wall.

"They've lost over two thousand of their numbers and half that again from their tamed monsters," Brandt explained as they jogged up the Wall. Defenders watched with fear in their eyes, happy they were far enough from the moving army that they didn't have to engage. Somebody had to hold the rest of the line. "If they've split evenly in three, each group will have a little over fifteen hundred demons. We can't know for sure where the Demon Lord is. I think we should wait back and have Orrin [Teleport] us in when we know for sure. He should be our priority."

Daniel slipped around two burly men wrestling a barrel filled with arrows across the Wall's walkway. "We can fight with the others until we find the asshole. Even if we stay on the Wall, I can't do nothing."

June held her robes up with one hand as they moved. "Do we have to run? Orrin can [Teleport] us to the next designated point."

Orrin chuckled. Months ago, he would have made the same complaint. He still didn't like running, but the muscles in his legs had come a long way from the sedentary boy who landed in the woods naked. "We want everyone to see the [Hero] and his party heading into the danger. They'll spread the word that Lady June, the [Pyrocaster], is with them. People see Madi and know that Lord Catanzano has his own daughter fighting for them. It would be quicker to [Teleport], but a few minutes running gives hope to the people on the Wall."

June didn't speak for a full minute as they continued to run. Her next words were quiet. "I may have underestimated you all."

Daniel slowed to a walk and threw his signature smile at the fire mage. "We're used to it. It's fun surprising people. I think we can walk from here. Orrin, can you find us a good spot close to a staircase and a [Teleport] area? If we need to move farther up the Wall, I don't want to jump over the side."

"Attack at will!" the captain in charge of this stretch of the Wall yelled. Arrows, spells, and a few larger thrown weapons sailed through the air. The demons were two hundred yards from the Wall. They'd stopped and planted shields in a row along their front line. Some wood or metal mages were casting magic, growing the demons their own little wall to hide behind. The demons had left their camp and dug in for the assault.

Orrin saved his mana, only casting [Lightstrikes] when he saw an opening. His natural mana regeneration made the spells cost nothing after a minute. Madi, likewise, sent out her butterflies to rain havoc only once. Brandt and Daniel requisitioned bows and spent a few minutes with the other defenders, taking potshots at random demons who stuck out behind their shields. June sent two fireballs flying out. One burst against the shield wall, flames licking up the side but not burning anything. The other sailed over and curved down, but a blast of wind magic sent the fire back into the air, dispersing her spell into nothing. She kept watch after that.

Thirty tense minutes passed with a slowing number of attacks between the two sides. Daniel was antsy, and Orrin could feel even June's desire to attack.

"What are they waiting for?" Madi cursed under her breath. "Brandt, can you find someone in contact with Crius? Are the demon contingents settled in or attacking?"

Brandt nodded and ran back to the captain. He knew the woman, thankfully, and returned quickly with his report. "Crius is in contact with Captain Yawer. All three divisions of the demons are in a holding pattern. There is concern they might be trying to tunnel under the Wall."

June smiled at that. "I'll be back."

Daniel moved and placed himself in front of her as she stood. "Our party sticks together. What's the plan, June?"

A frown of annoyance flickered across her face, but she relented. "My [Fire Snakes] can dig through earth. I can find any holes they might dig and fill them with flames."

Daniel nodded and waved to the others. "Let's go. We'll wait around June and help however we can."

June tilted her head. "You will likely not gain any experience from this route."

Daniel shrugged and pointed to the stairs. "We're here to save Dey, not gain levels. Let's go."

Once they found a spot that June accepted as workable, Daniel positioned Madi, Brandt, and Orrin around her. She sat and placed her fingers in the grass. Orrin sniffed the air, glancing down and seeing the smoke curling up from where June's fingers sank into the dirt.

"This will take a few minutes," June said distractedly. "Shake me if we are attacked."

Standing in a ready circle around the mage, Orrin smirked at his friends. "This is nice, huh? Anyone want a cup of coffee?"

"Orrin, I swear, if you pull out a cup of coffee while we're waiting for a fight, I will hold you upside down and shake you," Daniel threatened. "We're going to take this one step at a time. I need you all with me. I'm finding it easier to ignore the siren call of the demons when we have a plan and stick to it."

Orrin nodded seriously. "I hear you, D. We stick together, no matter what."

Daniel smiled. "Rule two."

Madi turned to look over her shoulder, catching a glimpse of June sitting with her eyes closed. "What's rule two?"

"We're a team and stay together," Orrin answered her. "Rule one is survive."

Brandt chuckled. "That's a good rule. Do you have more?"

Orrin didn't answer, but Daniel spoke after a few seconds. "Find a way home."

Madi and Brandt exchanged a look but didn't comment.

"I've found them," June murmured. "Six tunnels that can support two men walking side by side. Sir Bennett, you should report this immediately."

"No," Daniel cut in before Brandt could leave. "Leadership knows it's a possibility. June, can you do anything about the tunnels?"

"I could collapse one or two. I might be able to send a [Blaze Serpent] down another. They are spread out too much."

"Could me or Madi help?" Orrin asked. "I can use [Map] and figure out roughly where the tunnels are."

"Once I attack, they can change directions. They've already dug to a few yards away from the Wall. Unless you have a spell that can target everyone inside, the best option is waiting until they surface. We can have people waiting to throw magic at them." June opened one eye and looked at Orrin. "You simply don't have the spells for this type of attack."

"I can use [Vivid Lightshow]," Madi offered. "If I start them off small like you taught me, I can get hundreds into a tunnel before igniting the butterflies."

June patted the ground next to her. "Try to feel the mana in this area. I've tweaked it so you should be able to follow the path. If you can't find the end, drop the spell and try again."

Madi sat quickly and put her palm over the quarter-size hole in the ground. Her eyes closed in concentration.

Orrin's eyes flew through his own spells. *Maybe if I combine [Toxic Touch] and [Water Reservoir], I can make poison water and fill the tunnel? Nope. I've tried that before. Just [Water Reservoir] and [Boost] it until I fill the tunnel? How many gallons of water would I need?*

"June, how big are the tunnels? How many gallons of water would it take to flood one?" Orrin asked.

"Tens of thousands of gallons," June responded. "I know your spells, Orrin. This isn't your fight."

Orrin ground his teeth in frustration. Madi gasped, a smile blossoming on her lips. "I did it. I made it to the end. Should I cast the spell now?"

June opened both eyes and looked at them all. "This will create chaos. Be ready."

Chapter 67

Chaos was a mild description of what happened as June and Madi cast their spells. Orrin kept an eye on his friend, watching her mana tick down as she flooded one of the six tunnels the demons were building under the Wall with her new spell, [Vivid Lightshow]. Using her class, [Superior Prism Conjurer], Madi charged the butterflies with different functions based on their color. Orrin couldn't see the explosions of fire, flashes of light, or searing lava burning through flesh, but the pallid look on Madi's face was enough to know she knew what was happening.

"Talk to me, Madi," Brandt whispered as she shivered on the ground but kept her palm over the hole that June had dug for her with her fire summons. "Stop if it's too much."

"No," June ordered. "Don't stop. Her spell is more destructive in a small space than we knew. She can collapse the entire tunnel."

June's own mana was flowing down two other pathways as she spoke. She also summoned a flaming constrictor snake at least ten feet long that began eating down a third hole. "I need the path thicker for my [Blaze Serpent]," she answered Orrin's unspoken question.

Shouts from the Wall caught Orrin's attention. Brandt glanced up as well, torn between staying with Madi and the need to know what was happening.

"Brandt, take Daniel and report what we're doing to the captain. Have her report it along to Silas and the others, then get back down here. Find out what's happening, too." Orrin took charge, giving orders. "Madi, don't overdraw. You need to keep some mana for the rest of the fight."

Madi kept her teeth clenched. "Just a bit more. I can reach the end of their tunnel."

Daniel and Brandt ran toward the stairs as Orrin rubbed Madi's back. June's shoulders slumped, and she wavered in place.

"June?" Orrin reached out, steadying both women. "Both of you should stop. You're overdoing it."

June didn't answer. She clasped her wrists together and opened her hands, pointing her fingers at the larger hole. "I have enough for this."

A blast of fire mana emerged from June's hands, crawling and growing into her giant snake. It funneled into the ground, burning a hole big enough that Orrin had to drag both women from their spots on the ground before they fell in with the slipping dirt around it.

Orrin put mana potions into both their hands as Daniel and Brandt took the stairs two at a time on their way back down the Wall. June's hand shook, and Orrin helped her put the glass to her lips. Madi drank her own and rested on the ground, her arm over her eyes.

"Flames erupted from two different spots in the demons' formation," Daniel reported as they ran back to their party. "I swear I saw some of Madi's butterflies, too. Are they okay?"

"We'll be fine in a minute," June answered for them both. "That was impressive, Lady Catanzano. Good job."

"Did the tunnels collapse?" Brandt asked, moving to help Madi sit up. "They didn't have time to get all their forces into the holes. A few captains didn't even realize their numbers were shrinking behind those shields. An [Earth Mage] noticed what they were doing on the most northern demon group and reported to the others. Every [Earth Mage] not working on the Wall's defenses is searching for tunnels now."

June stood, steadying herself against a tree. "I received experience for two hundred and thirteen demons. I don't know how many are injured, but those three tunnels are closed to them now."

Madi shivered uncontrollably, then turned and held Brandt, her head nestled into his neck.

"Madi?" the [Knight] whispered apprehensively. "What's the matter?"

Her words were muffled against Brandt's chest, and he held her closer, rubbing her back.

Orrin raised his shoulders, waiting for Brandt to explain.

"Her tunnel collapsed on the demons. She's getting experience still as they suffocate and die," Brandt whispered, covering Madi's ear with his hand. "She leveled to thirty and just hit a hundred kills."

Orrin checked his [Map]. The lines of red stretching from the demon entrenchment to the Wall had pulled back or disappeared altogether. "I think they gave up. The other two tunnels are empty."

June shook her head. "The demons will push back fast. They don't have much daylight left."

Madi squeezed Brandt once more, then straightened her back. Her hands moved to her face before she turned back to them. "Orrin. I hit level thirty."

Orrin smiled. "Good job, Madi. That should get you a few more points in one of your stats. I'd recommend at least one in con, since I can boost your others, but it's up to you, of course."

Madi didn't stop staring at Orrin. "I'll get to that, Orrin. Maybe . . . you can use [Calm Mind] on me? I'm feeling unsteady after that much mana use."

"We should get back to the Wall," June suggested, looking around. "Orrin's [Map] might be the best way to track the demons for now. The use of these noncombat skills in a fight is changing my opinions on a lot of things."

Madi nudged Brandt and whispered something. He nodded and moved to June's side. "Lady June, would you come with me to report to Captain Yawer? I think your perspective would be welcome."

Brandt and June started walking, with Daniel right behind them. Orrin took two steps before Madi linked arms with him. "You are hopeless at picking up hints, aren't you?"

Orrin looked at Madi's arm around his own and blushed. "What are you talking about?"

"I was trying to get some alone time with you, Orrin," Madi whispered. "Thank goodness Brandt is quicker on the uptake."

Orrin's brain ground to a halt. The train didn't just fail to leave the station; it exploded on the tracks. "Um . . . What?"

"I hit level thirty, Orrin. I completed the Quest, but the reward is unavailable. Can you do your Administrator thing before we get back to the Wall? I didn't want to ask in front of June."

Orrin's hamster wheel started spinning again. "Oh. Yeah. Of course."

He reached out as she flipped her screen for him.

Quest Complete
Obtain Level 30
Reward: [Hero Kit Level 4] Unavailable Reward

"Wait, why are you blushing?"

Orrin ignored her and pushed at the notification with his mind.

Unlocking Limited Reward Set for Nonadministrator
Increase Constitution Stat +3
Increase Will Stat +3
Increase Intelligence Stat +3
+5 Ability Points

Optional: Edit Reward with Administrator Points?
Yes or No?

That's new, Orrin thought before whispering to Madi, "I can edit the reward now, too."

"I'll take the extra constitution for now. It's safer to do that and tell June that you've used your spell on me. I'm not sure we can trust her with all you can do just yet."

Orrin laughed. "Ironic."

Madi slapped his chest with her free hand. "Don't tease me, or I'll tell Brandt you thought I was hitting on you."

Orrin held his hands up in surrender. "You win."

Madi stuck her tongue out. "Let's hurry. I want Daniel to give me the next Quest before he kills the Demon Lord and we all jump another twenty levels. You realize that I might hold the record for the shortest time going from level one to thirty? It's supposed to take years, not weeks."

Orrin listened to her plans to reach level fifty within the year and held his friend's arm a little closer.

Instructions were relayed down the Wall, with several groups splitting off in different directions as Orrin and his friends moved north along the stone pathways. Torchlight cast long shadows from the guards watching the darkness ahead of them.

"They're sure this time?" Daniel asked for the fifth time. "Somebody actually saw the Demon Lord?"

Brandt pulled a face in Madi's direction before answering. "Yes, Daniel. Lord Tarris himself identified the man. Niko."

"His class is [Demon Lord]?" Daniel said, pushing between two archers without an apology. "He's not a scary demon someone mistook as the leader?"

"Demon Lord isn't a class, Daniel. He's a [Metal Enchanter]. From what the Guild was able to put together, he'll be able to work with metal magic like a mage but may be able to use spells to power his armor, weapons, or even constructs. It's not a class that is well recorded," Madi answered.

June smiled. "Metal melts with enough heat. We should find Phoenix team and strike together."

"You're free to join them if they'll let you," Daniel said before tripping over a spear that had fallen across the walkway. "Damn it. Pick up your weapons, people."

"Daniel," Orrin chastised, moving forward to slow his friend down. "You're being an ass. Calm down. The report said he's in the middle group. It's only a bit ahead from here. They are still recovering from their assault."

After Madi and June plugged up over half the tunnels from the third group of demons, their section of the Wall remained mostly free from attacks. The northernmost group was hit the worst, with the smallest number of [Earth Mages] to locate the demons as they dug under the Wall. Phoenix team's presence in the area was the only thing that saved them from having to abandon that Wall completely.

Lord Tarris and Lady Timpe worked with the thousands of defenders to keep the middle group at bay. Madi's father, Silas, was still working with Phoenix team to close the underground paths farther up the Wall. Daniel's team was notified as soon as the Demon Lord's presence was confirmed.

Night was truly upon them, with the new moon shedding no light upon them. Orrin's hopes that the demons would retreat for the night were shattered when they heard the yelling ahead of them.

"Breach!"

Orrin barely cast [Gust] in time as Daniel used [Shooting Star], rushing forward. The air at his back and his own increased dexterity kept him right behind the [Hero]. Daniel slammed into a dark shape with horns stretching back and over his head, knocking the demon back off the top of the Wall. Orrin was there a moment later, targeting five more demons with hits from [Decrease Dexterity]. Four went down and were dispatched by swords, axes, and a hammer. The fifth snarled at them before launching herself off the edge of the Wall toward Dey.

Daniel held his hand out and used [Gravity Well]. The demon's arms were outstretched like she could soar, and indeed, Orrin thought she was flying as she hovered in the air.

"Kill it," Daniel insisted. "Can't hold much more."

Two swords stretched out and stabbed the unmoving form in the air. A spike of ice longer than Orrin's arm speared through the demon's head, snapping her neck to the side. Daniel grunted and fell to his knees, letting the spell end. The demon's body fell into darkness. Orrin heard a meaty splat a moment later.

"Thank you, [Hero]." One of the swordsmen panted from the sudden exercise. "They came out of nowhere."

Orrin glanced over the edge and found no ladder. "How did they get up here?"

A mage wearing dark-blue robes with her hands in her pockets looked over as well. "I don't know. They weren't here one moment, then attacking in the next."

"They flew," the hammer-wielding man in a leather apron said, spitting over the side. "Good to see you taking care of Gertrude, [Hero]. Thank you for the assistance."

"Jovi, is that you?" Daniel smiled as he clapped the blacksmith's back. "What are you doing on the Wall? You should be making more weapons for us to use."

"And let the children have all the fun? Meh," Jovi snorted. "I have enough apprentices to take our orders and hit the steel. I will protect Dey with my own hands." He hefted the hammer back on his shoulder.

Introductions were quickly made, but the [Ice Mage] waved a hand. "Back to your posts. Back to your posts. We don't know if they have more coming our way. I doubt those were the only flyers they had."

Orrin fervently hoped she was wrong.

Chapter 68

Lady Timpe waved for them to sit as soon as they entered the small leadership tent. "We don't have much time. There are several reports of demons that fly bypassing the Wall in the night. We believe they will try to dig tunnels from our side to connect with the rest of the Horde and bypass our defense completely. Lady June, our [Earth Mages] were able to find the tunnels once they were close to the Wall, but the reports state that you found them well before. Would you be willing to teach us how?"

June was already shaking her head. "No mages you have could replicate my spell. You should be asking Orrin. His [Map] skill worked just as well, if not better, than what I can do, anyway."

Lady Timpe's face pinched in confusion before settling on Orrin. "Yes, the [Utility Warder]. [Map]? What could a tracking skill do against demons?"

Orrin was reminded again of how little the adventurers of this world thought of utility skills. "[Map] has extra options to view your party, monsters, and even traps, but enemies show up as red dots. Anyone you bring out with the skill will be able to help watch the Wall for approaching enemies."

Lady Timpe gestured, and one of her assistants ran out of the tent. "That solves one problem. We'll station a few [Mappers] or [Trackers] up and down the Wall. That doesn't solve our problem with the demons that got through."

"That's not our problem," Daniel said politely, his temper better controlled in front of an authority figure. "We need to find the Demon Lord. If we kill him, this should all end."

Lady Timpe shook her head. "There is no guarantee that is true. We could use your help with finding these loose demons. If they have the entire night to take position, I fear what will happen in the daylight."

"You have other teams that can play cat and mouse," Daniel argued back. "I was told that Lord Tarris saw the Demon Lord. Will you help me find him?"

Lord Tarris sat in a corner, rubbing his temples and nursing a cup of tea. "I will. If that is what the [Hero] chooses as his path, I won't stand in the way. You bet the lives of everyone on the Wall with this decision, though. If we are caught in the middle, there will be no easy retreat."

"If I kill the leader, the rest will flee," Daniel said, so confidently that Orrin almost believed him.

Lord Tarris sighed and stood, moving slowly. *Mana overexertion,* Orrin realized.

"The demon was a [Metal Enchanter] named Niko. Multiple high-level demons were talking with him when I spotted him. His level was too high for me to discern, but he looked directly at me when I used [Identify]," Lord Tarris explained as he drew directly on a map of the Wall. "If the forces are arranged the same way, I saw him here—" The lord marked a spot slightly to the left of center, near the back of the demons' placement. "He wore black and green armor and had a cape with the same crest used on their flag. He had a metal bo staff and boxes strapped to a bandolier across his chest. He smiled when he saw me."

The man whom Orrin had watched cast amazing magic and end another lord of Dey shivered. "His eyes were like ice. Even at that distance, I knew I would have no chance in a fight with him. We should bring in all of Phoenix team. Along with Dragoon, Lily, and the—"

"Thank you, Lord Tarris," Lady Timpe said softly, taking his arm and helping him back to his seat. "That's all we need. Rest."

Orrin watched the strong woman settle the frail man in his seat again before she returned with a small shake of her head. "Lady June, should I send for the rest of your team? I have never seen Lord Tarris . . . react so poorly before."

"Please do." June nodded, watching Lord Tarris. "He was rattled but will recover after a good night's sleep."

"I fear that none of us will sleep much tonight," Lady Tarris sighed. "I will send Dragoon and Lily into the Pass to hunt for the demons. Will you strike tonight, [Hero]?"

Daniel cracked his knuckles. "As soon as possible. I'm tired of him hiding. I'm going to kill the Demon Lord tonight."

Orrin pulled his last prebrewed pitcher of coffee from his [Dimension Hole] and filled cups around the table while they waited for Phoenix team to arrive. Daniel gave him big puppy eyes until Orrin sighed and pulled out cream and sugar as well.

"You're the best," Daniel praised him, while pouring half the milk into his cup. The large triple scoop of sugar that followed made Orrin grind his teeth.

"You're the worst," Orrin grumbled as he threw himself into his chair. The hot, nourishing liquid filled his mouth and soothed his mind. "How long until Henrick and the gang get here?"

Lady Timpe peered over a stack of reports she was reading, taking in the entire team drinking around her camp desk. "Can you all wait somewhere else? I have an entire army to marshal and important meetings to call."

Daniel sipped his sugary monstrosity and sighed. "I miss whipped cream. Orrin, can you get a skill that makes frozen blended coffees?"

Orrin shivered in disgust. "Lady Timpe, I will personally drag the [Hero] from your tent and throw him over the Wall, if you allow it."

June was talking with Lord Tarris in the corner, trying to console the man. It seemed that his encounter with the Demon Lord put a fear in him that was not easy to shake. It was surprising for a man whose family had been in charge of dungeon eradication for generations. June raised her voice slightly. "Orrin, you can practice your mana exercises. Daniel, you, too. Both of you. go outside, keep an eye out for Henrick, and bring him to me when he arrives, please. Madi and Brandt . . . you may finish your drinks if you sit quietly."

Daniel held his cup between his hands as the night wind blew against them outside the tent. "Why did we listen to her? She's not in charge. This is my party."

"She does have a higher level than us, but I agree. Totally uncalled-for," Orrin responded, nodding at his friend. "Once you finish your coffee, you should go tell her that. I'll finish my drink and wait for Henrick."

Daniel's next sip was slow, and he slurped a few drops into his mouth. "Maybe we can complain to Henrick when he gets here."

Orrin took an even smaller drink of his coffee. "He'll know what to do."

The boys stood outside, nursing their drinks until Daniel sighed in relief. "Phoenix team is here. Hey, Rasha. Hey, Thram. How are you doing, Henrick?"

Henrick's armor was dented and scored, with an entire section along his left arm missing. He was also covered in blood. Thram and Rasha weren't as banged up, but both looked dead on their feet.

"Is June inside?" Henrick asked, not waiting for an answer and sweeping into the tent.

"Of course, go right ahead and ignore us," Daniel grumbled and raised his cup to his face, only to discover there was no more liquid left. "Damn."

"Hi, you two," Rasha greeted them with a loopy grin. "Thram can fly now."

"No, I can't." Thram shook his head and pushed Rasha ahead of him. "She got conked on the head and saw me jump down to save her from certain doom. Keeps swearing about flying figures in the sky."

Daniel and Orrin exchanged a quick look. *Oh no.*

Orrin sent a [Heal Small Wounds] into the woman, checking her pupils for dilation. He didn't know exactly why that was the practice or what he expected to find, but he remembered that was something doctors did with head wounds. "Rasha, was it Thram flying or someone else?"

"Thram did get skinny when he flew." Rasha leaned in conspiratorially. "He's getting quite chunky in his old age."

"That's enough from you," Thram bellowed and shoved her harder toward the tent. "I'm the proper weight for a dwarf, and chunky is not how you describe a person. A soup, maybe. Not a friend. Get in there."

Orrin turned to Daniel. "You think she saw demons fly over the battle?"

His friend ran his hand through his hair. Even after a full day of sparring, fighting, and running, he could have walked off a movie set with that hair. "Yes. We should probably go in and tell them."

Orrin nodded. "It's a good excuse. You want to go in first?"

Daniel held open the tent flap. "After you."

Orrin wasn't scared of June. She was his teacher. She knew his origin and magic better than he did. It was because his coffee was delicious. Yes, that was a good point. He raised his cup in the air. "I'll meet you inside. I'm just going to finish my coffee."

Daniel narrowed his eyes in suspicion but stepped inside the warm tent.

Orrin took two sips before Madi stuck her head out. "Get inside, you dolt. We're going over the plan."

Lady Timpe held a switch. The long, thin piece of wood flicked through the air as she snapped it down on the map spread out between everyone.

"This is where Lord Tarris spotted the Demon Lord," she began, looking at the man snoring in the corner, completely wrapped up in blankets. "It is unlikely he stays in one location, but it is the best chance we have. Dragoon team, along with Lily and Hornet, are searching the Pass for the demons that flew over the Wall at twilight. The Horde split their forces, and the [Hero] wants a chance to take the fight to them. As I don't seem to have control over Phoenix or the [Hero]'s team, I've decided I may as well use the opportunity."

Moving the end of the stick to the section of the Wall they currently stood on, she pushed a few Kala marbles into place. "I am committing four hundred melee and two hundred mages to attack this contingent of demons in one hour. That will be near midnight. They are all volunteers for this mission and have strict orders to strike and retreat immediately. This is a single dagger thrust at the enemy, not a full battle. If we can draw some away from those shields they've reinforced, I will have the mages with mana left over do what they can, but most everyone is exhausted from the earlier raid."

She dragged the makeshift pointer down the Wall. "You should approach from this direction. There is an escape hatch here—" Lady Timpe tapped a spot about a ten-minute walk south of the command tent. "Dragoon and the rest of you can advance on foot. I believe a member of the [Hero]'s team can use [Invisibility]?"

"[Camouflage]," Orrin answered. "It'll work even better in the dark, and I can put it on everyone before we go."

Henrick nodded and took over. "If we make contact with the target, I will draw his attention. Thram will work crowd control, forcing any reinforcements away. I would like Lady Catanzano to assist. Her spells are flashy, and we can use that to draw the attention from the main fight. Rasha has enough mana for one bombardment if we can draw enough close together, but that is not the primary objective."

The [Paragon Knight] drew his shoulders back and stood straighter. "If Daniel, June, and I can wear the Demon Lord down, he can use his sealing skill to end this. Orrin, I think you would do best keeping in the shadows. Use any chance you have to slow the Demon Lord or any of the others around him down. I've been told you can [Teleport] and heal? Use that to your advantage. I want you as the fifth man on both teams. Swap out if someone goes down and get them back over the Wall if you can. Can you do that?"

"As long as they're conscious," Orrin said, accepting his role. Unless things went bad and he had to use [Blood Mana], which June had expressly forbidden.

"[Teleport], healing, and he made the spell orbs?" Lady Timpe muttered. "What else has Silas been hiding from us?"

Daniel grinned over the table and gave Orrin two thumbs up.

"Get some rest if you need it," Henrick ordered. "Let's end this."

Chapter 69

The night crept in behind them, covering the Wall in darkness as Daniel, Orrin, Madi, Brandt, and a reunited Phoenix team skulked toward the demons. Orrin's [Camouflage Ward] kept everyone's edges blurry. He'd also made an impatient Henrick wait inside the Wall safe room while layering wards on all eight of them. He didn't have a [Metal Ward] and hoped his stinginess with his ability points wouldn't bite them later.

"Patrol ahead," Henrick whispered. "Hold here."

They crouched low, and Madi made a gagging noise. Brandt moved to her side, lifting her gently and setting her closer to Orrin.

"Shh," June hissed.

"Sorry," Madi muttered, clearly ashamed. "My foot went right through the chest of a dead body. I thought it was mud."

They waited until the allotted time, waiting for the attack from the Wall.

"They're late," Brandt whispered. "Do we go back if—"

"Don't worry," Thram grumbled in his low voice. "I see them moving. They'll want to get as close as possible before they start."

A challenge rang out, followed by the whistle of an arrow. Staggered yells from far away picked up into a thunderous choir of war cries. The defenders of Dey announced their attack, sending magic at the shield wall even as men with weapons ran around the sides to strike demons on watch.

More arrows rained down from the Wall. Orrin saw the patrol in front of them get pincushioned. *Those are the elves. Nobody else can shoot accurately from that far out.*

It was good to know Leanthun's charges were there to help, and Orrin briefly wondered how Finley, Amir, and his other friends were doing. He didn't have long to ponder, as Henrick raised his sword and jogged forward.

The thrown-together camp behind the shields was nothing like the well-ordered structures that Orrin had spied on before. Barrels of water were knocked over and dry. Trash littered the paths they ran down, and the tents were little more than canvas pulled tight over hand-dug pits. Orrin moved quickly with the others, ignoring the few demon guards watching on tiptoes near the front of their camp.

Why push the demons out of their protected encampment? Orrin thought, jumping over a pair of legs jutting out from beneath a nearby tent. *If I were in charge, I'd keep back. Retreat to the safety of the camp when the assault didn't work.*

Daniel glanced into a pot over a cold fire as they moved along. He shook his head. Orrin changed directions and took a look himself.

The metal cauldron was huge, easily big enough to fit twenty gallons of soup inside, however, it was bone dry. Broken bowls and cutlery littered the ground around the iron pot.

Are they running out of food? It hasn't been a week.

Henrick advanced along the footpath created over the day through the camp, pointing toward a group of demons yelling orders. Orrin nodded but wasn't sure the man even saw him. It didn't matter, though. Thram's spell was the only signal they had prepared.

The dwarf shook out his sleeves and began drawing in the air. Orrin disregarded the opportunity to study the man's earth magic, instead watching for any roving patrols. It was incredible they'd made it this far in without a single thing going wrong.

Orrin flinched as the thought crossed his mind, waiting for karma to come knocking, but Thram finished his spell and the earth rumbled. Stone walls, similar to the ones he'd built before, grew from the ground so fast that Orrin would have missed them if he blinked. Whereas the previous earth spell created thick walls to keep the demons pinned, Thram's focus on this casting was numbers. Boxes of stone and rock sprang up around individual groups of demons, corralling them away. Several weapons crashed through Thram's earthen panels, and spells joined in a moment later.

"There." Daniel pointed to a demon twirling a rod that glinted in the faint spell light. "That's him."

Orrin couldn't say who moved first, Henrick or Daniel, but it didn't matter. Both of them broke through parts of Thram's defenses as they ran toward the Demon Lord.

"Good luck," June said with a smile toward Madi and Brandt, acting like she was dropping her kids off at summer camp. "Try to focus on your mana. You never know when you'll have a breakthrough."

Orrin chased after Daniel, with June at his side. Rasha's lightning spell, which she seldom used, jumped through several demons, pulling their attention toward herself, Thram, Madi, and Brandt. Madi's butterflies lit up the night, burning through demons, settling on still-sleeping forms under their tents and creating flashes of light that had Orrin squinting as he tried to keep an eye on Daniel.

Spells flew over Orrin's head at the group distracting the surprised army behind him. Henrick's plan was working in part, as with [Camouflage Ward] running, nobody was targeting Orrin or June.

Orrin felt the mana shift in front of him and barely hit the dirt in time as an explosion of ice magic, waves of fire, and dozens of arrows flew through the air. June cut the ice in half with a slice of her left hand, absorbed and redirected the fire with her right, used the fire to burn the arrows before they struck her, and continued running as if nothing had happened. Orrin scrambled to his feet and chased after, now last in line to reach the Demon Lord.

At least twenty demons fought Daniel and Henrick as Orrin stepped into the melee. Bodies already littered the floor. June created curtains of fire that moved like Thram's walls of stone, forcing some enemies to withdraw and go around. Her wand hand moved through the air like a conductor, with a demon dying or burning with every swish.

Orrin used his debuffs indiscriminately. [Decrease Dexterity] and [Decrease Will] were his first choices on every target he could see. He used [Split] to speed his casting and began using [Decrease Strength] and [Decrease Intelligence] next. With so much movement, he couldn't be sure that he hit everyone, so Orrin tried [Identify] on one to be sure.

Every third or fourth demon created feedback in Orrin's mind that rattled his eyes in their sockets. He started prepping [Heal Small Wounds] beforehand, just in case. Most demons in the area were above level eighty, with two above level one hundred.

"June, that one with the staff and that one with the ax. They're the most powerful besides the Demon Lord," Orrin shouted as he got close to June. She didn't answer, but the fires around them shifted and started moving toward the two demons that Orrin pointed at.

Orrin ignored the thumping in his heart as he watched Daniel get knocked back again and again. Henrick's feet were inches deep in the ground as the metal bo staff fell on his shield with a steady beat that hit like a bass drum in Orrin's ears.

He used [Identify] on the demon to be sure.

Niko Daenkuris	[Metal Enchanter] Level ???
HP: —	MP: —

Orrin cast his debuffs on the horned man, throwing a [Lightstrikes] out for good measure. *I'm not missing out on the Demon Lord experience.*

Daniel moved like a bolt from a crossbow back at Niko, using the combination of skills that made him an immovable wrecking ball. The demon turned his staff slightly, tripping Daniel. He didn't even watch as the [Hero] fell and tore up the ground for several yards before coming to a stop. Niko used the momentum to swing overhand and push the [Paragon Knight] farther into the ground.

"June, you might need to help Henrick," Orrin yelled, swinging a summoned [Ice Sword] under the guard of a demon with twin daggers. The longer reach of his sword let him tap the blade against the demon's leather armor. Ice mana exploded across his chest, halting his movement for half a second. Orrin sank his [Fire Sword] into the exposed throat of the demon, twisted it, and then let it explode. The demon's neck burst open, and a rain of hot blood splattered Orrin's face as the head rolled to his feet. "That was disgusting."

He looked around for his next target and was surprised to see most of the demons were gone. A few stood just beyond the flashes of light but weren't moving to help.

"Henrick, time to go high." June's voice rang out over the field.

The knight didn't respond but jumped. Orrin gaped. Henrick sprang fifteen feet in the air wearing full armor. The superheated air next to Orrin let him know what was coming. He felt his [Fire Ward] strip away in an instant as he threw himself to the side as well.

June's [Blaze Serpent] grew to the size of a small semitruck, destroying everything in its path as it carved flaming death toward the Demon Lord. It passed directly underneath Henrick, just as he started to reach his maximum height and fall back to the ground.

Niko's arm blurred as he ripped something from his chest and threw it at the giant fire snake. Orrin heard something clink, then had to close his eyes as the world around him flared bright. The night was gone, and, in its place, sunlight filled the space around them. When he finally cracked an eye open, his jaw dropped.

June's [Blaze Serpent] was frozen in ice. The fires burned bright inside, the obvious light source for the area around them. As Henrick landed, he charged not at Niko but at the snake. His sword hacked at the ice with an intense flurry of blows.

"Daniel. Orrin. Target the ice. The spell is still active," Henrick shouted. He paused his strikes only to deflect and push back the remaining demons fighting with the Demon Lord.

June was on her knees, holding her hand out and trembling. Her spell drained her mana continuously during use. The Demon Lord had trapped it somehow, and she was unable to unsummon the spell.

Orrin's [Gust] launched him at the ice-snake statue, and his [Fire Sword] hacked at the ice. It barely dented the material. Orrin's mind tickled, and he let [Mind Bastion] activate.

[Fire Sword]'s description talked about not being quenched in the bitterest of cold but was barely touching the ice. During their pillaging of the Dey Guild's storage, one of his friends, Emily, had taught him that his [Ice Sword] could survive regular fire, but magical fire could still destroy it. It made sense that the same would be true for his [Fire Sword]. If he couldn't hurt the ice, that meant it was ice mana. Orrin knew ice mana. He practiced with it regularly. Maybe . . .

Orrin stopped swinging and rested his hand on the ice.

"What are you doing?" Henrick shouted. "We can break through. Just a bit more. Hurry."

Orrin tuned out Henrick. He ignored the rings from Gertrude and Henrick's large sword vibrating through the ice. He closed his eyes and let [Mind Bastion] help as he examined the mana signature of the spell under his fingers.

The spell's mana funneled down into a different mana type. Orrin didn't recognize it. *It has to be metal. He wears metal boxes. Like grenades? Where is it?* Following the channel, Orrin began gathering mana in his chest. A lot of mana.

Daniel's sword stopped hitting the ice. Orrin couldn't take the time to check on his friend. He trusted Daniel. Rule one: Survive. They'd get through this, if Orrin could just . . . There!

Under the ice covering the flaming snake, a metal container with one side open. He pushed [Gust] at the ice, using the ice mana signature inherent in every spell to bolster it. There was no person connected to the static ice mana keeping June's snake trapped. It was pure and clean, and Orrin could steal it for his own.

The ice cracked.

Orrin opened his eyes.

Daniel guarded Henrick's prone form with Gertrude. He held the flat of his blade with one hand and the handle in the other, turning his sword to be a shield. Niko was swinging his staff down.

Orrin shouted and summoned an [Ice Sword] in each hand. He stabbed one into the exploding ice mana around the snake. It burst apart, and June's summon disappeared. He could only hope he'd been fast enough.

Niko's staff hammered down on Gertrude twice as Orrin rushed to his target. The mana swirling inside him was too much, and he felt his joints freezing, cracking, and refreezing with each step.

"Another [Hero] ended by demons. How fitting," Niko laughed as his staff flew through the air.

A villain monologue? How cliché. Orrin groaned in pain. His second [Ice Sword] moved in front of Daniel's sword at the last second. Niko's metal staff struck ice, and Orrin unleashed the whirlwind.

Chapter 70

The basic principles of Orrin's [Gust] and summoned sword combination were simple. The air mana moved through the ice or fire mana, creating a combination of moving cold air or blasting superheated wind. The understanding of mana signatures and how the two mana types interacted allowed Orrin to tie the two spells together. It was like he held a needle in one hand and a thread in the other. If he could put one through the other, he'd have a new tool.

The difference from that analogy came from knowing he held a needle and thread at all. Or what a needle was. That was before knowing he was blindfolded in a room filled with scorpions that would sting him if he didn't move in a very particular way.

Orrin's thoughts about the combination of mana over the last few days and the limited practice he'd been able to do had led him to one conclusion: Magic was hard and dangerous.

His original plan was to simply explode away the ice mana slowly killing June. He could use [Gust] to push it away from him and his friends, which was the only reason he'd even opened his eyes. Orrin wanted to make sure he didn't accidentally kill Henrick. Daniel would survive. Somehow, he always did.

The glee in the Demon Lord's eyes as he rained blows down on his friend burned the original plan to the ground. That happiness at killing Daniel sent Orrin down a thought process that might never have occurred to him otherwise.

Orrin *wanted* to kill that fucker.

He was holding the equivalent of thousands of mana points of ice mana in his hands. Orrin knew he'd survived mana cycling through his body before. He needed to absorb it, take a few steps, and release the deadly package back to sender.

Orrin screamed in pain as his fingers turned to ice. [Mind Bastion] was on. He shouldn't have felt pain, and still, the cold around him bit into his eyes and froze the water on his eyes. Orrin pumped [Heal Small Wounds] into his face and hands.

"Orrin?" Somebody touched him, and warmth generated along his skin. "Open your eyes, slowly."

June's mana broke through the cold, and [Mind Bastion]'s pain shield booted back up. He coughed, and flecks of icy blood stained June's robe.

"Did we win?" Orrin glanced around. It was still dark. He groaned when he heard weapons striking each other in the distance.

"You nearly died. You saved me and somehow got between the demon and Daniel. He's fighting him still," June summarized quickly. "Can you sit up? Henrick is hurt badly. We should retreat while we can."

Orrin checked his own status. He had frostbite on his fingers, but they were healing over as he pumped more [Heal Small Wounds] directly into the blackened skin. His arms were shaken from deflecting Niko's strike but not broken. He rolled to his side and saw Henrick barely breathing.

"I'll get him back up," Orrin promised. His mana was about three-quarters gone, but he wasn't going to leave anyone behind. "Where are the others?"

"Brandt and Madi checked to make sure you were alive and ran to help Daniel. Thram and Rasha went, too. The demons have backed away from the fight. I don't know why, but they aren't attacking. We should get back to the Wall and have all forces mobilize," June continued ranting, but Orrin ignored her.

If they're pulling back from the fight, Niko might not be popular. The other big demon said they couldn't hurt the Demon Lord, but accidents happen. Maybe they don't want to be here.

It was a shot in the dark, but Orrin trusted his gut. He poured almost the rest of his remaining mana into healing Henrick. The man groaned and sat up. "Where's my shield?"

"Blasted away into pieces, I suppose," June answered angrily. "What were you thinking? After all the times that I've lectured you on mana, the child figures out the best way to bring down that mana trap. When we get out of here, I'm going—"

"Maybe chew him out later, June?" Orrin suggested. "We need you both. Did Niko get hurt at all from that? I can't imagine he got away easily."

June shook her head. "I didn't see. I was more worried about you and Henrick. Daniel is holding his own now, so that would suggest the Demon Lord is hurt."

Orrin rolled his eyes and stood up. His armor was in tatters, and he ripped the last hanging strap off, letting it fall to the ground. "Let's end him. Are you with me?"

"Orrin, I've told you. We shoul—"

"I'm with you," Henrick growled and slapped his hand into Orrin's. "I don't have a shield, but I'll pick something up as we find them."

Orrin summoned an [Ice Sword] and handed it to Henrick. "Better than nothing."

June sighed and rummaged in her pocket before pulling out a shield and a replacement sword for Henrick. "Upgraded copies of your lost ones. I was going to give them to you when we hit level eighty, but I suppose this is as good a time as any."

Henrick smiled as he handed Orrin back the summoned sword.

Finding Daniel wasn't hard. The sounds of battle over the field had completely stopped except for one place.

Orrin watched as Daniel fought Niko, the Demon Lord, with pride. His own attack had frozen the demon's right arm to the elbow, and it was clearly messing with the man's response time. He could barely hold the staff in both hands, lacked the strength to turn Daniel's strikes, and guarded the arm in obvious fear.

"Target his right arm," Orrin ordered the two members of Phoenix team as they ran toward the fight. "He might surrender if he loses an arm."

Thram must have been low on mana, because he only occasionally sent a spike of earth up from the ground to halt Niko's retreat. Brandt covered Daniel's openings, halting Niko's staff with his sword on most attacks. Madi used her spear to harry the Demon Lord. She cast no spells but didn't look overdrawn. Rasha had a bow of lightning and was loosing arrows of electricity at her target.

Orrin threw one of his [Ice Swords] at the Demon Lord as he walked forward, hoping to scare the man. The staff caught the blade and threw it toward Thram. The dwarf scurried to the side, barely avoiding the rebounded attack.

"He's got lots of tricks, Orrin. Don't toy with him," Daniel said, breathing heavily but grinning ear to ear. "I knew you'd be up in no time. Nothing can kill you, huh?"

"We'll see about that," Niko shouted and attacked but was knocked back. His bandolier of metal boxes was gone, and his eyes darted around for escape or help. "Once the rest of my troops get here, you will all die."

Orrin cycled one mana pool, refilling his bar to full. He checked his status bar that he'd created and smiled. He might be able to get away with one more. If he needed it. Orrin started healing his friends.

"You know, Niko— Can I call you Niko?" Orrin spoke to distract the demon, but the Demon Lord failed to take his eyes off Daniel. Henrick started to circle behind him. "I'm thinking the rest of the demons want to go home. You came here and admitted that you weren't expecting all the new Walls. You set up camp but abandoned it. Every try at getting past us failed. Do you have troops left to come to your rescue? Or have they already pissed off back to their homes?"

Orrin wasn't trying to get under the man's skin. He only wanted to distract him as Henrick got in position. The dip in his weapon and heavy breathing betrayed the demon, though.

"Wait, am I right?" Orrin asked in disbelief.

Niko shouted and pressed his attack on Daniel. The speed was beyond impressive, but with Daniel and Brandt working together, every strike was deflected. They didn't try to block, but simply moved the staff off-center a bit. More arrows hit Niko, but most bounced off his armor.

"I will kill every abomination on your tiny peninsula." Niko foamed at the mouth as he struck over and over. "I will fulfill my destiny and regain the rightful place of the demons. I was promised glory, and I will not fail him. You will bow or di—"

Niko overextended just as Henrick moved in. One of Rasha's arrows hit his frozen arm, shattering it. As he screamed in pain, Henrick's sword went through Niko's back. Madi's spear pierced his inner thigh. Gertrude slashed his stomach a moment later.

"Now, Daniel," Henrick said as he pulled his sword out of the demon's body. "Before he dies."

Daniel raised a hand and bands of white sprang out, wrapping around Niko's chest. He had gone quiet with the multiple hits, a silent scream etched on his face. As the white bands compressed, Niko's scream pierced the night.

"What did you do to him?" Rasha shouted, covering her ears. "Is that a spell he's using?"

The Demon Lord's chest collapsed, crunching loudly as bones snapped. The metal of his armor squealed in protest as it bent. Ropes of darkness from beyond their tiny circle of light streamed into Niko's body as he began to swell. The bright rings finally cut through his armor, metal falling to pieces around him. Niko lived for ten relentless seconds before the bands broke him in two.

"That was different," Daniel said, shock on his face. "Why call it a seal if it just kills the guy?"

The body fell limply to the ground. Henrick reached down and picked up a white metal ball. "What's this?"

A whip of fire snapped out from June, making Henrick drop the ball. "Henrick Jordan, what have I told you about picking up unknown magical items?"

Daniel hesitantly reached down and wiped some blood from the brightly glowing orb. "Did I just catch a Pokémon?"

Orrin tried to make a joke, but the ringing of notifications in his head stopped him.

Quest Complete
Defeat the Demon Lord
Reward: Recalculating . . . Demon Lord defeated after Dark Horde attack . . . Recalculating . . .

"Come on," Daniel cried, stomping his foot as he read the same notification. "Is the system a rules lawyer? We killed the guy. Give me my experience."

A ding pulled Orrin's eyes back to his screen.

Quest Update Complete
Defeat the Demon Lord

Reward: 500,000 XP

Orrin was pissed the system was just now changing the rules, but the level notifications softened the blow. "Half the XP? What a load of bull. It even took away the other reward. No Essence? That's not fair."

Madi was practically dancing, reading through her own system prompts. "I'm happy with half the experience. What other reward? The Quest you shared only gives experience."

Orrin frowned, glancing over at Brandt. "You didn't have Dark Essence as a reward with the XP?"

Brandt shook his head just as Daniel whooped.

"Yeah, baby. Looks like the killing blow gets the spoils. Dark Essence obtained, whatever that is," Daniel bragged.

June's movement was abrupt. She stood in front of Daniel, staring at him with wide eyes. "What did you just say? Dark Essence?"

Daniel tripped moving out of June's reach and landed on his butt, the small shiny ball in his hand dropping to his side. "Damn it, June. I thought you were a demon. It's just the Quest reward. It was on the display the entire time."

Orrin searched his store for Dark Essence, then just Essence, but nothing appeared. "Whatever it is, we can deal with it later. We should get out of here before the other demons realize Niko is dead."

He moved to touch his friends, readying a [Teleport]. June held up a hand to stall him.

"Dark Essence is linked to Demon Lords, Orrin. It is the magic feared by all," she explained, and Orrin noticed her wand held down against her thigh was pointing at Daniel. "Is he still a [Hero]?"

Daniel stood and brushed off his pants. "Of course I'm the [Hero]. I just defeated the ultimate bad guy like a boss. Dark Essence doesn't even do anything. It says 'Locked' next to it. Let's get back and rest. I think everyone is a little on edge after that fight."

He bent over and picked back up the ball made from his [Demon Seal] skill. Daniel's eyes glazed over, and his lips moved silently as he read another notification. A small frown drew his face down momentarily before he forced a laugh. His eyes nervously danced over the members of Phoenix team. "Can Orrin [Teleport] us back already? I'm exhausted."

Chapter 71

Orrin jumped his party back before returning for Phoenix. The demons surrounding them didn't move or speak, creating an eerie atmosphere that Orrin was more than happy to escape. June began to pepper Daniel with questions immediately, but he shrugged and kept telling her he didn't know any more than she did about the Dark Essence reward.

"June, leave it," Henrick said warily. "We can find out more in the morning, but everyone is tired. Let them rest. They earned it."

Orrin barely paid attention as Brandt led them back to their tent. Orrin's eyes were awash with glee as he read his level notifications. The first few boxes were from the demons he helped kill. The few hundred XP barely made a dent in his path to level thirty-three.

Experience Gained: 500,000 XP
Level 33 obtained!
+10 AP
Level 34 obtained!
+10 AP
...
Level 45 obtained!
+10 AP

Another box contained his stat point increase.

Congratulations on obtaining Level 40!
10 stat points have been awarded.
Usable Stats for Utility Warder:
Strength
Constitution

Dexterity
Will
Intelligence

A separate box for the level-forty Quest appeared as well. Orrin let out a sigh of relief as he realized he wouldn't miss out on the level-fifty Quest. Losing that extra reward at level thirty still irked him. He quickly moved to fix the unavailable reward.

Quest Complete:
Obtain Level 40
Reward: [Hero Kit Level 5] Unavailable Reward
. . .
Administrator Access Override
Reward List Patch
Select your reward:
Upgrade one spell or skill
Increase Strength Stat +5
Increase Constitution Stat +5
Increase Dexterity Stat +5
Increase Will Stat +5
Increase Intelligence Stat +5
+10 Ability Points
Change Class

Optional: Edit Reward with Administrator Points?
Yes or No?

"I have ten points to distribute," he mumbled in his cot. His urge to bump his will up more was tempered by his recent injury. He dropped all ten into constitution, reasoning that he could use the edited Quest reward for will if he wanted to bring the stat up more. It felt nice to see two of his stats at the same number, though.

Orrin looked at his new status.

Orrin	Utility Warder Level 45 (24,540/51,000)	Ability Points: 147
HP: 998/1,000	MP: 856/1,043	Admin: 1
Strength: 9 (100)	Constitution: 40 (100)	Dexterity: 11 (100)
Will: 40 (100)	Intelligence: 11 (100)	

One more blinking light down the list pulled his attention.

> **[Teleport] Level 2—teleport to any known point within fifty miles. 25 MP per person (10,000/10,000)!**
>
> **Would you like to upgrade [Teleport] for 10 AP?**
> **Yes or No**

The ferrying of supplies and troops had made the experience bar for the skill fill up faster than he'd ever hoped, and the jumps around the battlefield had likely pushed him over the edge. He selected the upgrade to see how much farther the upgrade would let him travel. It might be worth taking if it increased to one hundred miles. He was tired of having to do two jumps to move through the Pass.

> **[Teleport] Level 3—teleport to any known point within 250 miles. 10 MP per person (0/50,000)**

Orrin let out a low whistle. *That was a lot of mana before the next upgrade.*

Daniel turned over in his cot. "Are you still awake, Orrin?"

"Sorry," Orrin whispered. "I'm going over my system notifications. The [Teleport] upgrade is sick. I might be able to get from here to the elven forest in one jump."

Orrin waited for Daniel to say something witty, but his friend was silent. Their small tent contained just the two of them. There was room for Brandt, but unknown to Lord Catanzano, he was spending the night in Madi's tent.

"Daniel?"

"We might need to go there in the morning. I need to talk with Arandir."

Orrin sat up and turned the small camp lantern up, chasing the shadows away as he swung his feet off the small bed. "What's going on?"

Daniel pulled the thick blanket over his shoulders, hiding half his face from the light. "Remember how I got the Dark Essence reward, but it was locked?"

"That's what you told June," Orrin said slowly. "Did you lie to her? Is it dangerous?"

"I didn't lie," Daniel responded quickly, blinking as he showed more of his face from under the covers. "It was locked when she asked. But . . ."

"Out with it, D." Orrin felt a sense of dread fill his stomach. Daniel was being shy about something, and his friend was anything but bashful. "What did you do?"

"I picked up the Demon Lord Seal. That's what the metal ball my skill created out of that guy's corpse is called. As soon as I touched it, Dark Essence unlocked," Daniel said, then rushed the next words out. "Here, see for yourself."

A blue box filled Orrin's view.

Dark Essence Unlocked:
Compatible Seal Accepted.

Would you like to absorb Dark Essence?
Yes or No?

"Obviously, you should pick no," Orrin said, scrambling to sit all the way up. "That's probably how demons become a Demon Lord. Remember the [Hero] book that Silas gave you? It said that Demon Lords spawn from places of Dark Essence, right? We should go tell June, or better yet, destroy the seal."

Daniel shook his head and waved a hand, throwing another box to Orrin. "Keep reading."

Dark Essence—Demon Race Administrator Access

"Oh, shit." Orrin couldn't think of anything else to say. "That's going to cause trouble."

Acknowledgments

This is the part of the book I write once the last period is placed, my brain is fried, and sleep calls like a siren beckoning me toward the dark waters. I forget someone in each book, so this time . . . Thank you to everyone. Yes! That means you!

To my Patrons, Royal Road readers, and Discord buddies. Thank you. You keep me honest with deadlines, messages to make sure I'm alive when I schedule a release wrong, and comments to point out the many mistakes I make drafting each book. I couldn't ask for a better group of extended friends. Special shout-out to Alan M. for questioning my confident and completely wrong assumptions and saving me from making a mistake. I owe you a beer or three.

To my family at Podium Entertainment. Julie, Brian, Leah, Christina, and Sara. Four books down! You've turned me into an honest-to-God author. Each one of you is a saint in disguise, making miracles and fulfilling dreams. Thank you.

To Nick Podehl. You've become as much an owner of this story as me. The incredible dedication to your craft leaves me in awe each time I hear a new character's voice. You are one awesome guy, and I wouldn't have anyone else on my side.

To my friends and family. Thank you for the continued support. Knowing random people I've never met read my book is a heady feeling. Hearing those close to me discuss theories and ask questions that you know I won't answer is humbling.

To my boys and Sarah. I love you.

About the Author

SourpatchHero is the author of the LitRPG series I'm Not the Hero. When he's not writing new stories, you'll find him spending time with his two sons and his wife, reading, or playing video games. He resides in Virginia with his wife and two kids.